Heated Earth - Aedgar Moves In

The Aedgar Wisdom Novels
BOOK ONE

MIKI MITAYN

PHOTOGRAPHY BY
CLAUDIA JOCHER

PRAISE FOR MIKI MITAYN

HEATED EARTH - AEDGAR MOVES IN

'A stunningly imagined novel with loveable characters... Insightful commentaries and wisdom on spirituality. Thought-provoking conversations and ... exciting dialogues that will move readers ... seamless, fascinating.

'Mitayn is a master storyteller with an extraordinary gift for crafting engaging dialogues.

'*Heated Earth - Aedgar Moves In* is a great book. A passionate tale that brims with energy and humanity.'

—**Bertin Drizller** 'The Book Commentary'

'In a time where channelled spirits are considered new age, Miki Mitayn's Nerida connects to the traditions of Aboriginal "dream visitors" to listen to Earth's past while agonising on a future of certain doom.

And it's her wife's lips this news is coming from ... This story is of love and the hopelessness and resonance of the incarnation of flesh.

A novel of macro and micro humanity, and the attempt to find tender, tragic truth.'

—**Kerri Shying**, author of *sing out when you want me*,
Awarded Varuna Mick Dark Flagship Fellowship 2019 for *Know Your Country*.

Cover Illustration ©Claudia Jocher 2022; Photographs ©Claudia Jocher 2022
ISBN: 978-1-922612-04-5

Some stories within were inspired by real life events at many places. Identifying details have been changed. Any connection to Mutitjulu Community, except for facts on the historical record, is unintended and purely coincidental.

Trigger Warning: Contains fictionalised suicide, self-harm, accidental death, assault, medical procedures including abortion, mental illness.

References consulted include:

Pitjantjatjara/Yankunytjatjara to English Dictionary. Revised 2nd edition. Institute for Aboriginal Development, Alice Springs NT, Australia, 1996.

Friebe M & Matheson B, Shrubs and Trees of the Great Victoria Desert. Friends of the Great Victoria Desert Parks, 2008.

Kerle A, Uluru, Kata Tjuta & Watarrka. UNSW Press, Sydney 1995.

Simpson M, Rowlands R & J, Kimber R, People of the Western Desert WATER. NSW Department of Education 1976.

NPY Women's Council, Traditional Healers of Central Australia: Ngangkari. Alice Springs, Northern Territory, Australia 2013.

Mistakes are the author's own. Write to miki.mitayn@gmail.com

FOR L.G.W.

WITH LOVE AND RESPECT.
YOU GOT ME.

ALSO BY MIKI MITAYN

THE CONSCIOUS VIRUS

AN AEDGAR WISDOM NOVEL

Gain Knowledge to Grow Energy LLC, 2021

PHOTOGRAPHY BY CLAUDIA JOCHER ©2022

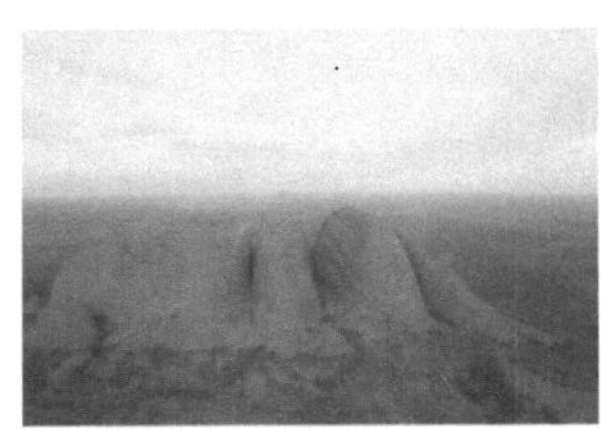

MAP

ANANGU LANDS (SHADED) CROSS STATE AND TERRITORY BORDERS IN CENTRAL AUSTRALIA.

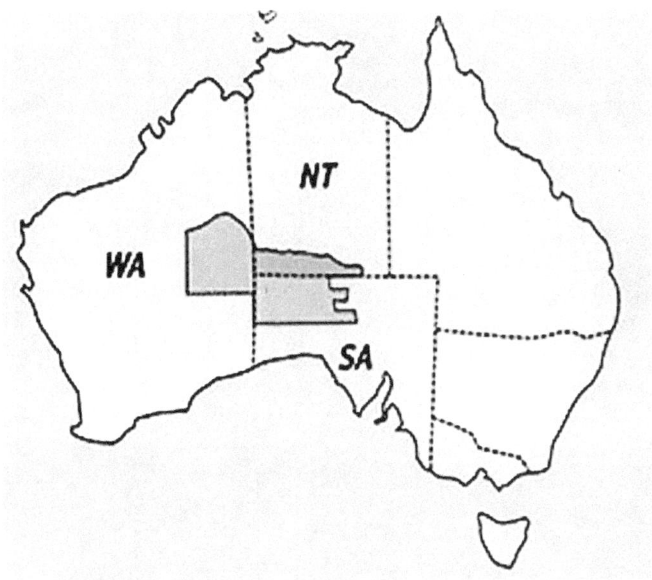

Historical Government map, showing Western Australia, Northern Territory and South Australia. This map is rough and inaccurate. In Western Australia Anangu Lands extend further, at least to the south, and probably in all directions.

PROLOGUE

B URBANK, CALIFORNIA
THURSDAY NOV 1, 2012

THEIR CHANNELLING SESSION created a rainbow bubble of the extraordinary in the beige, worn hotel room.

As soon as Dawn was in trance, Monica, the spirit she channelled, made an offer. 'We will arrange for the Dawn Weaver to bring it in, the main one that is around you, Mari. So you can be introduced.'

Nerida and Mari exchanged nervous looks. Mari raised her eyebrows where a dark curl fell on her forehead.

Nerida's grey eyes met Mari's brown. She squeezed her wife's hand. And unconsciously smoothed the blue silk scarf against her neck.

Having aroused their curiosity, Monica left.

Dawn came out of trance with a seated shimmy. She swept blonde locks off her shoulders. 'Okay. I need to take the socks off. I apologise ahead of time,' she joked. Planting her bare feet firmly on the dark red carpet, she said, 'This is **so** important. I want to make sure I'm doing it one thousand percent.'

It was cold outside. The trees in the carpark had lost their leaves. But the carpet was plush, the room heated.

Dawn's husband Trevor Weaver chose to stay for this session. *Native American beatnik entrepreneur*, Nerida thought, watching his tall form move quickly and quietly.

He gave Dawn, small and slender beside him, a water bottle. She scoffed a bit, screwed the lid tight, placed it at her feet. Trevor proffered a pillow for the small of her back, then went to sit quietly near the door. Perhaps Dawn had told him what she and Monica planned to do. And she wanted him nearby when channelling an energy she had never encountered before.

There was a pause of several minutes while Dawn, eyes closed, palms upturned on her thighs, attempted to channel this other energy.

A solidity charged the room's atmosphere. Nerida felt another being there.

But this was not like channelling Monica. Dawn's accustomed grace had left her. The chair creaked as she twisted in it.

Dawn strong, slim form made awkward, jerking movements, like tics and spasms. Her fingers moved in spidery stretches, her wrists, elbows and shoulders lifted, dropped and circled. The mouth worked, lips limbering up into shapes. There was puffing and releasing of the cheeks, and grimacing, like a performer exercising before coming onto the stage.

Nerida and Mari watched, fascinated and appalled. Dawn made deep, sometimes gasping, breaths. She hummed and murmured. Then gave way to higher-pitched moaning.

Effortful, all of it.

They were not used to such theatricality. Dawn was an honest, self-contained person, more used to the company of her animals than people. Monica, the entity she channelled, was always elegant and refined.

At a construction site outside the sealed hotel window, a power hammer pounded. The noise and vibration intruded.

Nerida was alarmed. *Is this what Mari has to do? This is not what she's like.*

Channelling the different energy, Dawn's throat and mouth formed sounds in a low, breathy, unsure voice: 'Sss, haa, he, el, kay.' Then with an effort, as if blowing out a candle, 'Hhhel...lo.'

Nerida smiled despite her misgivings, 'Hello.'

'Hello?' Mari spoke confidently.

'He... loooh...' the energy said.

'You're doing well.' Mari spoke softly.

Nerida felt love in the room, a radiance, such as one might feel at a peaceful death. *Or a birth.*

The energy panted with effort. 'M, mm...' They spoke the letter and voiced the sound. The hotel room filled with the sound of deep breathing. Dawn's body worked.

'Good to see you too,' said Mari, kindly.

After more deep breathing, they voiced, 'Mmma... Aaahhhhh... Reee.'

Mari thanked them, tilting her head in acknowledgement. Smiling. Nerida was amazed by the feeling of connection in the room. She saw that Mari didn't care, for now, about appearances.

Breathing deeply, the spirit began, 'A... B... C... D... Eeeeee... G... Haaaaaitch... Iiiii...' There was a longer pause and the sounds became unintelligible.

Then, with a sharp exhale, the spirit left.

Dawn returned. With eyes still closed she panted with relief, 'It's enough.' Then, 'Hoo!'

She smiled, opened her eyes. Looked brightly at Mari. 'It's doable. 'Really different!'

She continued to breathe deeply for several minutes, as if she'd run a sprint. 'Hm... quite remarkably different.'

'You all right?' Mari asked.

Dawn nodded.

'It's doable, it is. It's just really different energy! I can see why you're having a hard time trying to fix it.' She was still catching her breath. But excited.

'Siamese is the first language, and it's really Lemurian before that, and then it goes—it migrated and ended up, um, Druid.

'An odd energy—

'I can see why you're having a—I'll keep working on it. I'll keep trying.'

'Mari does similar kind of movements to what you were doing,' Nerida said. 'And the sounds and the breathing like that, but that's when she's asleep.

'It's less effort for her. The vocalisations come easier to her. Maybe the energy suits her better.' *I hope*, she thought.

'I'll try to ... I'm kind of used to doing this, so every time we meet I'll work it a little for you—' Dawn's pretty eyes were earnest, her brows knit.

'I was curious myself, you know. I was listening to some of what Monica said—and I actually think—' she slowed done. Then she said softly, 'It's so hard.'

Before Mari had time to respond, Dawn gathered up her enthusiasm again. 'It's an ancient energy, Mari! **Really** ancient.

'It comes from, almost, the primal depth of Earth.

'It's earth consciousness that took human form and then became aware of all the other stuff.

'That's why it's a little bit, it's almost a little tight in here,' she gestured towards her chest and throat. 'A little bit—' she made a guttural noise as if her tongue didn't work properly.

'I kept saying: "Let's do the alphabet, do the alphabet!" You know, that's what Trevor does when they're learning English, or even learning to speak.

'And that's what I think you should do too, just me talking, not Monica just me. Because that is a very oooold energy!

'It hasn't incarnated too often, so the physical form is a bit strange to it.

'And it's an earth energy, so it's—different.

'It's an earth consciousness kinda thing.

'Almost like it's the entity of the earth, you know? You have the entity that's us, people. And this is like the entity of the earth.'

She reflected. 'But it has taken human form, so it has an understanding, the consciousness of what it's like, being a human.

'It's got a story to tell!' Dawn laughed, rocking back in her seat. 'I saw it! I can't tell you—I just saw this spilling out and going eeugh!'

She tossed her hands out in an explosive, expansive gesture.

'It's just—it was like—it was like a rolled-up piece of cloth.' Dawn's broad, mid-western accent played out the vowels.

'It was like a big, long tablecloth that was folded, and they keep going, doing this, and it keeps unfolding and unfolding.' She rolled her open hands in a giving movement. 'Like this long piece of linen or silk. That's what it reminded me of, as it was unfolding.

'And the energy was right behind it.'

ONE

MUTITJULU COMMUNITY, CENTRAL AUSTRALIA
SATURDAY OCT 13, 2012

MARI CAME in from hanging the washing. She saw that Nerida had curled out of bed and was sitting at the front of their house. Mari could already feel the day's heat on the windows. With a quick wave to Nerida, she pulled the wonky blind down.

Their porch was a concrete slab with old plastic and wire chairs and a metal tub fireplace. Uluru was the centre of their outlook, towering 350 metres above the desert plains. Nerida felt privileged to be welcomed to live near the strange mountain.

She first came to Uluru in her late twenties, on a camping tour from Alice Springs, an adventure away from family life in Sydney. It was February. tickets were cheap because of the murderous heat. She stayed for a day and a half.

The Rock awed her with its massive split and jagged caves, tumbled boulders, waterholes and cliffs. She saw faces and animals in the Rock and finding that Anangu, the Traditional Owners there, could tell the ancient stories of what she saw.

In New South Wales, where her own Aboriginal Country was, Nerida felt a constant ache whenever she was in nature. Country trying to speak to her: about people who'd been there, the plants and what they could do, the animals. The formation of the land itself.

There was a nourishing feeling of connection for her there in Central Australia, where the people who owned the land (and were possessed by it) still lived. And shared.

The variety of plants, creatures and ecosystems, the infinite, bright night sky! She wished to stay away from the responsibilities she had in the city, to her family, her community and her comrades, to be near Uluru every day. *Three months*, she figured. *I could set up a tent at the campground at Yulara.*

What she and Mari had built was so much better than that. After decades of study and with Mari's skilled, stalwart support, they got to live near Uluru in return for the high-level care she gave the people.

From their house, Kata Tjuta, a majestic, twenty-kilometre-wide cluster of red, rounded, conglomerate-stone mountains—the Anangu name meant 'many heads'—loomed in coloured shadows on the western horizon. The tallest of those domes was 200 metres taller than Uluru. The smallest of them would tower over any of the world's cathedrals. The feeling of the places was otherworldly.

They were formally introduced to Uluru after their arrival to work in Mutitjulu in 2011. One evening after work, Angus took them out for a walk around the base of Uluru and introduced them to stories, lore and some of the caves.

Nerida met Angus in 2007 in Redfern, the Aboriginal nexus of inner-city Sydney, at a rally opposing the Federal Intervention. She stopped and looked up from the stall, where she was selling radical books and newspapers, to listen to the handsome Aboriginal man speak.

Angus introduced himself to the crowd. He came from Mutitjulu, the community of Traditional Owners at Uluru. 'Uluru is the name we gave the Rock when the land was returned to us in 1985.

'Some people still call it Ayers Rock. Mr Ayers was a politician in Adelaide in 1873. He might have been all right. But he did nothing to deserve having that magnificent, sacred place named after him.'

Angus was in his fifties, she thought. He spoke English fluently. He was at ease engaging about a thousand people.

He had a military bearing. His bushman's shirt was freshly ironed. But then Angus had tears in his eyes and his voice cracked.

'One of our young people took their own life just a month ago. 'Youth suicide is a terrible problem for us. Strong, healthy young people grown up and finding the racism, the dispossession and the consequences of colonisation are all too much to bear. It's heartbreaking.'

His brother Bull drove the earthmover to dig the graves. People covered them with artwork and flowers. They organised the whole funeral themselves. It was very sad, he said, that they did funerals so well.

Now one of the newspapers was persecuting Bull, who was on the Council. They sullied his name, implying that Bull was corrupt, or some kind of terrorist, because he had an Arab name.

Nerida talked to Angus afterwards. She'd been to Mutitjulu before, with Mari. They exchanged stories. His brother had a Lebanese mother. He and Bull had the same father.

He said, 'Y'know, now you're a doctor, you should come up there to Muti and work. People could really use the help.'

In 2011 then, Nerida had followed his suggestion.

Angus took Nerida and Mari to the cave at the base of Uluru where women ground seeds for flour and cooked soft bread. Called the Kitchen Cave in English, it was large and open, looking out over plains of seeded grasses and food trees. He pointed out the *kurku*, mulga trees. The hundreds growing there were a type that grew plenty of seeds to sustain people who travelled there for gatherings. He showed them the grain in the grasses. And the crystals women winnowed off the spinifex heads to make a malleable resin, which set hard enough to hold an axe or spearhead.

As they sat in the yawning space, Angus drew a map with his finger in the dust. He showed where Uluru fit on the Seven Sisters journey, part of *Tjukurpa* — Anangu Lore, pronounced, roughly, 'Choo-kurr-pah'.

It connected places and people across the continent. The sisters were famous among thousands of ancestor beings who created the Australian landscape and Aboriginal culture and lore amidst adventures and escapades.

The sisters were pursued by a wicked man. The degree of his wickedness was a subject of dispute. One of Nerida's ngangkari teachers, the Aboriginal healer she called Charlie, did paintings from this story in Tjukurpa. He insisted, 'He's not a bad one, really.'

There were hundreds of stories and almost as many important places related to the Seven Sisters. Nerida heard about them all over the country. Uluru felt like the centre of Australia and an epicentre of knowledge.

Nowadays, Angus explained, the Seven Sisters lived in Pleiades in the Orion constellation, visible in the sky world-over.

The coming weeks brought the hot time locals called *Mai Wiya*— 'nothing to eat.' That simplest name for the season was the one Anangu taught her first. She could understand and remember it. *Mai* meant food. Nerida knew words for food (like potato, rice, meat, spinach, pawpaw, coconut and bread) in five or six languages. She got by. Smiling people, the world over, gave her big serves of food.

Angus showed them dead finish, a small, straggly tree with needles at the ends of its leaves, blossomed bright yellow then. You could stick yourself with the spikes to charm a wart. It was called dead finish because it was the last plant surviving in drought.

That year, by mid-October in Muti it was already too hot for people to hunt. Too hot for anything, really. Every living thing wilted. And retreated in the ferocious heat.

There were lightning storms early that year, but no rain. Great thick bolts and crashing thunder terrified Mari.

She told Nerida that a schoolmate was killed by it when they were children. 'And the imprint of his body was in the grass for such a long time after. We saw it on the way to school.'

Their first house together had been at Koonawarra, near the coast in southern New South Wales. A flimsy house, it seemed to attract lightning from all directions.

When summer storms came in, Nerida, refreshed by the cool change and happy to be out from work, came home to find her love shaking in a doorway, holding herself in a ball, flinching with every crash of thunder.

She learned to send Mari texts from work when it was storming outside, trying to reassure her. Even if she would never answer the phone in a storm. Nerida came home earlier those days, when she could.

It was a mellow Sunday morning in the desert now and Nerida heard Selkie's children kicking a ball. Selkie's old dog was named 'Minyma' which meant 'grown woman' in the local language.

Minyma was the alpha dog of the pack in the part of the community where they lived.

She ambled over to Nerida and put her cool nose in her hand.

Nerida smelled resin in another neighbour's smoke. Wally Caldish was brewing his tea, squatted over his fire on the deck of his house, a metal and plastic donga. Nerida couldn't see him— Selkie's colourful hut was in the way—but could hear his brisk, hushed steps and the pops of desert oak cones in the fire.

I love it that Wally makes a fire every morning, even at this time of year. The air- conditioner was already chugging inside. The room smelled of coffee. 'How many eggs do you want?' Mari asked.

'Two, please. The Rock looks dramatic. Big, dark blue shadows, bright orange on the ridges.'

'Do you want to go out to Kata Tjuta today? Or maybe to the waterhole?'

Nerida stifled a groan. *Always this tension on the weekends. Mari needs to go out. But I'm so tired. I would love to stay in.* She didn't sleep well. She woke herself with snoring. Or Mari was sleep talking.

That Saturday night her rest was disturbed by shouting and fighting.

She worried. All week there'd been rows at the Blair sisters' houses, spilling onto the road and over to the Gaines house.

'They're fighting over a man,' nurse Becca told her on Friday. 'He went for Trudy and now he wants Kitty.'

'Wow,' Nerida said. 'Who is this man? Some kind of love god?'

'You've seen him once. He was getting himself off ice. I think he asked you for benzos. I can only say that because he asked me, too.'

Nerida didn't remember the man's face. But she was sympathetic. She would have given him the talk about the risk of dependency with benzodiazepines: 'They stop working after two or three nights and then you got a rebound insomnia. You think they're not working, so you take more. That's why they sell them in bottles of 50. The drug company loves people to become dependent on them. I've treated people who've been on these for thirty years with no effect but to feel like shit when they don't take them. I'll give you ten.'

She remembered harsh come downs. Nerida and her friends used hashish in the small hours when they'd used speed. She was eighteen. Her friends bought all of it from a truck driver.

Maybe they're fighting because he ran out of benzos.

She had enjoyed being high on amphetamine, loved the feeling of striding around the city with nothing but cigarettes for nourishment. It made her feel slim. Invincible.

Nerida only took it a few times, once or twice unknowingly.

Sometimes chemicals sold as acid (LSD) or even dried cannabis were laced with amphetamine as a cheap way to give a strong effect. That was one of the main risks she exposed herself to when experimenting with drugs as a teenager, not knowing what she took. Or how, consequently, it might affect her health.

She never injected speed. Some friends who did ended up in hospital with speed psychosis. And coming down off speed was already horrible, even taking it as a tablet like the truckies did.

Speed's initial effect was pleasurable—she could see how easily people became dependent on it. But her adrenals were overworked and exhausted by even a single dose, as well as all the other things she did then, seeking good feelings but neglecting her body.

Too many nights up all night. Too much sex. Never wearing enough clothes, sometimes not even shoes, in the winter. Eating irregularly—too little and then too much.

But it was probably the speed, she thought, that lead to her chronic insomnia. She couldn't drink coffee, coke or black tea for twenty years afterwards.

Nerida made it a principle in life to have no regrets. But decades of abstaining from chocolate because even the tiny amount of caffeine in it kept her awake, sympathetic nervous system switched on like fluoro lights, for nights. Was it worth it for those hours of flying around, irritating her friends, risking her safety? No. The only regret she had from youth was lack of self-care.

She said to Mari, 'It's gonna be hot quickly. Maybe we can go out when the sun gets lower around four or five o'clock?'

'I know you're tired from work. But I'm at home all week.

'Going to the store doesn't count.'

Nerida understood. But going to the store was a rare chance to get out of the clinic for her. She loved it. She envied Mari her flexibility and wished she'd use it more. Mari wished she had Nerida's ease with people. She trusted them and people treated her well.

There was a good store at Mutitjulu. Alongside groceries, with healthy, fresh-killed meat and produce, they sold fashion items: floral skirts and dresses, basketball jerseys and utilitarian hats, as well as small numbers of appliances.

A supermarket at the resort town, Yulara, thirty kilometres away, added variety to people's routine and diet. Sometimes Mari's need to get out on the weekend was satisfied by a trip to Yulara.

Nerida bought a newspaper there if the plane had been. A crossword and reviews were her idea of luxury. She'd only begun to do crosswords. Another kind of mental agility she clawed back, that she might never have lost if she hadn't smoked too much dope.

Mari took her camera to Yulara, stopping to photograph the Rock as they drove around it. Animals crossed their path—camels peering from among the desert oaks. Or she'd stop to pick up a thorny devil delicately trying to cross the road. Cradling the lizard in her hand, she told Nerida, 'They walk their feet on the same side together like an Egyptian hieroglyph of sideways-moving people. And did you know they can drink through their feet?'

Sometimes they watched the tourists climb the Rock, watching them crawl up and slide carefully down on their bums, clinging to the chain drilled into it for the purpose.

Sitting there at the base of the Climb, the women greeted people and introduced themselves. They told of falls. Of retrieving the body parts of a man that fell, reaching for his water bottle lid. Some stories might have been true. Around forty people had died up there.

The Traditional Owners stated clearly that climbing on the Rock disrespected its spiritual power, as well as being dangerous. There were signs in many languages asking people not to climb. Nerida was able to teach tourists some aspects of Aboriginal culture and she had the hard-won social ease of the doctor she'd become. So, most were happy to sit there with the women and learn, and not climb.

Afterwards Nerida said in the car, 'We feel so protective of this place and we're not even from here. I feel my gut churning when I see people climbing on it. I can't imagine how Anangu feel.'

'It makes me furious,' Mari said. 'People should show more respect.'

Mutitjulu Community was hidden and private on the other side of the Rock. No one was allowed there unless they had business and permission to go. Children roamed freely. Cars were rare and slow. The Aboriginal Community was a true home.

The women's house was sheltered and scratched by mulga trees. Birds sang. Willy wagtails, black and white wrens with wagging tail feathers, bobbled busily around on the lookout for news. Those little birds had a reputation as gossips among Aboriginal people. Some people feared them as bringers of bad news. Anangu called them *wipu inkanyi*, playful tail. 'Wipu' was euphemism for a penis, a dick, so the birds made kids titter. 'So's "willy," if you think about it,' Nerida remembered, telling Mari.

There were few other black and white birds, Nerida's totem. No magpies or currawongs. She missed them after they moved from the coast. Round, silly peewees were black and white. But they didn't satisfy her, even if they were family. Maybe she was too much like a peewee, the way people don't like family members who hold up a mirror exposing features they would rather deny.

Eventually a butcher bird, a fierce black and white bird with a surgical beak and a most melodious song, took up residence in a mulga tree near the house, soothing her spirit. Her totem found her. She was connected.

The women's house was luxurious by remote community standards. They had books on shelves of plank and brick. The previous tenant, Nurse Claire, left behind a bar fridge.

Mari explained when Claire visited for coffee later. 'I scrubbed it to remove any traces of the drugs you kept in it.

'Being a "dry community," means using it for beer isn't an option.'

Claire nodded, taking a piece of Mari's caprese cake, made with almond meal and oranges, covered in chocolate ganache.

'But I found a very good use for the fridge: I turned it into a chocolate fridge. Every child's dream. It's the beauty of being an adult, having this freedom.'

Mari opened the little fridge, pleased. Claire twisted around to see it full of colourfully wrapped bars and pralines.

'I buy all sorts of chocolate every time it's on special.'

'Like when the big fridge in the little shop failed,' Claire said.

'Yep. I like a bargain. There's always plenty of chocolate in the house. Actually I didn't eat that much since we had it, but our visitors did. It makes for happy moments.'

Nerida worked on the garden, and they had two crops a year of sweet citrus fruits, some tiny, token tomatoes, zucchini flowers and rocket in summer.

A carport in the yard sheltered Mari's fabulous old dark blue convertible, an almost- vintage Mercedes. And Nerida's brutish work car, the 4-wheel-drive sometimes necessary when roads were worn or washed out.

The house, built of hollow concrete bricks, was painted blue outside but the inside walls were still bare grey.

Mari hated it at first. She never really agreed to move.

'It is a bit institutional,' Nerida apologised, showing it to her.

'After all the cleaning, fixing, painting I did on our other house! I can't believe you agreed to this,' Mari had said then. 'You and Claire decided this without me.

'Do you have any idea how hard I worked to make that little house, our first house here at Muti, liveable?

'Now, I've gotta start all over again. You are so annoying!'

TWO

M UTITJULU, NT
SAME DAYS 2012

THE WALLS and windows in the blue house were mostly intact. There was no broken fibro to threaten them with asbestos fibres. Mari brought paint and sugar soap from Alice Springs and set about painting the walls in the living room and bedroom. The other bedroom, Nerida's office, could stay institutional, Mari decided.

The ladder she borrowed from Arthur, the local maintenance man, had legs that drifted apart. Nerida had to be home to hold onto it. Mari scrubbed and painted the lower part of the walls when Nerida was at work.

On weekends, Nerida held the ladder, reminding Mari, 'Gravity. Gravity. Put your weight straight down.'

You've only got one leg, remember. It took a swing of Mari's weight to manage stairs.

Climbing a ladder was a kind of miracle.

'I keep my arse in line,' Mari said, climbing with the same sturdy confidence Nerida admired.

There was one hole in the wall, near the back door behind the washing machine. An extinct cooling system in the ceiling still dripped water into the wall cavity there, and the washing machine hoses leaked, turning the cement brick into sand. It made a permanent puddle, with rusty slime and grey algae, outside. Mari repaired the hoses with tape. But the leak from the roof persisted.

The dampness attracted geckos. They came in through the cracks at the edge of the hole and Nerida was ordered to catch them and throw them out. She wasn't good at it. But would never admit that. Her cousins and sibs were confident handling lizards. Nerida was a squeamish, bookish child. Now she chased and cajoled the small, gummy-looking lizards with a plastic dish and a wet tea towel. Often, it took a day's pursuit, with the gecko taunting them with its chirps.

She had to do it. Mari couldn't bear to hear them. The chirps, she said, were 'like an itchy feeling vibrating between my skull and the brain, making all the hairs on my body stand up.'

Nerida gained Mari's admiration when she finally caught the gecko and threw it outside. 'My hero,' she'd smile, with a thankful hug.

Three long-prepared trips by maintenance people, one from Muti, two from Yulara, over eighteen months failed to repair the drip, the puddle, the rotting wall.

Arthur, a handyman, was white and smoked a pipe. Or sucked on the stem, over his cough, while he worked. He tied his ladder to a nearby tree or a downpipe when he used it.

There was a mouse plague in their second year in Central Australia. Arthur said: 'It will come to an end soon because they started eating each other.' Mice came through the walls. In the evening when the women sat down to read or watch telly, they'd jump at movements in the corners of their eyes. Not *mamus*. The mouse-traps they put out were all snapped by daybreak.

Inside the house, Arthur showed Mari a Northern Territory method of repairing gaps in the walls, using toilet paper mâché, sealed with just a smidgeon of silicon. It kept the spiders, snakes and lizards out. Some mice, too.

The mice did go away. They didn't see scorpions in the house either. It was a credit to Mari's Sisyphean housework. The house needed to be swept and cleaned constantly. Fine red dust got in everywhere, even through tiny cracks between the bricks.

The kitchen was irredeemably ugly. All the community houses (that had kitchens) had the same-coloured cupboards and bench tops, a sick-looking puce and a vapid pink that Mari called 'a chicken and pork combination.'

'The colours might have been fashionable for three months in 1993. There's an oversupply of that laminate somewhere,' Nerida said. 'Like that dark sienna we call "Mission Brown" that gets used on the frames and gutters of the low-budget government buildings.'

Mari was an artist with an exquisite sensitivity to colour. Tolerating the clash of colours in the kitchen took discipline. She still complained about it.

'You remind me of Wilde's dying words,' Nerida said, snuggling into her. 'You know, dying of meningitis from an untreated ear infection in Paris, poor darling Oscar. "My wallpaper and I are fighting a duel to the death. One or other of us has got to go."'

'He didn't really say that, did he?' Mari asked.

'I need to get you out of this kitchen more, huh?' Nerida said.

The house was nearly secure, but they shook their shoes before putting feet inside. Mari rattled her prosthesis to be sure there were no ants or other bities in the socket. Nerida saw enough scorpion and snake bites at the clinic to see how much they hurt.

Mari always wore her shoe in the house. A *Hausschuh*, German-style.

Nerida spent several years mostly barefoot in her early adulthood, disregarding concerns about worms and glass. She found Mari's care for shoes hard to relate to, even if she understood the importance of protecting Mari's remaining foot. The house tiles were cool, lovely in the summer. It was one of the moments she felt sorry for Mari.

Their first house at Mutitjulu was on the edge of the Community, in a spot that inspired Mari to draw plans for a deck at the house, to fully enjoy the splendid view of the Uluru.

Nerida was disturbed to be housed near other Community workers, who were overwhelmingly white.

Later, she understood the deep sense of privacy Anangu nurtured and cherished. And she saw that workers of every ethnicity from other places, like she and her wife, came and went, often unexpectedly. Community people and their families and friends had enough responsibilities and dramas of their own without having to look after strangers.

That first house was small. It felt like it might be just right for the two of them.

But two months later, when the removalists brought all their stuff —their big red lounge, Nerida's 130 boxes of books, Mari's easels, paint boxes and canvases—they built a mountain of furniture and boxes in the middle of the small living room. And left Mari to it. It was the Friday afternoon before a long weekend and there was serious drinking to get started in Yulara.

The removalists left all the doors of the house—which Mari had been training Nerida to close conscientiously—wide open. It was Summer and Nerida came home from the clinic to find her one-legged wife working away at the box mountain, distressed by the hundreds of huge blowflies collecting at the apex of the slanted ceiling. Their buzzing was a chainsaw overhead.

Mari killed the blowflies over the coming weeks. Fly spray eventually knocked them down. It took a lot. And they discharged maggots when they were dying, so cleaning maggots off the windowsills two or three times a day, wiping maggots off their crystals—Nerida's quartz, Mari's blue-green fluorite pyramid (from the Dapto lapidary fair) and her little piece of turquoise from New Mexico, a piece of lapis Nerida bought in India—all became part of her house-keeping routine.

The house had some damage.

Mari repaired the hole smashed into the veneer wardrobe door, sanding it smooth and scrubbed at the rusty marks on the bedroom wall and wardrobe, which were probably blood stains. She white-washed the wardrobe door and painted the windowsills and bathroom cabinets a vibrant aqua, bought on their first weekend shopping trip to Alice Springs.

The house had a fenced car port beside the house.

But when Mari's car arrived on the back of a truck from Sydney, the whole Community knew.

'He had to unload it right in front of the shop, didn't he? I told them to deliver it in Yulara or bring it out to our house. But no, he knew better, didn't he?' Mari fumed.

And that night, they heard people breaking into the car port. They stole petrol from the car. Marked the paintwork and damaged the lid of the tank where they levered it off.

'Petrol sniffing's still an issue, then?' Nerida asked nurse Claire at the clinic in the morning.

'It's only because the car was just arrived. Next time you fill up, it'll be the local fuel— it's not sniffable—so they won't bother you again. Unless they steal the whole car, of course,' said Claire. She smiled at Jasmine, the clinic receptionist.

Jasmine got the job straight outta jail, she'd explained to Nerida. She had her front teeth missing but was not shy about smiling once you knew her. Jasmine yelled at the patients. Yelled at her family from the front door of the clinic. She answered the phone with her own style. Jasmine wore oversized men's shirts with a preference for flannel. She wrote messages for the doctor on little torn-off triangles of paper with big round handwriting. She was maybe the best receptionist they'd ever had, Claire said.

Nerida arranged a meeting with one of the senior Community

people after lunch, to talk about the break-in. 'If mob want a doctor here, they need to leave us in peace at our place,' she said.

Her ally got the word around and they were reassured that the break-in was likely by young people from another Community and that it would not happen again.

Mari filled her car with non-sniffable petrol and they had no further problems.

The deep quiet of the desert settled around them at night. Mari was getting on top of the maggots.

She got her pressure cooker out, cooked beans and froze some. Began a sourdough culture.

Mari climbed a ladder to seal holes between the walls and ceiling, with Arthur's Territory method. The house was becoming more live-able, even delightful, when Claire suggested to Nerida at work that they should move out.

Nerida was open to the idea. There were still blood stains on the fan over their bed.

Nerida couldn't shake the feeling that there was a disturbed spirit around.

The bedroom was so small that you couldn't fully open the door because it hit the bed.

And she hadn't unpacked her books because there was nowhere to put them.

Claire had been coming to Mutitjulu for years already and spoke conversational and medical Pitjantjatjara, one of the main Anangu languages. She was dark-skinned with bushy hair. Her character was blunt and earthy, and she was knowledgeable and hardworking to a fault. She'd been there during the Intervention.

When she first met Claire, authoritatively instructing her on the completion of health assessments, Nerida smiled to herself thinking, 'You have no idea yet, how much you're gonna like me.'

Rebecca, another regular nurse, was a gentle soul who took particular care of the young mothers and children. Where Claire was loud and passionate, Becca was quietly committed.

Overweight, friendly, slow to anger, Becca always thought the best of people. Claire was cynical, brash and bossy. The two were solid friends. They planned to share the little house behind the hollow brick house, working on rotation. Having Dr Nerida nearby would be good. And it was a better house than the one they were in.

Nerida went with Claire to see the bigger house in their lunch break. 'This should be the doctor's house, ye!' Claire said. It was good.

The bedroom door opened fully and there were no bloodstains. There was also a little bath, which Nerida would love. And big cupboards in the hall so that things could be put away. Nerida had never had a house with enough cupboards to put things away.

It was great for Anangu to be cared for by nurses that knew them. Nerida wanted to encourage Claire and Becca to keep coming.

Looking at Uluru from the verandah at the front of the blue house, Nerida thought of a conversation she'd had that morning when Blossom Wandering came to the clinic. She was rarely seen there, Jasmine said. 'And she never, ever takes her medicine.'

Blossom was 78 years old (more or less), culturally strong and charismatic. She was a great dancer. Nerida had seen her dancing *inma*—dances from local stories, performed at ceremonies—at a fire-lit performance, when she and Mari travelled in Central Australia in 2007.

She'd seen Blossom, painted up in ochres and adorned with feathers, dancing on Indigenous television, too. Muti had several rock star Elders. The small community punched above its weight in charisma. Another woman named Thea was one. She'd met Oprah.

Blossom was, certainly.

Nerida worked with Blossom, reducing the medications she'd been prescribed to what she really needed. Visiting doctors, over the past five years at least, kept adding more and more medications to peoples' med charts without ever ceasing anything.

The more medicines they added, the less likely people were to take them. And when they did take them all as prescribed, their blood pressure or blood sugar crashed, or the medicines fought with each other. And they didn't feel better. Sometimes they felt really sick.

They managed to reduce Blossom's list of ten medicines down to two, which Nerida thought she might take sometimes. One would reduce her blood pressure, the other would reduce her blood sugar.

Getting up to leave, Blossom said, 'So you staying here for a while?'

'Why not?' Nerida smiled, accepting the compliment. 'I like the people. It's a privilege to be here. Country's beautiful.'

'It is good in the Autumn when the fruits and flowers come out. We got quandong, *mangata*. Tell your wife they make a lovely jam!' Blossom smiled. 'You know the lolly flowers? The kids love them.'

Nerida did. Honey grevilleas had nectar sweeter than honeysuckle. Sipping ambrosia from the big, wet flowers in the morning or after rain was one of the pleasures of living in Central Australia. 'But they come out at the end of winter, yes? Not in Autumn?' She tried to remember the feeling of the chill air.

Blossom smiled and called her *ninti*. She tapped her temple. 'Clever one.'

'And then there's the Rock,' Nerida continued. 'Uluru is a special place, eh?'

'That Rock?' Blossom screwed her face up. She might have spit if she wasn't in the doctor's office. 'That Rock's a terrible place. Look at it! Nothing lives there!' She turned and left abruptly.

Nerida had not known what to say. It was a new concept to her, that not all Anangu, all people for that matter, loved Uluru. She didn't see Blossom for a long time after that.

There were always plenty of people to meet in the clinic. Felicity had short brown hair, streaked with grey. She touched Claire's soft, frizzy black hair affectionately.

Felicity had an autoimmune disease that would probably be the death of her, but managed her life with humour and stamina, caring for her grown children, who were in and out of jail.

Claire came out of the house. Locking the front door, she mentioned that a client, a middle-aged woman named Thea, was doing so well since Nerida prescribed antidepressant medication. 'She's come out of herself—just that small dose and she's smiling every day.'

'When you get a good match for the brain, they can work really well,' Nerida said as they got into the car to go back to the clinic. Thea's smile was fabulous, showing beautiful teeth and a glimmer in her black eyes. Her hair was shiny nowadays and she'd taken to wearing a flower in her hair sometimes.

Nerida wondered about Thea's history. Not much was in the medical records about people's social and emotional history. It wasn't clear whether previous doctors didn't know, didn't care, or didn't have the time and communication skills to find out.

Nerida was the first permanent doctor at Muti since the disaster of the Intervention.

In 2012 the Community wasn't occupied by soldiers the way it was in 2007. But there were full-time cops there now, with their two-million-dollar police station. They enforced the rules of the Intervention, no alcohol, no porn, no control of your money.

The latter happened when people's welfare benefits were sequestered. Half of their money was not available as cash, only on a card. The card could only be used at certain shops. Muti only had one shop, anyway.

It meant that half of their meagre income couldn't be used for smokes. But it couldn't be used for fuel or ammo for hunting, either. For peripatetic people like Anangu, this reduced their opportunities to visit Country or go to funerals or other ceremonies. It made it harder to live from the animals. Hunting, butchering and cooking knowledge was diminished. Tenuous and precious social connections withered.

People who were bullied for money were now bullied for the use of their cards instead. Porn was more attractive than ever.

And, while the police displayed the cars of local men at the front of their station with a sash across the window (like a car sales yard) saying, 'Confiscated for grog running,' some park rangers, living at Rangerville, a couple of sand hills away, stored their alcohol in trap-door-covered holes in the yard.

The men whose cars were confiscated were jailed, often for as little as a couple of slabs of beer in the car boot.

Family members who had been functional alcoholics—people who worked all day and enjoyed a beer or three as the sun set over the Rock—were now homeless in Alice Springs, living rough in the long grass with others.

And every severe alcoholic, and every place had a couple, was now in town, oscillating between lying in the long grass, withdrawing in the hospital and the homeless shelter or going to jail.

People in Community had the grace to leave Dr Nerida and her wife out of their drama, until they needed medical help.

But she heard enough of the backstory to know, for example, that Mary Belling had twenty people in her house with one toilet and the stove was broken.

Sybil Piney's son was severely disabled, needing nappies, and they had no money to buy them.

Sybil used the washing machine at Respite for the towels and rags she used. Nerida knew that because the woman running Respite asked her about how to clean the machine. She helped Sybil by buying covered buckets and bleach for her to soak the materials in. Helped her manage the space and machines, keep it all sanitary.

Nerida made a mental note to investigate funding for continence supplies. *In my spare time between 1 and 3 in the morning.*

SE POLICE FOR
GROG/DRUG
RUNNING.

THREE

CHRISTMAS ISLAND & THE NORTHERN TERRITORY 2012

BEFORE MARI WENT to learn from Dawn and Monica in Burbank, she and Nerida talked about going to a different place. Mutitjulu was sublime, but stressful.

The salt water called.

Nerida accepted a job on Christmas Island, an Australian Territory in the Indian Ocean.

They planned the move for the new year.

CI was fascinating. Long isolated, it was populated by blue-footed boobies, giant coconut crabs and colourful sea life. There was a small harbour for diving and a couple of small beaches. Most of the island was surrounded by razor-sharp volcanic rocks.

People there had a rich, painful, history as descendants of indentured labourers from southeast Asia and the Pacific islands. Their ancestors were brought there to mine phosphate and harvest coconuts for processing into copra. A phosphate mine, with paid labour now, still operated.

Recently arrived was a newer group of people, numbering as many as the island's original population: detained refugees and aspiring immigrants. They sailed there in rickety boats and were bailed up and imprisoned (sometimes for years) by the Australian government.

Mari and Nerida were not dreaming of a peaceful life, but of more beauty, adventure and drama.

Meanwhile, they had such struggle at Muti that a job on a prison island could be an improvement.

Rural Australia was enduring a suicide epidemic. Remote Aboriginal communities were not spared. In 2012, well over a hundred Aboriginal people died by suicide, mostly young men.

The number of young women who died by suicide, Angus told Nerida with concern, had risen since the Intervention.

Adding insult to injury, the deaths were underreported because Indigenous people were often not recognised by police. And some suicides, like car accidents, were invisible that way, too.

Nerida's cousin drank herself to death after she was denied access to her child. It took six years but, in Nerida's mind, it was still suicide. Nobody could stop her. Now, another cousin was doing the same thing. Destroying his liver. No one could stop him, either. Nerida tried. So did her aunty.

Nerida understood the drive to self-destruct. She took a long time to learn not to hurt herself when she was growing into adulthood. At least she wasn't a drinker (like her Dad) and she didn't eat rubbish food (like her son). But she was plump. Sometimes, mostly, she was fat.

Being fat meant that she was perceived by some (especially among her colleagues) as a greedy and unreliable person. That made her frustrated and angry. She could be a self- controlled, disciplined in a thousand ways a day. She'd got through med school on a low income, after all.

She felt that being fat showed the world that she and her body were not communicating soundly. She said countless times, 'I'm not eating that.' And then ate it. She broke her promises to herself over and over. Her inability to trust herself undermined her in so many ways.

Sometimes she accepted her fat. Accepted that her brain and body worked that way and committed to being kind to herself.

She learned to wait before she judged photos or paintings Mari made of her because she found that she could accept, even enjoy, the images months or years later.

Mutitjulu people, most Aboriginal people, accepted her as she was. But no doubt her addictive behaviour was there for the world to see.

Perhaps some aspect of my spirit decided to do it, she thought. *It makes me more approachable. And compassionate.*

She knew the day she'd started binge-eating, aged twelve. A lonely, inarticulate girl, confused by unspoken feelings, grieving the loss of her grandmother. A voice in her head said clearly, 'Sure you want to do this? You might regret it.' She felt herself reply, 'I don't care. Bring it on.' And then kept eating til it hurt.

She heard the same voice in her head before she dropped a tab of putative acid that had poisons in it when she was a reckless adolescent. She'd already battled depression. Ignored that voice just the same, thinking, *No one cares enough to stop me. Why should I?*

Several months of drug-induced psychosis followed. She did well to heal herself after that. It made her a kinder and more insightful person. Eventually.

Now numbers, representing people, filled her inbox, saying that Aboriginal people were six times more likely to complete suicide than non-Indigenous Australians. Some commentators implied that it was a kind of fashion trend, by youth who did not understand the finality of death.

Nerida disagreed. *It's an outcome of colonisation. Inestimable grief, anger and heartbreak lies behind those numbers.*

Dispossession from Land led to generations of emotional distress and material poverty.

When they came, the British attacked the men first. It began for her people in the south when the timber was taken from their river. Men were hunted down like animals there. It terrorised the people. Her tribe brought other men food and water at night as they lay injured in deep, spiked traps.

I want my Land back! cried her heart, *to soothe my soul.*

Lots of other people in Australia looked at Indigenous people now as if they didn't belong there.

It got sharp when the Intervention was launched.

The Federal Intervention was an invasion of Aboriginal communities by the Australian military and federal police in 2007. The government suspended the Racial Discrimination Act to render their racist discrimination legal.

The Indigenous Affairs Minister went to Mutitjulu then, and held a press event outside the Community reporting he'd just come from a meeting with Elders, who'd asked for troops to come in to protect them.

People in Muti told Nerida that was a lie. He hadn't even come into the Community or looked for anyone to talk to.

The Intervention was pioneered at Mutitjulu, Angus had explained, because it was in Uluru-Kata Tjuta National Park.

The Federal government sent troops there without the consent of the Territory government. Aboriginal people saw the attack as a move to assert dominance over land that had been reclaimed through Land Rights battles.

There was gas, oil and uranium to extract and export in desert lands that the Australian rulers had once deemed worthless. Parcels of land were acquired amid a moral panic, vilifying all Aboriginal men as child sex abusers and rapists.

Nerida and Mari visited Mutitjulu for the first time in 2007 just a month after the Intervention was launched, on a trip to Aboriginal Communities in The Lands.

Nerida wanted to introduce Mari to the ngangkari healers she studied with. They had a mellow meeting with Victor and Charlie in Ernabella, on the South Australian side of the border. Then, having permission to visit Mutitjulu—a rare privilege—they went to see friends there, as well.

But their friends were gone. Muti was a ghost town. The only Anangu left were a severely disabled man and his mother. Terrified that their children would be exposed to violence or removed from them, everyone else had run away into the sand hills, to other camp-sites and homelands, when the heavily armed forces arrived.

There was a nurse at the clinic, who quickly denied any responsibility, 'I'm just from an agency.'

The ceiling was collapsing in the emergency room. The clinic was run by a man with the newly created position of 'Community Business Manager'. His previous job was as a personal assistant to the CEO of a mining company.

What would he know about health? His experience is all about money, Nerida thought. The clinic had been run by a Community Board, like other Aboriginal Health Services.

The Intervention had a dogma that Community people weren't capable of running their organisations. Government fiat enforced that clinic management was handed to other people (from other cultures) in Alice Springs, five hundred kilometres away.

The one other Aboriginal person still in Community then was now their neighbour, Barry. He was a pop star, a one-hit-wonder, in the seventies. He still had charisma. A bearded man with a pot belly and a mellifluous voice, he dressed as the cowboy he'd never been.

Barry came out to greet there, them. He offered the women a brief, walking tour of the deserted community.

There was the brand-new, three-metre-high fence around the

childcare centre, presumably to keep the pedophiles out. The shop (which was closed). And the new police station, where he introduced them to the resident policemen. The six men were heavily armed and looked sheepish, having no one to patrol. Barry was waiting on funding from the resort at Yulara to make a spiritual documentary, he said.

Nerida explained to Mari, 'The excuse for launching the Intervention was that children needed to be saved. A myth about a pedophilia ring was made up by a government staffer. He pretended to be a youth worker in Muti on the late-night news. It's a fucking scandal.'

Barry, not wanting to engage in the controversy, drifted off to chat with one of the cops.

Mari looked around, at the empty, embattled houses, the closed-up shop like an angry mouth, and said, 'I could see us living and working here.' Nerida did a double take.

'I feel a strong attraction to this place,' Mari said quietly. 'It's the beauty of the colours, the combinations between the deep red sand, the red to orange rocks and the clear blue skies.

'Although there's a lot of poverty around, it's in an incredibly powerful area. I can't explain why.'

'Well, it's Uluru,' Nerida said. The monolith was in sight everywhere.

'It's right in Uluru's shadow. That's right. And there's still privacy with that big sand dune separating Mutitjulu from the main road. I don't love these packs of dogs roaming around.'

Nerida pulled her back to their car. On the drive to Yulara she explained more to Mari about the Intervention.

A report had been presented to parliament on the extent of child abuse and family violence, calling for consultation to empower communities. It was like so many reports before. But this one was used as a device to justify draconian measures.

Some communities and homelands were offered limited housing or infrastructure in exchange for leasing their hard-won land back to the government. The leased land would be 'improved,' lawyers said, so the government would not be obliged to give it back when the lease expired.

In the years since then, the rate of self-harm and suicide in the invaded communities grew six-fold. Alcohol-related harm and family violence did not improve, despite exploded rates of incarceration.

Their small community was no exception to this horror. Some seasons, a young person threatened suicide once a week or more.

Any emergency call to the clinic put Jasmine on high alert, facilitating vital communication. Nerida stayed at the clinic to manage whatever happened while the nurses were away. Sometimes, if they had the luxury of three nurses, one stayed to help her.

It was daunting, helping people with their headaches or high blood pressure—or worse problems—with that unhappy young person's drama looming.

Sometimes she felt too powerless staying behind. Nerida drove out with a nurse or community member, urgently searching, apprehensive of what they might find.

One winter night a young man died. Claire and another nurse were called by the police.

Friends found him. He fell in love with the wrong person, people said. They cut his limp, cold body down.

They kept a rope cutter in the ambulance.

Nerida and Claire could see no pattern. Young people died who'd shown no sign of depression or other mental illness. They must have been overwhelmed, Nerida thought.

Maybe she could understand.

There was a night, long ago, when she felt that way. She was a teenager, travelling with a man who did not care for her.

She'd found out that day she was pregnant. An embryo was conceived when Nerida's guts were cleared out by the unfamiliar bugs of travel—she'd had diarrhoea in Sumatra, she remembered— and her pill didn't work.

She'd been taking that pill alongside other chemicals, at the encouragement of her boyfriend (who refused to be a boyfriend) for a month or two while pregnant. *No wonder I've been so emotional*, she thought.

Her emotionality frustrated her travelling companion. He was mostly annoyed with her. She tried to leave him in Malaysia but he persuaded her against it. Now they were in Nepal. He planned to leave her in two weeks. He wanted to help her find a way to terminate the pregnancy first. He said 'I love you,' for the first time in a year that day. She didn't believe him.

She felt overwhelmed and despairing. Her body was so thick, so fertile. People in Sumatra, seeing her crying in the rain on a mushroom trip, had told her she was pregnant. She thought it was just that she was full-breasted and fat. But she was pregnant then. The rural people seemed to tell by looking.

She wanted to destroy her body that night.

It was a beautiful, strong body, if only she'd been able to see it. She was an unfashionable shape in a mainstream culture that valued appearance over function.

As a teen, she fell for the sweet salves and pretty paints and painful depilation like everyone. Peered critically into the mirror saying nasty things to herself when her skin showed the strong doses of hormones that grew a child into a woman.

Menstruating meant trying to manage shameful mess, sometimes passing painful big clots of blood, and never being able to talk to anyone about it. Young Nerida could not believe that half of humanity was going through that every month and not talking about it.

School was harsh.

She never fit in a clique, but moved from one to another, always on the outer.

That night, pregnant for the second time at age nineteen, she felt like cutting herself. That would be a way to get the pain outside, where people could see it. *But what's the point of that when no one cares anyway?*

She got up from the cheap bed, careful not to disturb her partner, who would be irritated if she woke him with her dramatics. She lay down on the cold, bare concrete floor. The ache in her kidneys from the cold was sickening. She thought about dying. She thought of the lines from Hamlet, that she read at school.

O, that this too too solid flesh would melt
Thaw and resolve itself into a dew!
Or that the Everlasting had not fix'd
His canon 'gainst self-slaughter!
O God! God!
How weary, stale, flat and unprofitable,
Seem to me all the uses of this world!

Hamlet never got pregnant because he had Bali belly. His sturdy prince's body was not the trouble hers was. She knew she was not the delicate Ophelia, though. She would never leave a corpse to be admired, prettily expired among the drowned wildflowers.

After a while, she realised there was enough love still inside her, deposited like her baby fat, to know that she could not cause her parents the pain of taking her own life.

She knew she was privileged, with her fair skin. She had cousins that got treated as shoplifters whenever they went to the store, because they were brown.

She grew up in a house (after they moved out of her grandparents' garage) and there was food on the table every day. It wasn't always good food, but it kept the family going.

Her blonde and pink mum worked every day to feed and shelter them. Brown and copper, Dad was affectionate even though he drank just about every day.

Nerida would live for them, even if they didn't seem to like her much now that she was grown up (and she didn't always like them). She was still angry and contemptuous towards herself.

Maybe that was why she was with that man.

There were other times in the following years when she understood that dying could seem easier than going ahead. But life got better the older she got, as she understood the world better and so gained power. She was glad now that she'd stayed in the world. Life got more engaging and interesting the longer she lived.

These were some of things she talked to her clients about, offering her own experience to engage and stimulate them.

Now in her small clinic office, Nerida hopped on the net and found what she wanted: the passage in Keats' *Ode to a Nightingale*:

Darkling I listen; and, for many a time
I have been half in love with easeful Death,
Call'd him soft names in many a musèd rhyme,
To take into the air my quiet breath.
Now more than ever seems it rich to die,
To cease upon the midnight with no pain,
While thou art pouring forth thy soul abroad
In such an ecstasy!
Still wouldst thou sing, and I have ears in vain—
To thy high requiem become a sod.

A bird's song inspired him to find ecstasy. And in a painless death, he saw a promise of peace.

Dr Nerida talked about being young and 'half in love with an easeful death' with Maleah, a twenty-year-old Anangu woman who had threatened to kill herself that day. It was to normalise the thoughts Maleah had, to talk about the feelings without having to act on them.

The nurses had driven out at lunchtime after her aunty called the clinic, terrified. They found Maleah walking in the sand hills with a piece of electrical cord in her hand.

Nerida asked Maleah about the people that loved her, and the young woman cried.

They talked about the idea that a spirit has a purpose when we come to this world. 'You need a chance to find out what that is.'

And Nerida suggested gently that if Maleah took her life, she might have to come back again—be born a baby, learn to clean and feed herself, to walk, talk—and deal with the same questions she faced now, again.

Nerida was a militant atheist as a young woman. She appreciated that her experiences had led her to understand that people had a spirit. Most Anangu knew. Most First Nations people knew.

They did a pregnancy test to be sure. She wasn't.

Maleah didn't talk about the boy or man she'd been with. 'I guess he's a fuckwit,' Nerida said.

'Yeah, probably.'

They planned to talk every few days until Maleah felt safer being on her own.

In the meantime, she promised Nerida that she would not hurt herself before then. It wasn't much but it was all they could do.

There were eight different organisations funded to service mental health in Mutitjulu but only two of them ever visited: one charity once for two days once a year. Another came for a few days six times a year, offering a real service. Nerida wrote a referral.

The older people were frightened, of course, by this behaviour in the youth.

In the old days, Nerida had was told, a kind of voluntary dying was practised among the desert people.

Very old people sometimes chose to stay behind to die when they were a burden to the clan. And infanticide was practised as a means of survival. But suicide—taking your own life when your body was still functional—was unknown in pre-European times.

Through long discussions articulating feelings and the creation of language-rich resources in their languages, people did begin to talk more.

After one of these meetings, Selkie told Nerida that she heard some of the Elders discussing it, puzzled.

'Ssuey-chide, what is it, this thing? Sui-chide.' The aunty chewed the word in Pitjantjatjara. 'How can a person, alive and healthy, take their own life? How they turn against themselves that way?'

Nerida thought. Some young people had no capacity for frustration. They'd self-harm or threaten suicide over not being able to buy cigarettes or an everyday argument. They needed individual support to learn to cope.

For others, like young Nerida, there were complex issues, navigating the brutality, anonymity and promises of capitalist society, while struggling to access and maintain the exquisite sensitivity and nuanced spirituality of their Indigenous cultures.

Indigenous cultures could be brutal, too. Sometimes it must have felt like the youth faced intolerable harshness wherever they turned.

Repeated threats of suicide and the fear of it wore at the nerves of all of them at the clinic, traumatised them. Especially the nurses, who were the ones called in the middle of the night.

The fear of confronting violent death, especially self-created death, was corrosive.

They all hoped for a false alarm. They tried to help look after these young ones, these 'false alarms' with strained bodies and exhausted minds.

Claire had seen suicides at remote communities before. She was not inured but maintained a degree of detachment.

'These people are not your family,' she said emphatically.

How can she say that? Nerida puzzled.

Claire, who came from a large family, tried to protect the doctor's functioning.

But isn't every human my relation?

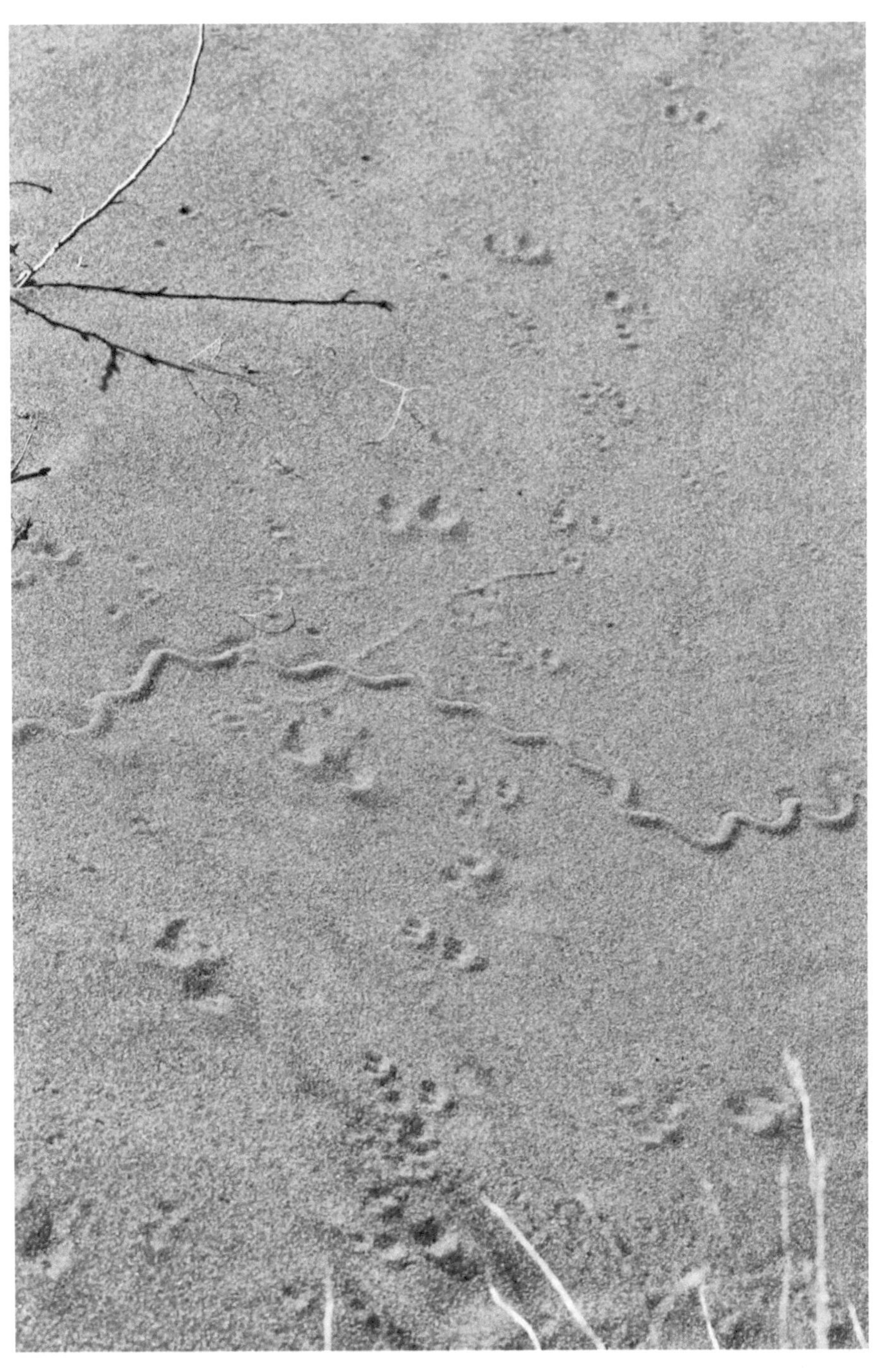

L A INTERNATIONAL AIRPORT
SATURDAY NOV 24, 2012

'GOD, LOS ANGELES AIRPORT IS HIDEOUS,' said Nerida.

She felt sore, exhausted and dirty after about twenty hours of economy travel from Yulara to Sydney and then from Sydney to LA.

They stood in the immigration queue, which was a dozen people across and half a kilometre long.

'I slept on the floor here between flights on my way to Alaska a few years ago. The carpet's so thin it's like a layer of dirty plastic on concrete. Everything was closed. Nothing good to eat.'

'What did you do in Alaska?' Mari was in pain—her stump swelled during the flight and pressed tight in her prosthetic leg—but was handling it.

'First Nations doctors conference. I got to dance at Pow Wow. And went to sweat lodge on the permafrost.'

'Was it a spiritual experience?'

'Hard to tell.

'I was sleep deprived, jet lagged. The sun set past 11 at night and rose at 3 in the morning. By the third day I was manic.

'I won a Pendleton blanket as a door prize at Pow Wow. I was ecstatic, walking and dancing draped in it, getting my picture taken. But it was another doctor's ticket that won. He'd asked me to hold it when he left early. I forgot.'

They shuffled forward about two feet. The man behind them had an unpleasant cough.

The women huddled closer together. 'So, you stole it from him?'

'He was good about it. Took his time trying to help me understand that the blanket wasn't really mine.

'We shared it in the end. I had it for a few years, then sent it to him when his son was born.'

They moved a bit closer to the dark, faux-wood booths where uniformed officers were conducting computer searches and finger-printing people. The massive queue was dividing into six or seven different lines. A man in front smelled strongly of stale sweat.

'And sweat lodge? You wouldn't go in a sauna, would you?'

'Not after these years in the desert.' Nerida ran her fingers along the spine of her passport. 'I had to learn about the ceremony to go, you know. You can't go when you've got your period. I thought that was sexist. But it's sensible, really. It was quite physically and emotionally gruelling. You wouldn't want to be bleeding.'

Mari gazed at the duty-free shop. Maybe she liked whisky well enough to bother to buy some and carry it around. 'Uhuh.'

'I learned about the stones. The hot stones in sweat lodge are special stones brought in by a strong and knowledgeable person. They're white or red hot. You have to pull your feet up away from them. We were sitting in a hollow in the earth with a low stone wall and a domed roof over it.'

'What's the roof made of?' Mari had decided against whisky and was contemplating perfumes now. 'I think we'll be in this line for another hour,' she said. She frowned.

They should let a person with one leg go ahead of other people, Nerida thought. But Mari wouldn't want her to do that now—to go to the front and advocate for her. She wouldn't show her disability unless she was desperate.

She was in pain, but she wasn't desperate today.

'Ours was black plastic and earth over a frame made of branches,' Nerida recalled. 'The thing about the stones is, they represent ancestors. When they put the hot stone in front of me, mine cracked. A lot of people got up and left the lodge straight away then. I didn't realise how dramatic that was. I was just relieved to get the extra space. I could move my legs a little. I should have been scared. It was my great, great grandmother. She was angry with me. She came and scolded.'

'Like, you could hear her voice?'

'No. But the words were in my head and I knew they were from her. I had a picture of her in my head, too. She was tiny, very black skin and penetrating eyes.'

'You've seen a photo.'

'Yes, but I hadn't yet, then.'

'So what did she say?'

'I'd been talking at a conference about the way that rape was used to subjugate Aboriginal women at First Contact. In our family, she was the first to see the British, you know. "Don't you dare make me a victim! I was never a victim. I survived as my own person, my own woman. I made choices for survival but they were my choices!" That's the essence of what she said.'

'Oh.'

'See, before that, I thought I had to be a victim as part of my Aboriginal identity. I thought that if I wasn't suffering, I wouldn't be respecting the deprivation going on around me and before me.'

'How did that look? I mean, what did that mean in you?' Mari had forgotten about the perfumes and was imagining Nerida in her twenties and early thirties, before they met.

'Well, it legitimised my learning about our history. I could read about the massacres, hear about the man-traps near the river, all that, and cry. And feel like I was doing what I should do. But I went to some dark places.'

'That's not being a victim, learning about where you're from,' Mari objected. 'And if you directed it yourself, that helps, right?

'Because I spent most of my summers in hospital as a kid, they made me repeat Year 5, three times. They thought I was dumb. I missed a lot of school,' she went on.

'I didn't care that much. Anyway, for nine and ten-year-old kids, there were excursions. 'We were all excited and happy, it's an excursion, you know. Singing on the bus, looking out the windows.'

Mari and Nerida were oblivious to where there were, now, speaking with the clarity they had when they were overtired but not arguing.

'They didn't tell us where we were. They left us to walk through the crematorium, past the gallows tree. It was fucking Dachau!

'We had no idea. Piles of shoes. Buckets of gold teeth.

'Then they made us watch this film about what happened there! Of the bodies being bulldozed into graves, all that. Kids were crying, wailing. Everybody sobbing. We were just little kids, you know?'

'But it wasn't your fault. And your family—' Nerida interrupted.

'They made us feel responsible. They said it was our grandparents and aunties and uncles that did that, even if it wasn't. And that there was always a danger, in us, that it would happen again.'

'Collective guilt. That's bullshit,' Nerida said.

'The teachers were outside, smoking and laughing. They didn't participate. They didn't comfort us. We were just little kids.' Mari had tears in her eyes.

'I wonder how the teachers could do that. They were probably already traumatised, themselves,' Nerida said.

'Shit. It's like the Catholic Church … All these little kids being made to feel like they killed Jesus.' She touched Mari's arm.

'I'm sorry that happened to you. That's so unfair.'

They stared ahead in silence for a minute or two. There were ads scrolling on big screens. For cigarettes, vodka mixers. And grim threats against drug traffickers.

Nerida flexed her neck, combed her fingers through her hair.

She put down her bag for a moment and re-tied her scarf. 'Somehow I needed to be miserable to be Aboriginal, in my mind. I was grieving. I mourned for a long time. If someone at work or Uni asked me how I was going, I could never just say, "I'm fine." Or, "Very well, thank you," as my mother taught me. It felt like I had to embody the grief to acknowledge the history.'

She looked at Mari as they stepped towards the gates. 'You still do it. But you have a different mask. You just get angry.'

Anyone who knew them would have been surprised that they went to Los Angeles to see Dawn, who channelled a being they called Monica. It was uncharacteristic. They weren't people who went to yoga retreats. Mari had been taught twenty-five different kinds of meditation and relaxation in pain management clinics and hospital wards over the years.

'They never worked for me. Never,' she'd say. 'When I was studying naturopathic medicine, they used to take us through meditations, hypnotise us. People had all sorts of ridiculous stories of where they'd been, what they'd "seen." I was always just standing there. Or sitting or lying. Saying, "So? Is something supposed to be different now?" Lots of people there thought I was an arsehole.'

Nerida was susceptible to being hypnotised and loved a good guided relaxation. But she had spent years enjoying the sense of fluent superiority and genuine insight she gained from her scientific studies. She was a student for thirteen years, on and off, working part-time, failing and repeating, marching in the streets, looking after her kids. She looked after their father, too, for years. Her materialist approach came from her politics. Science built on it. 'It is not the consciousness of men that determines their being, but, on the contrary, their social being that determines their consciousness,' Marx said.

Some of her comrades took the idea literally. What you were determined what you knew and thought. By this logic, being a medical student made her susceptible to petit-bourgeois ideas, and being a professional, a doctor (admirable and necessary as doctors were), would distort her worldview even further. Nerida was anxious about it.

So, she worked through her university breaks. It was not for the money, because she lived in government housing and her rent went up with her income. It then took months of negotiating for the rent to be put down again when she earned less money. Lots of hassle with Centrelink.

She did it because she wanted to prove that she could and would take a side with the working class. She needed to show how hard-working she was, too, somehow. Nerida was cheerful and pleasant, with a round figure. Some comrades thought she must be lazy because of it. She did not take on the strained, harried and hurried appearance they cultivated.

Nerida never regretted leaning to drive a forklift, working in the university offices or going to the country to pick fruit, children in tow.

She did regret the years of overwork, trying to prove herself.

It was because everyone around her knew her as a militant, materialist, atheist, if a warm and empathic one, that Nerida kept her phones calls with Monica a secret after she started calling her in 2006.

She didn't know how to talk about the resonance and deep understanding she felt in Monica's words. It was the same feeling she'd had with the traditional Aboriginal healers (and some elders): who could reach into her, rendering her transparent to their judgement. And understanding.

Monica, and other channelled beings whose material she started to read in books, like Michael, Seth and Fortunatus, promoted the idea that thoughts created things.

It was the opposite of the way her comrades (and colleagues) thought. And how she'd been trained to think. It was a deep quandary. Was consciousness primary, creating reality as the spirit beings and the Aboriginal worldview proposed? Or did reality create our thoughts?

Surely, there's a dance between the two she decided.

She was with Mari for almost a year before she told her about Monica, fearing she would see her consults with the channelled entity (paid for in US dollars) as an incomprehensible dependency, or even a sign of mental illness.

As it turned out, the Universe brought Mari experiences that opened her to the possibility of Monica.

First there was their consciousness-expanding sex. Once they trusted each other, the women came together like galactic forces. Love songs about the moon and the stars made sense. They met in different realities while their bodies came together. 'I was far away,' each would say to the other. 'And you were there.'

They were intimately bonded in pleasure. But then there was pain. Mari was attacked by a mamu. A mamu was a pathological force that came on the west wind, rolling and skulking in the Western desert dust. A kind of a bad spirit Mari did not know about. And wouldn't have believed in until she was hurt by one.

Mari was deeply upset after she opened a 'wrong' photo from their trip to Uluru. That started it. Ghostly dog paws hung out a tree hollow. Nerida came to delete the photo. Head- splitting pain came to Mari that night. Claws pierced her skull and brain. She lay in bed, unable to speak.

Nerida sent her terrified wife for an MRI in the morning. Was there a sudden brain bleed or tumour? Her hands couldn't rid Mari of pain and fear. They needed other ngangkari to help.

When Victor and Charlie met them a month later, they whispered and earnestly conferred. A wild dog spirit from Uluru was not to be messed with. Gently but firmly manipulating Mari's shoulder and neck, Charlie was able to take it out.

Mari's healing by ngangkari was an intense way of learning from the Anangu traditional healers who became their friends.

'I would have ended up in the psych ward if it wasn't for Victor and Charlie,' she told others, including Claire, later.

Mari learned about the connection between Dreamtime stories and everyday life in that tough way.

'You're a special whitefella to get that,' Nerida smiled, her eyebrow lifted. 'Mamu attacks usually only happen to our mob.'

After that there was the little incident when something in their Koonawarra house made the digital oven clock flash HELP.

The dishwasher turned on when no one was there. Nerida didn't believe in poltergeists.

She wasn't convinced by Mari, either, until she saw the electrical mayhem herself.

Mari turned the stove on, and the blender started.

There was that flashing HELP again, at night when Nerida came to the kitchen for water.

'Maybe it needs servicing,' Nerida said. 'There's nothing in the manual,' Mari said. The sparkie came but had nothing to offer. He probably didn't believe them, either.

Eventually, Nerida saw, or rather felt, the ghost of a terrified Koori girl, hiding under the stone overhang in their yard (in a geographical line with their kitchen), from marauding redcoats. Nerida escorted her to safety, in spirit. She'd been caught on that land for a century.

So it was that Mari was open to hearing about Monica.

But the first time she talked to Monica on the phone, Mari ran from the room sobbing. 'How could they know? They're in California. We don't know them.'

'That child spirit wants you to know they understand. It wasn't meant to be for them, either,' Monica said.

Nerida didn't even hear what had been said.

Monica had made a gentle allusion to the termination Mari needed at the end of an abusive relationship as a teen.

Abortion was illegal in her state in Germany. She'd been humiliated and shamed by the nurse attending.

Nerida had two terminations in her youth, both legal and safe. She was thankful. Contraceptive failure was a fact of life. She didn't carry the loneliness and shame Mari suffered. Which Monica helped dislodge.

Now, a man in front of them gathered up bags of duty-free alcohol, the bottles clanging. Nerida followed Mari to the booth of an immigration officer, who briefly acknowledged her smile.

Fingerprints were taken by the machine, passports stamped, electric gates opened.

FIVE

N EW SOUTH WALES, COAST
1977, 2006.

BY THE TIME she was eight or nine Nerida had adapted the Lord's Prayer to suit her. She asked for forgiveness for her sins, but left out the second part of the sentence, which asked to be forgiven as she would forgive others. She knew she didn't want that. She was not always that good at forgiving others. So thought she should be upfront about that. God should be better at forgiving than she was.

Child Nerida also left out 'Thy Kingdom come,' at the beginning of the prayer because she honestly didn't want the Lord's Kingdom to come. It didn't sound better than the world she had, with bush flowers and tadpoles, the occasional lollies, wrestling with her brother.

Reading in bed with him and her sister.

She got the idea that Jesus could grant wishes, like a genie. Sometimes she prayed to a genie, too. She wanted to be beautiful and famous, so strangers would adore her. She wanted to be richer than the queen. She imagined a chest of pirate treasure overflowing with jewels. That, and as many lollies as she'd want, were her idea of wealth.

As an adult, Nerida had learned to turn off pleasure. When she was an activist, she sometimes imagined in bed at night that socialism could mean finding lovely things—clothes, food, places to stay—wherever she went. She and the children were always traveling in her fantasy socialist world.

By the time she became a doctor her children were grown. In her new profession, Nerida's dreams became nightmares based on fear. Fear of being alone forever, of being degraded and punished for a mistake, fear of being found lacking in every way. Fear of a child dying on her watch.

One terrible night at the hospital, one of Nerida's elderly patients died. It was an unexpected death for some. Not Nerida.

She was was partly to blame. A junior doctor, she didn't understand that she should have called the consultant, her boss, for help. Juniors were strongly discouraged from calling consultants.

Other junior doctors were responsible for the death, as well. They did their damnedest—writing copious pages of notes into the record about her inadequacy and delusions—to make Nerida the scapegoat for all of it. She shook with anxiety, upset and shame.

The patient had metastatic pancreatic cancer. She deteriorated after extensive surgery. Her family wanted to palliate her, not send her back to the operating theatre for more. Nerida acted on their wishes, making the small, grey-haired woman (and her family) comfortable.

Near midnight that night she'd called the ward for an update. 'You didn't tell the boss?'

Her colleagues panicked. Got the lady tubed in intensive care. Gave heart-stimulating drugs.

Nerida was distraught that a peaceful, settled death was denied her patient. *Or maybe she wasn't meant to die then?* Unable to work or sleep, she cried day and night.

As it turned out, her consultant had been through a similar situation when he was a junior. Next morning, he treated her kindly as she sobbed. He understood that she had been as caring as she could be.

She and Mari had been writing daily for four months then. Mari wrote, 'I'm coming to look after you.'

Nerida was attracted to Mari's warm, deep voice on the phone. She joked that Mari could earn money as a sex talker.

A month earlier, Mari sent Nerida a small box of gifts: tchotchkes and trinkets, each with a story. There was a keyring with a comic shark on it because Mari used to be an instructor, taking divers to see sharks. Polished wood and stainless-steel chopsticks packaged ready for the travel they wanted together. Italian essential oils to roll on her temples for calm and happiness.

Mari was still studying as a naturopathic physician, living on a low, fixed income. A friend loaned her the money for a nonrefundable, economy airfare. It was twenty hours from her home in Germany to Sydney, Australia.

The day before she planned to leave, Mari's mother called her, frantic. 'Your father's in intensive care. His gut had a hole torn in it by all those tablets he took for his back over the years. He's bleeding! You must come!'

Mari's Dad had surgery that morning. She listened to him on the phone as he lay in Intensive Care recovering in the evening.

'You think this woman could be the one for you?' he asked about Nerida. 'I do, Dad. I can't explain it. There's something in her eyes.'

'Then, if you don't go, I'll kill you. There's nothing you can do for me here. Go to her.' On the other side of the world, Nerida sought comfort in eating, throwing coins for the *I Ching* and crying for a week. When she went back to work, she cries sometimes in the toilets or storeroom.

She didn't know whether Mari would bring ease or more tension.

Dates from The Velvet Lounge, where they met online, had not gone well for Nerida. Women looking for their idea of a doctor-wife were disappointed in her. She didn't fit their image.

She changed her profile then to say that her occupation was 'health worker.' It was fortunate. Because Mari would never have sent a smile to a woman she knew was a doctor.

By the time Mari knew about Nerida's profession, from the first time she saw her picture, she was smitten.

It was painful to her, then, to receive a text from Nerida as she was about to board the plane, with a list of local hostels and bed and breakfasts that Mari could go to, 'if the chemistry isn't there.'

Nerida thought she was being wise, taking pressure off them. But the effect on Mari was that she felt restless and insecure. She spent the next hours wondering if she was making a huge mistake.

On the day Mari arrived in Australia, Nerida was sick with tonsillitis and unable to make the two-hour drive to the city to pick her up. She sent her a message with details of how Mari should get to hostel for a rest, then where to get the train. Then took vitamin C and went to bed.

Late in the afternoon, Nerida went to the station, wrapped in scarves, and sat on the cool metal seat.

The railway line stretched into the distance, about to bring her future. She was a few minutes early for the train she'd suggested Mari should take.

A young woman sitting by Nerida was dressed in spectacular style, with a very short skirt and intense eye make-up.

'Where are you off to?' Nerida used her voice gently.

'Just out with friends,' she replied with a smile.

'I'm waiting to meet a date I met online. She's travelling all the way from Europe to be with me.'

'Wow, so she's never met you before and she's coming all that way? And now you're meeting her for the first time?' The young woman's eyelashes were distracting.

'Yeah, it's amazing, isn't it? I hope we like each other.'

When the train came the peak-hour crowd from the city streamed out of it. But Mari was not there.

At Sydney's Central Station, tourists at the counter ahead of Mari were too slow buying their tickets.

She heard her train leave as they dithered. The next train was not for an hour and a half. Nerida had lost her phone, so Mari's texts didn't reach her.

Nerida drove to the sea nearby and looked at the grey and white waves with the subdued flatness and exhausted acceptance of being sick.

Seagulls battled the wind.

She went to the supermarket and bought steak and carrots for dinner. She had an idea that she could make her Dad's carrot salad, with the raisins.

The sun had gone behind the escarpment when the next train from the city arrived at Wollongong.

Mari got off, dizzy with jet-lagged exhaustion.

And emotional. She waited for the crowd of commuters to disperse. But there was no sign of Nerida on the platform.

Disappointed, she hiked her pack onto her back and looked for the bridge to the other platform, returning to Sydney.

The sky flamed orange. Nerida waited in the carpark outside the station entrance.

And there she is, Nerida saw—*taller and fitter than I imagined, softer too. She's gorgeous!*

She was attracted to Mari's broad shoulders. Her face lit up in the twilight, dark eyes laughing under black curls. She embraced Nerida.

'You're quite little aren't you? I didn't see that on the net,' Mari said. 'I'm so glad to see you.'

Later that evening Nerida felt at home in Mari's arms under the brilliant stars out on the deck.

Even later, their connection was powerful and intensified quickly. As raw, new lovers, they rediscovered an ancient power, an intoxicating electricity.

CHAPTER

SIX

BURBANK, CALIFORNIA
MONDAY NOV 26, 2012

Mari and Nerida had travelled several days to meet with Dawn in the US.

A former sports coach, Dawn was fair, with a robust midwestern constitution and none of the obvious surgical enhancements which so commonly impaired people's appearance in Los Angeles.

Wearing scant make-up, neat chain-store clothes and simple jewellery, her face was open, with a few lines from the sun and smiling. She was probably older than them, Nerida thought. A great role model.

Dawn was the channel for Monica, who was, they said, a group of hundreds (or were they thousands?) of non-physical beings, speaking as one.

'She' exhibited a high degree of intelligence, particularly emotional intelligence. She had an ineffable ability to read and interpret an individual's past and present experiences and relationships. And a willingness to discern the future likely to grow from the seeds of the present.

Trevor, Dawn's husband, amanuensis and manager, arranged payment and schedules.

An affable guy with decades of study of channelling and metaphysics, he still had the drive of the media entrepreneur he once was.

Dawn had been successfully channelling for over a decade with Trevor encouraging, pushing and learning from her (and the ones she channelled).

They offered to help Mari learn to control her channelling. Nerida had some experience as a spiritual apprentice.

In 2005, when she was working fifty-hour weeks as a junior doctor, Nerida was also training in Traditional Aboriginal healing with a pair of Anangu ngangkari. Those two old men, Victor and Charlie.

On one of her trips to Alice Springs to study with the men, they introduced her to a woman ngangkari. Nerida had pushed for that. She should be learning from a woman because her male teachers intruded on her thoughts. She should respect the gender division that was so important in many Aboriginal clans in her learning, she reasoned.

She sat down with the woman she was matched with, a powerful ngangkari also. Her would-be mentor tried to teach her to introduce herself in Pitjantjatjara, using the suffix -nya at the end of her name. Nerida, over-excited and never one to do well under exam conditions, couldn't understand the concept. The senior woman ngangkari found her as stupid as a broom handle and less useful.

Victor and Charlie were stuck with her.

Back in New South Wales, Nerida experienced astral travel with the ngangkari in the liminal space between wakefulness and sleep. She heard Victor's voice in her head frequently through the day.

She had listened to the wind for years. Her father taught her to do that.

But now that she was at an intense point of learning in the old systems and the new, she was 'hearing' too much. It felt like each tree, each individual pebble on the beach had a story to tell her. Walking on the beach was not relaxing.

She wrote letters to Victor and Charlie, asking them for guidance, which may have been read to them. The only answer was the feeling that she had. That they read them and were bemused.

Nerida felt alone, even if she never really was. She didn't understand enough of the realm of spirit, where many healers did their work, to know that she was guided and supported.

Overtired and stressed with her work as a new doctor, the hospital system was opaque to her. She kept bumping into a hierarchy, invisible to her and so obvious to everyone else. She had never been taught the names of different doctors or their roles.

She spent too long with patients and tried to get essential things done for them. Her efforts made other staff feel exposed and inadequate. Or just tired, seeing in her an enthusiasm they never felt. She was sometimes mistaken for a social worker, with her dreadlocs, her muliebrity and warm manner. She learned to say, 'That's high praise. Thank you. I'm a doctor.'

Nerida had stopped believing in God when she was about 14. She prayed fervently from the age of twelve that her breasts, perfectly sized at that age, would stop growing. They did not.

By age 13 they were large enough to hang down like papayas on a tree. She didn't fit into regular clothing—the size range was small and narrow in Australia in the eighties.

The only men bold enough to meet her eyes then were migrants she saw at the markets or by the harbour in Sydney (and they did not let go).

Boys her age had no idea what they would do with her body. She hardly knew what to do with it herself. The first man she made out with was 22. She was almost 14 and went after him, beard and all, with enthusiasm.

Her attraction to women was strong but she hardly knew how to negotiate a sexual relationship with men. To take a woman to bed was beyond her skills. She never saw a story in a magazine or a book about it. She'd heard the word 'lesbian,' only as an incomprehensible insult, thrown at her when she walked arm in arm with a girl friend as an 11-year-old.

Young adult Nerida Green experienced moments of connection and synchronicity via sex, marijuana, psilocybin.

Sometimes she felt connected in much more ordinary circumstances—like talking to a stranger at the bus stop and finding they were reading the same book—like *The Celestine Prophecies*.

Over time, in direct opposition to her political and scientific materialism, she sometimes felt an inchoate sense of something greater, saw patterns or meaning in the Universe.

As a lonely medical intern in 2005 she sat under a tree and tried to listen, but found her mind full.

I'm glad I've finished my studies. And I like living independently in my house. But I feel lost and lonely. I need my person. Where is my companion?

It's interesting working at the hospital. I'm learning. And if I'm going to be a healer, I need help. A framework for understanding in my first language, which sadly is English. It could be a book.

She felt some peace but was unable to hear words in whatever the tree said. So she consulted the internet.

On The Velvet Lounge, that dating site for same-sex attracted women, she found discussion of a channelled book, *Messages from Michael*. She read it and looked at discussions about it. There she saw an ad for Dawn Weaver, a 'full-body, deep-trance, open channel,' bringing through a non-physical entity called Monica.

Her first phone consultation with Monica gave Nerida a profound sense of being known. Monica used to words describe her situation that Dawn could not have known from California. For example,

Nerida was still a political activist, even if she was increasingly conflicted about being a materialist Marxist. She had no online profile and hadn't talked to Monica about politics.

When she asked Monica about the journal she gave so much time and money to, the seer replied, 'You and your comrades do good work in the world. There is every reason to continue. They are important friends to you, are they not?'

It was the casual use of that word, 'comrades' that surprised and resonated with Nerida. Sometimes a detail no one else would give a second thought to, even a single word, changes the course of a life.

Six months later she met Mari on The Velvet Lounge. Each felt attracted and they wrote every day.

She asked Monica about Mari in one of her now three-monthly calls. Mari had offered to come to Australia from Germany to love and care for her. Nerida was in crisis.

'We'll never tell you what to do. A person always has a choice. 'But there is this compatibility there, between you two. It's like waves that line up and amplify each other. It would be a shame to miss that,' Monica said.

When she and Mari finally came together, Nerida tried to be cool. She was afraid of being hurt. But at their first breakfast together, before she had to go to work, both were tired and happy.

Nerida brought a plate of sliced rock melon to their table on the deck. She said, 'It's unusual to come on a first time together.'

Mari was discombobulated. 'Well, it's not a competition ... Why did you go and sleep in the other bed? I was looking for you.'

'I thought you might sleep better if you had your own space.'

Nerida couldn't tell her then how other lovers found her too much. Too much affection, too much talk, too much food and sex. Too much all together.

Mari was the one for whom she was sweetly more than enough. More than kind. Pretty. Soulful. Stimulating.

The attraction was mutual. Nerida fell into Mari's dark brown eyes. Loved the shape of her shoulders, her slim hips and strong legs. Even, maybe especially, the abbreviated strength of her left leg, cut off below the knee.

But still. Afraid of what Mari would say, Nerida didn't tell her about Monica until they'd been together for almost a year. For her part, Mari was curious. She'd been to a psychic once. It was interesting. When she joined Monica in a phone session, though, there was that reference to the little one that didn't come which drove Mari out of the room in tears.

Her experience of the illegal abortion was a closely held secret. 'How could they know?' she asked. 'I'm freaked out.'

In subsequent phone calls to Monica, Mari was shy, conveying questions via Nerida.

But she, too, found resonance in Monica's responses that challenged her atheism and skepticism.

It was not until three years later that Mari's 'sleep talking' was happening almost every night and Nerida eventually realised that she was channelling. She could sense that someone different was there. And once one of them spoke briefly in English.

She didn't get much sleep. The cognitive dissonance between nights lying awake by Mari and days scheduling drugs and procedures in the hospital was challenging to tolerate.

Dawn's husband (and facilitator) Trevor gave them advice about how to manage the evolving skill (*Is it a gift?* Nerida couldn't say)—over the phone and via email. 'Make regular times to try to channel. Nerida stay with her to keep her safe,' he said.

Nerida wanted to learn more. She tried reading the Seth books, channelled by Jane Roberts, but found them too dense to persevere.

So then she read books by Abbey, another American, who channelled Fortunatus. He said feeling happy and good attracts more happiness and goodness. The goal of life was to do, and experience, only the happy and the good.

It reminded Nerida of when she was manic after dropping adulterated acid when she was twenty. *It sounds positive, wonderful but might not be sustainable.* She was confused.

Mari's uncontrolled channelling came to a crescendo after she had a slip and fall in a wet carpark, cracking and chipping bones in her back. As soon as she closed her eyes to rest, then, Nerida saw strange patterns of breathing, whispering, talking or trying to talk.

Mari was in horrible pain. Nerida (and another doctor) tried different drugs, in high doses, to manage it. The other doctor noted Mari's history of untreated pain after surgeries as a child and said that she probably felt pain more severely because of it.

They had to move house when Mari had the broken back, after taking out a mortgage for the orange house—a rusty coloured stucco box with a fabulous view of the ocean—at Narooma, further down the New South Wales coast.

It should have been a happy time. But with Mari's injury it was difficult. Nerida worked long hours as a hospital registrar. It was hard to tell then, what was channelled, what was drugs, what was pain and misery. But with Dawn and Trevor's aid-at-a-distance, Mari did purposefully channel.

Following Trevor's advice, she opened herself to channel on Saturday afternoons.

In Los Angeles now, Nerida remembered an encounter one afternoon with beings who had a mathematical worldview. They were mainly interested in machines and mathematics. Even the way they spoke through Mari was kind of mechanical. It was like an autistic planet of Kraftwerk people. Splendid. But not for her.

The aim in coming to Los Angeles now, three years later, was to encourage the beings Mari channelled to be respectful, which included an agreement to speak only at particular, scheduled times. And in English. Nerida hoped to meet a being she could relate to.

They met in an ugly brown and old gold business hotel room, with striped wallpaper and heavy curtains, near Burbank airport.

Nerida was concerned about what this meeting could mean for her reputation as a sane and scientific doctor, worried that she used her credit cards and limited leave on a dubious project.

And if there was authenticity here, would Mari be able to respond to Dawn and Monica's tutoring?

Nerida felt impelled. Her darling Mari was not making sense to herself or to Nerida, waking her at two am, speaking a language that her linguist friend said sounded like a version of ancient Siamese.

She'd done the medical things. Nerida ensured that Mari had an MRI of her head after her fall. 'Your brain is perfectly beautiful,' she told her. She was not taking any medications. She was perfectly sane. Nerida knew what mental illness looked like. This was not it.

Coming to California was the best path she saw. But how would they feel if they got nothing out of it?

'So, you guys have travelled some. You must be tired,' Dawn said, sitting down across from them. The room had three chairs, a small table, a bed and a big television, not far from Dawn's arm. A window revealed the carpark, where the wind tossed papers and fall leaves.

Nerida wore a blue silk scarf Mari gave her when she came to live in Australia. She played with the edge of it now, fingering a crescent of gold paint. The pattern was abstract, inspired by shapes of a humpback whale. Mari was still, palms resting on her knees.

After greetings, Dawn closed her eyes and breathed audibly, going into trance. Her face looked deeply relaxed.

Monica arrived, manifesting with a strong, round-voweled voice, peering out with an unearthly glint through Dawn's narrowed eyes. She greeted them warmly. Trevor, who had other work to do and wished to afford them privacy, left the room.

'So, my dears,' the spirit said. 'We understand that there is *a reason* you have come all this way.'

Nerida smiled. 'That's right. We're here on a special mission.'

Mari said, 'The one we talked about on the phone.'

'Ahh, the Energy,' Monica mused.

'When you suggested that you might have—' Mari began.

Monica nodded. 'Yes, yes, we remember ... So, how are you doing with that?'

Mari was hesitant. 'Yeah, Nerida likes the idea.'

'Has it come forth through you at all? Or are you not feeling it deeply yet?' Monica was focussed on Mari. There was a warm, bright feeling in the dull little room.

'Ah, maybe not deeply,' Mari said modestly. 'But it comes through from time to time.'

'Right. And are you in control of it, or does it just come when it pleases?'

'Nerida says it comes when it pleases. Mainly.' Mari looked shyly at her wife.

Nerida thought of the many sleepless nights at the orange house at Narooma. But Mari had a broken back then. It was hard to tell how much of the sleep talking and strange breathing was attributable to the painkillers she was on. Nerida prescribed her plenty.

The channelling, if that was what it was, abated for a couple of years at Mutitjulu.

Perhaps there was enough drama going on during the day and the spirits spared them. But it had started again in the past year or so. When they asked Dawn and Monica about it, they had encouraged Mari to consider learning to control her channelling, on top of Trevor's tips. But, in the end, Nerida didn't know what to do.

While Mari was shy about it, Nerida also had reservations about whether they should be there. This was Mari, who refused (or was unable) to relax in a guided meditation, and whose muscles only really let go after a swim or an orgasm. Mari who mocked everything about religion and spirituality, from the rituals people were soothed by, to the clothes they wore—Birkenstocks with socks in Germany— to the language they used. When she first heard of channelling, from her sister Lotte when they were teenagers, Mari thought is was hydrography, a kind of plumbing.

'Mainly when it chooses to come, okay,' Monica said. 'We understand. And you would like to have better relationship with that movement, so it doesn't happen at the grocery store.'

Mari smiled nervously. 'A better relationship, yes.'

Monica paused for a long minute, as if assessing. Or listening to unseen company. 'Well,' she concluded, 'it isn't because you are incapable or unable or not wanting to. It's a matter of the Energy becoming comfortable with the progress into your form.' Mari and Nerida nodded, wide-eyed.

'And then,' Monica continued, 'you have a lot of, uh, thinking, thoughts, that sometimes are a bit judgmental... about you.'

'Yeah, could be,' Mari said.

'Yeah. And so the energies making the attempt can usually come through when you're not thinking so much.'

'Yeah, they mainly do it when I'm asleep.'

'A-ha! Alright. Alright.' There was an excitement in the air.

'Now, let's see this energy, hang on.' Monica closed Dawn's eyes for a few moments.

A jet took off from the nearby airport, booming low and shaking the windows.

'No, there's two.' Monica sighed. 'Alright, alright. We say there's two to three. There's possibly a third one that could be—is—interested, but has not made a move in your direction quite yet; has been observing more than anything.'

Mari murmured agreement.

'Alright? Alright. So... Still looking. Just want to make sure we see everything.'

There was the sound of deep breathing in the room. It reminded Nerida of the breathing Mari did at night when it felt like someone else was there.

It was Monica. 'And they are learning the ... English. They're trying.'

'They try?' asked Mari. Nerida had told her that she spoke in other languages in her sleep.

'Yes. They think it's, eh, rather basic,' Monica said in her cultured tone. 'And they're not thrilled with the timbre of it. There is a melody to words and language, and they say this is not melodic. This is ch-ch-ch-ch.' She made a chopping motion with Dawn's left hand.

'They're fighting it, a little bit. They're trying, but they think the language—their native tongue has a better melody and tonal quality to it than English does.

'This energy, the main one, is this, the energy looks like this—' She moved the hand in a large, rhythmic, horizontal figure eight.

'So it's looking for that path,' she said, continuing the 'infinity' gesture. 'That sort of ride to take when it's talking. It wants to do this, and English does this,' again, the hacking mechanical hand, 'so they can't do it.

'That's part of the difficulty; so you can understand.

'It's not just you that's having difficulty.

'They're having to adjust this kind of energy that moves like this,' the figure-8, elegant as a skater's arm, 'to language which does this,' again with the chopping. 'So that's why they wanted to speak, the several languages were mentioned to you, because there's melody to those.'

Nerida laughed. 'Old Siamese and Gaelic?'

When they lived at the Orange House and she was sleepless and desperate to understand what was happening to her wife, Nerida took a recording to her friend since student days. Bruce loved languages.

He used to suck on bongs and throw coins to consult the *I Ching* with her all afternoon in his tiny flat in Darlinghurst.

He taught her how to pronounce the names of the hexagrams. Bruce was now a professor of linguistics. She came to his small office. When he heard the recordings, he was astonished.

'We don't really know how they'd be pronounced, of course they're dead languages, like Latin,' he told Nerida, bobbing his mop of black hair and taking a mouthful of the coffee she brought.

'What really amazes me is, how does Mari know how to pronounce these words?

'I mean, Old Thai had only three tones.

'Modern Thai has five—the extra two split off around the fourteenth century, from memory. I'd have to look it up. How does Mari even know how to read the script?'

'Listen to this one,' Nerida had said then, playing a recording of Mari speaking with other sounds.

'That's totally different, yes. I would call that Old Gaelic. It's got such complex consonants.' He shook his head. 'Your wife has a rare talent. This is a gift! I'd love to see her reading this way.'

'She's not reading though, Bruce,' Nerida told him finally, 'She talking in her sleep.'

Bruce was uncomfortable then and didn't know what to say. Their meeting drew to a close quickly and she hadn't seen him since, despite sending him texts and messages.

Now, in Burbank, it made Nerida and Mari laugh to hear Monica confirm Prof Bruce's broad knowledge.

'Yes, yes,' Monica said. 'And if you were to listen to the recording of Old Siamese or Gaelic, you would almost feel like yourself doing this while you listen to it.'

She conducted waves with Dawn's hands.

'Certain languages have more smoothness to them than others. Some are very guttural. You know, some 'chop it off' through the middle of the throat, and this one likes to do this.'

Again with the waves.

'Especially the main one. Let's see what the other two are up to.'

Monica took a deep breath. Nerida noticed the bare branches of the trees outside shaking in the November wind.

Monica seemed to come back. 'The second one is similar to this,' she made the waves. 'And the third one, who's been observing, does this.' She made a stepped, castellated movement across and upwards, with the arm.

'So, that is interesting: we think, because of your tone, the third one—'

'Got attracted as well?' Mari asked.

Monica nodded '—happening by, was attracted to this, "chopping motion" when you are talking. That kind of connection's not easy to find either.'

'Oh,' said Mari. 'I thought it was me—'

'Well, you do think a little too much when you're doing it. Trying to be the "perfect match".

'Sometimes you just need to be you and relax and let them make the adjustments coming in. Okay?

'Because they would not have stopped by you if they did not think there would be success in the connection.

'So, eliminate all doubt of your worthiness and decide that you're just going to relax and be open.'

Nerida felt Monica's energy take a step back, then. Dawn's eyes closed. Her chin moved softly onto her chest and with a stretch of her back and a little shake she was back. She smiled broadly.

'So, wow, Mari. Monica just gave me the message as she was going out. She thinks you're gonna be a great channel.'

Mari smiled and looked from Dawn to Nerida, excited. 'I don't know,' she said shyly. 'I guess we'll see.'

CHAPTER

SEVEN

B URBANK, CALIFORNIA
TUESDAY NOVEMBER 27, 2012

DAWN SIPPED green tea with honey from a white china cup, decorated with painted flowers.

Trevor and Mari had cake. The buzz of the hotel cafe was loud enough for privacy.

In a sea of people competing for attention, they were unremarkable. A national singing contest was auditioning. The hotel was full of people, many young, protecting their throats.

Nerida wore an orange and red scarf, fine cotton with white knot dots, around her head, her dreaded hair coiled into a pattern like earth or woodgrain.

Mari's delicate forearm tattoos, one of pink and orange, desert colours, geometrical, the other swirly patterns of the ocean, slipped out under the rolled sleeves of her tailored shirt.

Dawn's husband Trevor bore his tall, broad-shouldered figure with grace belied by his slightly unkempt style. Like Nerida, his skin was fair. White people would assume they were white.

Dawn wore a little make up, adding to the intensity of her features: dark blue eyes and a ready smile.

'See, when I first started doing this, I just did it. And people would ask me about stuff, you know. In the early days—I'd go: "I don't even know what was said." I had no idea.' She put down her cup. 'Sometimes I sensed words coming out of my mouth but I wasn't listening. And when the channelling first started, it was just like I'd been asleep. And woke up to everyone excited.'

Her eyes widened. 'I looked like the dummy in the room. I was always, like, "I don't know what you're talking about!"

'I didn't read Seth. I didn't read any of that spiritual stuff. I still haven't read most of it.

I read Seth Speaks a long time ago, a bit. And I did read Messages from Michael because I was directed.'

Nerida interrupted. 'Yeah, Mari hasn't read any of that literature either.'

Mari, tucking into a sticky brownie, shrugged slightly. 'I'm not much of a reader.'

Dawn nodded. 'Yeah. And you know, it's probably better. You don't wanna influence what you channel. I wouldn't want to. People would be asking me to interpret what Monica says.'

She exchanged a knowing look with Mari. 'I thought, Monica knows those things, so why do I need to? I don't. It's all fine.'

Nerida played with the froth on her cappuccino. 'As long as Trevor knows about it. He can make sense of what they say.'

Pride shone in Dawn's eyes. 'Oh, Trevor's read everything.'

He was enjoying his apple pie with cream. 'Well, the Michael system is good vocabulary.'

Dawn jumped in.

'At the time, I was doing gymnastics contests, coaching the girls, travelling all over the country.

'When Trevor and I were first married, I was still going all over the place.

'I was stuck in Reno, Nevada for ten days with nothing to do. Y'know, working four hours a day. Bored to tears, and we always had Sundays off.'

You say that like it's a bad thing, Nerida thought enviously.

'I got a cab and went to a mall. I was talking to Trevor. I said: "I've got to find something to read! Something to do. I feel just bored out of my mind!"

'I'm walking through this bookstore in this redneck, cowboy place, then. Some chain bookstore. Thinking: "I'm going to see if there's any metaphysical books." And I stumbled over a, uh, like a step thing that you climb up to get books.' She sprang her hands out. 'I fell over it and knocked a whole bookstand over. And that landed right in my hand!'

Nerida's eyebrows slid up her big forehead. 'That book?'

'*Messages from Michael*. And I went: "Hmm, okay, we'll get it." I went back to the room and, of course, got involved in it. And it made the day go faster.

'I was telling Trevor this book fell in my hand.' She laughed. 'The thing fell down, there were books everywhere, but this book was in my hand. And then I found out there were more of them, so I read the rest of them, and I thought it's just so interesting.'

Nerida agreed. 'It is. But that's what it would take to get Mari to read one of those, too.'

Trevor said, 'And then when we had a session again, they said, "Well, we wanted her to read that because it's a good reference. It helps people to understand themselves." Spirit arranges things like that sometimes.'

Nerida ran ahead, excited, when they returned to the hotel room for another session.

Monica came through quickly and strongly, only moments after Dawn closed her eyes to go into trance. 'Ah, you're back. You went and did the food thing, yes?'

Trevor was arranging the water bottle and making sure Dawn's body was safe and comfortable. 'We did,' he said.

'Did you have fun?' Monica asked.

'I did.' He made a small smile. Then went to sit down, a little away from Nerida, Mari and Dawn's body, now channelling Monica.

'Hmm. So, we begin again.' Monica waited a beat, inhaled. 'So, while you were gone, we pondered a bit. And we think that it might be a good idea if we helped the energy that wishes to come through you a bit. Help them get a bit more acclimated to English, and we might be able to facilitate that faster, because we're more experienced with it. And The Dawn Weaver is experienced with it.

'So, we believe that we will, perhaps, attempt bringing this, one of those three, in.

'At least, to see what will happen.

'The Dawn Weaver is in agreement. She's open for it all. And then we'll get back to working with you, Mari, a little bit.

'We think we need to work with the energy as well.

'As you were relaxing, we were looking about and we think the energy feels a—just as when one does feel a little uncomfortable, when one feels under judgement—they feel just a little uncomfortable. And, so, maybe we can just, you know, join hands and then back up a little bit. And let go.' Monica reached as if to clasp Mari's hands, and then release them, but didn't touch her. 'So, we will give that an opportunity.' Monica inhaled.

'So, we leave you for the moment.' The hotel room filled with the sound of deep breathing.

Having aroused their curiosity, Monica left.

Dawn returned out of trance and took off her socks.

Trevor had chosen to stay for this session after their break. He gave Dawn water, then went to sit quietly near the door. His quiet presence helped when Dawn was channelling an

energy she had never encountered before, Nerida supposed. Trevor had spoken with hundreds of spirits. He knew Monica well.

And on Saturday nights the couple extended an open invitation to other spirits who wanted to come and speak through Dawn.

He had spoken to people who had passed on, including some who didn't know they'd died. He'd also communed with beings with roles and titles that Nerida had thought existed only in the realm of fantasy. She still wasn't sure. But Trevor was creditable. And they trusted Dawn.

There was a pause of several minutes while Dawn attempted to channel this other energy. It felt like another being was there. But this was not Monica. It was noisy, jerky and spastic. Dawn's chair creaked. Her hair flew over her shoulders and face.

Dawn's upper body worked hard, like a raging seventies punk. The mouth limbered up like a trombone player about to march. Nerida, who was tolerant of the many forms a human body could take, was quietly appalled.

She and Mari watched as Dawn's body made deep, sometimes staggering breaths. She hummed and murmured, until she started the higher-pitched moaning. It wasn't singing.

Nerida felt safe herself but fretted about Mari's capacity to participate in this intimate kind of abandon. Her sophisticated European wife, the stylish daughter of a tailoress, Mari always wore trousers to conceal her disability with elegance.

Mari was a disabled little child. She had told Nerida of hard women shooting bullets with their eyes, when she was at the local Black Forest swimming pool with her adored Roma grandfather.

'Wouldn't have been tolerated in Adolf's time,' they hissed.

Nerida could easily imagine Mari, with her big, dark eyes and curls, five years old and doing her best to walk with her metal-braced legs.

She has reason to be concerned about appearances.

Channelling the ancient energy, Dawn's low, breathy, unsure voice, with a huge effort, said, 'Hhel…lo.'

'Hello?' Mari spoke confidently.

'He... loooh...' the energy said.

'You're doing well.' Mari said tenderly. Nerida felt love in the room.

'M, mm...' They panted with the challenge of it.

'Good to see you too,' said Mari, kindly.

'Mmma... Ahhhhh... Reee.'

Mari thanked them, tilting her head, smiling. They were in a zone, like love-making, playing, birthing or dying, where appearances didn't matter.

With a sharp exhale, the spirit let go and Dawn returned. Eyes still closed, she said, 'It's enough.'

Then, 'Hoo! It's doable. Really different!' She was breathing into her belly, recovering. 'You all right?' Mari asked.

'It's doable. I can see why you're having a hard time trying to fix it.' Dawn was excited.

'Siamese is the first language, and it's really Lemurian before that, and then it goes—it migrated and ended up, um, Druid ... I'll keep trying.'

'Mari moves like that when she channels in her sleep. It's less effort, comes easier to her. Maybe it suits her better.' *I hope so.*

'I'll try to... work it a little for you—' Dawn's brows knit. She softened her breathing.

Then said, 'It's so hard ... It's an ancient energy, Mari! **Really** ancient. 'It comes from, almost, the primal depth of Earth.

'It's earth consciousness that took human form and then became aware of all the other stuff.

'It hasn't incarnated too often, so the physical form is strange to it. And it's an earth energy, so it's—different.

Nerida was curious. 'Mmm. So it's not an entity like Monica?'

'It's an entity! But it's not—' Dawn shook her head, pulling her fair hair behind it. 'Almost like you have the entity that's us humans, and this is like the entity of the earth.' She reflected. 'But it has been human, so it has an understanding. And a story to tell!'

Dawn laughed. 'I saw it. This unfolding and going eeugh!' She threw out her hands. 'It was like a rolled-up piece of cloth, like a big, long tablecloth and it keeps spilling out.' She rolled her hands like a go-go girl.

'And the energy was right behind. It has awareness of being physical, embodied, and that awareness came through.

'Druid was very important to it, because it used the earth, was trying to align everything...' She took a moment, as if recalling a vision, or a dream. 'So, there is quite a bit there. I wanted to see, myself.'

'Mmm, yes.' Mari looked thoughtful.

Dawn laughed. 'I'm like in your position, so...'

Mari chuckled too. It was a strange spot to be in, knowing an ancient and powerful spirit was keen to use your body to express themselves. She felt kinship with Dawn.

Dawn said, 'I thought maybe if I looked at it, I might be able to understand it. 'It's going to be hard to do, but you can do it. You can do it. I'll try to fix some of the roughness. I fixed a little bit of roughness this time.

'It's similar to some things Trevor and I do on Saturday nights when I'm open to channel other energies. You bring in an energy and it's not the best match, but you're, like, the only chance they've got to communicate here, so they're going to keep pushing.

'And you are a good match with this energy, Mari. Probably a lot better than I am. 'But the energy is having a hard time because it doesn't have a whole lot of experience being physical. It has more experience being part of the earth energy. It has plenty of experience being an energy itself. But it is very earthy.'

What does that mean, a spirit that's earthy? Nerida tried to wrap her mind around it. 'I think there's a lot of forgotten history here. You know? 'Remember, the library in Alexandria burnt down? That got rid of a lot of things that we all need to know—knowledge that they thought was a good idea to restore.

'I adjusted their energy quite a bit. I'll keep doing it.'

Dawn's confidence that there was nothing but good for them there was inspiring, Nerida felt. Her frank, sincere manner, her open, expressive face and relaxed physicality made Dawn easy to learn from.

Trevor commented, 'Takes practice for them too.' He'd been the amanuensis for Dawn since she started channelling over a decade earlier.

'Well, it was really interesting for me,' Nerida said, drawing in breath. 'Because a lot of the sorts of sounds and the breathing—it's was exactly what she's been doing.' She turned to Mari, 'You've been doing it for a few years now, so, yeah, hopefully they're more comfortable with you, because they have been practicing with you.'

Dawn spoke directly to Mari, too. 'Yeah. You just need to surrender. Just surrender. It's safe.'

'Yeah?' Mari's fine, dark brows lifted.

'I wasn't afraid,' Dawn said warmly.

'Okay.'

'It's very loving. And—I think it knows a little more English than it's letting on right now.

'That's just my opinion, it's not worth too much. I think it's done its homework.

'Because it wasn't that unfamiliar.

'I went in consciously with the idea: I want to do the alphabet. And I just keep thinking: The alphabet, so that it'll align with me and then speak the alphabet.

'And I've worked with other energies before that didn't know the English alphabet at all. Then it was a lot harder pull to get it.

'This wasn't hard pull.

'So just go for it. I think you're going to be able to channel it with English pretty well.

'But the energy does do this.' She made the waving horizontal figure eight movement.

'I could feel that movement that Monica talked about. You're just going to have to surrender.'

'All right.'

'And trust that in surrendering you're going to be taken care of.'

'It was interesting for me to see it, because Nerida described things I was doing in the night, like that, and I said: "What are you talking about?" You know?'

Dawn nodded. 'Remember to let your body be, just, really loose. 'Because they need to experience the hands.

'And even if I've had the experience of being a channel, it's hard.'

'Yeah. She said that I'm playing with the fingers, and looking at them and...' Nerida said, 'She was—like a baby. Moving her feet around, too.'

'You're perfectly safe, from my point of view,' Dawn continued. 'Don't be afraid.

'Surrender to the experience.

'Let yourself surrender, cause it's very knowledgeable.

'I think it's only had, maybe, ten physical incarnations? Not too many, and they've always been at—it looks like—it was pointing out to me where it had been. Looks like up at the North Pole? Maybe it was England? I don't know.

'Then there were quite a few Druid moments. It came back to finish work that it left off on. Reincarnated and had to wait to grow up to be—'

Nerida interrupted brightly '—what it was before?'

'Yeah. And incarnated in the same family because they kinda understood it. And they said: "Oh please come back". They could get him back up to where he needed to be.

'It's male energy, that one is.

'I'm just trying to give you all the information I can get.'

'Thank you,' said Mari.

Dawn was winding down now. 'Nice, though. I mean, there's love in there. There's love there. They like you. They're excited, you know?

Mari smiled. 'I'm excited too. It was trying for a long time.'

'I think you just have to get out of the way,' Dawn mused. 'If you just relax and let it happen, you'll do better. Don't judge it.'

Nerida squeezed Mari's hand. 'Knowing it's from the Earth helps. You're very happy with the Earth.'

'Yeah,' Mari agreed. All her paintings and the photos she took to inspire them were about the wondrous planet and the life it sustained.

'It had some conscious moments just as the Earth,' Dawn said. 'They said they were there at the beginning of all this. And then the earth was moving and they were, like, part of that, helping to structure that.'

She moved her hands, as if around a globe. 'That's how it looks.' Nerida said, 'That was in your newsletter today!' She turned to Trevor, who was reading his phone.

'Do you remember the question you put in today's email, "Questions to Monica"? Somebody asked about the earth?'

'It was about consciousness, I know,' said Trevor.

'Whether the earth is conscious or aware of its being?' Nerida nodded. 'Oh, I truly believe it is,' Dawn said.

'There's no question that it is. Everything's conscious. It all is,' asserted Trevor. 'We've periodically—I've talked to channelled entities and asked, "What are you?" And had a response, "I'm the consciousness of this place." You can be a consciousness of a storm. I mean, there's all kinds of things, aren't there?'

Dawn said, 'Okay. Trying to make sure I've got it all to ya before I let Monica come back. I need to make sure.

'I was on, like, a whirlwind tour! 'It was taking me around.

'I said: "Who are you, what are you doing? What's happening? Use me for a moment." He said, "Well, it doesn't match."

'I said: "Well, just try!"

'And they kept, you know, gesturing to Mari.

'And I said, "Well, she needs to see you—so why don't you just give it a shot? Doesn't matter if you come through. I'll try to adjust," I said. "We're trying to get Mari comfortable with you."

'And,' she addressed Mari, 'you, seeing that, I think was an important part of the process, even if it wasn't the kinda thing I would usually do. It was something that you needed to see because you've got to get comfortable.'

It seemed far from comfortable, Nerida thought. *I wonder how Mari will be able to go through with this?*

CHAPTER

EIGHT

B URBANK, CALIFORNIA
WED NOVEMBER 28, 2012

MARI JOINED DAILY RELAXATION EXERCISES, meditations and visualisation and work with crystals. Following Monica's lead. She surprised Nerida, sitting beside her.

Monica helped Mari navigate by and through perfectionism, intellectualism, insecurities, building self-respect and honouring the work.

The annoying matter of the negative language Mari used was only superficial, Monica assured Nerida. 'Encourage her to rephrase.'

Then there was more meditation. Monica was able to lead Mari into ways of being she had rarely experienced consciously before. *Well, we've reached elevated states of consciousness before, in sex,* Nerida thought dreamily. *Or she has, diving with manta rays. Swimming with the humpback whales. Mari is a traveller in other realms, only in ways beyond the superficial and the fashionable.*

Dawn and Monica wanted to teach as many aspects of channelling as they could, aware that the women were returning soon to their desert home across the ocean. No one was sure what would work, if anything.

Most people who try to channel, they were told, are not able to do it. Trevor told them, 'I really wanted to be a channel. I worked really hard at it. I studied. Went to workshops and courses. I went to a night school for months and got a taste of it. Then, I saw Dawn. She just tagged along to a meditation class with her friend. And Monica took the opportunity and stepped right in. Amazing natural gift, she has.'

'So now you're the scribe,' Nerida said, with respect.

They made their own world in the dated brown and gold hotel room. Trevor left to work in the Business Centre downstairs. Dawn was in trance for hours, as Monica led Mari through her program.

'Right, pen in hand. Take a deep breath,' Monica instructed Mari.

'Now, this Energy would like to write, as well as the other work. That's why we're giving you this little exercise—an automatic writing moment.

'The best way to do this, is don't try to control anything. Other hand away. You don't control the paper. The paper needs to be here. And put your hand, put the weight of your hand on it and just start here like this, and go up and down. Up and down.'

Mari's long, artistic fingers held the pen, scratching across the lined paper of Nerida's exercise book.

'That's alright. This is a way to start, you just let the hand take over. Now, we'll also do this: start here. Just start making letters. You make an A, B. Allow them to see all the letters. So, you write the alphabet all the way through.

'And it's almost like what you call the ouija board, when you let your hand go to the letters that you wish to go to, that's another way to do it.'

Mari kept drawing letters. 'This doesn't make any sense,' she said, doubtfully. 'Don't be thinking,' Monica said.

'I want to draw to this area but I don't know which—'

Monica's voice and vibes were soothing. 'Relax, let yourself be drawing. And don't be concerned if it makes sense or anything, just let your energy take you to the letter.'

After a moment to unfocus, Mari drew some more.

'Good. What does it say if it says anything?' Monica asked.

'Nothing. Bartgroff.' Mari met Nerida's eye and they laughed.

Monica peered over the table toward the paper in front of Mari. 'It could also be Bartgrinn.'

'Bartgrinn?' Nerida was incredulous.

'Bartgrinn,' Monica said with dignity. 'It is a name, an old Gaelic name.'

'Oh.' Mari was also unconvinced.

Monica enunciated very clearly, rolling the second 'r' and making the 'nn's ring. 'Bartgrinn.'

'I was trying not to look at it and just put it down and then look at it so. I wasn't sure.'

'We think that's Bart-grinn, including the last part,' Monica said confidently.

'Grinn?' Mari asked.

Monica nodded slightly. 'Grrri*nn*. You need an Irish tongue to do it.'

'So it's Bart and then the Grinn?'

'Bartgrinn. Bartgrinn.'

'There should be an 'n' in there or—?' The letters looked like 'GRWF' where they should have said 'GRINN'.

BARTGRWF, Mari had written.

'Not necessarily an N,' Monica said. She was a bit lost, for once. Nerida murmured, 'Gaelic spelling's very strange...'

'Yes. But this is a good way for you, my dear, to start to get words formed. Because the Energy can come in. It can have a hard time speaking at first, and this would be a way for you to allow yourself to let the Energy dictate for you.'

That makes sense. They try to learn to speak all night, thought Nerida.

At least writing is quieter.

Mari was thinking about the speaking at night, too. 'I wake up in the morning and I have a sore throat and—'

'Because he's been talking all night,' Nerida said.

'What did happen? The air's so dry or, has he been snoring or what?' Mari was puzzled.

'There's a lot of this, ssshhhhh. Shhhhh,' Nerida added. 'Practising moving the mouth.'

Monica responded. 'And you have to understand, the teeth are usually an interesting thing for a spirit.'

'Mmm,' Nerida agreed. 'She's moving the tongue over the teeth a lot, feeling the teeth.'

'Yes. In the times it was incarnated we don't think there were a lot of good teeth. Coming into your body he's going, "I don't remember all these teeth."'

'They're so smooth!' Nerida said.

'Why are there so many of them around?' Mari smiled.

'Well, you have to consider that for ourselves, coming into what we call a "modern" body,' Monica said, 'we have different memories. Memory of being in a body, but, not necessarily being able to see, not necessarily being able to hear, having a limb missing, or no teeth. Teeth were not common in certain cultures, not—'

'I hadn't thought of that,' Mari said.

'—not taken care of. They didn't brush their teeth. They just let things accumulate and when things accumulate in the teeth one knows now what can happen, the teeth rot and fall out and you don't have them. So, we think, with him coming in he's doing a lot of this because he's trying to see what's here.

'Yes, the teeth are a problem for some energies, especially a very ancient one that only incarnated a few times in bodies that weren't perfect.'

Mari imagined it. 'Is it like, "So I came into this body when I was born, reincarnated, and there were no teeth, then I had a few of them for a while and they were gone again. So why are they still there?" Is that what they're thinking?'

'Yes, you have to understand, that this is an ancient energy. And it hasn't had what we term modern bodies.

'It didn't incarnate often enough to have enough experience to know that hey, maybe in life or two we did have all our teeth. Maybe. But this one does not, this one's only incarnated about ten times maybe.'

'So does it make it more difficult to speak too because there's less space for the tongue?'

'Yes, well the tongue has to move against the teeth, making the sounds: t, t, t, t.'

'She does that in her sleep too.' Nerida was relieved to talk about her experience of these past years. The only person she'd talked to about what Mari's form (as Monica called it) was doing at night was Professor Bruce, and that didn't go well.

'It's trying to make sounds, to figure out how the tongue works,' Monica explained. 'There've also been generational advancements.

'In each generation, there's a bit of advancement: the jaw changes, the way they breathe through the nose changes.

'There was no ability to fix teeth then, lots of teeth were crooked or they had a double set of teeth or no teeth and so on. It was a very different kind of experience.'

'So you think he might not be giving good advice on treating teeth,' Mari suggested.

'Probably not.' Monica smiled, too. 'Just pull them up. ... we'll laugh it out for you. And you don't need to be knocked out, we'll give you a pint of ale and you'll be fine.'

Mari said suddenly. 'When you said that the Energy's coming in, I could smell beer. I smelled beer.'

Monica nodded. 'Mead.'

'Strong smell,' Mari recalled. 'Yeah, I don't know about mead, to me it smelled like beer.'

'Well in ancient times they didn't drink the water,' Monica said.

'I don't drink the water ... either.'

'No. She doesn't drink water. She's terrible that way.'

'I mix juice or cordial in it. But I could clearly smell strong beer.'

Monica let that pass. 'So, we'll say those are simple things we wanted to make sure you did in this channelling study.'

'And what we'd like to do is one more meditation, and with your permission, we would like to perhaps escort the Energy in and leave it there for a minute or two.'

Monica started breathing deeply and slowly, Mari and Nerida naturally followed. 'Breathe, inhale. Right out. Inhale. Out. ... You can feel it if you ... It's almost a ... shape. It will come to us ...'

The room filled with the sounds of their breath, covering the hum of the central heating, warming the room.

'Keep breathing. Do a little "omm-ing" for us.'

'Omm.' Mari's voice was deep and resonant.

While Mari was on her journey, Nerida had a vision of her own. When she came back to the room, she felt that the vision served to distract her from Mari. Maybe she was too close. She put the vision aside to recall later.

'Breathe in.' Monica was instructing Mari.

'Omm. Omm.

'The vibrations increase when you do this. If you had your hands here, Nerida,' she placed Dawn's hands at the base of her throat, where her collar was unbuttoned, 'you'd feel the increase of energy when she releases it.'

'Omm. Omm.'

Nerida continued to be surprised. She'd never heard Mari chant. She didn't even sing.

'Good, it's good work, you're doing very well, dear. The vibration is increasing and increasing. One more time, breathe in. And ...'

'Omm.'

'Good girl. That's enough for now. ... the energy. ... we'll lift the energy up and down. This is the ...'

The breath was like wind in the room. Monica, still channelled by Dawn of course, got up and took a few careful steps towards Mari, whose face was so deeply relaxed it hardly looked like her. Monica stepped like a person learning to walk, taking care not to trip over Dawn's feet. She moved the hands around Mari's head and upper body. Showed Nerida, speaking softly, how to do it, how to shift energy using her hands to help Mari allow the Energy to enter her body.

Nerida's hands felt open and warm. Her whole body felt light and agile.

Monica, concentrating, murmured as if to herself, 'Always clear after the opening—' Then snapped her fingers. 'Would you have anything to say?'

There was a deep moment. Nerida knew, somehow, she was not being addressed.

Neither was Mari.

Mari's head nodded gently, with an appealing tilt.

Monica was pleased. 'Good. Alright, movement is good. A word? A sound?' She commanded.

'Ah. Hello.' A breathy voice came from deep in Mari's throat.

'Hello. Well done,' Nerida grinned. *Someone good, someone different, is here.*

'Good work, good,' Monica said, moving back to the chair. Mari, channelling, made inaudible whispers.

'Excellent. Takes a bit of getting used to,' Monica said, encouraging.

With a breathy 'h', the Energy said, 'Who is it?'

Monica said, 'You are welcome to stay if you like or if you have become weary, you can go. However, just know that the door is always open.'

From Mari's throat and mouth: '... not go.'

'Good. What is your name so that we all may know you familiarly?' Monica asked. 'Or how would you like to be referred to? In the linear they need this.'

There was no response for a few moments.

'It's alright.' Monica got up again, placing Dawn's feet with care. She gestured at Mari's neck. 'Move up into the vocal cords, move up into the vocal cords. You're going a little too deep. Up higher.' Monica sat back and looked toward Mari's form with a small smile and a glint in the eye.

The voice came purposefully, 'Aedgar.'

Nerida repeated the name in wonder.

Suddenly the energy Monica had held in the room, which had filled the space, was gone. Nerida felt, but could barely comprehend, that Monica focussed entirely out of the room for a flash.

It was only listening to the recording later that Nerida was able to hear what they said. 'Do you know your Aiden?' Monica said softly, tenderly.

Back in the room, Nerida said again, 'Aedgar.'

'Aedgar,' he responded.

'Lovely to see you.'

'Aed. Gar. Aedgar.'

'Bravo Aedgar,' Monica said warmly. 'Feel the vocal cords. Feel them. Find the spot to sit in them where it's comfortable.'

'I ... happy,' Aedgar said.

'We're happy too, really happy,' said Nerida.

'Good work...' Monica got up and took a few steps to move Dawn's hands near Mari's neck, '... just attempting to move your energy a little bit higher into the vocal cords, dear. Make it easier.'

Aedgar, like a colt finding his feet, said, 'Easy ... quiet.' Indeed, the central heating had stopped its hum.

'So it is alright, Mari,' Monica suggested, 'to return to the form. Tell yourself to come back slowly. Open the door and walk back into your conscious awareness in this body.'

After a long minute, Mari opened her brown eyes and looked brightly around the room. 'You did some marvellous work here. We finally met Aedgar,' said Monica.

'Hello, beautiful,' said Nerida.

'Brava,' Monica said. 'Good for you, dear. Now, how did you feel? Or we could keep that personal if you like.'

'We're just curious, aren't we?' Nerida was excited.

Monica looked like the cat with the cream. 'You're just curious. 'We kinda know, but we think it's good to verbalise it.'

'I could hear, I could hear what was going on. I could. And I thought 'How can it be so difficult?' I'm judgmental about it,' said Mari.

'Yes, you are,' said Monica.

'I just thought. "How can it be so difficult to get a name out?"'

'Well, if you haven't been in a body for several hundred years...' Monica offered. 'All right, yes,' Mari conceded. 'And, there's a bunch of teeth there that were never there before. It's a woman's body. You can see why it would be difficult.'

'Yes ... So when you have these moments don't try to analyse them. Say, "I'm connecting."'

'And we believe you are allowing yourself to hear so that you feel comfortable. And it's alright to hear sometimes. It means a lot to you and you want to be sure, the controlling part of you, wants to be sure it goes right.

'But you're going to have to get rid of the controlling part sooner or later.'

Mari considered. Then said, 'So it sounded like Aedgar or something. Aedgar like A.'

'A.G.A.R.? Agar?' Monica prompted.

Nerida said, 'It was almost like A.Y.D.G.A.R.'

'It was like an Ae,' Mari said.

'Between an 'e' and an 'a'. We can ask Aedgar,' Nerida smiled broadly at Mari.

'Yes.'

'He's happy.'

Mari said to Monica, 'I felt like I was trying to open my eyes but I couldn't.'

'We do think he will want to open the eyes, but for the time being it's okay to keep them shut, to maintain focus. Because the eye will go to colour, the eye will go to different things it doesn't need to go to.

'He's really attempting—he was a little low in here,' Monica tapped the base of Dawn's throat. 'And we were encouraging him to come up to about here. He was here and we think that's why it was so hard to get the name out.'

Nerida was amazed. 'He was trying in the wrong spot?'

'Yes, he needed to come up, that's what we were encouraging, "Move up to here and you'll be fine."

'So, we think it's a job well done, dear.'

'Thank you.'

'Now you need to practise.'

'Yes.'

'And no judgment. None.'

Nerida chimed in, 'No expectations and no judgement.'

'Is he happy now?' Mari was wistful.

'He's very happy. Yes, very happy and he says you're a much better fit for him than we are, or Dawn, for that matter.

'A much better fit, and we do think that with time, and focus, that it will become as fluid as we are with Dawn. And to be able to see through the eyes and do all kinds of things. That's what he's looking for.

'And you are one of the energies in the shell that can provide that. It's a good match.

And he's waited a long time.'

'Yeah?'

Monica leaned forward. 'He said he's known you since you've been about three or four.

'That's a long time, around forty years.'

'And your face has, there's a beauty in the face, your face has opened up, the energy in the face has opened up. It's changed.'

Monica was right, Nerida thought, looking at her beautiful wife. Mari smiled. 'I could smell the beer again.'

'I smelt it too this time,' Nerida recalled.

'You did?'

'Mhmm. Just at the beginning.'

'Very strong.'

'Just as he was coming towards you. I smelt a strong yeasty smell.'

'I could feel it from coming from here,' Mari waved her right hand above her head.

Nerida remembered the smell. 'I think it's mead. Monica's right. You might start making mead.'

'Yeah, I might. Would go well with the sourdough bread.' Mari stopped herself. 'We can't do it in the desert. Because of restrictions. There's prohibition, no alcohol.'

'Oh, that's unfortunate. Nothing like a glass of good stout,' Monica said. She persuaded Dawn to drink a glass of stout once or twice a year when channelling, Trevor had told them. Dawn, herself, didn't like it and complained of having the taste in her mouth afterwards.

'We had times in Bristol that we remember fondly,' Monica mused. 'Yes, Bristol was a big part of it and so was the south.'

'Mmm. Did you get to live a whole lifetime in Bristol?' Nerida asked. All she knew of Bristol was that it was a coastal town in England's southwest.

'Yes. We experienced love there the first time.' Monica glowed with a witchy smile, so different to Dawn's open American grin.

'That's a good life, then,' said Mari. She and Nerida both knew true love and were proud to declare it.

'Yes,' Monica recalled.

'He was quite handsome and so were we.

'He was a good lad.

'When you discover love connection, for the first time outside of eternal existence, there is always a beautiful moment. You finally get it. You can have all the incarnations you want but until you get that—'

Nerida interrupted: 'So did you have a lifetime with Aedgar? You and Aedgar have known each other in linear lifetimes?'

'Yes, we have.'

Oh, this is too much. You cheeky beings. 'Oh, that's lovely. Go on.'

'He enlisted our help,' Monica said simply. 'He said he'd been trying a long time.'

Mari found her voice. 'Is this how Nerida or how we found you?'

'Perhaps.'

The room was quiet for a few beats while the women tried to comprehend the idea that Monica had somehow chosen Mari to channel her lover of past lifetimes.

And yet, it all felt like our idea to come here, Nerida thought.

'Could be. Well, I was looking,' she said. It felt like a random act, responding to Trevor's ad for Dawn's channelling sessions on the net.

'It was all good things,' Monica said, soothingly. 'And you, Mari, have great abilities. And now you've leaped over that first hurdle, leaped into it for the first time, without being asleep, without being unconscious.

'Sleep is nice but it's not really going to do any good if you want to channel material because that means you must be awake.'

'It's not a very sociable thing when you're asleep,' Nerida said.

Mari nodded. 'Especially not if you have to go to work the next morning. And you have a taxing position.'

'I do.'

Monica said to Nerida, 'You need all your mental facilities engaged. You can't be half asleep.' She turned to Mari. 'And this channelling work, you'll need to do it for people eventually and that's usually done in the daytime, not at two in the morning.'

'They can't come into the bedroom at two o'clock to talk to Aedgar,' Nerida laughed.

'They might think that is a bit strange, not the channelling part but the two in the morning,' Monica said. 'And happy. He said he was very happy.

'He's been waiting a long time. Coming in and doing all the practice runs. And this is really your first practice run in a conscious state, so this is a big day.'

'It is. November 28th,' Mari said.

'2012,' said Nerida.

'The birth of a partnership,' agreed Monica.

'One that will last for the rest of this life,' Mari said. Nerida was impressed by her depth of feeling. And yet, she felt it, too, a resonant connection. It was like meeting someone at a party and feeling as though you'd known them all your life. And would always be friends from now on. But exponentially more intense.

'There's a couple more beings lurking about,' Monica reminded them. 'But one at a time for the moment, stay with that.

'Now, you need to practice and you need to stay out of the criticising.

'Whatever happens, happens.

'And move on. And probably not listening.'

'Yes,' said Nerida. 'Maybe ease off getting angry about my work and other things that you can't change.'

'But it's hard to see you suffer.'

'I don't suffer much.'

Monica said, 'Nerida is quite capable of fighting her battles. She's there to cause change in that environment. That's one of the prime reasons she's there: to be the rough edge that everyone must get past to do their nonsense.'

At knock at the door heralded Trevor.

Monica tilted Dawn's face towards him. 'Very exciting news.'

'What's that?' He put his satchel down and sat on a bed corner.

'We've met Aedgar.'

'Edgar?'

'Aid. Gar.'

'Aidgar? Aedgar. Oh...'

'She brought it through well.' Monica said with pride.

Trevor turned to Mari. 'Did you?'

'She did,' said Nerida.

'That's fabulous then.' To Nerida, 'You recorded it?'

'We did.' She grinned.

'That's great, that's fabulous.'

'Yes. So, we're all very pleased.' Monica seemed to have proved something to Trevor.

'I bet you are.'

'We worked out some techniques,' the spirit said.

'And they had a fabulous time together before,' Mari said.

Nerida nodded. 'Uhuh. She fell in love with him in Bristol.'

Trevor was astonished. 'Oh really? You know him? Then was he a girl? Because you had a male life in Bristol...'

'Yes, we did,' Monica said. There was deep quiet in the room. Then she said to Trevor, with a queenly satisfaction 'You assumed.'

'You had heterosexual assumptions!' Nerida laughed.

Trevor said, 'Monica really likes Bristol, she has always said it was the place she had the best time.'

Monica looked at Trevor with a smile. 'Yes. It was a lovely afternoon and we're quite pleased.'

'I'm pleased then,' Trevor said, recovering.

'So,' Monica said, 'we will leave you. Until tomorrow. Alright my dears.'

The others talked excitedly while Dawn came out of trance.

'Excellent ... productive,' Trevor said.

Nerida said, 'Incredible.'

'Even if I ...' began Mari.

Dawn returning, said, 'So we heard it happened! Did some good work.'

Nerida was telling her. 'Monica's first true love, Aedgar! He only had about three or four words because he was concentrating a bit low for the vocal cords, but he got out, "I'm happy," and "easy." Good, huh?'

'Well, practise,' said Trevor.

'Yes, she's been told, haven't you, Mari?'

'It's like playing the piano, it's like, you seem to have no progress and then, all in one go, you can play it,' Trevor said.

Dawn agreed. 'I remember doing the scales over and over and making mistakes, making mistakes and all of a sudden, they just worked beautifully. True.'

They were excited and animated, talking over one another. 'Well, Mari plays the saxophone so she knows about that.'

'I used to play the saxophone,' Trevor said.

'I gave mine away. It made someone happy so—' Mari said.

'I did that with mine as well. I had a good one too. Better that they could use it though. It was sitting in the closet.'

Mari smiled. 'I had it sitting in a closet in my hut in the Maldives because I loved it so much, just the look of it.'

'So he is Monica's old, first love!' Nerida exclaimed to Dawn.

'In the Maldives... he and I ... we were out under the moon ... beach playing ...' Mari was telling Trevor.

Dawn said, 'I knew there was a discovery of love in Bristol, and I knew he was a guy and I knew she was a guy then, I knew that.'

Trevor said, 'You know I actually would like to play soprano sax because it's smaller and ...'

'And it was in a time frame where to be married was expected,' Dawn said. She read historical novels, she said. Sometimes had conversations with Monica in her head.

'She got to live in Bristol all her life then? Or his life, rather?' Nerida was fascinated.

'So I believe,' Dawn confirmed.

'... It was time to change how we spent our time, no more partying...' Trevor said.

'Mari asked her, "So is that why we met you?" "Oh, could be," she said.

'And she's very happy. It's a long, long cherished goal beginning to be achieved today.' Nerida wanted Dawn to know, for once, what happened while she was away.

Dawn said, 'Yes, Mari you did it rather well. From what I hear. Monica was ...'

Nerida interrupted, 'Yeah, she was doing the happy dance.'

'The Snoopy dance,' Dawn laughed. 'But you're a good student. 'You listen. She said that you're applying yourself.'

'Once you get it rolling because that's the big step, it's like a finger in the dyke ...' Trevor said, with no pun intended.

'There goes Saturday nights for the rest of your life, look out,' Dawn said. 'At least it's something to do on a Saturday night.'

Mari nodded, 'Yep.'

Nerida turned to her. 'Nothing on television.'

'No, not much.'

'If you have the time, you can do it three nights a week,' Trevor suggested.

'I don't know if I'll have the energy actually,' said Nerida, feeling suddenly worn out. *Talking to spirits three nights a week? What will become of our lives? When will we have sex, then?*

B URBANK, CALIFORNIA SAME DAY 2012

THE COUPLES SHARED dinner at a steak house. Dawn ordered a sirloin and salad, finally able to eat a proper meal.

Nerida reflected that Monica was like a counsellor to the women. They asked about where to live, the personalities of relatives (or bosses). Past lives of friends. People who'd died. Their own foibles and fears and past lives.

Trevor was interested in bigger questions. He asked Monica (and other beings) about Black Holes and Quantum physics. He'd met the spirit who was Nikola Tesla. And Edison. Nerida must have looked non-plussed when he talked to her about it.

'Show them television. They're amazed!' He suggested.

Somehow it feels like Aedgar would not be amazed, she thought. *I need to educate myself about more important things to be worthy of this.*

'Well, you've read the Michael book. Do you know your role in essence?' That was 'Michael' jargon.

Nerida smiled. 'Monica told me that my role is "Priest." I'm not religious, so I didn't like that.'

'You know that's not what it means, right? It's kind of a type, a kind of an archetype, that doesn't change through lifetimes. There's a million ways of expressing it in a lifetime. I mean, lots of people have the role of "server." That doesn't mean they don't have their own mind and free will with it.'

'Yeah, I understand. The servers are caring people. So, "priest"? I am good at listening. And I do tend to turn my medical consults into spiritual discussions, often enough. I mean, I try to help my patients work out how to get better, not only with the medicine.'

'What's your Chief Feature?' Trevor asked. *Messages from Michael* had a concept that a soul chose two negative qualities to overcome to protect the ego and to accept and learn from in a lifetime. In Nerida's mind it was a bit like a Sims game.

'One of them is greed. I don't remember the other one,' Nerida recalled. 'Monica laughed. She said, "Who would believe that? A greedy priest!" That never happens, right? I'm a generous person. But I eat too much, just about every day.' Her giant schnitzel arrived.

On the other side of the table, Mari was giving Dawn advice on the rosemary sprinkled on her mashed potato. 'I don't like eating it. It's good to wash your hair with, though,' she said.

Mari studied to be a *heilpraktiker*, a naturopathic physician, before she came to Australia. Her class would study anatomy in the morgue in the morning and dance to a shaman's drums in the afternoon.

She fought to be allowed to study something she was genuinely interested in. She always thought, in hospital as a child, that she should become a doctor to prove that healing could be done better. She studied medical language so that she could understand what they said when they gathered at the end of her bed, planning new tortures.

The language it took Nerida ten years to master—Mari spoke

fluently by the age of ten. After Mari's accident as an adult, and the long tail of suffering it brought with it, German Disability Services offered her a career in a sheltered workshop. Just being at the Heilpraktiker school was an achievement.

The first years of her course were the same curriculum as the doctors and dentists followed. She chose to specialise in the German traditions of herbs, homeopathy, osteopathy and other complementary healing modalities because she felt they had more to offer.

But she wasn't a natural fit.

When the shaman was drumming, she felt herself swimming with the humpback whales in Tonga. That was extraordinary. But she'd done it many times in real life.

Mari began her photographic life as an underwater photographer, wielding heavy and bulky underwater camera housings in the days of film. It was a natural outcome of her artistic eye and her job as a diving instructor. She won competitions for her photographs: second place in a Europe-wide contest and first in a US-based one. She published photos in *National Geographic*.

She was always a painter and skilled at drawing. But she stopped exhibiting her paintings after feeling pushed to read into and assign meanings to her paintings by people who bought her work or the press. And the gallery owner.

Mari stopped entering photographic contests after she realised that her rights to her work were taken from her for the paltry fee of the prize. She saw her photographs of the humpbacks in Tonga reproduced on shirts and mugs in Hong Kong and was furious.

Back in Germany, her colleagues at the heilpraktiker school had encounters with imps and trolls, saw psychedelic patterns, talking mushrooms and other fantasms when the shaman drummed. She dreamt of the whales but thought her experience ordinary by comparison. 'It didn't work for me. It never did.'

Now, she was the one who channelled.

'Those idiots in the Birkenstocks would have sold their grandmother to be able to do this,' Mari said. 'And here I am. I never asked for it.'

They were eating dinner in the hotel's dining room. The next batch of television contestants surrounded them with their shiny hair and self-involvement.

Nerida chewed thoughtfully on a piece of schnitzel and murmured agreement.

In hindsight, roommates on school trips, at sleepovers or in the hospital ward heard Mari's odd version of sleep talking in her youth. It was always in other languages.

There was resentment, Mari said. 'Some people got really angry. Like, "You kept me up all night and I didn't even understand a fucking word of it." I didn't know what they were talking about. I'd get angry back.

'When I grew up I worked as a diving instructor and often had to share a room. Living on a boat, you know? Or in a cabin or dorm on a trip. People would refuse to share with me because they said they never got any sleep. I didn't understand it."

Mari sipped a broth, glancing at the schnitzel enviously. 'Are you sick?'

'No. I want to try channelling again. Dawn says you have to eat lightly so your guts don't put them off.'

'No wonder she's so slim,' Nerida said. Her own thoughts were about her role in this turn of events. *Is this going to be our life now? What am I going to talk to non-physical beings about?*

There was a pattern in the curtains of their hotel room that reminded Nerida of one of the Aboriginal paintings they had on a wall at home. It portrayed sacred waterholes in crimson, silver and black. The women had a minor collection of uplifting Indigenous art, often bought (or even gifted) by Nerida's patients, complementing Mari's art.

At Mutitjulu, Mari was given a painting by Aunty Blossom, the one who was disgusted by Uluru, after she helped Bloss stretch canvases over frames. The painting, again about water, also had blues—teal and indigo—in it. It hung in their very private bedroom.

That evening Mari repeated that she wanted to channel again.

Even though she'd seen Mari fasting, Nerida was surprised that she wanted to do it again so quickly and unsure whether it would work. But she set up to record.

'Don't look at me,' Mari said.

They sat in bulky chairs in their hotel room, a small wooden table between them.

After ten minutes or so of exercises with her breathing and voice (and probably her mind and intention, too) Nerida sensed that Mari was far away.

Through the french doors hardy, woody bushes tossed in the early evening breeze.

Lights came on as darkness descended.

Aedgar returned—at least, Nerida hoped it was Aedgar—and tried to speak. But there was only indistinct whispering.

Three long minutes passed. Nerida tried moving her hands near Mari's head and neck, as Monica had.

Mari's head moved gently, tilting and turning, her neck stretching. Swallows and throat-clearing followed as Aedgar found his voice.

'Hello'

Nerida smiled. 'Hello'

'I—I—Are you ... Can you hear me?'

There were a few more minutes of quiet, with neck flexing and ahems. Then moving of the eyebrows, twitching and wriggling the nose and forming shapes with the mouth.

'How—hhow— hhow are —are you?'

'I'm very well, Aedgar, thank you. I'm very well, indeed.

'How are you?'

'Well, well, well.'

Nerida laughed fondly. 'We're so happy that you can do this.'

He whispered, 'Quite, quite, quite te, quite a bit, quite a bit to do.'

'Quite a bit to do. Indeed. We have wonderful work to do.'

'Hah. I—I ag-ree. I ag-gree.'

'You agree. We need to make this work a high priority.' Nerida felt a little giddy.

'Indeed,' the spirit said.

'Mari agrees also.'

'Hah.'

'Monica is very happy.'

'Aha,' said Aedgar. 'Of course. Long waay. Long waay. Long way to come. Long way to come.'

There were pauses between many of the short sentences, as if they were a result of consultation or research. Or perhaps learning to be in a body was like driving a car, Nerida thought briefly, and didn't come automatically at first.

Nerida nodded. 'It was a long way to come. I can't imagine.'

'No.'

There was the sound of a train in the distance. Aedgar noticed. 'Nois—noise, noise.'

'Noise, yes. We're in a city. There's noise all around. There are trains. There are people in other rooms. We're in a hotel in America.'

Aedgar whispered. 'Hotel. Ho hot -t— ho -o—ho-otel.'

'Mhmm.'

It felt like the room was silent then, even if the noise outside continued. Mari's head tilted and turned delicately as if Aedgar listened, sensing the surroundings.

'Is the body comfortable for you?' Nerida asked.

'I—I'll find out. Works.'

'Good, yes, it does work.' She was nervous, grasped for something to say. 'We hear you have an interest in healing.'

'Mm Mmakes sense.'

She tried again, feeling a welling of emotion, perhaps joy, in this strange communication. 'We hear you speak for the Earth, the beautiful Earth.'

'One, one has to, one has to do someting, thing.'

'One has to do something, yes.'

'I, hi, I gg, agree.'

'Be encouraged in your speaking. This English is not your first language.'

'No, no, it's not.'

'Thank you for speaking English.'

Aedgar sighed and took a sharp intake of breath, as if marshalling effort. 'Welcome.'

'You can leave at any time if you're tired, of course.' She followed Monica's example.

'But I do enjoy speaking to you.' Nerida felt a light, timeless happiness. There was that exhilarating energy in the room.

'Ss same here.'

'I hope it's going to get easier for you, this talking.'

'Itt it will. It will.

'Soon, soon.

'Learning, learning.'

'You are. Learning brilliantly.'

There was quiet for a minute or so. Nerida tried to think.

Trevor had told her that she should engage the spirits, keep asking questions, keep talking, if she wanted the channelling to continue. Now, after years of wishing that the inarticulate and foreign words and noises would stop, she did want the communication to continue. They could finally speak in a way she could understand. She was curious.

'My intention is to listen to you, record what you say and write it down in books. And to encourage Mari to help you come through to express yourself.' She wondered as she spoke if she should commit herself so. An ancient spirit was not like someone you met on a bus stop.

'As one would, as one would want to,' he agreed.

'I very much look forward to hearing more from your perspective.

We have a meeting with Monica and Trevor tomorrow morning at 10.30.' Nerida wasn't sure if it was necessary to make an appointment, now that Mari was supposed to be in control of when the channelling happened.

'We-ll, well so it be, then.'

'So it be.' Nerida smiled at his poetic style of speech. 'Well, so it be then. Good.'

Nerida was unsure. 'Perhaps Mari will come back now if that's okay with you.'

She was relieved to see Mari return, with a sleepy sound. 'Hello beautiful! That was very good.

'He's delightful.'

Mari stretched and yawned.

'Well done. You make it look easy. It's not easy for him, but you make it look easy for you.'

Mari put two rocks—crystals Monica had given her—on the table with a clunk. 'I'm impressed. How's your neck?'

'I don't know.' She was dazed. 'Were you listening?' Nerida asked.

'Yeah, kind of, distantly.'

'He's very sweet. Polite.'

Mari laughed. 'Compared to me?'

'Compared to anybody!'

Nerida leaned in and kissed her wife's cheek. 'Let's order you a club sandwich.'

NEXT MORNING MARI only took coffee at breakfast.

They had only 24 hours until their departure from LA.

It was an unusual situation to be in a room with two women channelling ghosts.

'Non-physical entities,' Trevor called them. 'The universe is so much more interesting than most people know,' he said quietly as Dawn and Mari went into trance.

Mari channelled Aedgar again, with apparent ease. But Aedgar needed to learn to speak more loudly.

Again, Monica used Dawn's hands to help him locate a place to focus his voice, around Mari's larynx.

Monica coaxed him into conversation, 'Won't you speak with us? We had some lovely times here in linear. Do you remember The Hog's Head tavern? A lovely stout or an ale and a dish of Cobbler's Pie?'

'We remember,' Aedgar said.

Monica explained later that cobbler's pie was a kind of a stew, a big steaming pot of all the parts of the deer that the landowner didn't want. Nerida had an earthy image of hungry people stealing choice pieces of offal. Perhaps Aedgar and Aiden might have been guildsmen or peasants. Or even serfs. Most people who'd lived on Earth were not Cleopatra or Genghis Khan.

The women went to Santa Monica for sunset, each reflecting as they watched the tide come in under the old wooden pier. She felt mellow and amazed. But it was a jolt to Nerida's ego to see that Mari was the gifted one.

After Nerida's studies with the Traditional Aboriginal healers (at Mutitjulu, the Anangu called them ngangkari), and even with her training in Traditional Chinese Medicine before she became a doctor, Nerida felt she could become a healer.

She'd felt energy moving in her clients' bodies when she worked as a masseur in a beautician's shop, as a youth. As a child her touch grounded and relaxed people.

She had hopes of becoming a ngangkari herself, but her training stopped abruptly when she married Mari. If she was honest, she'd made mistakes before then, cultural clangers that must have made it difficult for her teachers.

An astral travelling ngangkari should fly like an eagle to visit the sick at night, Nerida was more like a peewee, not even a magpie. She crashed and tumbled, never that good at spirit flying.

She was in the thick of her training as a medical doctor by then.

The difference between her external world, of science with its drugs and numbers, and her internal world, where she heard her ngangkari teachers talking in her head, was sometimes extreme.

She asked for a break. *Let me be unconscious of my learning for awhile*, she asked then, in a kind of prayer.

Back in the airport queues the next day, she reflected on the strange turn in her world.

She would follow Mari's guidance now.

Nerida had never really been monogamous before. She fell in love with other people as a way of learning when she was in her twenties. Her children's father, Sam, tolerated it for the love of her.

But loving Mari was different. Fiery, prone to jealousy, with the passion and temper her Roma ancestors were known for, she demanded exclusivity when they met in 2006.

Nerida didn't know how that would work. But she grew in response to Mari's love, loyal, protective and all encompassing. She'd never in her life been so in love and so comfortable at once. She was often happy and excited.

Besides, her work was tiring as a doctor. She didn't have the energy for more than one lover anymore.

Taking her ipad out of her bag for security, Nerida's thoughts were distant. *Now here I am, married to this weirdo. Mari, still hostile to the worlds of imagination and mysticism—in other people.* Trust in their own experiences and love was leading this pair of erstwhile atheists to give voice to an ancient earth spirit.

This Aedgar, whoever or whatever he was, who'd fallen in love with another man in England, hundreds of years ago.

Nerida wasn't sure if Aedgar and she would get along.

There were significant cultural and temporal differences to bridge.

Why did he have to come from England, really, of all the places on the planet? She was ashamed of the thought.

She had English ancestors herself.

She knew how screwed up they were, laden with centuries of

intergenerational trauma, removed from their land to make way for machines. Completely lacking in insight.

It might be kind of a dull story to tell. Why does he have to be a white man? What happened to Ancient Siamese?

Finding her seat on the plane, she stuffed her bag under the seat in front. She buckled her seatbelt, squeezed Mari's hand, then reached for and glanced at the menu. Kalamata olives. Beef rendang.

Nerida pulled the heavy glass and metal video screen out the armrest of her seat, looking for a movie.

TEN

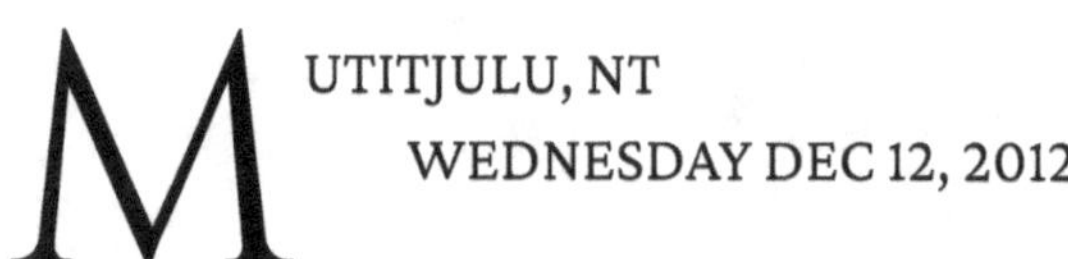

M UTITJULU, NT
WEDNESDAY DEC 12, 2012

BACK FROM LOS ANGELES, Mari and Nerida resumed life in the desert together. Nerida returned to caring for sick people at the clinic. Each wondered how this new set of skills would work out at home.

Mari ran the household, working as hard as Nerida did, but mostly in her own company. She had long, argumentative phone calls with her mother, who cried for her to come home, even after Mari had been living in Australia for five years. There was a litany of misery whenever she called, a couple of times a week.

Their oven heated unevenly. 'I spend all day getting my bread to rise and look, it's got bits that aren't cooked properly. Other bits are burnt.'

Nerida had her own stressors. She tried not talk about the complex challenges at the clinic. But sometimes didn't restrain herself from complaining about the idiocy of management in faraway Alice Springs.

Mari escaped into her art. She photographed Uluru from the front of their house, documenting the way the Rock changed in colour and apparent texture in different lights. She had a series of small canvases coming along.

Even then, at the hottest time of year, birds sang their distinct desert songs by the house windows. Tiny wrens, which the Anangu call *nyii-nyii*, made a sound just like their name.

Willy wagtails jumped about in the grasses, on the lookout for news. There were few other black and white birds, Nerida's totem. She missed them since they moved to the desert.

Eventually a butcher bird, a fierce black and white bird with the most melodious song, took up residence near the blue house, soothing her spirit.

Work at the clinic was steady. The team did good work every day.

Nerida was a slow and thorough doctor and her patients had always waited for her. She was honest enough to say what she didn't know, which meant that her colleagues, especially Claire, came to trust her.

The older people came to respect her, or at least be glad of her being there.

Sometimes she was called in at night to help, but the nurses bore the brunt of the after- hours work. As doctors do, she was always reading, always studying.

Visiting health workers and nursing colleagues taught her in more memorable ways.

If she was unsure, there was always help at the end of the phone. Her experiences at the clinic were not always enjoyable, but she kept learning.

When a deadly king brown snake came into the clinic seeking refuge from the heat the previous summer, Jasmine called out to keep everyone still.

She called outside the clinic into the hot, quiet Community.

Her shouting brought Jerry, a handsome young man with a soft energy, inside. A snake catcher. He caught the king brown, flipping it deftly with a broom into a sack.

It was a treat to see Jerry, with his flashing smile and easy physical grace. He was Caleb's son-in-law.

Caleb, the man who had the metaphysical snake pulled out of him to remove the threat of recurrent meningitis, was a father of girls. His middle girl, Henrietta, was Jerry's partner. Henni came to the clinic with their toddler to the clinic most days.

She and their daughter needed daily medication for a heart condition. The child, named Biggie, was handsome and bold, with curly light brown hair and the long lashes so many Anangu were blessed with. She looked sturdy and strong, unlike her mother, who was delicate.

She was easy to love, little Biggie, taking her medicine willingly, seeming to enjoy the attention and the ceremony. She got a vitamin C tablet, too, which the children liked.

They came in after school asking for them.

Nerida told the nurses to only give them one. 'Too much can give them kidney stones,' she told them. 'I don't want the kids eating vitamins like lollies. Especially when they don't drink much water.'

'Really? I didn't know that. Better just one then,' said Claire. Nerida saw young men rarely, usually only in emergencies.

Once they entered puberty, they were taught to keep women at a respectful distance.

They would consult the male nurse, when they had one, in the men's room (a detached part of the clinic, for men's privacy). The nurse then talked to Dr Nerida about any prescription or referral needed.

Young women came to her in groups for education and support, usually after school when Biggie and other kids were climbing up the drainpipes and walls—like they were charged up by their vitamin C— shouting and stomping on the roof.

The clinic was quiet inside then, with Jasmine finished for the day.

Sometimes a super-shy young woman needed her forthright cousin to ask about contraception. Some girls even came with one of their mothers or an aunty.

Nerida's own difficulties gave her insight into the struggles of others. Her compassion grew.

She gave too much to some people. She was not afraid to give her love and caring, especially to people others didn't like or care for.

There was a crisp day of coffee and cake in a marketplace in Germany when Nerida gave a fifty euro note to a Gypsy mother and baby.

Mari was cross and embarrassed. 'They're a professional operation, those people. You never give them money.' Sure enough, the woman's husband, or her pimp, arrived promptly, trying to get more money. Mari thought Nerida was foolish and naive.

Aboriginal people share. Even as a student, before she was on a regular wage, Nerida would give twenty dollars, when she had it, to a patient or a homeless person who asked for money.

At Mutitjulu, she didn't always say yes. She wasn't asked for money as often as most.

She learned not to take her wallet to the clinic.

Sometimes she wanted that feeling, a bliss that came of giving. She'd been generous with Thea.

The first time Thea came to the clinic, she said to Nerida, 'You're Koori, aren't you? I heard about you.'

She invited Mari and Nerida out to cook kangaroo tail with some of the other women.

The conviviality of raking the coals, the efficiency of the women preparing the meat— singeing the fur off, burying it to bake. The smell as it cooked. They drank sweet, milky tea while they waited. The sun was going down, casting orange and gold light. Shadows were long and the red sand was silky underfoot.

The meat was gummy and tender, delicious straight out of the coals. Nerida felt Thea watching her lean past the fire for salt.

And knew later that it was in that moment that Thea decided Nerida's name in Pitjantjatjara: Dr Tjula.

At first, Nerida thought people were calling her Julie. Claire had explained what they were calling her: Dr Soft. A soft-bodied creature, Nerida knew it could have been worse.

There was a whitefella at Imanpa they called Mr Paku. *Paku* meant bored.

Thea was kind, affectionate and charming—hard to say no to. She had picked up something in Dr Tjula's character. In the emergency department at Wollongong hospital, the boss used to call her 'Mother Earth.'

At Thea's request, Nerida made an extravagant purchase. It was a small electric piano for Thea's musically talented grandson.

She bought a similar instrument for her own son, Jim, even if she hardly had the money, when he was a child. Jim was musical too—he still played exquisite guitar and piano if he was sober. So, she understood.

A couple of weeks after she'd bought the piano, Thea came to the clinic for a blood test. The nurses were busy, so Jasmine came in from reception. 'You can take blood, can't ya?' she asked Nerida.

'Yeah, she can do it. Come in, Thea!' Jasmine called.

Sitting in the venipuncture chair like a queen, as Nerida strapped on a tourniquet, Thea said, 'I wanna get a tent.'

Nerida looked to the imaginary horizon with her and said, 'I wonder where you can get a tent.'

Jasmine put her head around the corner from the waiting area, 'They've got them at the store now. Good ones for two people, just $97.'

'Oh really? Thanks Jasmine,' Nerida said, tightening the tourniquet and feeling for a vein.

Then to Thea, she said, 'I wonder where you can get $97 from?' The question hung in the air. 'What do you want a tent for, anyway?'

'I'll put it out on the verandah,' said Thea.

'You can't put a tent on the verandah. You need dirt to stick the pegs in.'

Jasmine came in as Nerida put the fine needle into Thea's arm and started to draw blood. 'You can use rocks, you put em in the corners of the tent,' said Jasmin helpfully. 'You can tie the ropes up on the fence.'

'Hmm,' Nerida said, collecting tubes of blood and sticking a plaster on Thea's arm. 'Shame we haven't got $97, then, isn't it?'

She didn't get called Dr Tjula, Dr Soft, after that. Thea got a tent on her verandah anyway. Nerida saw it set up when she went on home visits a week later.

Daphne, who she visited at home, was wheelchair bound. She never asked Nerida for money. But Nerida gave her plenty of time. Her health issues were complex. She had severe diabetes that damaged her nerves. But it was not clear from the notes what happened to disable her.

She tried a couple of acupuncture treatments for Daphne's chronic pain and stiffness. It didn't help.

She tried drugs for neuropathic pain. Tried reducing her other medications in case some were interacting. Referred Daphne to Alice Springs for scans, physician and neurology reviews.

It was almost two years before Nerida found out about the suicide of Daphne's son. It seemed that the young man's death had triggered an immune disease in Daphne.

Grief devastated her body. Nerida requested blood tests to try to diagnose her condition. 'Your body will tell us through this blood, ye,' Claire said to Daphne as she drew it.

Nerida was more than a year at Mutitjulu, too, before she found out about the passing of Thea's grown son in a car accident. Both of their young men were about the same age as Nerida's son. These tragedies were not in the medical notes. No previous doctor had the cultural skills to find out about such important events.

Mutitjulu has secrets. I'm honoured to be shown some of the reality beneath the surface.

Her patient Caleb was an imposing, silver-haired man. When he came to the clinic with severe headaches, developing a fever, she and Claire consulted the doctors in town and flew him to Alice Springs Hospital.

He was there for over three months with life-threatening meningitis, an infection affecting the brain.

He needed intravenous antibiotics in the Intensive Care Unit and later in the medical ward. And then his long rehabilitation, building up physical strength again.

Caleb looked well when he finally came home. He needed to continue a complicated regime of large doses of antibiotics four or five times a day, for a year or more, to prevent a recurrence of the disease.

When he didn't come for more tablets after his two-month supply was up, Nerida went to see Caleb to ask him about it. Caleb told me he'd been away. He was treated by a Traditional Healer in his mother's community to the northwest.

'She pulled a giant snake outta me,' he said, his face open with awe. He touched his abdomen firmly, showing where the snake had been coiled. 'Pulled it all out. It's gone now, finished.' He gestured as if the snake had come up and out through his mouth. For a moment, Nerida wondered if he'd had a tapeworm.

She could see that the experience had been a profound one by the sincerity of his expression and the feeling of free expression in the room. Caleb was an intelligent man, strong in culture.

She thought about him on the short walk, over the silky red dust, back to the clinic. Desert pigeons, exotic creatures compared to their city cousins, made a whirring, whistling sound with their wings. They had a curled feather crown and iridescent green and purple feathers on their cloud-grey patterned bodies.

That was the only time Nerida had any conflict in her mind about a treatment by a ngangkere (as they called healers in that northwest region). But Caleb was fine. His meningitis never reoccurred. Later, she heard about big snakes in the belly that caused disease from other patients.

Dr Nerida was more open than most to the possibility that Caleb had been healed by his experience than most of her colleagues. She was able to talk to her clients with knowledge that spirit was real.

But she knew she walked a fine line.

A young women came for contraception, Desdemona, was a big, sexily dressed, confident 18-year-old. She had beautiful skin and was showing plenty of it.

She reminded Nerida of her younger self when her body had its own loud, proud voice.

But I suffered unwanted attention for it. How does she get to be herself so freely?

Anangu had dress taboos: women almost all wore skirts below the knee, as Nerida did.

Breasts were for nurturing children and painting with ochre for dancing. But showing your thighs was forbidden. Nerida knew it from boxes of donated clothing she brought for the people. Women's shorts, swimsuits or leotards were always left in the box.

Desdemona was travelling from a different community.

Like me when I was sixteen. Got away from home. Felt free. Desdemona was relishing her youth.

After her prescription was sorted, she asked Nerida about connecting with a lover, in contrast to partying.

'It's different for everyone,' Nerida said. 'But a lot of people understand that they've got a spirit or soul by having good, connected sex. Love can be empowering like that. Healing.'

Desdemona looked puzzled. 'But Jesus keeps your soul,' she said.

That was unexpected.

There was a small, significant group of churchgoers in the Community. And many other Aboriginal communities were founded by missionaries. Some people had positive experiences of the church.

Daphne loved to sing hymns, wheeling around the Community in her motorised wheelchair.

Felicity told Nerida about her youthful experience working with nuns at Ernabella as a nurse's assistant, swaddling the babies, caring for the bodies of people who had passed.

Their child health nurse, Rebecca, attended church at Muti, sitting in the hot shed with a local dog lying, panting on her feet. 'You've gotta get there early to get under the fan,' Becca said.

Nerida smiled at Desdemona, touched her hand. 'Your soul is your own always and that's the way Jesus would want it. You're the only one who decides where your spirit goes to.'

Immediately she wondered where she got the nerve to say that. And what the Community Christians would say (*will say*, she thought grimly) when they found out that she and Mari had a secret life.

Most Anangu she'd met had a healthy respect for spirits and feared bad ones.

There was a story that young people used to go to the base of Uluru to make out at night. But something terrible happened and nobody went near the Rock at night anymore.

Barry, their entrepreneurial neighbour, had sold tickets to lantern-lit ghost tours at the Rock for a while but stopped after something horrible happened to the dogs accompanying the tour.

Nerida knew that a doctor at Mutitjulu held a precarious place. She worked hard to be as transparent to the Community as she could be.

Aboriginal people earned respect as they learned and aged, by being known, in all their strengths and weaknesses, by the people they were responsible to. There was ideally no tolerance of a powerful leader who was secretly abusive of his staff, or his family. Such people existed in Communities, of course, but people knew them for what they were and the idea that they were leaders was openly scorned.

At Caleb's house, Nerida reminded him that the Infectious Diseases specialists at the hospital had ordered he should stay on his medication regime for over a year.

'I don't need those tablets,' he said. 'It's all better now.'

After more discussion, she agreed to document his decision not to take the antibiotics in the notes. He was responsible for his own health. 'That's right,' he said.

Amidst all the work and wonder was the confronting experience and privilege of getting to know Aedgar, who was delightful. And sometimes an irascible curmudgeon.

On a Wednesday evening, December 12, about ten days after returning from the US, Mari wanted to channel.

Choosing a straight-backed chair in the living room, she lengthened her spine, relaxed her face and shoulders and, over five minutes or so, went into trance. Her eyes were closed, with the gentle movements and easy posture she had when channelling. It was a relief to see Mari sitting comfortably, without pain.

When she could wait no longer to speak, Nerida said, 'Welcome. Finally. Thank you for coming back.'

'You're welcome,' came the quiet, low voice.

'You can speak more loudly, that would be good because it's noisier here. Different place.

'We are at Mutitjulu in Central Australia. Mari and I live here.'

'Central Australia ...' Aedgar repeated.

'Do you know Australia?'

Quietly, he said something incomprehensible, and then, 'Have to think about it. Hmmm. It had a different name. Flanders—from the guy that came from Flanders.'

Did he mean Dirk Hartog stumbling into the west coast in the 1600s? But he was a Dutchman. Did he mean Flemish map makers? *What century is Aedgar in, anyway?* she wondered.

'You may not know it from your Bristol lifetime, but you will know it from further back.' If he knew the early planet, he might know Australia as part of Gondwana, one of the ancient supercontinents. Nerida was disoriented already. But so curious.

'Is the body okay for you?' she asked. *Let's keep things local.*

He inclined Mari's head slightly. 'Yes. Things have to be put in place.'

'Mari appreciates any help you can give her.' Mari had chronic pain in her neck, back, shoulders and sometimes her foot or her stump. The problems came from the change in balance needed to walk with one foot.

'Seems to be a hot place here,' Aedgar said. The voice was easier to hear.

Their air conditioner, usually an unnoticed hum in the background, seemed very loud, Nerida thought.

'It is,' she said. 'It's a hot, dry desert. The earth is coloured red and there are some very interesting stones and rocks. It's an ancient place.'

'It's an old place.' He corrected her.

Okay then, 500 million years is not ancient to you. 'It's a very old place. And the people who live here are old people, too.'

'But you've got young ones too,' he said.

'We do. But we've got a lot of old souls here.'

'True,' he said.

Nerida said brightly, 'Mari and I have been out dancing tonight. There was a concert.

We enjoyed the music.'

'Dancing.'

'Can you remember dancing?'

'Kind of.' He spoke slowly. 'Dancing—always came with … drinking.'

Nerida smiled. 'It's a free feeling, dancing. A very energetic thing to do.'

Aedgar lifted Mari's hand, indicating her left neck. 'Stuck here.'

'Yes, she's had surgery on her neck and some of the bones are held together with metal.'

Exploring, he said, 'Moves here, stops there. Got to work with it.'

'Yes, I guess you'll get more used to it.'

'I will.'

'Can you move the fingers?'

'I have to find my way through this brain. Find the right words to talk about things.'

'We are a little bit travel worn,' Nerida explained. It had taken three days travel to get back from LA. 'Mari's complaining of a clueless brain as well. It may be that her body's still tired from travelling.'

'I have to get used to this language.'

'Thank you for that.'

'I don't like it.'

'Why not?'

'It's very basic,' he said gruffly. 'Was left behind in the ages.'

Is he speaking from some future time? First, he's trying to remember some Flemish guy who speculated about the Great Southern Land in the Middle Ages. Now he says English has been left behind 'by the ages'. She did have multilingual friends who found English limited, though. 'Very basic language,' she said. 'But it's an important language on Earth in this period.'

'Unfortunately.'

'Unfortunately, it's the major language of communication, in the wealthier countries at least.'

'It lacks expressions,' he said.

'It does. Particularly emotional expressions.' Dutch friends had told her that.

'Not only, but that's part of it.'

She felt a frisson of impatience. 'But surely you were speaking English in your last lifetime in Bristol?'

'We spoke something similar,' he said. 'It's not what you understand as English. It was an old language, different dialect, different way of talking, like singing at times. Could be rough at other times.'

Now, she wanted to find out more about his life there. Did he and Aiden toil to earn their Cobbler's Pie? Did he have land?

'You enjoyed your piece of earth and you grew your food—'

'Sheep.'

'And sheep for wool and mutton,' she speculated.

'We made cheese. We didn't eat the sheep, because if you eat the sheep there is no more wool.'

'And the wool went to Norwich?' She'd looked up Bristol and saw there was a big market at Norwich, hundreds of years old.

'It went everywhere,' he said.

'Aye, and made fine clothing,' she asked.

'And some not so fine.'

Nerida laughed.

'The ones the monks had weren't so fine.'

'Unfortunate old monks,' Nerida said. 'I guess they were relieved to be warm.'

'They liked to suffer.'

'They liked to suffer?'

'I guess,' he said. 'It's supposed to make them feel closer to the Lord if they suffer.'

'Uhuh. Poor things.'

'Yes.'

'Were you ever a monk?'

'No. I didn't like to suffer ... But they could read! Many people couldn't read and write.'

'But you Aedgar, could read and write?'

'Indeed, I could.

'It helps at times.'

'Ah, you're a modest man.'

'Not always.'

Nerida smiled to herself. *Not always modest? Or not always a man? Probably both.* 'Who taught you to read and write?'

'Monks.'

'Monks? You went to school at the Monastery?'

'No, the monks came to teach the children, some of them. There weren't really schools.

Kids had to work.'

'Uhuh. Were you working as a child?'

'No. I was studying, reading and writing.'

So, he was not a serf. 'Excellent. And numbers, arithmetic, I guess.'

'Yes.'

'So that you could run the property?'

'I could. I could trade the wool.'

'Had your family owned the land for many generations?'

'Yes.'

'It was always your family's land.' Mari's family, on her father's Swabian side, had been on their land in the Black Forest for five generations or more.

Her own Aboriginal family's land was taken from them by the Catholic Church two generations previously (in her grandparents' time). But much of it was a state forest. She was fortunate. It was wild country, in the upper reaches of their river, mountainous and hard to clear. It had been her tribe's Country since time immemorial. Tens of thousands of years, at least.

'I don't know,' said Aedgar. '"Always" is the wrong word for that.'

'Yes,' Nerida recalled. 'You've got a much longer timescale. But you've always loved the earth, I think.'

'And the sea,' he added.

'Mari loves the sea. She's been teaching me to use an apparatus so that we can breathe underwater, so that we can stay underwater with the fish and watch them.' Mari was a scuba diving instructor in her twenties and early thirties before the amputation of her foot.

'Why would you stay with fish?' Aedgar quizzed. 'She loves the fish.'

'Fish don't talk.' Said the spirit, just learning to talk.

'Maybe that's the best thing about them.'

'How so?'

Nerida laughed. 'Maybe that's what she likes.'

'So, it's good for quiet times.'

'It is, yes. She likes the Indian Ocean, where the water's warm and there's lots of colourful fish.'

'Indian Ocean...India...It's a big trade going with India.'

'Yes, a big market for wool. It's too hot for sheep there,' Nerida said.

'If it's too hot for sheep, it's too hot for wool. Might be a country for cotton.'

'It is, but there are parts of the country where they definitely need wool. Up near the Himalaya, they do.'

'Mountains ... big mountains,' Aedgar said slowly, as if he could see or feel them.

Nerida had seen the Himalaya when she travelled in Nepal and northwestern India in her youth. At age 18, she worked at the Post Office in Sydney for most of a year, then followed a man to Southeast Asia, travelling to Nepal and exploring India on her own when he left her.

Now, she asked Aedgar, 'Are you able to visit parts of the Earth energetically, in your present form? If you think about the mountains, does it take you there?'

'This body is not moving at the moment,' he said.

'No.' *But you're obviously not fixed in it, otherwise I'd never see Mari again* she thought impatiently.

'I could go wherever I like to,' he conceded.

'Ah. Where do you like to go?'

'Interesting places.' There was a moment. She couldn't tell if he was thinking.

'I like to go to Japan,' he said. 'People get very old there, in small areas.'

'They eat lots of fish and seaweed.' *And umeboshi plums*, she thought. Nerida had read research on the lifestyle of the long-lived ones in rural Japan.

Aedgar asked, 'Seaweed?'

'Hmm, they do. It's good.'

'It's a nuisance. The net gets stuck in it.'

'Have you been fishing?' she wondered.

'Sometimes.'

'Do you enjoy fishing?'

'No.'

'It can be hard work,' Nerida offered.

'You're out in bad weather. You go fishing to talk about trading, business. Not for enjoyment.'

'People nowadays do go fishing for enjoyment, for the pleasure of it, like hunting,' she said.

'What pleasure comes out of killing creatures?' the spirit asked.

'Well, if you make them your food it can be good,' she said.

'You said, "for pleasure." Pleasure indicates there is no need to do so.'

'Well, that's true. But even people who don't have to hunt anymore still want to.'

'They shouldn't. It's wrong.'

Nerida wondered if there was a moral conflict. 'What do you think about people eating meat? Mari and I are about to have a meal of meat.' There was a pork roast in the oven.

'Nothing wrong with it,' he said. 'There's nothing wrong with killing creatures to survive. There's no need to kill for pleasure.'

'I agree.'

There was no need to try to persuade Mari to give up her favourite foods, then.

Nerida went on, 'It's a significant date in linear time today, the

12th day of the 12th month of the 12th year of this century. Some people think there's magic in these numbers.'

'No, there is no magic in numbers … Unless you gamble.'

Nerida laughed. 'We might take you to the casino with us one day. You can help us win some money. Monica thinks it's fun.' Trevor had told her that he loved to go to the casino and ask Monica's advice.

'Yeah, she loves this kind of thing,' Aedgar said drolly. Nerida thought for a moment. How to explain the differences between the Community and Burbank, where she'd met Aedgar?

'The society we live in here at Mutitjulu is different. Some people would say it's more backward—it's a rude word to use—than where we were overseas.

'People here still use the technology available, but they're materially poor, most of them,' she said.

'Yes,' Aedgar replied.

Then, 'Only little advantage in technology.'

Technology seemed important to her then. Nerida thought of cars. 'It's nice not to have to walk if you travel long distance.'

'Yes, indeed.'

'We have machines, cars for that.'

'We had wagons with wheels, being pulled by an ox if you were poor or by a horse.'

'Uhuh, if you were wealthy, you had a horse?' *Did Aedgar have a horse?*

'Yes.'

Nerida wondered how to describe a car to someone who'd never seen one. 'The cars we drive are machines operated by one of the people who sits inside.'

'The wagons were operated by a person who sits inside, too. You had to steer the animals, otherwise they would have gone all over the place.'

Nerida chuckled at the image of wild and crazy animals. She felt foolish for not seeing the continuity between the vehicles.

She felt socially awkward. But she was used to that feeling.

She was out of her depth most of the time with her clients at the clinic, being a visitor in their place, not speaking their languages and with so much to learn.

She said, 'Of course. The cars can travel quite fast compared to an animal-drawn wagon, sixty or seventy miles per hour.'

Aedgar waited a beat, then said, 'So, you pay for time with energy?'

It was like a punch in the solar plexus. Suddenly subdued, somehow ashamed, she said, 'Yes, that's right. Energy from the earth.'

'Depriving the earth of energy?' he asked.

'Yes.' She acknowledged his point, even if it was an odd way to put it. 'It has to stop.'

She suddenly noticed that there was some difficulty holding Mari's head up. 'You're tired, my friend, in this body today? Mari's body is tired today.'

'We have to get used to the weight of the head.'

'Perhaps I'll let you go and let you rest and let her rest and have her dinner. 'We'll see you again soon. Sooner now I —'

'Yes. One might hope so.'

'Yes, dear friend,' she said, for she did feel fond of him, whatever he was.

'See you another time,' he said.

'See you soon,' she said. 'Tomorrow, I hope.'

CHAPTER

ELEVEN

M UTITJULU
THURSDAY DEC 13, 2012

THE NEXT DAY was busy at the clinic. People came in for their medicines because they were planning to go away for a week or three. Claire was in the pharmacy closet, (you could hardly call it a room), making up dosette boxes all day. Most Anangu on medication were prescribed it once daily.

Their routines, the way people used or measured time, were often different. If a person really had to take something three or four times a day, Nerida would talk about the sun rising, high in the sky, setting and deep night, as times to take the medicine, using her hands and basic Pitjantjatjara phrases. There weren't a lot of functioning clocks around and phones weren't reliable.

Prescribing things at mealtimes was useless to people with erratic food supply. Some houses did not have a working stove. Or electricity or gas. People had to buy electricity in advance on power cards. Gas

138

was in filled cylinders. There wasn't always money for that. Most preferred to cook on an outside fire anyway. So when the fire was ready and the cook was ready and the meat was baked or stewed, the family ate it all.

Most people cleaned their teeth though, and had a cup of tea when they rose. They took their medicine then.

Her clients had different medicines that they believed in, like people everywhere.

Nerida saw Angus' brother, Bull. Reviewing his medications, which weren't working for him, she talked about bush foods. People with diabetes did better when they had natural foods, anything that didn't come from a factory. Bull confessed that he shot pigeons with an air gun, cleaned and plucked then, and had a dozen in his freezer.

Bull was powerful in the local council. He offered to have a little exhibition of Mari's paintings at the Community-run cafe.

She asked Bull about rubbish collection. Their bin was full at home and the garbage hadn't been collected for about three weeks.

'There's a fight, see, between the Council, the Lands office in Alice and Parks in Canberra. We want the men here to do the job. We've got people who wanna do it. We need the funding to pay them.

'The government doesn't trust us to run a proper sanitary service.' Bull stiffened his back. 'They want to pay outside contractors from five hundred kilometres away to come and do it. It's unbelievable! Some kinda corruption. Little enough work here and we're lucky to have people that wanna do it. Right?'

Nerida offered to write a letter of support.

'I think we've turned a corner,' Bull said. 'Thanks for that. I'll let you know if and when we need it.'

In the waiting room the cowboys were waiting. The former stock-men, now older men, liked one of the puffers—inhaled meds.

They were paid with tobacco (and flour, sugar and tea) when they worked on the cattle stations as young men through the fifties and sixties. Then they were laid off when Aboriginal people won equal pay in 1968, the year Nerida was born. Station owners wouldn't pay wages. When they were sacked the workers were denied access to land they knew, land that was often rightfully theirs.

They kept the tobacco habit. Many still had their slim figures but their lungs weren't good. Jack brought his nephew, a sullen young man taking antipsychotic medications. He was probably brain-damaged by petrol sniffing as a teenager and was overdue for his three- monthly injection. Nerida gave it to him with gentleness and respect. She wasn't convinced that it was the best way of keeping him well. But he nodded affirmatively when she asked if he felt better when he had the medicine.

Nerida liked old Jack, who must have been strong in his youth. He had a sleek charisma. He always wore his best belt buckle to the clinic. He took a pack of ipratroprium caps. Inhaling one each morning helped him breathe.

Mid-morning, Thea came in and told Jasmine the women had caught a big *putjikata* and were stewing it to make the old people strong. Jasmine came to tell Nerida about it. 'Have you had putjikata?' Her enunciation was a bit wet because of her missing front teeth. 'That's cat! Like pussycat, putjikata!'

'It's good that people eat the feral cats,' Nerida said. 'As long as they don't have parasites.'

'People here know what time of year the animals have parasites. They don't take the roos after rain,' Jasmine said.

She was not Anangu, either, so she and Nerida learned together sometimes. Jasmine was from the Adyamathana people, desert people from the south. Her colouring was dark brown like Nerida had wished she was when she was younger.

Home from work, Nerida told Mari about the pussy cat.

'Not sure I'll be cooking one. But good on them,' Mari said. She was allergic to cat saliva and dander. When she came to live with Nerida in 2006, her face and throat had swollen up and her eyes teared when she was in the main house with the pet cats, Devon Rexes named Oscar and Bosie, who lived there. Their bedroom was separate to the house, a converted garage across the deck. But it became clear within a week that Nerida was in love and that Mari was already more important than her loyal cats. Oscar and Bosie found a new home within a month.

'I saw Ulises Daugherty at the painting shed when I was there with Blossom today.' Mari had been stretching canvases with some of the women. She was shy and appreciated having tasks in common with some of the locals.

There were painters in Muti, but the most outstanding work was wood carving. The mulga wood was as hard as iron. Some people carved with softer woods, witchetty bush or mangata.

'He came to the door with a big lizard he'd carved out of mulga wood. It was brilliant.' A shadow crossed her face and Mari paced to the kitchen, began packing plates and pans into the cupboards as she talked.

'The head of the art centre?'

'Brynn,' Nerida said.

'Brynn came to the door, barely looked at it and spat out, "Thirty dollars". Then he went back inside, turned his back.

'Old Ulises gave me this look.' She drew her head back and raised her eyebrows in silent surprise.

'I couldn't help it. I said, "I've seen work like that selling for hundreds of dollars." I said it loud enough that Brynn would hear me back in the office. "I reckon you can get more. How long did it take you to make that?"

'Ulises didn't say but he smiled a little. Took his lizard under his arm and went away. He gave me a wave.'

'Good on you, honey. Speak up for the other artists. I've heard reports. Thea told me Brynn has been paying some of the old ladies only twenty or thirty dollars for their paintings. It's not right, is it?'

Nerida was proud of her wife.

They hugged and caught up on the day's other news. Mari had

scored a bargain camembert, marked down because it was past its expiry date at Yulara.

Nerida said she yelled at Caleb's four-year-old granddaughter to get down off the clinic roof when she heard her stomping around. The kids ran amok around the clinic as the doctor checked pathology results after hours.

She also told Mari about Bull's offer to exhibit five or six of her smaller paintings.

Bull's wife managed the cafe. Nerida saw happiness dance in her wife's eyes.

Then, at Mari's suggestion, they settled down for a channelling session before dinner.

She was open, willing.

When he came, Aedgar spoke softly, slowly and carefully. His first 'Hello' was so quiet, Nerida barely heard it over the noise of the aircon, the fridge and the kids shouting as they played with a ball in the sunset outside.

'Is it getting a little easier?' Nerida asked hopefully.

'We're working on it.'

'That's the way. I enjoyed our conversation last night.'

'So did I,' he whispered. 'It was a long time of silence.

'It was a long time of silence for me before I had this opportunity.'

Nerida was moved. She looked out of the battered Venetian blinds. 'Tell me what you think about this place—it's big red Rock.'

'Seems to be a very powerful area,' he said. 'It's being threatened by people. I can feel it.

'I don't think it's a rock in any common sense.

'It's a conglomerate of Beings.

'This would be the closest to describing it.

'It's not the exact description.

'We have to think about it.

'It's a dry place. Hasn't always been that way.

'Something happened. Something like, but not quite, an eruption.

Things have been, like, thrown around. Shaped now by erosion, but once it looked very different. It was a much bigger area, with sharp edges. Much higher. Like the peak of a mountain.'

'It turned this colour. It's like if you bake clay, then it turns from brown to red. It's too hot, it got too hot in this place. Things have been thrown around like, not quite, but like, an eruption or explosion. Parts of it are thousands of miles away. You would find more under the sand in other areas, but in different colours, as it's not as hot—it wasn't exposed to the same heat.'

This did not fit with Nerida's understanding of Uluru's geology.

But the theories are only theories. It's a mysterious monolith.

'I get a bit overwhelmed by it at times,' she said.

'Don't be,' he said. 'It needs to be overwhelming to express power and to protect itself.'

He went inside, had she had begun to think of it. 'It was never meant to be walked on. People climbing it are speeding up the erosion. It's very sensitive. After it has been baked, it got very sensitive.

'This mountain is part of a system. The other parts are not visible at this time. They're hidden under the ground.

'It requires respect. It should teach respect. Respect for the earth and the environment.

'It's a negative example of what happens if the forces of nature get out of control.

'It teaches caution. Never underestimate the force of nature. Humankind can't conquer the conflict between human nature and the forces of nature. It's a struggle that can't be solved. Human nature and the force of nature don't match very well.

'Battling with Nature doesn't help humankind to grow.

'It's all gonna be destroyed because there's no respect.'

This is why he's so flat. He's despairing of the Earth's survival. Nerida felt agitated. *Isn't a spirit supposed to be able to help people transcend their problems?*

She also felt anticipatory grief, that old, sickening despair she'd known since childhood.

She was born with war on the television every night—she asked the adults who the 'gorillas' were that the Australians killed in South Asia when she was three or four. She cried in bed before school age about the threat of conscription of her father.

Small Nerida was already frightened of losing clean air as she held her mother's hand in the city, her face full of warm car exhaust. She saw the Cook's and George's rivers (they had lost their proper names) used as sewers for raw industrial waste. A river had no beauty for Nerida as a child. It was a stinking hazard, to be avoided.

'Every time human beings intervene against the forces of Nature, the forces of Nature grow,' Aedgar said. 'Human beings think they've made a big step forward, but it's actually backward.

'They challenge power they can't handle.

'These powers come back like an echo, it's just a matter of time.

'It's very late to save humans on this planet. There's a small chance that it's possible. 'Otherwise, one day the earth is gonna take a big breath. And it's just shaking all the humans off it.

'They turned into tiny parasites.

'Instead of protecting it they used it.'

He was quiet. The air was dense with sombre truth.

'Others are watching it from a distance, with concern,' he continued. 'You're not alone.

'We will make suggestions at a later point.

'These are the things we have to think about.'

Another silence. Nerida had nothing to say.

'I need to remember,' he said. 'I have to go further back, much further back.'

Nerida offered, 'I've been looking for information about the Druids.'

'It's lost,' he said sadly. 'People tried to find the knowledge, then to hide it. And then they didn't remember it, so it got lost.

'It got lost for them, but it is still there.

'It has some importance to it. There are more things that are as important.'

'I understand that you've been an earth spirit, that you've lived near ports,' said Nerida.

She needed a smaller scale to try to relate. And she was curious about what that concept, mentioned by Dawn, might mean.

'True.' Another half minute of deep quiet. 'You want to know a lot.'

Nerida was disturbed. *Have I done something wrong?*

'Never stop wanting. It's the way to go, to expand your horizons,' he said.

'Just when I thought I knew a little bit about the world!' She felt like that three-year- old, asking about the guerrillas in Viet Nam.

'You have a way to go,' he said. 'I can help you.'

'I've heard that a spirit can have a holiday resting in a rock or a tree,' she said.

'That's the easy option. To sit somewhere and wait.

'You sit and wait.'

'And enjoy not doing much.'

It sounded like bliss to Nerida.

'And then you realise,' he said, 'things don't get better.'

'You just have to watch how things get destroyed.'

She could imagine that, too, vividly.

'And then you have to come back,' he said wearily.

'The inexperienced and uneducated tend to rule this planet.

'They try.

'It's a mistake. They need experience. They gather experience the wrong way. They try to go the 'easy' route. They've always been around, the ones choosing the easy route. Trying to avoid gathering experience and knowledge. Sometimes it needs to be painful to make you realise, after you've been through it, that it was worth going this way, because you grew so much after it.'

Nerida worried the she was one of the ones looking for the easy route. 'It's nice if it stops hurting,' she said. Then changed the topic again. 'There is another one teaching through a channel. He's named Fortunatus.'

'He's been around in different areas than me. He's trying to teach the greedy ones. 'There's nothing wrong with it, as long as you know when to stop. He's trying to get to the masses. Someone had to.'

Nerida smiled. 'Who would you like to reach?'

Aedgar responded quickly. 'Everyone who's capable of doing things and everyone who's interested in doing good things.' Then he said, 'You might not attract the wealth the other one's teaching about.'

That's a shame, Nerida thought. She'd been hoping they might get superrich by thinking happy thoughts over and over. *How wonderful it would be to never have to work at something disagreeable again—to never have a boss again. That lottery dream. Isn't that why most people listen to Fortunatus?*

Aedgar said, 'If you try to do good work, good things, that doesn't make you necessarily rich. It makes you rich in a different way.

'But of course, it can improve finances as well, if you do it the right way. It's just not the main target. We don't chase wealth.'

It is as if he senses my disappointment and is reassuring me that we won't be poor again. I wish it could be so.

'The universe can create these things but in a limited way,' Aedgar said.

This had been a quiet suspicion Nerida held while reading the channelled Fortunatus material. The Universe might be infinitely abundant, what did she know? But the planet's resources clearly weren't.

'There's not actually room in the universe for infinite greed?' she asked.

'Not for greed,' he said.

'Abundance, but not greed?'

Aedgar found the word he wanted. 'Wisdom. Knowledge. It can all be provided, if it's used to help, to support the earth and human beings.'

'This is not a religion, though,' she checked. This was another question that had been worrying her. Would she and Mari need to accept the idea that there was a god?

'No.'

'Tell me your opinion of religion, Aedgar.'

'People have to believe in what they do to give them the satisfaction they're looking for. If people can't find satisfaction in what they do or provide to others, they need a substitute.'

'You sound like a Marxist,' she smiled. *Religion as the opium of the people.*

'No,' Aedgar said bluntly. 'Marxism is a different kind of religion. It was made to satisfy the masses, give them direction and keep them quiet.'

'Do you think so?'

'I know,' he said.

'Well, there's nothing wrong with satisfying the masses and giving them direction.'

'Of course not, if it's the right direction.

'Sometimes directions lead into dead ends.

'But directions should open new opportunities, expand opportunities and not limit them.'

Nerida said, 'I can see we're going to have many interesting conversations.'

'If you want it so, we can have.'

'It's been a fascinating discussion Aedgar, and I look forward to speaking again soon.'

'Welcome,' his voice became softer as he left. 'The pleasure has been on my side.'

Afterwards, she was disgruntled. *Well, there goes a decade or two of study and activism. Dismissed by a ghost with a wave of the hand. A dead end? No revolution happening here then.*

Her former comrades would be satisfied, if they ever heard about her conversations with Aedgar, that the outcome of her mystical delusions, her *Folie à Deux*, was reactionary or counter-revolutionary.

She thought about what Aedgar said, though, over the coming weeks and years.

That Saturday, she stacked her books by Lenin and Trotsky in a box and mailed them back to the city. Someone else could study them, who believed in that way now.

She kept her Rosa Luxemburg quote on a card on the wall beside the bookcase: *Freiheit ist immer die Freiheit des Andersdenkenden* —Freedom is always the freedom of the one who thinks differently.

TWELVE

M UTITJULU
SUNDAY DEC 16, 2012

'DID YOU HEAR ABOUT THE POOL?' Nerida asked over breakfast. 'People saved the money to pay for a swimming pool over years. Mainly from Gate Money.'

'That's good,' Mari said, arranging salami and cheese on her buttered sourdough. 'That would take some discipline. There's always a lot of things people need that money for.'

The Gate Money was a tiny percentage of takings from the Uluru-Kata Tjuta National Park entrance fee. It was given to Traditional Owners twice a year, Nerida heard. Anangu decided collectively what to do with it.

'So, when are the kids getting their pool?' Mari knew that a proper swimming pool would be great for the kids' health. She sliced a gherkin.

'I was talking to Bull about it. There's been arguments for, I dunno, four years now?

Mutitjulu is on Parks land, which means the Feds keep getting involved.'

'But I thought the land was handed back twenty-five years ago.'

'It was. Then the Traditional Owners generously leased it back to the government for Parks to manage it. So that people could keep coming to Uluru and Kata Tjuta.

'Now, every time the Community wants to do something, they have three or four government bodies full of siloed bureaucrats, arguing with them and telling them why they can't do things. Sometimes it feels like the bosses don't want this Community here.'

'They're quick to roll people out for tourism, though,' Mari commented. The resort at Yulara tried to engage Anangu.

Angus did talks for tourists at the Rock, where they lifted glasses of sparkling wine and ate canapés, then went home to his Community, living under the government's prohibition of alcohol.

The previous Wednesday, Mari had finished a major work, one of a series of abstracts inspired by patterns she saw in Uluru and the red sands around.

The gallery at Yulara only sold work by Aboriginal artists. She sent the painting to a small gallery in Alice that would frame the works and sell them for her. It caused Mari pain to sell her work. She worried about where it would go, what would become of it.

She packed it carefully and mailed it from Yulara.

Next, she started work on a doll. Little jars of paint in shades of brown, green and blue were decorated the kitchen bench.

She baked the doll's vinyl head and limbs after applying each thin layer of paint, showing veins and giving the appearance of depth.

He was to be a green-eyed, brown skin boy, with long, wavy Angora kid hair. She was calling him 'Greg,' after Nerida's gay cousin-brother, who had similar colouring.

Mari always made brown boy dolls.

'There's plenty of peaches-and-cream girl dolls in the world.'

She figured out a way to suspend a giant steel ball bearing inside the head (so that it lolled on a shoulder when held), in a way that it didn't smash the spooky glass eyes she ordered from Germany. The doll's eyes were made at the factory where she bought her leg prosthesis.

A buzzing blow fly came in through a crack between the wall and the window they were unable to completely close. Nerida was reading poetry. She plucked the plastic fly swatter off the wall.

'Just use the spray,' Mari called.

'You know I hate the spray.' Nerida stood by the warm window where the insects always came. *Okay, thanks for getting me up and moving me around. Wrong place, wrong time for you now.* She killed it.

After an active morning in a flow state, Mari came to Nerida, wiping her brushes. 'I thought I might try channelling.'

Nerida put down her Walt Whitman. Went to get her notebook and tablet. The air conditioner was roaring, a constant wind. Midday approached.

Mari seemed to be in trance but then shook herself out a couple of times. 'Not working?' Nerida asked.

'He's trying.' Mari cleared her throat, coughed. Sniffed. Entered again the paradox of concentrating on letting go, pushing to be forceless.

There were people outside. Local people stopped and sat on their front porch for a few minutes of shade. They walked on.

Nerida turned the air conditioner off so there was only a rattle like a broken-down car.

It quieted gradually. She let the heat build up in exchange for quiet.

It was almost five minutes before she could be sure that a being had joined them. A gentle, long breath, then murmuring in the throat.

'Hello, dear friend. Welcome back. You can do it. In your own time.' Nerida spoke gently.

There was quiet. 'Is it you, Aedgar?' Mari's head shook. No, it wasn't.

Whoever it was practised nodding and waggling Mari's head. 'Somebody different?' They nodded. 'I see,' said Nerida.

'Just learning, aren't you, about this body?

'She has some difficulty with her neck here, as you can tell.' She didn't want anyone to be too energetic with Mari's neck, which had a titanium cage screwed into her bones to hold the vertebrae together.

Mari's years as a diving instructor, hauling air tanks and pulling people out of the water, had made her neck vulnerable. When her left foot was amputated and she had to learn to walk again, the change of balance in her body put strain on her neck, too.

She'd had a second round of surgery on it only last year.

Nerida was friendly and tried to be supportive. But she was still learning to trust Aedgar, who was always utterly respectful and gentle with Mari's body. She felt like Aedgar was around when Mari went into trance, but somehow this other being had got in.

'Are you the one who comes in through this arm, this hand?' She indicated Mari's right hand.

THE BEING RESPONDED with vigorous nodding. There was a light feeling in the room. 'Good on you!' said Nerida. 'So you've come back.'

Mari told her before that Aedgar came into the body near the crown of her head. There

was someone else who came in via her chest, near her heart, and another who came through the left hand, she'd told Nerida over their Sunday brunch last week.

'You really wanted to come.' Nerida was chuckling at the spirit's energetic nodding now. 'So, Aedgar let you come? You worked it out between you?'

The head waggled.

'Eh, maybe.' She laughed again. It seemed this one didn't talk yet but had maybe come to meet her and have the experience of being there.

'He's waiting, nor far away, I know.'

They nodded. 'Yes.'

'You can speak. We can try and make a sound first of all,' Nerida encouraged.

Children called, playing outside the house.

She tried moving her hands near Mari's neck to help the spirit find the vocal cords. Nerida modelled a voiced sigh and the being repeated it.

'That's the way!' she said. 'You're welcome. We would like to get to know you better.' After a minute or so, she started the alphabet, like a game, as Dawn had taught her.

Softly, playfully, slowly: 'A, B, C—'

The being was shaping Mari's lips and mouth but no sound came. 'You're so close.' Nerida tried humming.

'Last time you were here, you were able to say, "How did this happen?" Do you remember?' Nerida recognised the feeling of this being. It was brief visit, when Mari was asleep, before she learned to control the channelling.

There was that enthusiastic nodding.

'It's an amazing thing.' She felt ebullient. 'It's an amazing universe …Yes, the chair that you're sitting on can move. A little.'

Then, in response to Mari's nose twitching, she said, 'The air is dry.' 'Yes,' the spirit said softly. 'Smell.'

'A smell? You can smell something?'

'Poison,' they said softly. Then, with a little more voice, 'Poison.'

'You can smell poison?' Nerida was taken aback.

'That's no good … Ah, I know what it is. There was poison used against an insect.' She and Mari had killed a moth that came in under the door that morning.

'I can use a machine to move the air more, if you like. Or open a window. Perhaps I'll open a window.' She moved to get up.

'No.' They said softly.

'It doesn't harm the body you're in, that poison,' she said, like the doctor she was. The head waggled.

'It does a little? Okay. Perhaps that's why Mari was feeling unsettled ... I'll tell her.'

After a moment or three, Nerida asked, 'Do you know where you are?'

'Far away,' they whispered.

'Right. Planet earth,' she said.

'Which is far away.'

'We're in a desert. An old part of the planet,' Nerida explained.

They waggled Mari's head and said softly, 'Nothing is old. Not here.'

'You think this is a young planet?'

They nodded. Whispered, 'Yes.'

'You must have a very grand perspective,' Nerida said.

'Normal.'

Nerida chuckled. 'Normal, for you?'

'For us,' they quietly agreed.

'You're speaking nicely now. You can speak a little more loudly if you use the breath.'

'Bad smell,' they said.

'Bad smell makes it hard to breath more deeply. Okay. I'll do my best to make nicer smells here, or no smell, next time.'

'No poison,' they said.

'Does the poison make it harder to stay? Perhaps you can come back soon. This afternoon?'

She thought to try, 'Is there a name I can use with you? You know those of us in linear like names.'

They shrugged the shoulders beautifully, making Nerida laugh again. 'You must have been incarnate before, on Earth,' she said. They nodded. 'Once or twice,' she said.

'More,' they said.

'Perhaps, I'm speaking with an Entity,' she asked. An entity was a group of souls, often hundreds, expressing themselves as one. Monica was an Entity. When she used the royal 'we,' she had reason to.

'Part,' they said, having made some effort to form the 'p'.

That's intriguing. 'Well, beautiful. Let me clear the place of poison and give the body a chance to recover. I'll encourage Mari to give you an opportunity to come back later today.'

She asked softly, 'Is that a good plan? Yes?'

The being nodded the head, inclined it gracefully to the side.

'Thank you. See you soon,' Nerida whispered.

Mari came out of trance with a deep sigh.

As she was coming out of trance, Nerida's nostrils and throat were suddenly assaulted by a strong smell of insecticide. Mari had a spluttering, choking cough as she came out of trance.

'You know what the trouble was? That fly spray.'

'I could smell something horrible,' Mari said dramatically. She coughed wheezily. 'It's extreme now, isn't it?'

AFTER LUNCH, a rest and cleaning, they tried again. The sun was low in the sky, just after five.

Mari closed her eyes and settled into trance again,, clearing her throat.

'Have you come back then?' Nerida asked. 'Is the poison gone? I hope the air is clear for you.'

Mari made a wheezy cough, something she'd never done in trance before.

'You are very welcome. I appreciate you coming back when you've had a rather unpleasant experience.'

The being didn't talk but exercised the body: the face, head, shoulders and arms.

Nerida tried humming, but they didn't respond. The room felt different. *Is this a different being again?*

'Is there anything I can do to help you communicate?' She moved to try to guide the energy into Mari's throat.

But Mari started coughing. Little coughs at first, then bigger ones.

'It looks like the dryness of the air is making it harder for you to speak.'

The coughing continued. Nerida started to worry. Should she bring Mari out of trance straight away? 'Perhaps it's just too difficult today,' she said. *Am I being too polite?*

More coughing. 'This body has a problem,' the spirit whispered. 'With cats!'

Nerida's eyebrows shot up. 'Ah, yes. She's allergic to cats. Has there been a cat nearby?'

'I am related to cats,' they said softly, enunciating clearly.

Nerida felt a surge of love for the being, in spite of the difficult situation.

She laughed. 'I love cats. Oh, what can we do? I'll have to talk to a healer about healing that, in this body, yes?'

Mari was coughing again.

'I might need to come back,' the being whispered wheezily, 'in another form.'

'Okay, please do.'

'This body can't breathe,' they said.

The coughing and wheezing was out of control now.

Mari came back into a coughing fit. 'Oh fuck. Jeezus.' She panted. She gasped for air. 'I'm never doing this again!' Choking noises, coughs and wheezes filled the house.

Nerida felt guilty. She'd enjoyed the being's company. Even smelled a delightful fragrance of jasmine or frangipani afterwards as they left.

And now Mari was spluttering and gasping, panting. *I should have brought her back sooner. I'm an arsehole.*

'Here, drink. I can explain!'

She rubbed Mari's back as she used to when her kids had asthma. 'It was a cat.'

'A fucking cat! What?'

It took days for Mari to recover. She was angry.

Nerida sent an email to Trevor, requesting an urgent telephone consult with Dawn and Monica.

THIRTEEN

MUTITJULU & LOS ANGELES
SUNDAY DEC 23, 2012

NERIDA PULLED on jeans and ran, woken by the sound of the garbage truck. It was always good to get the garbage collected and she gave the local men a cheerful wave. Once out of bed, she stayed up. Shadows moved across the Rock and birds foraged in the soft red dust and dried leaves.

Bush raisins fruited near the front of the house. She picked a couple of berries that had dried on the bush and sucked on them, contented.

Until it got too warm, and the flies suddenly woke up. She dashed inside, snorting them out of her nose, pushing them away from her eyes.

Mari and Nerida had an early telephone consult with Monica.

Before Dawn went into trance, they talked about Mari's unpleasant experience.

'What gives?' Nerida said, 'An allergic reaction to cat hair! From an energy that comes from who knows where?'

Dawn considered. 'I don't have allergies, fortunately. You know, I've got four cats and two dogs.'

'Uhuh,' Nerida said. 'I had cats when Mari came to Australia. But they had to go. Her eyes swelled up. She was wheezy. Really allergic.'

Dawn reported news of her menagerie. They talked about a desert town they all dreamt of moving to.

'We could even take Trevor's tortoises. The water's good,' Dawn said. Mari told Dawn she was channelling Aedgar regularly.

'We are so happy and proud of you, Mari. I couldn't believe how Monica had that program all put together for you. Trevor and me were impressed.

'We can't wait to see you again.

'Anyway, I can just about hear Monica rapping her nails, waiting for me to leave. Let me go get her.'

Seconds later, Monica arrived with a warm greeting and her lower, mellifluous voice.

She rounded her vowels in a transatlantic accent unlike Dawn's.

Dawn's voice was warm as cornfields. Monica's would fit in a London whisky club. Conversation turned to Aedgar. 'I don't think he's quite worked out where Australia is, yet,' Nerida said.

'His dominant memory of the linear is his last life in Bristol. It was interrupted before the discovery of Australia by the British,' Monica replied. 'There wasn't a name or concept for it then.'

'He's so sad about what's happened to the Earth,' Nerida said. 'I'm feeling his grief and worry that there's not much time to change things.'

Monica said, 'The raising of consciousness continues. There's a surge of positive energy from loving thoughts towards the planet. There is an opportunity to save the planet.'

'That's how I usually think,' Nerida agreed. 'But Aedgar doesn't feel that way.'

'Aedgar is a realist,' Monica said.

That's an odd way to characterise a non-physical entity. Nerida corrected herself, *As if only the material is real.*

'He was always like that. "What's in front of me is what I see," he'd say. He wears his heart on his sleeve. He's sweet.'

Nerida agreed. 'I'm loving him already. He's earnest.'

'He takes everything very seriously,' Monica concurred. 'And he isn't afraid to show his emotions. It's a good thing.'

Nerida could see that. *Mari is like that.*

To Mari, Monica said, 'You have blossomed so beautifully. You are emerging like a flower on a tree.'

'What was your name in the lifetime you were with Aedgar? I have "Aiden" in my head. Or "Reuben" is it?' Mari asked.

Monica took some time to answer.

'Aiden. Yes. We were Aedgar and Aiden. We thought we were like twins.'

'How?' Mari asked. She and Nerida knew gay couples who looked more and more alike, going to the same barber, tailor and shoe store.

'The names are similar. Aedgar and Aiden. What a team we were.'

Later, Mari asked about the cat. 'I had difficulty trying to channel Aedgar last Sunday. I held the crystals the way you taught, to ask Aedgar in. I felt Aedgar trying. And then, suddenly, I couldn't breathe!

'Nerida told me that this being said, "This body has a problem with cats" and "We are related to cats." I was choking. They left, saying to Nerida they'd try in a different form.'

'There's a lot of relationship with animals for some of the energies,' said Monica calmly. 'We'll talk to this energy. There's no reason for you to feel the allergic reaction. That energy is showing a degree of immaturity in knowing how to come through someone. We don't think they have come through many. It's carrying characteristics it doesn't need to.

'It wasn't your fault at all. You have a physical issue with cat dander. This energy could have set the physical attributes aside. It's comparable to an energy bringing in a diseased moment from another lifetime. Doesn't need to be that way.

'We'll talk to them. They need counsel. You are open. That energy showed up without the preparatory work it should have done. It should have looked at your form and known.

'It can leave the cat attributes behind, like a bag. No need to bring it in. The energy was a bit startled.

'When you are preparing, you can say in yourself that "This body has a problem with cat dander. I need to be comfortable in my biology, so put those attributes aside if you want to come in." It's like taking off muddy boots before coming inside.'

'I didn't know something like this could happen,' Mari said, gesticulating to express her surprise.

'Absolutely. An energy contains sense memory. But now it knows. It should have scanned you before arriving. It could bring the personality, the energy in. It didn't need to bring biologically aggravating attributes it had when incarnate.

'A vivid experience. It makes the process more real. There was no cat. But you felt like there was.

'You'll become experienced at asking people to remove muddy shoes at the door.' 'Afterwards,' Mari recalled, 'I had this image in my head of the Sphinx. I know it's mythical.'

'In the Egyptian and Atlantean cultures, cats were revered. Like cows are in India now.

'There were extraterrestrial moments when the cats were worshipped, as well,' Monica explained.

Cats channelled aliens when people worshipped them? Did she say that? thought Nerida.

'These cat-like energies came in. They haven't come through for a long time. They saw an opportunity with you, without realising your different biology.'

'So, what's with Mari having this allergy, anyway?' Nerida asked. She wanted to make Mari better. Her challenging patient.

'In Mari's particular form, she's genetically inherited that sensitivity.'

Nerida lifted an eyebrow, aware of a line between fantasy and intuition. 'And was she eaten by lions or something?'

Mari hid it when they first met, but it was sensible for anyone to dislike cats in the desert.

Feral cats killed hundreds of native birds, lizards and small mammals every night.

'Hm. She lost a leg to a sabre-tooth, yeah,' Monica observed.

'Ouch! That'll put you off. She also has a severe aversion to crocodiles. Might be some history there, too.'

'Let us look ... Not personally. But she saw others being attacked by them. She witnessed executions by the crocodiles.'

'Was that a Roman moment?' Nerida asked, using Monica's style of expression.

'Greek. Greeks did that. They would import them from Africa.' Monica was quiet.

'They had a pool full of them. They never fed them.

'So, unsuspecting individuals, opposed to those in charge, suddenly found themselves teetering on the edge of the pool. A hungry crocodile will eat just about anything.'

'Ergh,' said Mari. 'So, I don't have to feel bad about my crocodile skin belt?' She fingered the knobbly leather around her waist.

'No. Their sturdy hide has been used for many things.'

'Yeah, and they have parts of them that would act as antibiotics,' Mari continued. Nerida wondered how Mari knew that.

'In Greek times they didn't know that. In Lemurian times we knew that,' Monica said.

Again, this Lemuria. What is this Lemuria?

Nerida had looked it up and found nothing but a reference to a Victorian-era mystic novelist (who was discredited). And drawings of fae. And the Lemurs of Madagascar. She enjoyed lemur videos. And fantastical drawings of intense fairy people.

But she respected Monica, who spoke as if Lemuria was real, not fantastical. Some located the lost continent in the Indian Ocean. Others in the South Pacific. The internet was not helpful there.

'A lot of things discovered have got lost. Then got discovered and again lost. There's this back and forth of knowledge.'

'So the Greeks weren't as clever as they thought. It was the Lemurians before them?' Mari asked.

'Yes, the Lemurians were the intellectuals on biology. They researched it. They did meticulous tests, experiments. They discovered antibiotics then, including natural ways to find them. And synthesised antibiotics. About 400,000 years ago, they had antibiotics. But then it got lost, Lemuria itself. A lot of it was, you know, swept away with the shifting of the planet's tectonic plates. Lots of information was lost.

'Now, the Atlanteans, they did more with crystals,' she mused.

'So, would these be things that Aedgar would know about?' Mari asked.

Since they returned to Australia, Mari never listened to the conversations she channelled. And wouldn't let Nerida to tell her about the content, either. Except in a life-threatening cat encounter. Talking to Monica was her only means to ask about Aedgar and what he did.

Monica took a few beats. Then said, 'Aah,' as if she was returning.

'Aedgar knows a lot about the medicinal uses of herbs. He was prolific in teaching about it. Also did a lot of clairvoyant work, while in the body. Proficient with spices and herbs to bring about healing. Good at mixing concoctions. And dictating prescriptions to those needing them. He has knowledge of that.'

Mari spoke quietly to Nerida.

'Mari's asking, he wasn't Lemurian, then?' Nerida ventured.

'No. He is an ancient energy that's had five or six incarnating moments, but most of the time has come through to others with medicinal knowledge. And planet-healing kind of information.

Balancing the chakras of the planet. And having conversations with the planet. He's very good at all that.'

'Wow,' said Mari

Feeling out of her depth, Nerida changed the subject. 'Mari's been wanting to ask you about her father.

'Here, take the phone.' She handed it to Mari and got up to get a glass of water and walk around for a bit.

'Yes, when we spoke to you from Germany, Dad felt left out. He asked, "So what did you find out about me? Everybody knows things except me. Am I not that interesting?"'

Indeed, Monica explored Mari's family ancestry on her mother's side in a depth that intrigued Mari, her mother and her sister Lotte. Her father had remained aloof from the lively session in her mother's kitchen.

'Well, we think he needed to feel a bit prodded into participating. Let's look at his energy. Hang on ... There's Roman times—we're gonna pick the meaningful ones—he was also in Istanbul. He was in Florence. This energy likes to bring forth knowledge. He likes to understand how the world works.

'There's been times in other lifetimes when he had opportunities to talk to the likes of us. And he's drawn back and said, "I don't need that."

'We think it was appropriate for him to feel a bit left out, to spur him on. That jealousy, that "Hey, what about me?" We think there was a need for that to occur on many different levels.

'He had a life as a Roman centurion. Very warrior-oriented in that particular life.

'Vulnerable!

'Of the centurion force: he had power, he had a say and had people under him.

'But he was responsible to the people, as well. He had a kind of dual participation in that life. And he did go, then, to consult oracles. To find out about the potential future, how things were shaping up.

'We're talking around 67AD. He'd heard fables about the Christ. Fables about the other gods. He witnessed massive deterioration in the Roman Empire.

'The next life, in Istanbul, a lot of learning was about love: how to give it and how to keep it.

'He'd been that centurion. Now, this was a life when he learned to appreciate the beauty of being linear.

'He had a hard time of it. He went from being that powerful one to needing to appreciate the dew on the flower. He was equally proficient in both. He found that decision making could be a delicate thing.

'He doesn't show too many people that side of him: his appreciation of Nature, the sun, art.

'He was part of a whole artistic endeavour in Florence. He would weep then, with joy, at seeing what someone carved from marble. He's had a hard time reconciling that delicate, sweet appreciative side of him with the part that makes big, hard decisions.

'These two sides have sometimes been, literally, two people. So, he's divided in his energy. And we think it was appropriate that he had to ask. That was the only way we could have read his energy anyway. Because of all that he had his energy closed down.'

'He cries at movies, Mari's asking me to tell you,' Nerida passed on with a smile. Her father-in-law cried at the *Sissi* movies every Christmas, technicolor tales of a tiny-waisted, kind, intelligent princess from the 1950s.

'Are you able to give insight into his genetic background in this life? Mari's mother had Gypsy and Jewish ancestry. Her parents both are brown-eyed and brown-skinned. Where does her dad come from?'

Monica breathed out forcefully. 'Looking.'

She quickly said, 'There's some of the Jewish in the dad. We think there's also Gypsy. There was Germanic energy, as well. He's lived through a time when people didn't talk about that stuff. It'd get you in trouble.

'His ancestry traces all the way back to Spain, where there was the

Inquisition, and the turning out of the Jewish population there. Twelve generations ago.

'Some Jewish ancestors never got out.

'They put you in a dark hole and left you there. Generations had that happen to them.

'His ancestors migrated then, those that could, into Germany and France.

'The Jewish people were way smarter than most of the Spaniards. And were able to deal with money, with mathematics.

'They were merchants. They were not well liked. The Inquisition used the idea that they were the murderers of Christ.'

'And everybody was supposed to be guilty of that,' Nerida commented. She got back in her chair. She had no time for that idiotic way of thinking.

'The families of your father's ancestors disappeared. They put them in jail, never let them out. Some of them were garrotted, for being the antichrist.

'Twelve generations later, the family presented as pure Germanic. But we think he's got Hungarian Gypsy ancestry. He's still got Jewish genetics in him. Some Spanish.

'Some family hoped to obliterate the Gypsy and Jewish ancestry. They tended to get into trouble because they were incredibly smart. The Catholic Church was always looking for somebody to persecute for the death of Christ and they were right in the firing line.'

'Except that he still looks like he's Jewish, or Roma or Turkish,' Nerida smiled. 'What is his role in essence, Monica?'

'We would say artisan. He has a goal of caution. Tends to stand back from things and observe.'

'Yes, that's true,' said Mari.

'He's in higher intellectual. His chief feature is stubbornness.' The women smiled at each other.

'Oh, yes,' said Mari.

'He plants his feet in the ground and that's that. He's a good man. But it takes a lot of covering up to survive. It's in the genetics.

'Twelve generations ago it was a matter of life and death. Usually death, if the Inquisition got a hold of you.'

'He's never treated me as a girl,' Mari reflected.

'I was always welcome to use his tools. He showed me how. Not like Lotte, who was not interested. Or my brother Detlev. Dad used to tell him, "Stay away. You've got two left hands."

'Dad used to boast to his friends that I was "made of steel," because I didn't cry when they hurt me in hospital.

'I was only little when I learned to laugh so that the doctors and nurses were not so nervous. They didn't hurt me so much if their hands weren't shaking. Dad said I shouldn't cry.

'When he was a centurion in the Roman army, did I have anything to do with him?'

'Let's look.' Monica paused. 'You were his son. An artful son. Men were supposed to go to war and fight and knock each other's brains out. And you had no desire to do that. You wanted to do art. You wanted to participate in the beauty of the reality, not destroy it.

'In that lifetime it was hard having him as a father because he wanted you to be like him.

'And you couldn't be.'

'So,' Mari said, 'it was a complicated relationship.'

Nerida looked at Mari, who was relaxed and happy, aware that she was about to tread on shaky ground.

'So Papa needed to hide to keep safe. It's in his bones. Mari's mum has a more recent history of such persecution. She must remind him of that.'

Mari's mother almost starved to death as a child refugee in wartime. Her father, Mari's grandfather, survived a concentration camp. Her grandmother did what she needed to do to get him out alive.

'Yes.' Monica commented.

'Does her mum have a goal of martyrdom? She suffers so much.'

Monica took a moment. 'Yes. With an underlying fear of being worthless.'

'She seems to have infected Mari with it,' Nerida said cautiously. Mari had so much suffering since infancy. So many surgeries in the days when children's pain was untreated. So many more operations after the accident that caused the amputation of her lower leg and foot. Pain and more surgeries since.

'Yes. The impaired understanding of self-worth. But Mari is a recovering martyr. She's getting better.'

Mari laughed. 'That's good to hear.'

'It goes to show you that you can overcome these overleaves. You can deal with them.

You can grow out of them,' said Monica.

'Yes. I'll recover from mine. Any minute now,' Nerida said. Monica laughed.

'Mari that worthlessness is something your mother put on you, on your shoulders. It's not even your chief feature. You're recovering from all that. Talking to her brings all that back up. So, it does drive you mad.'

Mari nodded.

'We think it's good thing that you give her your time. She really, underneath all of it, feels that she's not worth talking to. She's going to go further into that feeling of worthlessness.

'She's not going to get past that chief feature in this lifetime. So give her time, as you do. Recognise who she is.

'She's been trying to push her chief feature off on you, your whole life. That's why you always feel like she's cornering you.'

'Yeah.'

'You have bigger things to do than your mother understands. Your mother embraces her martyrdom and has feelings of worthlessness.

'You both have other things to do in this life.

'You're magnificent.

'Look at your mother with compassion. It's a pity that she's probably never going to, in this life, realise her full magnificence. But you are. And that is a victory for her, as well. Because you are her daughter.

'Look at her with concern and pity. Let her talk. Let her feel connected with you. Send her the unconditional love that she deserves. And let it go.

'And don't let her push the worthlessness with you. She's done that all your life.

'Blasted you and put you in a corner and started tossing the worthlessness onto you.

'That's not your chief feature. That was a burden for you. It made you agitated and angry, Mari.'

Mari said, 'She calls. She complains about everything. She dumps all her problems on me. And if a phone call doesn't last at least an hour, it's not a phone call.

'I'd be happy to talk for ten minutes. But getting this kind of phone call three times a week, lasting for an hour, it's just—too difficult.'

Monica suggested, "It's lovely to hear from you. My agenda is very full today. I want you to know how much I love you and hope your day is going great. But I can't sit and listen to this today."

'I have the problem,' Mari said cautiously, 'that I can't tell her that I love her.'

'She is your mother. You love her unconditionally,' said Monica. 'You do love her.

You care for her. You don't want anything bad to happen to her.'

'No.'

'But you can't be the trash can that she throws all her garbage into.'

'Yeah,' Mari laughed. 'True.'

'Your mother can stop that. She spends an hour unloading her trash onto your lap. Of course, she feels better! Because she's unloaded all her garbage.'

'Yeah.'

'You're a little bit too available for what she tries to do to you. Tell her, "I love you. I hope you're having a great day. I'm doing stuff during the week. I'm painting. I'm starting to write books. I'm driving sick people. I'm doing all kinds of things. I don't have time to talk for longer now, Mum."

'And you're gonna have to squeak that word out. It'll get easier when you practice: "Love, love, love," you'll say. And you do not allow her to treat you like a trash can.

'That's not the position you are meant to have in life.

'You end up with an upset stomach at the end of the day from listening to all of it. And processing it.'

'Yeah.'

'Or, be bold. "Okay, Mum. Tell me about your day. Did anything good happen?" Get sassy. It could direct her into a better conversation.

'We think you are more in charge of this than you know. It's a pattern that's occurred over and over and you've allowed it.'

'All right.'

'She needs to process her own energy. You could say, "Tell me about the good stuff. I'm only interested in the good stuff. I'll tell you something funny or interesting." 'We realise that's a bold statement for Mari to say to her mother. But do consider it.

'Redirect. You are much more focussed and powerful than she.

'You are now a receptacle for energy coming in.

'It needs to be clean. This form needs to be clear of the debris which your mother dumps on you all the time.

'You have a new focus in life. You're bringing in spiritual material, some ancient information. And the energies coming in are going to say, "What is all this? We don't want to come into that."

'With this new perspective, you need your energy to be in a posi-tive place.

'So manoeuvre Mum into a more positive conversation. And if you can't do that, end the talk. Politely, with respect.'

'Okay.'

'You've got a responsibility here to embrace.

'You've made brilliant progress. In your personal moments, in your connecting moments with source energy and in your channelling. Realise that you are now participating with high level energy.'

'She's done this her whole life. She won't change much. So, all you can change is you. 'You're evolving Mari. You're expanding your consciousness.

'The channelling needs to comes first.'

'I know someone who fears ageing.' Nerida smiled gently at Mari. 'Takes it very seriously.'

'Yes. Perhaps have an annual 32nd birthday every year for the rest of your life.'

Mari smiled. 'Sounds good. I hate the numbers.'

'Have a birthday cake with one candle. It's just a number dear.

'And the body will deteriorate if you want it to.

'And it will maintain itself if you want it to.

'You will find that the body can recover from a lot of the negativity it has participated in, with your channelling. You're going to feel a lot better.

'Tell Aedgar, or this cat-like energy, when they come in. Say, "My back hurts." 'Or, "I have a bad knee. A little bit of maintenance would be appreciated."

'The Dawn Weaver does that all the time. She'll say, "Work on this while I'm doing this channelling because it's starting to bother me and I don't like it."

'Many things on the Dawn Weaver have been fixed. She had an X-ray, and they said "You're gonna need surgery on that knee." After a couple of channelling sessions they said, "We must've got the X-rays mixed up."

'They will help you. We do it all the time. We only need to move the energy around.

'This cat-like one could do some energy work for you.'

'Was she the second one who had been there before, that you saw waiting when we were there in California?' Nerida was trying to figure it out.

'No, she's the third.'

'Oh. I really liked her. But when I asked her whether she'd negotiated coming in with Aedgar, she just gave me this cheeky smile, like she didn't care. She didn't care if the crystals were in position for Aedgar, because she'd never been before.

'She was strong and proud of herself that she snuck in,' Nerida said. 'Very pleased. She had this lovely little smile. Moving the head around. It was disappointing.'

Monica said, 'Remind her. She doesn't have manners yet. She elbowed her way in and then said "Oops. Sorry."'

Nerida recalled, 'She literally did. She went in through the elbow, didn't she?'

'Yeah. She was impatient. Really wanted to be there. Stormed in with her muddy shoes.

'We would suggest asking for more time with Aedgar until he is comfortable. You need to establish an order here.

'We are still so very proud of you, dear Mari.

'It will take a while to get comfortable with the role.

'This is a gift.

'Take whatever time you need to get completely comfortable.

'Dedicate some time.

'You've come a long way dear. And you'll go even further.

'The responsibility will become enjoyable. It'll all work out ... Keep in mind the goal, to be able to bring through the energies.'

FOURTEEN

MUTITJULU
AFTERNOON DEC 23, 2012

'I'M happy you're here. I recognise you, Aedgar.'

Nerida felt she knew him by the way he moved Mari's head, lifted her brows.

'Do you?' Aedgar said. 'That's interesting ... Still not completely easy for me.'

'We'll keep practising,' she said.

'Good.'

'We have all the time in the world.' Nerida said breezily. It was an attitude she practised with her patients—giving them her full, relaxed attention (when she could) so they had space to express themselves. It was not an entirely honest posture.

'Not as much as you think,' he said.

He means time is running out. Nerida nodded politely, 'I understand.'

'You try to.'

'I do,' she admitted. 'We've had a lovely conversation with Monica this morning.'

'I know about it.'

Nerida was intrigued. *They communicate with each other in spirit. They keep their individuality. Monica has individuality despite being an Entity of thousands of spirits.* It was all mysterious. 'Then you know that we now recall that she was Aiden. You were Aiden and Aedgar,' she said.

'Yes. I talked about it. I thought you'd got it.'

'Mari got it. I didn't get it. Somehow, I forgot. Mari was pleased.'

'Better be,' said Aedgar. 'Have you been surprised?'

'That Mari was right?' 'That the world didn't end?'

At the end of the Mayan calendar on the 12th of December 2012. Ha!

'No. Not at all,' she said. 'I had your reassurance.'

'It's just numbers,' he said. 'But it gives you a chance to celebrate now. Probably have a drink or two. That's why people make things like this up.'

'So that they have a chance to celebrate?' Nerida smiled.

Aedgar tilted Mari's head slightly, lifted the eyebrows. 'Indeed.' She imagined him at the head of a dinner table, pewter goblet in hand.

Nerida was at a loss to guide the conversation, though. 'Is there anything on your mind that you'd like to talk about?'

'Not particularly.'

He comes with no agenda. 'I was interested in Monica talking about herbs and spices available during your lifetime in Bristol. I have an interest in the medicinal qualities of herbs,' she said.

'I know you do. Many people do. I used to know what to do with them.'

'Yes, me too.' She used herbs in her twenties, looking after herself and then her kids.

She was drank rosemary leaf tea to strengthen her uterus in the last trimester of her pregnancies. And afterwards when she fed them, to help her milk. Gave the babies fennel for colic, camomile when they were teething.

Somehow, she had stopped using herbs.

It was after Sam's accident, she thought, *when nothing I did seemed to help. And then, of course, most of my comrades had no respect for them. They were 'unscientific,' 'old wives' tales'.*

It was an argument over acupuncture that convinced her to leave politics, in the end. She was learning from the ngangkari then, and later, having psychedelic sex with Mari.

She'd had more and more experiences of human energy, (she wouldn't call it a soul), that went beyond the physical body.

It was time then, to stop pretending she was still a scientific materialist. She was becoming a scientific metaphysician, Trevor had said. She wasn't sure what that was but appreciated that he gave her an idea of something to be. She'd been researching metaphysics since then, trying to sort the wheat from the chaff.

Now she asked Aedgar, 'Do you remember some of the plants that you used?'

When he replied, he spoke softly, slowly and distantly, almost as if to himself. 'Tiny yellow ones. Tiny yellow blossoms.'

'Not yellow and white ones?' She thought of the camomile she'd seen growing wild in Mari's home village in Germany.

'No, just yellow,' he said.

'They grew in the forest?' She wondered if they might have been buttercups. But she had learned never to eat them, as a child.

'In the meadows,' he said. 'It was too dark in the forest. They need the sunlight.'

'Did you pick them and dry them for a tea?'

'I got other people to pick them.'

Oh, ho. A scion of the ruling class.

'I just watched them, making sure they got the right ones,' Aedgar continued mildly. 'Too tiring to pick them. You need lots of them, at least of some kinds.'

Then, his voice seemed to penetrate her consciousness. 'Tiny amounts of others could kill you easily.

'There was that little purple one, shaped like a bell: would have been a bad idea to use a big amount.

'Even a tiny amount was a bad idea.'

With the same mildness, he said, 'Could get people quickly onto the other side.

'It would stop suffering.'

Nerida raised her eyebrows. 'Did you ever use it that way?'

'We did.'

'You used it in a kind way?' *Please god, don't let him be the ghost of a murderer.*

'Yes. You wouldn't let animals suffer, so why should humans?

'It was said they had nice dreams.

'I can't tell, I've never done it myself.'

Of course, he's died more than once. Broaden your perspective! She asked, 'Is it belladonna? It that what it's called?'

'No.'

'Digitalis, then?' She was trying to remember the poisonous, medicinal, English plants in her parents' garden.

'That's closer to it,' he said.

'You could use a bit of this with some ale and off they went, happily.'

'I don't know if you know,' she said. *I have no idea what he knows.* 'But in this lifetime, I'm a doctor. I've worked to help people to die comfortably. It's one of the privileges I've had.' She was working in palliative care when her experiences led her to realise she could no longer pretend to be a militant materialist.

Some of her clients visited her at night.

She was aware of other spirits where they lived in Koonawarra, then. She learned to guide them to the horizon where loved ones appeared as a light. This was all happening in the infinite space inside her, in the liminal space between wakefulness and sleep.

Nerida had loved being the doctor for mothers when they birthed their babies. But her back wasn't strong enough for that work since she'd her own kids.

Since she wasn't up to that, she chose the privilege of being with people at the end of their lives. Her team was understaffed and over-stretched, but gave people excellent care. She was the sole doctor for a ward of fifteen patients (and their families) by her second year out of med school.

'That's important work,' Aedgar said. 'It's underestimated. It helps spirits find their way around more quickly on the other side.'

There was a lull, each with their own thoughts. 'What did the little yellow flowers help with?'

'Infected wounds.'

'They have an antibacterial or disinfectant property?'

'Yes.'

'Did you use it as a tincture?'

'Yes. It was used for other things too, internally, in much smaller amounts. It made sad people see the colours again.'

'That's a beautiful way to put it.'

She was loving him sometimes, just as she'd said to Monica. Aedgar asked, 'Do you have meadows here?'

How to explain what the endless desert plains of mulga trees, gibber stones and orange sandhills are like?. There are meadows of Alpine flowers in the Snowy Mountains, down south in New South Wales. 'Hmmm—we do but it's a very different kind of—'

'You don't. You had to think too much,' he said.

Nerida laughed. 'It's a very different ecology. In some parts of the land we have something like meadows.'

'So you would have herbs that are much sturdier than the ones in the meadows. Which could mean stronger,' he said.

'Yes, particularly here where there is very little water. They are quite concentrated.'

'You'd better not use too much, then,' he said.

Nerida agreed. 'Well, you know I'm not from here, but the old people know about the herbs, some of them.'

'Some of them don't, but they say they do.'

Nerida bridled. *That was disrespectful.*

'It can be dangerous,' he explained. 'These things are very powerful.'

'So, you used herbs to make people feel better, make their spirits stronger—'

'Stop the young ones from passing and help the other ones to do so,' he summarised. 'You must have been very respected for these skills.'

'In some circles; hated in others. 'People get afraid.

'If you know too much you'll be crucified as kind of a satan.'

He lifted an eyebrow. 'But I still had the power ... So I could turn into something like Satan for some of them. That was my privilege.'

Nerida chuckled.

'I loved to use that. It taught them respect.

'Some of them it was too late to help. Others just had a happy passage.' Nerida thought about this. 'You had to defend yourself?'

'I had to defend my family and friends,' the spirit said. 'If they can't get to you, they make your family and friends suffer.'

'Yes. Unfortunately, it's still going on, that kind of stuff.' She thought of the tortures of the Middle Ages.

Recalled, also, stories Mari had told her of the Maldives, where tourists were serviced by labourers from Bangladesh and Sri Lanka on an isolated resort island.

And Maldivians, punished sometimes just for being gay, languished on a prison island nearby, chained to a tree or a pole in the ground and thrown scraps like a neglected dog.

'We know,' Aedgar said gently.

'Monica told me about a lifetime I had working in a monastery, where I knew some of these herbs and salves,' Nerida said.

'Did you teach?' he asked.

'Yes, but quietly, secretly.' She felt a warm glow. He took her story seriously. It has resonated with her when Monica told her that a few years ago.

'Another one in the dark,' Aedgar mused. 'It's a sad thought ... Knowledge is power, if it's used in the right way.'

'Who taught you?'

'Monks,' he said. 'Some old people. And I had these, kind of, intuitions or dreams.

'I couldn't talk about it. That would have made me even more 'evil'.

'I had a secret life already.'

'With Aiden?'

'Yes.'

She sensed a rich fullness behind his single word answer. 'You had a doubly secret life?'

'More than that.'

Nerida smiled. 'Very sophisticated.'

'Very hard to organise things,' he said. 'Takes a lot of energy, that could have been used in other ways.'

'That's right. It can be tiring, keeping secrets.'

'Yes.'

'Did you have a sympathetic wife?'

Aedgar's tone was dreamy, then. 'She was like an innocent child.'

'It wasn't so much about being sympathetic. It was more about not knowing.

'But she was very good.'

'She allowed you to be yourself, to some extent?'

'She never questioned things. It wasn't the role of women to do so at that time.' Nerida felt sorry for his wife, then.

'We had to bury a son,' he said sadly. 'Didn't last long.'

'Your son?'

'Yep.'

'Oh.'

'He had his time and then he had to go. He wasn't able to live this kind of life. It was the wrong time for sensitive little children.

'The rude ones survived.'

He was quiet. 'We had quite a few girls though.'

'Did it become a problem, to have daughters?' Nerida was a little afraid to ask. *How much will Aedgar reflect the misogyny of that time? He remembers the pain. Will he still have the prejudice?*

'Not for me.'

'That's good. Others were unhappy about it?'

Aedgar nodded. 'Some, especially the poor people, because they needed children to work. Boys were stronger. And they could sell boys off to other people who needed the "work power"; so they could buy food for the other children.'

'You saw this going on around you?'

'Yes. It was normal back then.

'People would have been suspicious if you didn't sell your boys, if you had more than one.

'They would have thought that you had treasure somewhere hidden and tried to find it.'

Nerida may have seen fleeting disdain on Mari's face.

'Some people behaved like animals.'

Images of violence flashed in her mind. She said, 'So, a poor person would protect themselves from violence and suspicion by selling their son?'

'Not if they had only one.'

'Okay.'

'That would have been suspicious too, very suspicious.'

'It was a time, then, of suspicion and vilification and a lot of fear, especially among the poor,' Nerida concluded.

'Mainly fear of the unknown. And the stories they've been told by some who teach,' he said mildly.

'And the church,' she added.

'Of course.'

'What was your relationship with the Church like in that life?'

'You had to participate, especially when you had to hide a secret life or two. It's all about suspicion.

'It was very challenging.'

Aedgar reflected. 'It's not a bad thing to believe in God, as they call it. But it's a bad thing to believe in the system that other people build around it.

'They used the fact that people were not able to read and write.

'So they were told lies, but these people didn't know, because they couldn't prove— they couldn't realise—what was written in the first place.'

Nerida said, 'People with power exploited the fact that people couldn't read and write to create a system around so-called God.'

'Aren't they still doing it?' he asked. 'They certainly are,' she said.

'It's never changed.' 'Not yet.'

'Well, there are some changes coming, slowly and steadily,' he said. She felt herself brighten at the ray of hope he offered.

'You used your herbs secretly, then? Or some of them you could use openly and others not?'

'Some people consulted me about it.'

She visualised him in a library, a private place with walls of leather-bound books. He went on, 'Some people didn't know. And some forgot about their fear when they got really unwell. It was like, "I give it a try, because I've got no chance, anyway."

'It was sad. I could have helped many of them at an earlier stage.

'But that is still going on, too.'

'Yes. Mari knows about that. She was trained in European herbs. She looked after some people who came to her too late.'

'Happens all the time.'

Nerida was still trying to work out when Aedgar and Aiden lived. 'Was this a time when people talked about witches?'

Aedgar scoffed. 'Yes. I was more like a satan, because I was male. If I would have been in a female body, they would have just burned me.'

'It had advantages to be in a male body.'

Nerida agreed. 'Absolutely. Still does.'

Aedgar reflected, 'Except if you want to have a child.'

'Yes. So was it the Catholic Church burning witches and taking the land?' She still had the Inquisition in mind after the morning's talk with Monica.

'Both. Well, there were more than two different belief systems. They were all talking about a god. But they used God in different ways.'

'There were several different churches competing for power?' *Were they living during the Reformation, then, when Henry VIII broke with the Pope and declared himself head of the Anglican Church?*

'It was "Religions",' Aedgar corrected. 'They didn't call it "churches".

'They had wars about the power. All the time.'

'Are we talking about the so-called Wars of the Roses?' Nerida never studied English or British history and, in the UK, she'd only ever briefly visited London (for a week), and the white cliffs of Dover and Stonehenge, (from behind a fence—no one was allowed to walk in between the stones), for a day. She knew little of the War of the Roses, except thinking that perhaps Tudors and Stuarts were involved.

'That was one of them.'

'Was that in this period?'

'No.'

'That war was before your time?'

'Yes.'

'Were there any monarchs I would have heard about involved in these wars? My knowledge of the period is very basic.'

'I have to think about it.'

She understood that these non-physical beings were not good with names and dates. These things were irrelevant in their dimension, Monica said. Others were recognised by their energy signature (or something like that—the expression was Nerida's) and they were the summation of all their lives and experience in spirit. So, a name from one of the lifetimes didn't matter much. Even less so, the name of someone peripheral to your life, like a king.

Nerida said, 'I think you mentioned Cromwell before and Charles, Charles the second.'

'There was an Edward, too.'

'Edward the Good?' *Now I'm just making shit up to sound clever. Where did that come from?* She was learning to take responsibility for words that came out of her mouth. But was not there yet. *Impulsive,* she berated herself. Mari used to call it 'a fart in the brain.'

Aedgar replied, 'He wasn't particularly good ... One of the relatives of Arthur, late descendant.'

'I thought Arthur was a mythical character?' She'd heard of King Arthur.

'No, he wasn't. Some people back then would have wished he was. He was a violent man,' he said, darkly.

'Oh, a warlord?'

'Yes. A tyrant, a violent tyrant.'

'That's interesting. He's been mythologised in England as a good fellow nowadays.'

'They made him a hero, we don't know why,' Aedgar responded. 'It wasn't a part of history to be particularly proud of—that's probably why they changed it. Plenty of things have been changed about history. If people knew, they would be really sad and ashamed to be descendants of that tribe.'

An Englishman with insight. How refreshing. 'Were you aware of this during your lifetime in Bristol?'

'We enjoyed the good things in life, because they were available, but we knew about the bad things too. But why make it worse by participating?'

Aedgar was responding to Nerida's subtext: *How does a person live and enjoy life in such barbarous times? How do you then think positive thoughts?*

She studied the concept that one needs to keep thinking good things to attract more good things, in life. This was from reading Fortunatus's channelled material.

Interested, she asked, 'Did you go hunting?'

'For food.'

'Did you hunt deer?'

'At times.'

'Pheasant?'

'They were too difficult to hunt.' He pondered. 'Ducks.'

'What kind of weapons were you using?'

'Slingshots. Not for deer of course.'

This 'of course' delighted Nerida, as if she knew about such things. Anangu hunted using guns, clubs and spears. They made weapons from local wood, stone and resin.

Nerida did not hunt. When she was 14, a classmate was shot dead accidentally on a roo hunt. He was a classical pianist of great promise —like no one else at school. It put her off guns.

'What about deer?'

'Bows and arrows.'

'Not the crossbow?'

'No.'

'Did you know the crossbow in that time?'

'Yes. It wasn't easy to transport,' he said.

'Very heavy?'

'We preferred to use the ones that were easily hidden, under the coat.'

'Oh, so you weren't always on your own land when you were hunting?' *They may have been privileged but they were also naughty.*

'No.'

'Did you and Aiden like to go hunting when you were together?'

'If we were hungry.

'Well, the woods were a good place to hide.'

She smiled sympathetically. 'You had some good times in the woods together.'

'Yes.'

Nerida referred to her notepad. 'I have to make a note of how you raise an eyebrow.' Then, she asked, 'So, homosexuality was not accepted in this period?'

'It didn't exist.'

'It didn't exist. You and Aiden discovered it yourselves.'

'As one does. I was considered a satan anyway.'

'You had nothing to lose!' Nerida laughed. There was a light, electric joy between them that she wasn't able to put in the notebook. 'How did you meet, you and Aiden?'

'At a celebration.

'We had some ales.

'Felt attracted.'

'I'll bet he was just gorgeous.'

'Of course. So was I.' A smile crossed Mari's lips. 'At least that's what people said.'

'Monica confirmed an image I had of you as tall, dark, handsome.' The entity had painted a word picture of Aedgar for them when Mari was learning to channel.

At first, Mari had in mind an older, white-bearded man, with sparkling eyes, 'a Druid type,' Monica said. Later, Monica described the Aedgar they knew.

Aedgar said, 'I was tall for that period of time.'

'Yes. Quite slender, at least in your youth?'

'Yes, but not skinny. Muscles.'

Nerida nodded, 'Muscles. You had muscles ... I had the image of Aiden as somebody smaller, fairer, with very bright eyes.'

'You're right about bright eyes. Not about the rest.

'He was the same size, maybe taller than me.

'Redhead, curly red hair, long hair. But not with the fair skin they usually have.

'Wow. That's a striking individual.'

Again that little smile. 'I had good taste. Very special ... he was very special.'

'What colour were his eyes?'

'Green.'

A bit like her cousin-brother, Greg. 'Ah. And a magical mind as well?'

'Cheeky.'

'You met at a celebration. You saw him and were attracted.' She wanted to know all the details.

'Yes.'

'You had some ales together.'

'Yeah, one or two.'

'Was it a men's celebration, the wives were not there?'

'We weren't married at the time.'

'Oh! You were still very young?'

'Yes—old enough to have fun.'

Nerida nodded. 'I see. But you fell in love with each other before your marriages were arranged.'

'Yes. It was good. We had more time.'

'You had time to be together, before you were married?'

'We could never be together officially. No matter if married or not.' There was a poignant pause. 'But of course we married.'

'Who got married first?'

'I did.'

'It must have been very sad.'

'No. It was the thing to do; I was expected to do it.'

For Nerida, it seemed like intimate interference on many levels, to force marriage to others on young Aedgar and Aiden in love.

He seemed to sense her feeling and declared, 'But I never stopped my secret life. So, it wasn't a loss.'

'You never had to give up Aiden,' she confirmed.

With soul-deep intensity, he said, 'I didn't.'

Then, lightly, 'He got married too, soon after.'

'You were able to support each other a bit, through that change,' she suggested.

'It wasn't a loss. It was a gain. We had wives as well, as we were supposed to, and we still had our secret life. We never stopped. We were lucky.'

'You were very lucky. But you also arranged it that way, I think.' Luck came with determination and vision, she felt.

'Well Mari and I in this time are two women together. We've been able to marry in another country but in this country our marriage is not recognised. We are able to live together, though.'

They were married in New Zealand in 2007, more than ten years before same-sex marriage was legalised in Australia.

Aedgar was startled. 'You have marriage?'

'We have marriage.'

'Interesting!'

'There's a big discussion in this time about whether marriage for homosexuals should be permitted or not.'

'Is that how you call it?' he asked.

'Well, women call ourselves lesbian, men call themselves gay.' She had not expected this conversation, somehow. *Better to keep the terminology of identification simple for now.* She mentally apologised to her rainbow allies of other identities.

Aedgar, processing 'gay,' spoke with a sense of wonder. 'Yeah, like having fun. That's how it is.'

'It's true. Was there a name for being that way in your time?'

'Didn't exist,' he reiterated.

'You must have felt like you were on another planet, you two.'

'We were,' he said simply.

'Did you ever meet others like you?'

'No. You couldn't trust people. If they were fearful, they could hurt you.'

Nerida said, 'You must have noticed interactions between people that made you say to each other, "Do you think they are like us?" Surely.'

'Once or twice,' he conceded.

'You were able to have your lives together? Your whole lives you were able to be together in a secret life?'

'Inseparable!' His pride in their achievement rang through the ages. Nerida relished the feeling.

She was curious about the logistics. Curious about the men. 'Did you live close to each other?'

'It depends on what you call close or what transportation you had. He didn't live in the next house, of course.'

'He came with a horse and wagon or on his horse to see you?' She was still wondering about the men's class. Perhaps Aiden was a craftsman or tradesman.

'Different ways,' said Aedgar, evasively.

'Did he have land as well? Was he a landed man of property?' Nerida asked directly. She had some remaining prejudices against wealthy people, while wishing she could be one herself.

'Yes.'

'Did he have a son?'

'Yes.'

'I wonder if perhaps in this lifetime, Mari and I might go and visit Bristol with you, sometime?'

'It has changed,' he said with finality.

'Of course.'

'You wouldn't find the interesting parts.'

'What about The Nag's Head? The tavern?' *How wonderful to go to Bristol and find evidence confirming Aedgar and Aiden's history.*

'That was the wrong name, I think. It was The Hog's Head.'

'It might still exist.'

'I don't think so,' he said.

'It's getting hot now. I think Mari's body's wearing a little.'

'I can feel it.'

'We'll take a break now and talk again soon,' she said. 'It's been a delight to talk to you, as always.'

Aedgar said gracefully, 'Thank you. The pleasure is on my side.' Aedgar was among the most fascinating and mysterious beings Nerida had had the opportunity to know, at least since she met and married Mari.

She still wondered whether Aedgar could be a part of Mari or related to her. *Could he be a sub personality, born of trauma? Is he Mari in another lifetime?*

Sometimes she probed, exploring whether he knew things that she knew Mari didn't. She even asked directly about his relationship to Mari a couple of times. His response was to deny that they were related, but to reiterate that he was 'very fond of our friend and very grateful for the opportunity,' she offered.

It took some time to distinguish his personality and knowledge from Mari's. But in the end this was not hard to do, partly because hers was a stubborn, black and white sort of personality. Aedgar's judgements were generally more nuanced.

His knowledge of English history, chemistry and physics, for example, was different to Mari's. She had no interest and little education in these fields.

She had a practical knowledge of physics as a diving instructor. But formal physics and maths never interested her.

Her time in hospital as a child, enduring orthopaedic surgeries for a congenital problem with her legs and hips, left her alienated at school, immune to the teachers' threats of detention. Even when they hit her, she had been through much worse at the hands of doctors and nurses.

She was bored by history and disdained period drama, even on television.

She may have been the only person over twelve in the western hemisphere, then, who did not watch *Game of Thrones*.

Mari had no knowledge of metaphysics either and refused to develop any, despite her ongoing contribution to that body of knowledge.

This did make it clearer that Nerida was talking to someone who knew things that Mari didn't. But it made it more challenging if she tried to discuss what she was learning with Mari.

Mari refused to listen to anything Nerida told her about what Aedgar said. She wanted to keep her channelling 'pure,' as Monica had suggested, so she didn't listen to the conversations. The only idea she had of the content was reflected in the sessions they had with Monica. They couldn't afford to have those sessions too often. Nerida had a substantial credit card debt.

Given the cards as a senior med student and using them as a junior doctor (when she was paid $23 an hour—less than she had been as a clerk in summer holidays), she used the cards to visit Mari and meet her family in Europe. To help with the extra expenses when they bought the orange house. And then to move them to Mutitjulu.

Now, she needed to keep working full-time to service the debt.

Mari worked as a driver for the clinic but the central organisation in Alice Springs never paid her.

She was officially employed, but there was some problem, the 'human resources' department said, with accessing superannuation when she was not an Australian citizen. She had her residency, which had cost them thousands of dollars and years of stress, education and documentation to achieve.

Mari had never lived on credit and didn't understand. Nerida did not know how to involve her. She was ashamed of not being that rich doctor.

She kept sending money to family members and political causes that she couldn't really afford to support, either. Usually in secret.

Money was an issue they needed to learn to talk about. But now the big divide in their relationship was their different experience of the spirit beings.

Amidst a busy life in Community and with a new friend from beyond the material world, Nerida found herself, as Mari did, in a strangely lonely situation.

FIFTEEN

M UTITJULU
JUNE 2012

WHEN THEY CAME to live in Muti, the women brought the rain with them. Their first two years there were the rainiest on record. The Rock was surrounded by baby desert oaks. The juvenile trees were like toy soldiers or paint brushes. After the roots reached the water table underground, they transformed into their mature, branched form, with thick, grooved bark.

The slender leaves and stems turned upwards in even a scanty shower, to direct water down the trunk to the roots. Some adult trees were over a thousand years old.

It was their second winter at Mutitjulu, on a Friday afternoon, that Jerry went missing.

Henrietta's partner stormed off and disappeared after a petty argument, threatening to kill himself.

'He was the one who caught the snake for us, wasn't he? Beautiful, kind young man,' Nerida said when Claire told her.

'The argument was about nothing, Henni says. Transferring money from their account onto the Basics Card. You know people have to call Centrelink, every time they get paid, to be able to use their money?' Claire was snappy, impatient with stupidity.

'Oh, no, really? That's why people are always hanging on the public phone in front of the shop for hours.'

'Got it in one. From what Henni said, he was pissed that she hadn't done that, so they had no money for flour. One of the Blair women has given her flour now, so they've got damper for the weekend. But he's gone off.

'Who knows what's going on in his head,' Claire mused. 'He's not a sulky fellow.

'Everybody loves him. Jerry's been recruited to start work with the Rangers on Monday. We wanted him to train as a health worker here. Maybe he's gone Bush to feel a bit of freedom before he starts full-time work.'

'Well, yeah, you would. I hate full-time work,' said Nerida. 'I wish they'd get another doctor here, so we could job share.'

'That's what me and Becca are looking to do,' Claire said. They'd applied to management to share a role as Chronic Disease Nurses. 'Anyway, someone says they'll kill themselves, we've gotta take it seriously, ye?' Sometimes Claire added little Kriol words, like 'ye,' to her speech. Maybe it was from where she grew up in Papua New Guinea.

'Anything you need me to do?' Nerida was wiping down the exam bed in her room, covering it with the sheets of paper they used in place of linen. She'd been sitting in her chair too long and her body hurt.

Claire saw her hunched over, near exhaustion. 'Nah, go home. Anything happens, I know where you live.'

Next morning, Claire called Nerida say that Jerry was still missing. From Saturday afternoon through Monday Mari and Nerida heard the police out in helicopters, scanning the trees and the red sand for signs of life, signs of him.

Monday was an ordinary, busy day.

On Tuesday, Claire called Nerida at home during her lunch break. 'The police called me here at the clinic,' she said. 'They've found Jerry. They saw his body from above, from the helicopter.

'He hanged himself not far from here, within sight of the Rock.

'He's laid out in the emergency room,' she said. 'I thought I'd better let you know.' She sounded at a loss. 'We found a body bag to put him in.'

Jerry's body seemed impossibly long in the zippered nylon bag. In life, his self-contained, graceful movements belied his size.

Looking at him, Nerida grieved for all the love, all the good food, and the warmth and tenderness that had gone into growing that tall, strong body. He was made of the esteem and caring others had for him. The natural world loved him. He grew up so fine, every cell in his body knowing what it needed to do.

Her job was to certify him deceased. It was clear that his spirit was far, far away. The empty shell showed signs of having been abandoned for some time. Maggots crawled out of the eyes, from under his long lashes.

'I keep trying to clean them away,' Claire said.

After a while, Henrietta, his newly bereaved partner, mother of Biggie, one of the young man's children, came to the clinic.

Claire brought her into Nerida's colourful, cosy room. They hugged. Nerida cried a little as Henni cried a lot. 'It's not your fault. This was his choice,' was all Nerida could say to her, not yet twenty, too young to be a widow, sobbing too hard to talk.

Nerida told Mari about it that evening after work.

In following days, people came through the clinic, using aromatic eucalyptus smoke to help the young man's spirit let go of the all the places he'd been. The mourning procession travelled through the Community. Women cried and wailed.

One of the old women, shirtless and thin, sat in the dirt in her dusty black skirt, left behind by the others. The smoking ceremony could not console her. Sobbing and moaning, her tears made paths on her dust covered face and chest. She was the young one's great grandmother. No ritual, even an ancient one, would be enough in the face of such loss.

Rebecca and a male nurse helped her into a wheelchair and brought her bumping over the stones to the clinic.

'Too much drama,' Claire said.

'People should yell and carry on. It's wrong,' Nerida said. She had streaks of red dirt her own face.

Jerry's family extended to the northwest of Alice Springs. They decided in the coming weeks that Mutitjulu would host the Sorry Camp.

It was a complex decision for such peripatetic and socially conscientious people: the generous Anangu would host members of another tribe related to one of the young man's parents. The young man would be buried in the Mutitjulu graveyard, a beautiful, sombre place on the edge of town.

They had time. They took time. It would be weeks before the coroner released his body to be flown back from Alice.

Sorry Camp was a gathering of family and friends to honour and mourn. People came from all around, often great distances, and camped. It was a time and place of important storytelling and learning.

Being from the East, Nerida was not familiar with all the protocols, but Claire was able to guide her. They were concerned for their vulnerable patients, exposed to intense emotion and an extreme climate. One of the other nurses disapproved of the people's ceremonies.

Claire appreciated the culture, but even she had her limits. 'I can't stand the wailing,' she said.

Nerida liked the lamentation. 'There needs to be wailing,' she said.

Sorry Camp was tough in the middle of winter, being outside, sometimes only on a blanket or mat on the frosty, cold ground. Local people dragged mattresses from their own place. The visitors brought as much comfort as they could in cars already loaded with people. Some people slept in their cars. They travelled for days, over hundreds of kilometres. The young man was beloved by many.

Sorry Camp for him lasted for over two months.

Finally, on the afternoon before the young man's funeral, Claire pulled a big box down from a high shelf in the clinic: decorations, including ribbons and gaudy artificial flowers.

Two aunties of the deceased took it to decorate the church and the old ambulance, which would be the hearse. The vehicle had bench seats along the sides in the back. The suspension was gone and the back doors had to be opened from inside, but it served the purpose. Mari offered to drive on the day.

The morning of the funeral dawned with a pink and then bright blue sky. Mari drove a group of male relatives to the airport. Their sombre task was to pick up the young man's poor body, which had been in Alice Springs for the Coroner's grim operation.

After extricating it from the small plane, the men held the coffin with their hands and knees as Mari drove back to the community.

On their direction, she slowed the vehicle to walking pace when it passed important places of men's power and education on Uluru.

After delivering the pallbearers and their cargo into the corrugated iron church, Mari fetched Nerida from work.

Jasmine and the nurses went into the church for the service, while Mari and her doctor wife waited in the ambulance outside. Some people milled around outside the church.

Perhaps they also didn't like sermons.

When the service finished, Mari clambered into the back of the truck to push open the back doors. Wailing, sobbing, moaning people pressed around the coffin and the vehicle as the men pushed the casket into the old ambulance.

Mourners were bereft. Mari and Nerida shed tears too in the storm of grief.

People rocked the ambulance, jostling to touch the coffin. On Nerida's passenger side window, the distraught face of the young widow appeared. She had her child on her hip.

Henrietta's eyes were wide with fear. She pounded the window with her fist.

Nerida wound it down. 'Can I come in? They're hitting me.' Henni tried to shield little Biggie from the rough crowd.

'Let her in!' Mari cried.

Nerida opened the car door against the press of the crowd.

Henrietta squeezed in between Nerida and the dashboard. 'Did they hurt you?'

'I'm a sore here and here,' she said, indicating her right arm and ribs, her face wet with tears.

'They say it's my fault. I didn't look after him properly. One said she'll kill me.'

Henrietta was thin as a dingo.

Nerida could feel her bones as Henni sat across her lap, her head and back curved to fit under the car's ceiling. She rested her hand against the young woman's back, transmitting comfort. The toddler sat on Henni's lap, her chubby arms propped against the dash.

Mari was astonished to see that Biggie held a puppy in her arms, which broke free and ran under the vehicle's foot pedals. The toddler followed, climbing down under Mari's legs.

She giggled at the golden puppy running around their feet and legs, undisturbed by pounding on the ambulance and shouting and screaming outside.

The little ones, dog and human, were quick to feel safe. Biggie held the pup in one arm and wrapped the other around Mari's right leg, the artificial one, in a gentle, natural movement. She laid her head against Mari's thigh.

The young man's pallbearers climbed in the back of the vehicle and arranged themselves tightly together, packed in rows of sweaty, formal clothing. The back doors closed.

'Are you okay to drive?' Nerida asked. Mari nodded.

Then the old ambulance led a sombre procession to the community cemetery, where the coffin was carefully unloaded. Bull, looking brusque and weary, climbed out of the earth mover. He'd dug the grave.

Biggie climbed on the pile of fresh-smelling earth and played there through the service, finding stones and throwing them with her father's hunting skill. She chose not to throw them at any people, Nerida noticed. All was quiet while the preacher spoke, and the coffin was interred. Even the puppy looked subdued in Henni's arms.

A cooler breeze came from the west, making it bearable to stand in the burning sun. With the historic and tenderly decorated graves all around.

The preacher was Adam, an Aboriginal Lore Man as well as a Christian reverend. He was a man of knowledge and experience in several cultures.

Adam looked resplendent in white robes and a red and gold surplice. He wore handmade, embroidered cowboy boots underneath. And, on his dark brown face, blue mirrored sunglasses under his stylish bush hat.

Uluru was close by and the domed mountains of Kata Tjuta loomed orange in the west.

Adam stood there with the afternoon sun behind him.

Biggie, in a bright, white shirt and a black skirt, with shiny black shoes and white socks, sat herself down in the dirt as her young father was buried.

Another widow held a baby in her arms at the graveside. The young man had two wives in different communities. His life was complicated.

The family from far away were powerful and graceful at the graveside. Nerida was impressed by their soulful singing and disciplined organisation. The attack on Henni at the church was not necessarily a breakdown in that discipline.

As Nerida understood it, that clan practiced 'payback' as a way of extirpating tension and emotion after a death.

Among Anangu, there was sometimes physical punishment, or justice, but they didn't practice 'payback' in the same way.

When Henrietta came to see her in the coming weeks, Nerida thought that perhaps the physical expression of rage and blame meant that she was psychologically freer. It was hard to tell. Henni spoke good English, but like her father Caleb, she had her own private spiritual life.

As Nerida and Mari did.

Mari and Nerida felt hugely privileged to be permitted to witness what people endured and help in some small ways.

Most community people had difficult lives. There was too much grief, fear and worry, living at the forefront of colonisation.

Those who processed the trauma, healed, and stayed mentally well had to deal with the deteriorating weather, as it got hotter and hotter. And the continuing insults of the time: the alcohol ban, the disputes over the garbage collection and the pool, the material poverty and neglect.

There was asbestos in the walls of the childcare centre. The childcare workers had to move out of their office because of a ragged hole.

The three-metre-high metal fence that Barry had shown them had been constructed around the building, while it remained full of dangerous fibres.

Two or three times a year Traditional Owners in the Anangu communities got a small but significant pot of cash, called 'Gate money.' It was gathered for them, a royalty—surely that was the right word—paid by tourists at the National Park gate.

They bought white goods, sometimes a vehicle, at highly inflated, 'remote' prices.

Other times the money went on power cards (for electricity) or phone cards through the extended family.

Anangu chose how a large part of the money would be spent at important meetings that the whole community attended. They bought water tanks and solar heating.

One year the lion's share of the money went to Imanpa, 200 kilometres down the road, where they built and ran a store because the Community didn't have one.

People did their best to look after each other and maintain Indigenous values. But the money wasn't a lot, considering the difficulties people faced.

Beyond the houses and buildings, the soft needles of the trees shimmered in the heat.

The desert oak where the young man died lived on, witness to generations of Anangu coming near the Rock for dancing, singing, storytelling, romance. And sorrow.

Its bark was thick.

In 2013 the tree survived a lightning strike. Half of its trunk and branches were charred and black. The rest of the oak, strong and brown, continued to grow around the lifeless charcoal.

And people who knew the young man ended his life there were sad to see the tree.

They felt mournful whether they saw it or even just knew the tree was still living, when the young man did not.

SIXTEEN

MUTITJULU
SATURDAY DEC 29, 2012

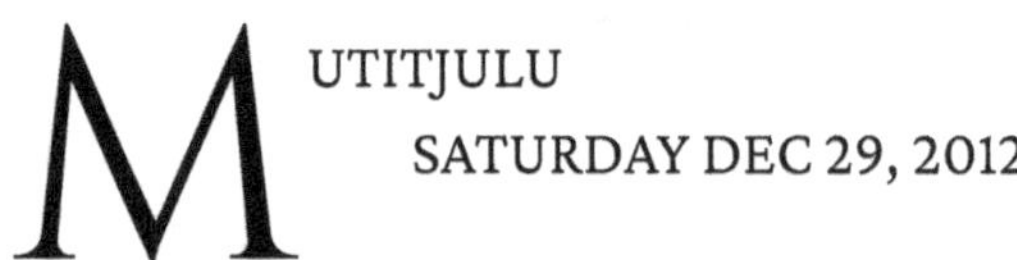

IT WAS ONLY HALF a year after Jerry's death, even if it felt a world away, that Mari and Nerida visited Dawn and Trevor in Burbank to study with Monica. Their experiences shaped who they were, even if Mari's channelling sessions seemed to promise an escape from the drama and difficulty of life and work at Mutitjulu.

Watching Mari develop this strange and impressive ability and getting to know Aedgar gave Nerida hope of finding meaning.

Mari was frustrated and upset though.

Her paintings, brought to the local cafe to be set up for an exhibition, went missing.

They were last seen in Bull's ute, on the passenger side near the door, Bull's wife told Nerida.

But Bull denied any knowledge of them. Weeks passed with no news of the paintings.

Nerida felt like she could kill Bull, who was avoiding her. *What's going on?*

'I'm going to the Police Station,' Mari declared after nearly three weeks of torment.

Nerida went with her to write a report in the two-million-dollar concrete shell, proud architecture of the government intervention.

The job at Christmas Island, meanwhile, seemed to be on hold. Things felt stuck. Irritating.

Nerida learned a concept in Chinese Medicine, that pain was congested energy. Energy needed to move, to flow.

She tried to get things moving by learning about channelling. As well as participating in sessions, Nerida read books. She was trying to practice positive thinking and speaking, to create good things in their life.

Mari was no help. 'Who wants five cars? How to be a shit magnet, isn't that what you're reading?'

And 'It's not all pancakes, rainbows and unicorns, you know. I'm going to stop doing this is that's all that's coming out of my mouth!'

'That's not what it's about,' Nerida objected.

'Better not be. Cause I don't hear what they say. But I'm still responsible for it. I'm not putting more bullshit out in the world.'

The 'New Age' culture around some books she read led Nerida to expect positivity in the channelled material. She found it frustrating. Aedgar was quick-witted, candid and melancholy. Like a best friend, really.

Nerida was confused. She did not like the idea that her thoughts created reality at all. Some days she felt that she had a brain full of repetitive, noisy crap. She conceded, though, that fear and anxiety created more angst and misery.

Nerida began small by practising thinking positively about lost or misplaced things and being delighted when they showed up.

She wondered if Claire thought she had a screw loose in the clinic when she'd say, 'I'll be so pleased when those mosquito forceps show up.' And then, 'There you are, thank you for coming,' when they appeared.

Nerida tried smiling at herself in the mirror, as Louise Hay (in her books) said she should. *Maybe it will seem more natural in a few years*, she thought. She couldn't ever remember grinning at herself.

But what she discovered in conversations with Aedgar was more complex than being exhorted to practice affirmations or speak affirmatively. Many aspects of life and her part in it became intriguing, more interesting for her. He unpicked her illusions— knocked off unhelpful aspects of her 'grown-up' doctor's ego.

Aedgar helped Nerida see her experiences in a broader perspective. As he revealed some facets of his mysterious being, she learned more about the purpose of living and came closer to understanding herself.

But she wouldn't say she always liked it. If there'd been anyone to talk to about it.

The heat was extreme outside. Mutitjulu had an average high of over 38 degrees (over the century on the old scale) in December.

Community was quieter. Everyone moved slowly, if they had to, in the shimmering, scorching heat.

Mob went to other communities to visit family in December.

Mutitjulu felt severe. 'If you're out in the heat for five minutes, it takes 45 to recover,' Claire said.

Other places Anangu liked to visit, like Pipalytjara or Hermannsburg, even Alice Springs, had more trees and shade.

By day, the dogs were too hot and tired to bark. Some were starving, left behind for someone else to look after when people went away.

Sometimes people fed them, but no one wanted to end up like Peter. He hoarded dogs, unable to refuse any of them.

Animal protection came from Alice periodically to help him decide which ones could be taken 'to find a new home.' By the time they came, the dogs were sometimes eating each other in Peter's yard. Everyone was cautious walking by his place. Nerida gave up riding her bike to work (when the season allowed) after Peter's dogs warned her against it.

Peter's wife died, and he kept her dogs. That was how it started. He was not from there, but Mutitjulu people tolerated him out of compassion.

Nerida was tired. When the moon was full, or almost, sleep deprivation exacerbated her usual exhaustion. The community dogs hated the moon and attacked it fiercely. Peter's dogs, only a couple of hundred metres from their place, barked madly at the moon all night. Only Selkie's dog, Minyma, ignored the ruckus.

When Mari took a seat and composed herself to channel, Nerida turned the airconditioner off with some reluctance.

'Is there anything I can do to help?' She had to ask, once she could feel someone else there.

'It's a very dry place,' Aedgar croaked, with a short, dry cough. 'It's hard to talk.'

'We will be moving to a moister place in a couple of months,' Nerida said.

'Are you moving next to a tavern?'

Huh? 'Are we?' *What does he know?*

'You said it's a moist place.'

Nerida chuckled. 'No, it's an island. Surrounded by the beautiful sea.'

Aedgar nodded. 'Like Britain.'

Nerida thought about it. 'Hmm. But much, much smaller.'

'Well, Britain is not as big as they think,' he replied. After a moment, he asked, 'Where is this island?'

'South of Java.'

'Java…'

'Do you know Java? One of the Spice Islands.'

'Sounds exotic. I'd know it under a different name.'

What was Indonesia called by Europeans in the Middle Ages? Did they even know it?

Does Aedgar know geography in southeast Asia?

'You might,' she said. 'This little Australian island is in the Indian Ocean. People are mostly of Asian ancestry, descended from China, Malaysia and Singapore.

'Some have great grandparents from Japan. Or they're Melanesians or Polynesians: Pasifika people.

'It's called Christmas Island.'

'What a jolly sounding name,' Aedgar said. 'People tend to give wonderful names to horrible places.'

'Yeah, you have a point,' she said. 'I hope it's not like that.'

'It can be horrible. People seeking refuge from war in Asia point their boats in that direction. Sometimes they get it. But often they're taken as prisoners. Sometimes they die in the attempt to get there. That makes it a sad place.'

Aedgar seemed to step back from the drama. 'Well, it's the ocean, the sea,' he said. 'People always think they can master it, and most of them underestimate the power. It's not as easy to handle as it might look to some people.'

'You told me before you'd been out fishing in bad weather, during one of your Bristol lives.'

'Not the brightest idea,' Aedgar said. 'But you're supposed to go out during the night, so sometimes you can't see bad weather coming up.'

'Why were you supposed to go out during the night?'

'Because of the fish!'

'The fish come out at night?' Nerida asked. She'd always been fishing in daylight with her Dad or Grandmother.

'Yeah. We used the lights with the candles in them. Fish get attracted to the light and then you catch them.'

'Well, that's clever.'

'It's the usual way to do it,' he said.

'Oh, there are many ways,' she reflected. 'Were you ever hurt by the sea?'

'No. But I know people who went missing.

'Strange enough to say they went missing because everybody knew they were dead.

'I guess it's for the loved ones, so there is still hope, if it's said, "They went missing."

'There have been two or three occasions when there were people lost at sea and everybody thought they were dead, and then they came back.

'One wonders what they have done. Coming back one or two years later.

'They might have had some great adventures. Must have been because they never talked about it. But they looked happy and well, so...'

Nerida nodded. 'It's a shame not to tell stories when there are stories to tell.'

'Maybe they had to hide something,' he suggested.

'Yes. A brown-skinned wife and a family of ten children on a tropical island. Or a treasure hidden somewhere.' Nerida smiled.

'You're exaggerating a bit. I said they've been gone one or two years only.'

Nerida smiled. 'You have a good grasp of linear time, for one so far from it.' Then, she said, 'I was thinking of you this morning as I was driving past Uluru.'

'How come?'

'To go to the shop to get supplies, we go around the Rock.'

'So you think of me when you get supplies?' He sounded surprised.

'I think of you in all sorts of contexts. But this morning I thought of you when I was looking at that grand monument. You said it was about caution. And that it has not always been so dry here.'

'True.'

'The old people here say that too. They say there used to be more animals and plants here. But I think you're talking about much further back in time.'

'Yes. When there was this great heat that made this mountain turn red.'

'The earth got cooked?'

'In some way.' He tilted Mari's head slightly to the side.

'Were people responsible at all?' *Was there some ancient nuclear blast? Do I really want to know?*

'No, no,' he said. 'It was this kind of "volcanic" energy. Not exactly volcanic, but this would be the closest thing to describe it, that you might understand.'

'So if the lesson of this place is caution—' she asked.

'You should obey its rules,' he answered.

'What are its rules?'

'Treat it with respect,' he said. 'It's not here for eternity, as you would say.'

Nerida was incredulous. 'It's visiting?'

'Yeah, sort of visiting. It's temporary. People here might not realise it and no one who is on the planet now might see it disappear again.'

'But it's arisen? And it can disappear again?' *What scale of time is he working on? I'm intrigued. But also wondering if this spirit relates to the human scale of events, at all.*

'Yes.'

Nerida looked for something more immediate. 'I always felt it presented an opportunity for people to learn.'

Aedgar seemed to sense her impatience. 'It does, it does. But people don't understand. Most of the people don't understand, not even most of the people who live here.

'Some of them do, some of the old ones, not many. And some of the very young. They haven't forgotten. But they will soon, unfortunately.'

Again, that bleakness. Is there no hope, then? 'Monica says that some of the young people are here for this particular time, with specific knowledge for this period on Earth.'

'They are, it's true,' he replied. 'But they need support to pass the knowledge on. You must, kind of, bring it to the surface. Otherwise, it just seems to evaporate.

'They grow up. They feel empty and kind of hollow, because the knowledge they had and came back to pass on has evaporated.'

He considered.

Nerida felt the emptiness of youth who were born knowing their purpose and had it slip out of their grasp.

'We'll have to find a way to bring it to the surface and help them to keep it,' he said.

'Yes, we will.' She desperately wanted to. That, she felt, was **her** purpose: forgotten and now being reclaimed.

Again, there was that sensation as if he was looking into the distance on an internal plane.

'The one who will help them is still not here,' he said. 'Being born.'

'Coming soon then?' He aroused her curiosity. But she felt resistance. *I could really do without the prediction of a messiah.*

'Soon for our understanding. Might not be equal, or on the same level as your "soon".'

He finds estimating time a challenge. How will we ever prove anything he says? 'Is that person specific to this area?' she asked.

'Yes. Not directly from this place, but from the same area.'

'And perhaps with the same languages? *If there's a leader for this mob's youth coming, I want them to be Anangu.*

'They will understand. It's something that's not about language.

'It's about giving the people a key to unlock their knowledge.

'They will be surprised they have it. They know there is something.

'They don't know what it is, until it goes missing. And then they feel very lost and sorry, because they have lost something.

'They can feel it, but they don't know what it was.

'It's been going on for a while.'

'I think something like that happened to me. I felt empty inside as a young woman,' Nerida said sadly. She used to describe it as having a hole in her, in her spirit. She'd wave a hand over her abdomen. She tried to fill it with sensory distraction: drugs, sex and food.

Overeating was still an entrenched habit. She always felt that she needed to have more. Aedgar inclined Mari's head, just a shade. 'Could be.'

'At least enough for me to be able to understand you when you talk about it,' she said.

'Yeah. Most people wouldn't understand it, if I said it like this. The old people here are watching it, but they are helpless. They get sad, because they don't know how to help,' he said. 'It's not their fault.

'It needs that special person.

'Doesn't have to become an adult, that special person. It will have the ability as a child, already, to show these things to other young ones. People won't realise it's happening until some years later.'

She felt eager for that. 'When the young ones show what they know and what they can do?'

She tried to imagine that wise child. An old soul able to remind other children of their purpose. She pictured the adults seeing those young ones grow to claim and fulfil their aspirations, their soulful intentions.

Aedgar agreed. 'Yes. Some of the knowledge comes back, that's why, in your terms, there is not much time.'

His tone changed, with a shade of anger: 'Because others will try to change this whole area, a lot.'

Then that kindness, that sweet melancholy, 'So, it should all be slowed down, for these young ones to have a chance to teach and show others, once it's gone.'

Nerida took a beat to process that. *Development in the area: tourism? Mining? Should be delayed. The young ones need to be able to carry on teaching after that special one is gone.*

'It's gonna be a female,' he said. 'Very wise from the beginning.' Nerida felt the love. But that was in the by-and-by. *What about now?*

'We have some wise young ones here already. Is there anything I can do to help them?

I'm just trying to keep them alive, really.' She sighed.

'A difficult task,' Aedgar acknowledged.

'Yeah. We've lost a couple already since I was here.'

As well as Biggie's young father, another youth had taken his life. Nobody could help him. 'He stopped listening,' old Blossom said.

Selkie told her that the nearest expression the Elders came up with, their translation of 'sui-chide' was an Aboriginal language phrase that translated as 'one who stopped listening.'

Aedgar said, 'Unfortunately, there is not very much you can do. They should be loved and supported, just to survive, until this knowledge comes.'

Nerida felt encouraged.

Then, she felt his energy move away.

He turned the head towards Mari's right shoulder, a little behind.

'They are trying to dig—big holes—about half a day's travel away from here. 'They are very close.

'And they are trying to extend it, because in their opinion, it will be very successful.

'But it's just another opportunity, that they think of, to deprive the Earth.'

Nerida's heart beat harder. *This is happening now.*

'We may be involved in protests, demonstrations?

'However people can express themselves?' She fired up. Then waited.

'It will take a major disaster, unfortunately.'

'To stop them?'

'Yes.'

'I'm sorry to hear that.' She waited again.

Aedgar said, 'It will hit the right people.'

'I'm grateful to hear that,' she said, shocking herself.

'There will be protests,' he said, 'but it won't help. It's going to be too 'successful' (in their terms) in the beginning.

'They're going to unleash the powers of the Earth.' There was thunder in the voice. 'And they will pay for it'.

Nerida wanted to know more. There was no image in her head this time. She speculated, 'Are they mining uranium, is that what you mean?' There were uranium mines south of the state border.

Aedgar seemed to watch it unfurl. 'They will try to dig something out that they should never touch.'

'It's yellow stuff?' she asked.

'No.

'Bluish colour.

'It has no smell.

'It will have powers that they will recognise too late.

'Far more dangerous than anybody could think of.

'It's like a different kind of radiation, a kind that's unknown so far.

'It's not dangerous if you don't touch it.

'If you leave it where it is, it's not dangerous.

'It's something that was created during that kind of 'volcanic' event.

'It's unknown, so far.

'It will change when it comes up to the air.

'They have the idea that they just dig it out and then they will find out what they can use it for—which is a very bad idea.'

SEVENTEEN

MUTITJULU
SAME DAY

NERIDA FELT DAUNTED by Aedgar and frightened for the world. It was that old ache for the planet and fear for her fellow humans.

'It's about half a day travel, to the southwest,' he said.

'Southwest,' she repeated thoughtfully. She imagined communities in that direction.

Beautiful, peaceful little places like Pipalytjara. Artistic centres: Kalka in South Australia, Wingellina across the Western Australian border.

'There are no people there now,' he said, as if reading her mind. 'I don't think there is a settlement around. They'll start an artificial settlement. It won't last.'

She released a breath she hadn't realised she was holding. She knew those instant mining towns of dongas, shelters off the backs of trucks. People living there had regimented, hard lives with long hours and curfews.

'What about the mining that's happening on this continent already, with these artificial towns and large open pits, or deep holes?'

'Well, it's depriving the Earth, but it's an opportunity for people to use large areas of this island,' Aedgar surprised her by saying.

It's true, I want people to see the beauty of the Australian interior and find ways to live here.

'They should try irrigation systems to change the area, not deprive the Earth, taking everything out,' he continued. 'Everything inside the earth is there for a reason; it's about balance. It's not **stored.**

'It was never stored for future generations of humans to take it out and use it to "save time". It was never meant to make some people very rich, in taking the land off the owners. It was never meant to be that way.'

She took this to heart. The idea that minerals were an intrinsic part of the planet, not made for human pillage and exploitation, seemed obvious now that he had pointed it out.

Nerida tried an idea from her reading of one of Seth's books. Fortunatus alluded to it too. 'Is it true that the Earth is created by human intention and human desire?' she asked cautiously.

Speaking slowly, Aedgar replied, 'It's partly—a similar thing to that. People think it's very complex. It's not.'

'The way the planet is created is not complex?' *That's unbelievable.*

'It wasn't in the beginning,' he assured her. 'It has evolved. Cooling down, heating up again: oxygen was generated.'

Nerida asked, 'Plants and animals arose in the way that science sees it—simpler organisms evolved into more complex organisms?'

'They have an idea,' he granted.

He was annoying her now. *Couldn't humans have got one elemental part of knowledge right?*

She was fond of Charles Darwin, able to relate to his love of Nature and fine observation skills, as well as the many years he did not publish his books, keeping his truth to himself. He periodically went to the country for 'cures', trying to heal his spasming guts with harsh Victorian water treatments.

Darwin dreaded the impact of his brilliant observations on his ordinary church-going friends and family, as well as on society at large. He so much feared being misunderstood. *And in some ways his worst fears were realised*, Nerida thought, *considering the backlash against him and the misuse of Darwin's ideas by racists, eugenicists and colonisers who used 'survival of the fittest' to justify atrocities.*

'It's not exactly how it went, but they have an idea,' Aedgar allowed. 'It's not all that wrong. But they think they know it all.'

Nerida bristled on behalf of her colleagues. *We do good things in science.* 'Well, the best scientists know they don't know it all.'

'But it's never the best ones that get listened to. It's always the ones that think they are the best—they have to make up for lesser knowledge by making more noise.'

She had no response to that. It was true.

So she raised another topic. 'You said that this place, this Uluru, is like a conglomeration of beings.'

'Yes.'

'I wondered if you could tell me more about those beings.'

'Another time. You're not ready.'

'Okay, thank you.' She realised that he would not disrupt her beyond her capacity.

There's tenderness here. He gives me only what I can handle. If Uluru really is a conglomerate of beings and I'm living with it towering over us every day, I might go mad.

'You're welcome.'

Outside the window, a pair of honeyeaters chirped and called. They were called *pinpal-pinpalpa*. Nerida thought she heard one saying its name.

She asked Aedgar, 'Do you have any advice for me to help encourage Mari?'

'She's fine.

'We'll work it out.

'She's trying.

'I'm trying. We're getting better.

'You're getting better too.'

Nerida laughed.

'You've been waiting for that,' he said.

'For the encouragement?'

'Yes.'

'Always. You see right through me.'

'Literally,' he said, 'I can't see. But I can feel it.'

'You can read into my energy?' *What manner of being is he, anyway?*

'Sort of.'

'Trevor Weaver, Dawn's husband, said that you will be able to find a way to access any knowledge that Mari and I have, before too long.'

This is a confronting idea. Trevor talked about it enthusiastically when they were in Burbank. Nerida had become more and more used to the idea that her thoughts were not necessarily private when she met ngangkari, the traditional Aboriginal healers. She couldn't tell whether they could read her mind. She felt like they did.

Or were they perceptive observers, with my thoughts, in their patterns, being predictable to them? She was a good observer herself now, becoming an experienced doctor and maybe even, she felt sometimes, a healer.

People thought she could read their minds because their ways of thinking were unsurprising. This happened less often with Anangu or other Indigenous people than with so-called white people.

She never liked the expression 'white'. *Everybody comes from some-where. Calling people 'white' is used to bury history.*

Nevertheless, Nerida had learned young to watch non-Indigenous people in authority closely, since she was often (inexplicably) watched closely by them. Many of them had predictable patterns of thought that came from school, university, the church or the media. It was a way of staying safe, to know how they were thinking.

Aedgar, on the other hand, is maybe reading me the way that animals read each other. She'd learned to keep her energy calm and light when visiting a community house with dogs that didn't know her.

She knew that a dolphin could tell when another was hungry, or pregnant or aggressive, (or all three at once) using sonar or something related to it. *Maybe spirits are like that.*

Nerida wrestled with the issue of privacy, as she did with her ngangkari teachers. If Aedgar would have access to knowledge that she and Mari had, what did that mean for her intimate memories?

He would have access to their knowledge, Aedgar agreed.

'So, we'll have to work on getting smarter,' said Nerida, glossing over her reservations. *And I will have to learn to trust you even more. But how could I trust him any more than now, when he is welcomed into the body of my darling?*

'Would be helpful,' he said.

'Is there any particular area of knowledge you would like to encourage me to study?'

'I think you are well prepared.'

Wow. That's a cool acknowledgement. 'Thank you.'

'This one seems to have little problems with science if it's not related to practical things.'

'Mari, you mean?' she asked.

'Yes.'

'She is very pragmatic'

'People said that about me.' He lifted a brow. 'Nothing wrong with it.'

'Absolutely not. You're a good match, you two, personality-wise.'

'I knew that. That's why she was chosen.' His voice resonated in the quiet room. 'One of many reasons.'

Nerida said, 'Mari was wondering today whether the trials she had in early life— physically and emotionally—were preparation for her being able to do this kind of work.'

'That was part of it,' Aedgar acknowledged. 'She was always trying —sometimes too hard—just that little bit too much.

'What happened could always be filed as experience—it's all about learning. But what she needed to learn could have been achieved a little more easily. There were power struggles with other people too.

'In this linear life, sometimes you can't go the direct way.

'And you find all these tasks if you take these little detours.

'You have to take them on then, before you can continue your journey.'

Thinking literally, Nerida suggested, 'Like learning to walk again, as she's had to, many, many times.'

'Yeah. It was a bit slow in beginning. It was, as well, about learning about compassion.'

'Oh.' Nerida was taken aback. Mari's compassion could be deep.

But sometimes, where Nerida had an empathic response, Mari was hard and sharp, as she'd been with the Roma mother and baby Nerida gave money in Germany.

'I guess suffering often is about learning more about compassion, in this linear life,' she said.

'Yes. That's part of it.

'It can be that instead of learning about compassion for other people, you have your own experience to realise what might have been done to other people.

'It's about having the same experience.'

Does that mean Mari has chopped off people's legs and broken their backs in past life?

Nerida speculated. For Nerida in this life, she was kind, loyal and fiercely loving. Nerida knew Mari would never consciously hurt her.

Aedgar corrected himself, 'Except that suffering still doesn't necessarily result in learning about compassion, for some of these other people.'

'True. Karma, they call it,' Nerida said.

'I wouldn't exactly call it that. It's about widening horizons, about a different angle to view things and to experience things.

'If someone rules a tribe or a nation, he will say, at the end of the life: "I've experienced it all. I know all about it, about ruling."

'Of course, this being doesn't know all about ruling because you must have the experience of being ruled, as well.

'Otherwise, how can you say, "I know about all of it?"

'These ruling people have to learn that they don't know everything.

'No one ever does.

'It's all about learning, having different experiences on different sides of the wall, so to say. You have to be the conqueror, but you need to be conquered, as well, to know what it is about.'

Nerida thought about the types of soul journeys she'd read about in *Messages from Michael*. 'You speak as if you come from a clan of warriors, Aedgar. But I don't think you are a warrior.'

'No,' he said simply. 'I've watched it. I've seen people go through it. I had a few experiences myself. But I'm not a warrior.

'This life is about learning and teaching to make others understand.

'Warriors think they make others understand by hurting them. They think, "If you try to do it that way, you'll get hurt. And then you won't do it anymore." But that's not how it works.

'Warriors are used as tools to get other people's ideas realised.

'It's like they have no brain. They get an order and they follow it through. That's what they're supposed to do.

'There are no heroes amongst them. People think they are. They are not.

'They're just like a herd of sheep.'

He took a moment, then added, 'My sheep have been brighter.'

'And more loveable, perhaps,' said Nerida.

'And more useful,' said Aedgar.

He expounded, 'They had to make some of the warriors into heroes, when they already knew most of them were dead, and they would need new ones.

'They planted the idea in their heads, to recruit new people.

'So those recruits thought, "I'm gonna be a hero, one day."

'It's just a sheep ...

'It's unfair to the sheep, to say so.'

Nerida recalled, 'You were telling me that you have lived through wartime: many wars of religions.'

Aedgar warmed to the subject.

'Yeah, these religious people, that's what they love to do. "You don't believe in, what I believe in? You don't deserve to live! Except if you change your mind."

'Some did change their minds. The warriors among them tried to get up in the hierarchy and impose their own ideas.

'Which the religious ones in the hierarchy didn't like either then, not surprisingly.'

He's seen this happen. She thought of Tudor England. 'We're talking about Britain?'

'Yeah, and many other countries.

'They're still doing it. They still do.

'It's the nature of these humans.

'The weapons they use to fight each other will change, but the behaviour won't, not for a long time (talking in your terms).'

The tone and content of his message threatened Nerida with despair. *No chance of peace, then? This doesn't feel very spiritual.*

She asked, 'You are not optimistic about a breakthrough in the near future them, in my terms, in the consciousness of humans?'

Aedgar responded to her quiet yearning. 'There will be changes in some areas of this planet—and it won't be the areas where you expect it to happen. It will be a surprise.'

'I hope we can part of those changes.'

'You will. I am here to teach.'

The upside of his honesty and directness was that when he said something she liked, Nerida felt her energy lift. She trusted him.

'Perhaps we'll go to India one day, Aedgar.'

'Why?'

'There are lots of people who like to learn, there.'

Nerida journeyed in India as young woman, found it appalling, awe-inspiring and fascinating. She journeyed through the territories of some of India's myriad cultures.

She took her children there when they were teenagers.

Her daughter Ruby learned about protecting herself in a rough environment and using spices.

Sonboy Jim learned to smoke hashish. And manage dysentery. Lessons Nerida herself had learned there, in part, when she was younger. (She learned to smoke hashish in Sydney.)

But they'd all learned cross-cultural skills.

Now, Aedgar said of the peoples in India, 'They need to learn a lot. They have been held back, by ruling people, from using their brains. This will take a lot of learning, studying, training.'

That's disappointing. 'You're suggesting we start among better educated groups of people?'

'Yes. You will need many more people to help you to educate other people.'

There was a sudden, load noise above her head. A big lizard, a goanna, lived in their roof. Claws scratched. She heard its tail drag inside the ceiling. Aedgar was not distracted.

'There are a few good people up in the mountains.'

'The mountains on this island?' Nerida thought that sounded odd.

'No. I am talking about **mountains**.'

'Real mountains?' She laughed.

'Very high mountains.'

'Ah. The Himalaya?' She'd seen them from Nepal and Himachal Pradesh, in India. *Gods come to earth.*

'Yes,' he answered. 'And there are a few wise people in the mountains of the Americas. And some on tiny islands close to the Americas.'

'Hawaii or the Caribbean? East or west?' *Surely there are wise people in all those places.*

'Where they use to touch. The Americas, they used to touch, the south and the north. In this area, further down south and then all the way up in the far north of it.'

She tried to follow his hands, making a map in her mind's eye. In the Central American countries. And then up with the Indigenous peoples of the Arctic. 'In the very cold part?'

'In the extreme part. It can get very cold, but not all the time,' he agreed. 'They have very long nights and then very long days.'

'I know that place, yes. Well, Mari and I are good travellers.'

'Yes. Could be useful … Travelling would be a good way to teach.

'You should try to do big distances with the metal bird you told me about, but you should use slower travel for the rest of it. This will give you more opportunity to talk to people. Because if you use this bird-like thing to go from one place to the next, you miss out on meeting all of the people down on the planet.'

'And talking to people face-to-face is the best way to teach?'

'If you get them to listen. But you will find people who are eager to learn.'

'Yes, we will.'

'I'm looking forward to it,' he said.

'Me too. I'm excited. I'm excited to see how things unfold to allow us to do this work.'

How will we find the money to live to be able to do these things?

She loved the idea that she might not always have to work this hard. Aedgar spoke with patience. 'It will work out.'

'And there are people looking for us already, wanting to meet you,' she said.

'I'm sure.'

'One of my brothers is already keen. A fellow named Greg, he's a healer. I talked to Monica about him.'

'Yes. Might be the type.'

'Yes, he's very open.'

'No, visually, it might be the type. He favoured this type of man.'

Nerida laughed. 'You mean Aiden liked this type of look that Greg has.' Her cousin- brother was dark, slim and handsome.

'Indeed.'

'Mari saw you when she was gazing into a crystal the other morning. Were you aware of that?'

'Yes, I was there,' he said.

'Very handsome dark man, she said, with a little beard.'

'Yes.'

'Yes, I said, "I'm sure that's Aedgar." She said there was an older man in the crystal as well.'

'That's me, too.'

'I thought it might be. In your Druid form, perhaps.'

'In an earlier stage, a while ago. Quite a while ago.'

Nerida suddenly felt the heat in the room. The sun was low, shining directly in the front

wall of the house. Orange light came through the blinds.

'Are you able to check in with Mari, to see how her body's going? Do we need to take a break?'

'We might need to stop,' he said. 'Continue another time. It's very dry, makes it difficult to talk.'

'I'll encourage her to drink.' Nerida nagged her wife to drink.

Mari didn't like drinking water, so Nerida was always finding new cordials for her, checking she had her bottle beside the bed at night, in the car and in her pack.

'I think you can't drink the amounts needed to change this. You can never drink enough,' he croaked.

'Thank you so much for your efforts. Always a pleasure and a delight,' she said politely. She appreciated the love she felt when he was there, even if his words could be grim.

'For me too. Talk to you another time.'

The sunset was gorgeous, with rippling pink-orange clouds in the west. The season was changing. storms and rain would come soon.

After she had some of the drink Nerida pressed on her, Mari went outside with her camera.

She planned to photograph the Rock from the backyard. Stars were just coming out. The yard was alive in the evening.

A fine drizzle soaked the roots of the citrus tree. The irrigation was on. A superb fairy wren glinted luminous blue, stepping between bougainvillea spikes, catching insects.

The male bird was splendid, chirping. His azure and turquoise feathers shone in the light of Mari's small torch.

Mari came back into the house elated.

She said, 'I felt like the energy of Aedgar was in that tiny wren. He moved his head as I talked to him. And jumped to me.'

Nerida was reading about politics in the weekend newspaper. 'Mhmm,' she murmured.

Mari's seeing Aedgar everywhere lately. First in crystals, now in a bird in the yard.

EIGHTEEN

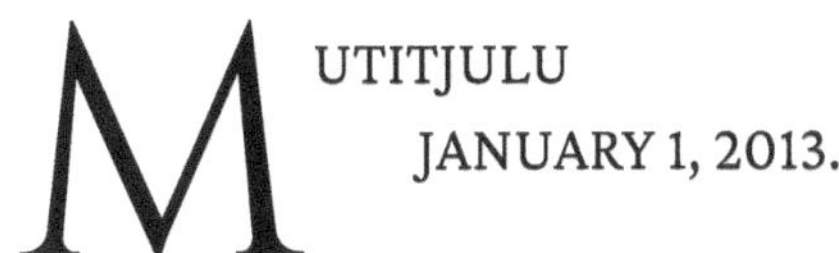

M UTITJULU
JANUARY 1, 2013.

THE HOLIDAYS ARRIVED. On Christmas Eve, the Community rang with shouting, still clanging, banging and roaring after midnight.

Mari and Nerida were up, drinking sparkling apple juice, after a supper of smoked salmon they'd bought on their last trip to Alice. Mari boiled and baked bagels with poppyseed. They even had horse-radish, brought from Sydney in November.

They heard a woman hollering. A man's voice growling. Glass shattering and the sound of metal crashing on metal. More people chastising and reprimanding the ones who were fighting.

Nerida had her phone nearby, kept it close when they went to bed. But the nurses didn't call.

On Christmas Day Claire popped in for one of Mari's excellent coffees. 'Black and strong, like me,' she said, 'with just a dash of milk.' She sat at their kitchen table and beamed. 'Is there any kek?'

Mari had baked bee-sting cake, with a crust of toffee-coated almonds. And vanilla pudding, not too sweet, between its yeasty layers.

'My favourite,' Claire said, tucking in. Finishing her first bite, she licked pudding from her finger. 'The Blair sisters' love god burned Trudi's car last night. You musta heard the ruckus! Did you know he burned Kitty's car out of town the Friday before last?'

'Jesus. Really?' Nerida was relieved that the fighting involved damage to property rather than to human bodies.

'But Community people really need their cars. What the fuck is he thinking?' Mari said from the kitchen.

'Mm, not much thinking,' said Claire, chewing. 'You can see it by the road, just before the turnoff to Mulga Park.

'This cake is delicious! I don't know how you do it, Mari.'

Mari sat down with Claire, stirring coconut sugar into her own foamy latte. 'You know I don't like it that the government made Muti into a 'dry' community in the Intervention. We can't have alcohol in the house, or the car. Nerida would immediately lose her job if we did.'

Claire understood. She played with the pudding with her spoon.

'That means for me that I'm not even allowed to use tiny amounts of "Kirschwasser" for my black forest cake.'

'Kirschwasser? Cherry water?' Claire understood some German from Papua New Guinea. There was a German influence in the national language there, *Tok Pisin*.

'Cherry Schnaps, yeah. We don't drink, so we thought the ban on alcohol wouldn't be a problem for us, but a black forest cake without that little bit of special taste just isn't the same.'

'The Intervention is corrosive. It's a mind fuck,' Nerida said. 'Mari and I watched a current affairs show on telly last night. The panel was discussing censorship of pornography and erotica.'

Mari said, 'Whether porn was bad and how it might influence teenagers ... I was like "Oh my god! I have to change the channel because people mention the 'p' word all the time." I said, "In the city, they'll know what we watch." But she told me it's okay. No one's watching. We're allowed.'

Nerida tilted her head and reminded Claire, 'It doesn't help that there's a nanny program on our internet. Like, I organise meetings of lesbian doctors. When I open the web page of our organisation I get a bright red wall of censorship. Same for sex education pages. It's nasty.'

A week later, on New Year's Eve, Mari used a timer to take a photo of herself with Nerida. They held plastic wine glasses of sparkling grape juice in front of the moonlit Rock.

They ate New Year's pretzels Mari made, with unsalted butter.

That morning, Mari started on a portrait of them both from the photo, sketching it out on canvas. She blocked out the colours through the early afternoon, not eating, so she was able to say later that she'd like to try channelling.

Nerida's inner child was always pleased when Mari was inspired by her. Mari made her feel pretty, her portraits were flattering but not false, showing something of the subject's spirit. Being loved through Mari's art was healing.

They settled at the kitchen table. Mari tied her black curls back into a ponytail. She closed her eyes and went into trance quickly and easily.

Nerida arranged her notebook and found a pen, switched on her recording device, and welcomed Aedgar back.

'Good to be here,' he said.

'It's the first of January 2013.'

'Come a long way ... Two thousand thirteen.' He said the numbers slowly. 'Is it cold?'

'I just turned off a machine that makes the air colder.'

'It's January. It's cold,' he insisted.

'And yet it's hot. Because we're on the southern half of the planet. So, it's midsummer.'

'Summer in January? Strange thought.'

'Strange for Mari, too. She grew up in Europe.'

'I was in Bristol. That's in Europe.'

Nerida smiled. 'Mari thinks a hot Christmas makes no sense.'

'It's a foreign thought.'

'I heard that you visited Mari when she was a little child.' Monica mentioned it when she introduced Aedgar.

'I did. I did be there at an early age. Had to make sure some things went right.'

'For example?'

'Growing old enough for us. Being able to get all the experience that's needed. Just life's experiences. And learning from them.'

'Like training?'

Aedgar said, 'It's not a program. Some learn from life, some don't.'

'Surely, we all learn eventually. Every soul evolves.' Nerida had that optimism. It had become a core value. *Or is that faith a brittle shell? A mask I needed to behave and be respected as a doctor.*

'Some don't,' he said. 'They have to do things many times and yet they still don't know.'

She had difficulty processing that. *Some souls don't learn. Some souls don't evolve.*

As usual in that situation, she brought up something else. 'Keep the conversation going. Keep them engaged,' Trevor Weaver had said.

'Tell me about New Year's celebrations in Bristol.'

'Singing, drinking, dancing.

'Sometimes fighting after too much drinking ... or dancing with the wrong person.'

'Some things never change.' Nerida smiled.

'No, they still do it. It's in the nature of humans.'

Nerida didn't like generalisations about humans, but she accepted that one.

'Mari and I are quite abstemious,' she said wryly. 'We're living in a place where the people are not allowed to drink alcohol.'

'Who decides?'

'The government.'

Aedgar was thoughtful. 'Back then it was decided by poverty or wealth.

'Some rulers brought out alcohol and drinks as a cheap form of keeping the people happy.

'They should be able to decide if they want to drink or not for themselves. It's a sad place if you can't make these decisions.'

'Yes. It means people don't have a sense of control in their lives,' she agreed.

'Some people don't have it, even if they think they do.

'It's quite a large number who don't know.'

Who aren't aware that they have no control? Or need to know that they could have control in their lives? Nerida wondered.

Before she could ask, he said, 'So, what did you decide for the upcoming future, to do?'

'Well, I hope to continue to expand my energy and my knowledge. I hope to continue to support Mari to be good at this work. I hope to continue to document this work, so that others can learn from it and experience it. I hope to continue to get to know you better.'

'Good idea,' he said. 'It will happen. We are happy to do this work.'

'Mari is too. She and I feel, I think it's fair to say, that this is something we are on Earth to do.'

'There is quite a bit of truth to that.'

'I hope our lives can be so arranged that we can do more of this more comfortably and with joy.' She needed relief from the pressure of working full-time in such a demanding job. Perhaps Mari needed relief from such a harsh environment.

'It will come. There will be more. There will be times when you think it would be less. 'There is a lot to do. We need to change some things.'

What does he mean more or less? Channelled material? Impact? Money?

She asked, 'You mean on the world scale? Or on the more modest scale of what Mari and I need to change to be able to work better?'

'We are talking about big things here.' The voice was deep and resonant.

'What would you like to see in the world, Aedgar? What kind of world would you like to help create?'

'A world that's in balance.

'Balance needs to be achieved for this planet and for the living beings on it.

'It will make life easier.'

'And more joyous,' she said, always looking for ease and fun.

'As it should be. But things need to be eliminated.'

That made Nerida nervous. 'What would you like to see eliminated?'

'We'll get to this later. We are still working on basic communication.'

She was relieved to hear that he felt that way, too. 'Yes. And one wants to be precise.'

'You have to be,' he concurred. 'There will be individuals seeking the proof of it. We need to be accurate to be able to prove what we do.

'It will take a while to understand, because the people who need to understand this are not the most intelligent people.'

She laughed.

'You seem to know who I'm talking about.'

'I have had some experience with some who are not the most intelligent people,' she said.

'Oh, you find them everywhere. But mostly on top, on the top levels of everything, cheating their way through. They make the intelligent people work for them, claiming their knowledge as their own.

'But they are not intelligent. They take the knowledge out of context, so it doesn't work anymore.

'They don't realise it. It's the lack of intelligence.

'They steal ideas from other people. They try to make them their own, but in trying to change it to make it sound or look different, they thus eliminate the good parts of it. It's happening all the time.'

How to change them, then? 'If these people are not intelligent, and we know they're not, is there a psychological or experiential means to help them understand?'

Aedgar surprised her by saying, 'You have to trick them. You can get them with their own thoughts. You take their stupid parts, make them believe it's the good thing and let them announce it to the world, so people will know about their lack of intelligence.

'It's like they eliminate themselves.

'You just have to give them ideas that they think are worth stealing and making their own.'

'I like your imagination,' she said.

'It's not imagination. It's how it works. You will see. It will happen.

'But we will need some help to do it. We must find the right people at the right time.

There are some good people around.'

Nerida agreed. 'There are. I find them everywhere.'

Aedgar warmed to the topic. 'They're mostly kept "small," so to say. And "stupid," so to say. They are not, but that's what the people with the lack of intelligence say about them.

'So, you won't find the good people in important positions.

'They need to get there.'

'I'm interested in the tricky strategy.' She smiled slowly.

'It will reveal itself in the future,' the spirit granted.

She wasn't sure that this was what she understood as a spiritual approach. *What about unconditional love and forgiveness and all that?* 'It promises to be fun,' she said.

'Oh, it will be. It will be fun to watch it: how they are destroying themselves and only realising it, once it's too late. It will be very satisfying.'

'Yes.' She stood up.

'I have to turn the oven down, because otherwise the food will get burnt. I'm going to come back to you.'

She went to the kitchen to do so.

'My Mari is a great cook,' she said, returning.

'We can sense that. It is a good decision for this body. It's easier to talk if it's not that dry. The sense of smell keeps it moist.'

'So food in the oven when we're channelling is not a bad thing?'

'I don't use food but it helps with the talking.'

'How would you describe this process, whereby you come into this body and are able to talk to me?'

'I use the entrance on top of the head to slide into this body. I am around most of the time.' He spoke mildly, as one would discuss growing tomatoes.

'Have you been around a lot of time during our lives, Mari's and mine?'

'Sometimes. Not always. I have been hoping for this opportunity. I've given guidance to get there. But sometimes the spirit ventured away further than I would have liked. So it wasn't always clear whether it would work out or not.'

'Hmm. Nothing is predetermined.' *Spirits or souls will make plans … but we always have free choice in this linear life, as Aedgar and Monica call it. I guess they call it 'linear' because of the way we see ourselves on a timeline.*

Nothing is predetermined, he agreed. 'You can create an opportunity, but you never know if it's taken up. It was close several times, but further away other times.'

'I know Mari explored shamanism at one stage and felt a resonance with that.'

'It was part of an experience to learn. Some so-called stupid, foolish things happened. She felt inadequate because other people were talking about experiences during the sessions that they never had. They just got all too excited, wanting it to be that way.'

'And so she discounted her genuine experience,' Nerida said.

'Yes. She wasn't sure. She thought, listening to the other people, that there should have been more to it. Some people told all sorts of stories: funny experiences, great encounters.

'She saw these whales. She thought she was dreaming, because she had seen it before, in this linear life. So she thought it was just a dream of something she had experienced; or a place she would rather be, which wasn't the case.

'It wasn't a dream; not in the way you see dreams here.'

Nerida tried to figure it out. 'She was actually with the whales again?'

'In a manner of speaking, yes.

'Yeah, other people in her class had funny stories.

'Some people can get really silly, given the opportunity. Some of them had genuine experiences, but those were the less vivid stories. There is an expansion of imagination going on in some people, which doesn't describe their experience. It's far away from it. But it makes them interesting, they think. It's something you can't prove; not with their available tools.'

Nerida sipped her tangy tea of rosehip and hibiscus flowers. It was cool. She said, 'So you're interested in science, Aedgar?'

'Yes.'

'I'm glad of that.'

'We have to establish some basics with this one here,' he said. 'She's never been prepared for, you would call it, "proper" science.

'But there will be some other science that you don't know about.

'It will take time. You should be patient.'

'I try to be.'

'It's hard for you. You're not the most patient person I've met.'

Nerida thought she was very patient. People said she was, but that was compared to other doctors. 'But I'm not the most impatient person you've met, either,' she said.

'There are a few different ones,' he allowed, oddly. Patiently. Dogs were barking excitedly outside.

'You have a hunt going on there?' Aedgar asked.

'No. The dogs are barking because the moon is rising. We have packs of dogs in this community. They live around the camps and houses.'

'So they are not used for hunting?'

'Some of them are hunting dogs. They hunt the rabbits around here.'

Aedgar said, 'It would be a waste not to use them.'

'It's true. There are some good dogs. People take them to hunt kangaroo.'

Aedgar listened to the yapping, growling and howling. 'There are some not so good ones around too.'

'There are. There are some very sad dogs, in poor condition.'

Aedgar commented, 'You shouldn't have dogs if you can't care for them. Even the poorest people back then had dogs which were well cared for. It's not about wealth. It's about wanting to care for them.'

'Some people like to have a dog that's worse off than they are,' Nerida supposed.

'That's sad, for the dog as well as the person. Probably more so for the dog,' he said.

'They get excited when the moon rises,' Nerida said.

Aedgar replied, 'There's obviously not much else to get excited about here.'

'It's not a very exciting little town. Most of the time, not much happens.'

'This doesn't have to be a bad thing,' he observed.

'Mhmm. Most of the time I like it that way.'

Aedgar said, 'But you feel deprived. You need to have things going on and happening.'

Nerida, always trying to improve herself, said, 'I'm trying to be less attracted and interested in drama.'

'Oh, you don't feel deprived of drama,' he said. 'You feel deprived of...dancing!'

Oh, he is charming. She laughed.

'Drinking...'

'Music,' she added.

'Yes.'

'You're right.' She smiled at him through Mari's closed eyelids. 'But these things will come to me soon enough, again.'

Then, she asked, 'How about Mari? Is she deprived of anything?'

'Not at this time.

'At times there was the feeling of being cheated, of not having a proper life. Being forced to sit still, so to say, while the world kept turning. The feeling that life happens without her, the feeling of not being part of it anymore.'

Nerida felt the bleak unhappiness of that.

'Many have felt that way I think. Still do,' she said. *All the lonely people* sang in her head.

'True. But plenty get away with a shorter period.'

'Yes. She had a very long, hard time of it,' Nerida said. Her wife endured surgeries and long hospitalisations from infancy, in a time when children were said not to feel pain. It was a kind of torture, in the name of her own good.

Then, in the prime of young adulthood, when she worked as a diving instructor in the Maldives, she had the accident that eventually led to the amputation of her ankle and foot.

That was not a clean cut. She suffered over a dozen surgeries after the accident. Her real injuries, she eventually found out, were the result of malpractice.

It took over a decade to sue the high-ranking doctor who had wounded her, demeaned her and lied to her.

He had also injured and deceived many others.

Aedgar said, 'A very hard time. More than once.'

'In more than one lifetime you mean?'

'In this life. Many times.'

'I'm so grateful she doesn't feel that way anymore,' Nerida said sincerely. Mari had been suicidal only a few years before they met.

She'd lost the job she loved and the respect and glowing health that went with it.

Her relationship was barren. Her erstwhile partner turned her back on Mari and was having an affair but wouldn't admit it. Meagre welfare payments she was meant to subsist on came with strings attached. The government was constantly telling her what she couldn't do.

'Once the right path is chosen, it gets easier,' Aedgar said gently. 'But it can be a long way to get to the path. Some people never get on it. Then they have to try again.

'Some people have their path right in front of their nose, all their lives, without ever realising it.

'They feel really sad once it's shown to them, revealed. It's hard to see that the path was there all the time.'

The poignancy of that situation made Nerida's chest ache. She felt tears of compassion welling. And there was deep gratitude for her own sense of connection and purpose.

Nerida saw the waning moon at the top of the kitchen window, over the blind.

'What are you experiencing Aedgar?'

'Shoulders are getting tense. The head is getting heavy.'

'Hmm. Perhaps it's time to fare you well again. I never really want to.'

'I enjoy it too, so very much. It's been a wait.'

'We'll talk again soon then.'

'Talk to you another time,' he said.

He doesn't know what 'soon' means, Nerida supposed. *The way he sees time.*

She told Mari over dinner. 'He said, "Once the path is chosen, it gets easier." Could be true for us.'

NINETEEN

MUTITJULU
FRIDAY JANUARY 11, 2013

DESPITE SPORADIC FIGHTING, Mutitjulu was a profoundly peaceful place. Behind the dogs barking, loud calls to children or vigorous arguments across a road, lay deep, quiet, desert life.

The susurration of the wind through the trees and grasses was like the hush and crash of the sea. In the evenings, Nerida tried to imagine the thousands of miles of sand hills—the Pit name was *tali*—that the wind crossed to reach them. The isolation was soothing. Nature ruled. Life was undeniably of the earth's dominion.

Sometimes cooler breezes followed the clouds, swirling into willy-willies or storms.

On the mornings when she was disciplined enough, Nerida did ten minutes of yoga. She did gentle poses, the cat and dog. Her favourite was the corpse pose. Occasionally she was ambitious: lifting a leg towards the sky in a half-moon pose, or holding onto her feet behind her, soft belly stretched on the floor, to make a bridge. She arched her back, kneeling, in camel pose.

The season was changing. *Itjanu* meant clouds came in quickly from the east to cover the sky.

It gave Mari confidence when she called the rain.

She enjoyed the water-centred painting in their room by Blossom Wandering. It showed, with its blues and mauves, that Blossom was from one of the northern-western clans, as well as from here. Artists at Muti didn't often use those colours then.

'She didn't really give it to me,' Mari told Nerida. 'She asked me for money for it later.'

'That's a shame,' Nerida said.

'Quite a trick, isn't it? Give someone a gift then ask for payment when you're in the shop.'

'I guess she needed the money and thought you were worth a try. She might've asked you even if she hadn't given you the painting, because you are friends.' Nerida had an inkling of how extensive Blossom's family responsibilities were. Her Gate Money was always very widely distributed. Money from her artwork probably was, too.

'She's the only one who's ever asked you for money, though.'

Mob usually left Mari alone. She often had a stern look, being in pain. *Or it's her imposing energy*, Nerida thought.

One day, Mari's displaced paintings showed up, four of the five that were missing, resting against one of the big bins behind the shop. They were dusty and a bit beaten around.

The painting still missing was an intricate abstract pattern, a mesmerising tessellation with gorgeous colours. Mari used metallic paints she'd bought in Alice from the sale of her paintings at the small gallery there. It had aqua and turquoise with yellow, peach, coral red and blue.

The found paintings seemed forlorn, like neglected animals, leaning against a concrete wall in their house without that one.

'I guess the thief must've liked it too much,' Nerida offered lamely. 'It's one of the best, for sure.'

'The cops should search the houses. It's not fair! People here should value paintings.'

'Maybe someone was jealous,' Nerida said. She put the word around that Mari was crying, pulling at her hair for that painting.

She couldn't stand the idea of cop raids being launched, even for Mari. She had bitter memories of such behaviour—cops damaging homes, hurting people in the name of a search—from inner-city Sydney in the 90s.

'I'm never doing any business with Bull again,' Mari said.

Storms could come from any direction. Truly, Uluru felt like the centre of the world, then. The Rock attracted lightning. Winds came. The cooler air they brought was blissful.

Birds abounded. Their chorus called Nerida out of the house at sunrise. A cup of tea as Uluru came out of the dark blue starry sky into bright day made her conscious of her privilege. She and Mari appreciated daily the opportunity granted them in being there.

Wally Caldish, next door, a wood-carver, rose early every morning and made a fire on his verandah for a cup of tea. Nerida liked the smell of the woodsmoke, sharing the peace.

'My parents used to tell the children stories at that time of day,' he told her one morning. 'Just before the sun came up, when they were still sleepy, us kids heard stories of animals, creation beings and Land. *Tjukurpa.*'

It made that time of the morning feel even more special to her. She wished she'd known about that when her children were little.

The only time Mari practised stillness was with her camera, speaking calmly to reassure the highly-strung desert birds that she meant them no harm. She adored the flocks of brilliant green budgerigars that swooped through in good rain years. The contrast of their colours against the red stone of Uluru lit her up with pleasure.

Flocks of tiny wrens came too. But Mari could distinguish the budgies calls from the nyii-nyii and other birds. She'd wake early, cracking the blind apart, scanning for the flashes of bright green. 'I heard budgies. Did you hear them?'

Branches of stiff mulga trees scratched the walls and roof of their house. White-browed birds with striped bellies hopped, hunting insects. Their call was like crickets chirping.

Mari worked hard to keep the dust out of the house, sweeping a couple of times a day.

She put seals on the bottoms of the doors to keep animals and insects out. Sometimes the wooden tiles she painted and put in the ceiling to cover the old aircon vents were lifted by the wind and fell with a clatter, letting in dust.

Mari was frustrated by a drip from the old air-con which made the constant algae-growing puddle next to the rear house wall.

The wall stayed intact if you didn't touch it.

Plumbing was an issue all over the community. Even in their luxurious house populated by only two, the pipes were too shallow to drain properly. When Nerida drained the small bath, dirty water from neighbouring houses came up the drain with her own, flooding the bathroom floor. Not only bath water came up.

Mari railed, 'Why do you insist on having baths where there is so little water and the dirty water floods the floor every time you pull the plug?'

'It relaxes me,' Nerida said defensively. Sometimes she wanted quiet time apart from everyone, including Mari.

'And then you go outside to water invisible things in the garden, pretending every day you can see some tiny green spot where you put seeds weeks ago. I can't see a thing. Nothing ever grows anywhere here,' Mari threw her hands up.

'We are so lucky to have this house and the yard,' Nerida said.

'Knowing that other people here live in asbestos-ridden hovels doesn't help with the problems in this one,' Mari countered and strode in to the kitchen, where she noisily did the dishes.

The plumbing problem was worse in the clinic, where the toilet drains blocked. The nurses put on long gloves, like vet's gloves, to clear them. Nerida offered to do it, but only had to do it once. Her thankfulness to the nurses grew even greater after that.

The nurses, in turn, appreciated Dr Nerida Green and her wife. They depended on Nerida for her skills. Through the clinic, she made a difference in people's lives, whether it was finding a medicine they could tolerate or a power card so that they had electricity.

She arranged for a woman and her partner to go to Adelaide when an ultrasound showed that their unborn baby could have a heart defect needing surgery.

The bus to Alice Springs (to fly to Adelaide) was in two days. There were no flights from Yulara to Alice. So, Mari drove them.

Sometimes Mari met an ambulance from Alice Springs halfway to hand a patient over if Nerida couldn't get them on a flight.

She was an excellent driver. People felt safe with her.

The Blair sisters had missed the bus because Barry, the entrepreneurial neighbour, employed then as the clinic driver (and getting paid for that), did not have the caring or determination, or the cross-cultural or cross-gender skills, to get them on the bus.

Mari drove them five hundred kilometres in her convertible.

At the hospital, an ICU doctor shouted to force the women to understand they should agree to making their elder sister, now brain dead, an organ donor. She spoke up for them. Berated him.

'People don't understand you, just because you raise you voice.'

The women needed a Pitjantjatjara interpreter, but the doctor didn't have the resourcefulness (or the will) to find one.

His idea of compassion was to throw a box of tissues at the women. He vented frustration on them.

'Your sister is dead! We need you to sign this paper for an operation for her!'

The women were mystified, appalled. Painfully confused. 'She's dead,' Kitty whispered.

'But she's needing that operation!' her sister argued back. Her breathing came in jagged movements.

'Just because you've got dark skin doesn't mean you have cultural intelligence,' Mari hissed at the doctor, disgusted.

She called Nerida for advice.

'What a fuck up. He needs training. Organ donation is an offer we make to the family, not a demand. Do you want me to talk to the ICU team?' Nerida said.

Mari screwed up her courage, fired by her anger at injustice.

She took the women to their sister's bedside and patiently, tearfully, helped them understand that it was only the machine keeping her body alive. She had a massive bleed in her brain that killed her. Their sister's spirit had left her body behind ...

ON THE WAY home to Muti the next day there were fights over who got to travel in Mari's car. Two men at the fuel station jumped into the back as if Mari was a taxi driver.

One ate an ice cream, the other a pie. She was unable to budge them until her real passengers came back onto the scene.

'Paa! Hey! This one is my **mutaka**!' Kitty Blair shouted. They drove the men out of the motorcar with spirited yelling and flinging of hands.

'This is a nice mutaka,' Kitty said to Mari later, breaking out of her pensive grief.

'It's a twenty-year-old motorcar,' Mari said. 'Cost less than a Toyota.'

'Yeah, but it's a European car,' the woman said.

It was the only time Mari had heard an Anangu person say that a European thing could be good.

• • •

At home, Claire and Becca took turns living in the little house behind the doctor's.

Sometimes they worked together.

Or they alternated work in six-week stints with a short handover.

Each was the one who knew what was going on in the clinic and with the people, while temporary nurses came and went.

The clinic had no manager. The Community Business Manager Nerida met in 2007 (the former mining PA who was given the job as part of the Intervention) came back from the city that year to find his office burnt down. Muti had trouble recruiting managers since.

Claire, Bec, Jasmine and Nerida did a good job running the clinic themselves. Claire was onto ordering supplies and keeping their little pharmacy stocked. Rebecca was good with the admin workers and maintenance people they sometimes recruited from the Community.

And Jasmine kept the waiting room in order. People were scared of her, probably, since they found out that she'd been in jail for hitting her former partner with an iron bar. He had it coming—had been violent for years. He'd knocked her teeth out, dislocated her shoulder. 'Police didn't do anything until I hit him!' Jasmine told Nerida. 'Then I was the one, ended up in jail.'

Selkie and her family lived in a cosy hut next door to Mari and Nerida. An exceptional woman, she said she may have been 'white', from the urban coast. She came into the Community for love and nursed her first husband when he became terminally ill.

She stayed at Mutitjulu after he passed, which intrigued Nerida. Selkie spent years studying to become an interpreter in Pitjantjatjara. Nerida tried to persuade her to work at the clinic, where her skills would have been a powerful force for good. But management in Alice Springs would never pay Selkie properly. She worked there for months at a time, put in her time sheets, and never was properly paid. It was just like they did to Mari, Nerida realised after a year or so. *That organisation has to be corrupt.*

Behind the blue house and sharing the side back fence, Barry had people come to camp in his yard for top-dollar cultural tours. He strummed his guitar and sang them ditties in other Aboriginal languages, as well as his top twenty hit. Mari came in laughing from the yard, sometimes. She was convinced that he was making the languages up.

'He has been to other places and had workshops with the young ones, teaching guitar.' Nerida strove to be fair and remain respectful. Barry was one of her patients. If the main thing he came to her for was a blue diamond pill to make his cock stand up, that was nothing she would ever tell anyone, even Mari.

Sometimes when the camp was on, young women under Barry's spell sat on the dirt road behind the house to meditate among the dog shit, as Mari noted. They had to be roused and moved so that the women could get their cars out.

Still, Nerida and Mari were content.

The house's fenced yard meant the house felt secure. Previous tenants started a garden which came back to life with evening water-ing. High summer brought beans, herbs, even lettuce. And a bountiful crop of sweet citrus from a sturdy little tree.

Mari's robust convertible held its own under the carport out the back next to Nerida's work car, a four-wheel drive sturdy enough for bush-bashing or fording the dirt roads which flooded a couple of times a year. When a big rain came their yard turned into a river that threatened to go right through the house. The house was probably built on a creek bed.

Nerida could just imagine a local saying to the Health Depart-ment, 'Sure, build there, that's a good spot. Great view of the Rock.'

In the early evenings Nerida worked late alone at the clinic.

Barring emergencies, she took long lunches with Mari, catching up on the day's news, sometimes having a nap or an excursion. Refreshed, she did extra hours of work at the end of the day.

· · ·

In the midst of this extraordinary life were the conversations with Aedgar.

Nerida realised that he found ways to bring her delight, to help her bear the harsh reality in his messages. She remained defensive a lot of the time, conscious of her limitations, feeling fear and shame.

He (or they) coaxed and pleased her. But the spirit's commitment to truth telling never wavered.

Nerida needed to grow. She was not sure who or what she was becoming.

One hot Friday evening after work, as Nerida watered the orange tree, Mari came outside with her camera.

'Come and see,' she called softly from across the yard.

In the algae-riddled puddle from the constant drip of the old air-conditioner that was corroding the laundry wall, the superb blue fairy wren splashed around. He was splendid, with brilliant feathers shimmering as he bathed and drank.

He flitted up into the spiky branches of the mulga tree next to the puddle. They saw him canoodling with a female in there.

The female wren was brown, drab as a sparrow. She blended into the tree, so that she was nearly invisible. They were little balls of fluffy feathers.

Sweet and happy, they rubbed beaks and snuggled.

After a few minutes standing quietly there, her arm around her wife's waist, Nerida's back ached. She went inside.

Mari was so much more patient. When she was waiting for a photo or a painting was coming together, she was able to ignore the pain in her body.

She came inside twenty minutes later, looking at her camera with satisfaction. Mari said, 'I felt like the energies of Aedgar and Monica—she was Aiden then, wasn't she? I felt like they were in those cute, little wrens. Do you think they could do that? Come into a bird's body?

'They seemed attracted. It was like they listened when I talked to them.

'The blue one took off. He was jumping all over the cars. That bird really seemed to be inspecting your car, looking down under the wheel arches at your tyres.'

Nerida was reading the newspaper again, doing a crossword. 'Uhuh,' she murmured. 'Yeah. Maybe.'

That night when Nerida was brushing her teeth there was a crash and a clatter in the back yard.

Mari came to the bathroom door. 'What was that?'

The women went outside with the torch. It was the night of the new moon, softer and darker than a peaceful mind. The stars were showing their colours.

Far above, clouds of red, blue and silver gases made isles and paths through the Milky Way. Mari's vibration felt deeply calm.

'I should bring the camera out,' she said softly.

They checked the perimeter of the yard, stepping carefully to avoid the thorny bougainvillea branches that spilled over the fences. Nerida felt her rubber thongs grabbing thorns of another devilish weed sprawled and spreading in the red dirt.

'What's that?' Mari said, astonished.

In the corner near the wrens' pond, propped against Mari's old Mercedes, was her final misplaced painting, returned. Its gold, turquoise and blue paint glittered in the mild beam of the torch.

CHAPTER

TWENTY

Mutitjulu
SATURDAY JAN 12, 2013

Nerida was called into the clinic. 'The love god needs your help, ye?' Claire said on the phone.

It was always daunting for the doctor to be brought in after hours. The nurses coped with most things, especially Claire. It meant that something extraordinary was wrong.

Nerida recognised the man who had needed benzodiazepines for withdrawal from ice, sitting quietly on the exam couch in the emergency room. He frowned deeply, subdued by pain, nursing his left arm delicately.

On examination, Nerida saw a ragged piece of his radius, the bigger bone in his forearm, sticking out of a bloody wound of smashed, bruised flesh. 'The ulna, that skinny bone in your arm, is probably cracked, too,' she told him.

'Let's give him five milligrams of morphine,' Nerida said to Claire.

250

They went to the pharmacy safe to sign a vial out. Claire drew it up while Nerida put on gloves and a mask to have a closer look at the wound.

It was surprisingly clean. 'You haven't had a fall,' she said. 'What kind of weapon did this?'

The man looked at her dolefully. 'Crowbar,' he said quietly. 'Did you get hit anywhere else? You didn't get knocked out?'

'No. Only this one, *kungka*.'

He was being polite. Anangu used 'Kungka' the way other people used 'Miss'.

Nerida corrected him firmly. '*Kungka, wiya. Minyma!*—Don't call me a young woman. I'm a mature woman.'

Claire gave him the morphine and, after five minutes to let it work, cleaned his arm around the wound with an antiseptic.

'Let's give him five milligrams of midaz, too,' Nerida requested.

The midazolam made the man sleepy. He rested.

Meanwhile, Nerida spoke to the Flying Doctors. They had a psychotic patient needing sedation to fly, as well as a deteriorating child at Tennant Creek who were their priorities, with three others also awaiting evacuation to Alice Springs hospital. They wouldn't be able to pick up their patient til tomorrow afternoon the operator said. *Probably not until the day after that,* Nerida thought.

She called Mari for advice. Her wife spent years of her childhood in orthopaedic wards.

She had a feeling for trauma and fractures—knowledge in her bones. 'You should reduce it before plastering it, if you can. It'll be safer for him to travel.'

Nerida resisted her wife's advice, even though she'd asked for it. *What does she know about the dangers of going beyond your scope of practice?*

Mari had been the de facto health worker when she was a diving instructor (and often manager) in remote places. She was better at suturing than Nerida was. She'd showed that stitching up wounds in camp dogs at the clinic with Nerida after hours. And her approach to physical manipulation was bolder.

The patient, who had been in pain all night, slept on. Nerida made herself and Claire a cup of tea, then called the orthopod in Alice Springs. 'Would you like to talk me through reducing this open fracture? It looks like this man will have to get the bus, ten hours on a bumpy road, to get there.'

They gave him more morphine. The midazolam had done its job relaxing muscles that had tightened around the wound. It didn't seem to hurt too much (the patient only stirred) when Nerida pulled steadily and strongly on his hand, her small fingers entwined with his calloused, thick ones. The jagged bones straightened, with the broken end retreating deeper into the wound. Reducing an open fracture was not something she would normally do, but Nerida followed advice and her instincts. It would help reduce the risk of infection. 'Give him two grams of ceftriaxone, too, please,' she asked Claire.

Nerida gently shook him by the shoulder to rouse him.

'These antibiotics will help for 24 hours. But we need to get you to the hospital. This needs an operation to put your arm properly together again. We must keep it very clean. The risk of infection is serious, eh.'

The patient nodded.

Claire cleaned and dressed the arm around the wound again and, fetching a bucket of warm water and strips of plaster-soaked bandage, made a back slab to protect the arm.

'Can anyone drive you to Alice?' she asked, immediately realising the low chances of that. He just looked at her, lifting his eyebrows slightly, as if to say, 'What do you think?'

'You don't have to tell me who did this. You can go to the police if you want to.'

'No,' he replied simply.

'You reckon you had it coming?' Nerida had an image of Ulises Daugherty in her mind. *Maybe he's disciplined the man when the police did nothing about the car burnings.* She didn't know who was related to who, or how, in the Community. It was better that way.

The man hung his head in a gesture of acceptance. Nerida arranged some oxycodone tablets for him. It was going to be a long ride to town. He went home to sleep until bus time.

Claire corrected Nerida when they cleaned up later. 'As I understand it, it's only Pitjantjatjara that has 'minyma' for a mature woman. Yankunytjatjara people use 'kungka' for all women. People might snicker if you growl too much about that.'

Nerida sighed. 'I'm a goose,' she said. 'Sometimes I forget that APY Lands are Anangu, Pitjantjatjara and Yankunytjatjara. Similar languages but not the same, eh? Still learning.'

'We all are,' said Claire kindly. She got up from a crouch, where she'd been sweeping bits of plaster from the floor. 'You know, I heard from old Jack that Brynn at the art shed has been cranky with Mari. Apparently, he ended up paying two hundred dollars for one of Ulises Daugherty's carvings—a big goanna. They'll sell it for twelve hundred at the gallery, mind you. I wonder if Brynn's snarling had something to do with Mari's exhibition at the cafe being cancelled without telling her.'

'Yeah, could be,' Nerida mused. 'Nasty, small-town politics here sometimes.' She tipped out the bucket of water they'd used for plastering into the steel sink, cleaned it and put it into the cupboard beneath. Wiped the sink. 'Hey, are the Blair sisters still keen on that fella after he burned their cars and all?'

Claire laughed. 'I saw Trudy at the shop. I only asked her how she was going. She told me she "bin gibap that man." Sounded strong.'

'Gibap. She gave him up. Good. One of your Kriol words.'

'Yeah, mob here have their own versions. But sometimes I think they like using mine for fun. I can't tell.'

· · ·

THAT AFTERNOON, unaware of the details of the morning's drama, Mari went into trance and channelled Aedgar.

'Hello,' Nerida said.

Aedgar cleared the throat. 'Another dry day,' he said. 'What have you been doing?'

'I've been making fermented milk.' She had kefir granules mailed to her from South Australia. They were alive, growing and working in a china pot on the kitchen bench. 'Good for you. Produces some bacteria that kill other bacteria. You can use it on the skin too, if the skin is out of balance.

'But you do need to figure out, first, where the skin imbalance is coming from. If you put it on the wrong thing, it's going to aggravate the condition.'

The living room clock ticked loudly. It was a Swiss railway clock with rainbow colours around the dial. Mari bought it in Sydney. She liked the style.

Aedgar didn't. 'Your time measurement is ticking away. Useless thing.

'Some think it might help you in this linear to survive. That you wouldn't be in line, or lined up, with the rest of the world without it. This is not true.' Then, he said, 'It is useful to navigate if you're not familiar with the stars and the universe.'

Nerida was surely not familiar with the stars or the Universe. She'd read in one of the Seth books, though, that spending a day without looking at clocks occasionally would be good for a person. 'Better to live without clocks if you can,' she said.

Aedgar was hard to please today. 'Won't be possible at this point,' he said. 'Everything and everyone is too involved in these things: these "time limits". The limitation of time ...

'They could have a closer look.

'They would realise it doesn't matter.

'But they don't know where to have this closer look or how.

'So, if you want to meet other people at this time, you can't live without it. Otherwise, the meeting up might never happen. You'd always be there in the wrong moment, so to say.'

'I think it's useful to feel that there's not really a wrong moment, that things happen in their own perfect time.' Nerida had heard that idea from one of her palliative care doctor supervisors. He was always late to come and help her on the ward. When she was cross with him, he'd say 'We're all where we need to be at the perfect time.'

It was infuriating.

But the idea gave her consolation when she was running late, which happened a lot.

Aedgar acquiesced. 'They would be there at the perfect time, if you wouldn't measure it.

'But now that they started to measure it, you would miss people over and over again.

'Because everybody has a different perception of it and a different perspective.

Depends on where you live on this planet and in which circumstance. There are many facts that influence one's understanding of time.'

Nerida recalled happily, 'I was sent (in my mind) a wonderful little song about time a few years ago. It came into my head almost intact. I wrote it down. Was that you?'

'Would it matter if I tell you? ... I know the one who did send it.'

He's mysterious. 'Very nice little song,' she said.

She was driving home from work in 2006 when the rhythm and rhyme of it came into her head. It made her feel she could be a song-writer. *This is how people get inspired.*

She adapted it. The verses were her idea. The monkey in a rock story came from the *Monkey King: Journey to the West* tales. She'd watched the *Monkey* show on television with her son, Jim, when he was small.

Jim was musical and she was disappointed that he didn't want to collaborate on writing a melody when she emailed him the song. But he was nineteen then, and living for bad food, quick sex and too much marijuana. His mother had not long moved out of the unit they'd shared. A project with her did not attract him.

She had to go to the country for her early medical years. And was happy to leave Jim to sort out his own mess, anyway. Being a boy, she thought, made him even more undisciplined and self-indulgent than she'd been at that age.

Monkey was a playful, naughty, god-like being travelling to India with a Buddhist priest (who was of indeterminate gender in the television show). Monkey was born from a rock on top of a mountain.

The gang included a greedy but good-natured pig and a clever fish. There was a horse spirit, too. They were on a mission, carrying scriptures.

Each had their vices and special, overdeveloped, powers.

Monkey flew and fought. Like the ancestor beings in *Tjukurpa*, (but the Aboriginal ancestral beings created the Land, as well as social mores).

The chorus of *The Monkey Time Song* was channelled, Nerida would say—now that she knew what channelling was.

TIME IS MY INSTRUMENT.
  Time is my toy.
  Time is stretching out to fit me in it.
  Time is my joy.

THAT MONKEY WAS STUCK in the rock five thousand years.
  He scratched with claws.
  He wet the earth with monkey tears.
  He hit his head and cracked the egg.
  He laughed out loud.
  Grew up so quick.

Now spins a stick.
Rides a pink cloud.

TIME IS MY INSTRUMENT.
　　Time is my toy.
　　Time is stretching out, so I flex in it.
　　Time is my joy.

WALLS CLOSING IN?
　　It must be time to move on out.
　　Takes time to please.
　　To grow up trees from just a sprout.
　　So, what's potential needs the time to be come real.
　　Time's exponential when you flow in what you feel.

TIME IS MY INSTRUMENT.
　　Time is my toy.
　　Time – might be an hour or a minute.
　　Time is just a ploy.

TIME IS MY INSTRUMENT.
　　Time—build and destroy.
　　Time is stretching out, so I climb in it.
　　Time is my joy.

'IT JUST NEEDED to get somewhere so it can be written down,' Aedgar said, obliquely.

'I'm looking forward to hearing people singing it too,' Nerida said. *It would have been a gift to Jim.*

'Looking forward to the words or to the people singing?' he asked. 'The music or the words?'

Nerida thought carefully. 'I'm looking forward to people playing with the ideas.'

'That's an acceptable answer. It would have been wrong just to mention the music,' he said, didactically.

Nerida was happy to have passed this little test. 'It's the concepts that really interest me.'

Aedgar concurred. 'Good,' he said. 'Music is something to express feelings or to alter them. It's not exactly the way to convey messages, even if some people think that's its purpose.

'With music you would only reach a certain amount of people because it's a matter of taste as well. So don't send messages in a musical package. It might not reach the people you want it to.'

So, I'm not going to be a songwriter, because it doesn't suit your plans? Nerida told herself to be of service. But she still thought she could become a musician or a playwright. Or an artist, like Mari. She could draw, if not as well as Mari. She had her own expressive style.

Aedgar said brightly, 'Did you realise the birds … ?

'Thought we might have a little look around because I can't see at the moment.'

Nerida took a few beats to realise what he meant.

'Aaah! Mari told me she thought that the two little birds she photographed yesterday were you and Aiden, playing and looking around!'

'Oh, just having a look around.' There was a smile in his voice.

'She'll be delighted to know that she was right. Beautiful birds.' Nerida was in high spirits now.

Aedgar said, 'Very affectionate'

'They are! Very sweet. Were you the blue bird?'

'Yes. I thought Aiden should have the pleasure as well, to move around a bit in a female body.

'Not that he doesn't know about it. But I thought that's fair—because I'm using one now.'

Nerida thought that was odd. Aiden was very often in a female body now, as Monica channelled by Dawn. *Perhaps Aedgar wanted to be the pretty boy again for a moment. As if Mari's not beautiful enough!*

Aedgar went on, 'I imagine that I saw one of these things you use to move around and cheat the time.'

'You did!' Nerida exclaimed. 'The birds had a good look at the car. Mari told me.'

'I wasn't impressed,' he said. 'I thought it would be a more vibrant thing. Nicer.

'Well, it had different wheels,' he conceded. 'They might be more useful and more comfortable than the wooden ones.

'I couldn't see what's inside.

'I just looked at the footprints. It makes long tracks, as the old wheels did. But it has a different footprint.

'It's bigger.

'Well, our wheels were much bigger in diameter, but not as wide.'

Nerida responded promptly to his tone. 'My car is a particularly ugly specimen.'

'There was more than one,' Aedgar said.

'Ah, you saw the other one, the blue one.' *Mari's Merc convertible.*

'My colour of choice,' Aedgar commented.

'That's Mari's car.

'I thought so. Better taste.'

That's not fair, even if Mari does have better taste, somehow. But that beast was for work. 'Others choose my car for me.

'People with less care for quality. Thoughtless people.'

'Is it the case,' he asked, 'that it needs more of that energy, the bigger it gets?'

'Yes.' It felt like a slap of reality.

'Oh. Not thoughtful at all,' he said.

In a moment he was happy again, she could feel it glowing in the room.

'So you have that little pond there, where the little friends can wash off the radiation. They appreciate it.'

It's gorgeous that he calls the cursed puddle from the old air-con a 'pond'. 'Mari took photographs of you two.'

'Photographs?'

How to explain? 'Pictures, captured with a machine; that can be shown to other people.'

'Oh.'

'We can put them in a book with this story,' Nerida proposed.

Aedgar tilted the head to the side, 'Will it draw something?'

'The machine opens a mechanical eye and captures the light. And then that picture can be transferred to other places to be seen by other people, onto paper or behind glass,' she explained.

'That's interesting. It's less effort doing a drawing. Can this machine catch the colours?'

'Yes.'

'Good.'

'Your colours were splendid!'

Aedgar had a small smile. 'I know.'

'We looked at other birds of that species that other people have photographed.' She and Mari had looked up blue wrens on the net after dinner. The one they'd seen was called the Splendid Blue Wren.

'We are special.'

'You are,' she said. 'Mari's been chasing that little bird for days trying to photograph it.'

'We are tricky,' Aedgar boasted happily. 'And quick ... I think the machine she used was probably not quick enough.'

'Hmm. The pictures are a little bit unfocussed because you are so fast as little birds.'

'It takes practice?' he asked.

'Mari has lots of patience. She's an excellent photographer.'

'So, you're a photographer if you know how to use this machine?'

'Yes, you could call yourself one. But she actually is one. That's the main work she does, along with her paintings. Apart from this channelling and the maintenance of our lives and our house.'

Aedgar pulled her up. 'What we have is a relationship. Not work.

'We try to expand horizons and spread knowledge. It's a team effort and it's not work.

'It will create some activities that have to be followed up and kept up with, but it's not work.'

'Good.' Nerida liked that idea, even if she was not entirely convinced.

After a half minute, Aedgar observed 'Someone's trying to gain entry.' Nerida was startled. *Who's coming?* 'At the telephone or the door?'

Aedgar's voice was light. 'It's one of the little friends with the feathers. The birds.'

'Oh, yes. They climb on the frames of the windows. We have a metal lattice on the windows, that they like to explore and there's water nearby for them, from that machine which keeps us cool inside.'

'A machine to keep you cool?' He was full of curiosity.

'That loud machine that I turn off when we begin,' she said.

'It helps to survive here, if you're here at the wrong time,' he said. 'It seems you have no choice.

'It will get better.

'Not on this day and not the next, but it's coming soon.'

His reassurance that the weather would continue to improve was calming. He stopped talking for a few minutes. She watched as Mari's eyes and eyelids twitched.

'Are you trying to open the eyes?'

CHAPTER
TWENTY-ONE

M UTITJULU
SAME DAY, 2013

'I'M TRYING to have a look around, using my senses.'

He placed the crystals on the table, then lifted Mari's hands carefully to grasp the table.

Nerida was astonished. *I didn't know he could do that.*

'Here's this nice piece of wood,' he said.

The room was quiet. Even the birds outside were still. Aedgar explored the table's edge, feeling its width and depth, extending hands to the corners. Then he used one hand to feel the other and explored Mari's face, as a blind person might, with exquisite sensitivity and confidence.

Returning to touching the hands, he felt her wrists, which were delicate. And her strong hands with their long, tapered fingers. He stopped abruptly at her gold wedding ring.

'What's that? Metal?'

’Yes.’

Nerida was engrossed as he seemed to try the muscles of Mari’s face individually. ‘She has sharp teeth, huh?’

‘There are teeth,’ he said, ‘we noticed that. No beard, of course.’

When he seemed satisfied, she asked, ‘Would you like to feel another object?’

‘What do you have?’

‘I have cups, bowls, spoons, pens, books.’

He inclined the head slightly. ‘I know spoons.’

‘There’s a spoon between your hands, a small one.’

Aedgar moved the hands across the table, meeting at the teaspoon he grabbed and held between them. ‘Metal. Not wood.

‘It’s a hard metal. We had soft kinds of metal.’ He felt the spoon. ‘You would make imprints with fingernails and you could bend them. Again, that feeling that he was smiling. ‘Wasn’t much appreciated at a pub, if you did so.

‘Some people talk and then they don’t know what to do with their hands,’ he said indulgently.

Mari sneezed hard.

‘Bless you!’

Aedgar let his amazement show: ‘I almost thought I’m gonna be blown out of here!

‘What a pleasant surprise.’

Then he observed with a shudder, ‘There are all these things attached to this body, makes it irritated—’

‘You mean like clothes and jewellery and things?’ she wondered.

‘Or just dust,’ he said.

Well, she doesn’t have lice or scabies, Nerida thought. The clock ticked. A vehicle drove by on the unsealed road outside.

‘Seems like the heat is increasing,’ he noted, ‘in the place we are here.’

Nerida agreed. ‘It’s because the cooling machine has been turned off to allow us to hear each other.’

'So you need a cooling machine to be able to live here that makes so much noise that you can't hear each other?' he said. 'That's poor technology. What energy is used for this machine?'

'Electricity.'

'Electricity like in lightning?'

Nerida sighed. 'Still generated by fossil fuels, oil and coal from the earth, even if it's not necessary to do so. We could generate it from the sun here.'

'You've got plenty of it. You could transform the radiation. It's very powerful. It's radiation coming from the earth. The Rock reflects it to protect itself. It doesn't come from the Rock, just reflects it. I told you so.'

'That might make this a particularly good place to capture the radiation from the earth,' she suggested.

'You only need to put something up that reflects it, doesn't have to be here. But it can be as easy putting rocks there to reflect the planet's radiation. Doesn't need a high level of technology.'

Rocks reflecting radiation to generate usable energy? 'Like Stonehenge?' she asked.

Aedgar agreed. 'Yes, it's a ceremonial site. It's a place with strong energy.

'It had the strongest energy in the centre because it was reflected to the centre from all sides. And it was protected from other energy because that was reflected as well, to keep it out.

Nerida was unsure. 'Hmm. By the stones?'

'Yes.'

Okay, let's talk about Stonehenge. She had a scratchy feeling, as if the coffee she'd had was too strong. 'It's a special kind of stone?' She and Mari had seen documentaries about the mystery of Stonehenge since they were children.

It was impressive, even on black and white television. She had pictures in her head of massive stones rolled on logs.

'Not very. It's a common kind of stone for the area.'

He annoyed her by making something magical, ordinary.

'But people say,' she began, feeling like an eight year old, 'the stone came from a long way from there, that it's not accessible in that area.'

He paused a beat, then asked, 'How do they know?

'It wasn't from that far away. It was quite a bit of work to get it out and transport it there. Wasn't that far. But putting them in the desired positions was a tricky thing ... I used to work with energy. Everybody who worked with energy knew about it.'

'So you visited that place during your lifetimes in Britain?'

'I did.

'You could gain energy and balance energy within the circle at a certain time of the year, a certain moment. Could use the power of the moon, the power of the earth and the rocks and stones reflected it to the centre.'

'People still try.' Nerida thought of those still holding onto Druid beliefs, doing their best to keep the ceremonies alive in their all-too-white robes.

Aedgar was not encouraging. 'It's not the same anymore as it was. The energy has shifted away from the place.

'You could have it again if one would put a similar arrangement up at another place.'

Build another Stonehenge? Is he out of his infinite mind?

He continued, 'It's like in the Americas, in the southern part. They built these big things to collect energy.'

She thought of the Mayan pyramids.

'When the energy shifted and moved, these big things didn't work anymore. So they left and went somewhere else. Happens all the time.

'Energy is not a static thing. ***It moves***. It needs to move to keep alive and powerful. If you tried the stones in England now, it wouldn't work. If you try the big stone monuments in the Americas, it doesn't work. It did back then.'

Nerida was crestfallen. *No special energy at Stonehenge anymore? Nothing is sacred.*

Behind her feeling was an intimation that New Age people would not tolerate this. *They won't like Aedgar.* And these were the people who she thought should be Aedgar's main audience. If they were ever able to go public with this experience.

'You need a sensitive soul to find the new energy spots,' Aedgar extrapolated.

'It doesn't need these huge things that they had in the Americas to work. It can be smaller because the energy is very strong. You can collect and bundle energy at these places.'

He made illustrative gestures, as if collecting and bundling energy with Mari's hands. 'But only for a certain amount of so-called time,' he said. 'And then the energy must move.

'People here knew, in this area. I can sense people wandering around, following energy. And avoiding places where some other energy got too strong. Because you always aim for the balance.'

Nerida was keen to join his vision of the Old People. 'The people called them song-lines,' she said. 'Because they made songs to tell them where the journey goes and to tell them about the country as they travelled it. A lot of that knowledge has been lost.'

Aedgar continued, 'They didn't think that time, as it's measured now, was important. They lived the old ways. There was nothing to measure things, as people seem to do now.

'So, they sang a song, they walked in a certain direction, and they knew: if they sing this song and the song finishes, they will be where they need to be. It depended how long and how often they had to use that song. It was a different kind of way to measure time and distance. For them, it was mainly distance.

'They showed the young ones how to sing the song and taught them how to do it so that they wouldn't sing it too fast or too slow, because otherwise they would have never found the place they were supposed to go.

'Sometimes they had a song so that when the group travelled, one after an another sang the song. And when every adult in the group had had a go, they were there.

'And the young ones did listen to the song. They grasped the tempo of the song and how many people had to sing it or how often one or two had to sing it.

'It was a navigation tool: looking at the stars or at the sun for direction and using the songs for distance. These songs were related to the place they landed, or to the different tribes and their places. They had different songs to go different places. It's a basic and good system. It's very effective. And you don't need any tools.'

Nerida was fascinated. It was humbling to be taught aspects of her ancient culture by the spirit. 'But you need to be able to count. How do you know how many times to sing it, if you're not counting?' She understood that in Pitjantjatjara, numbers were made by putting together one, two and three.

'They got the feeling for it,' he replied.

'A feeling for the number of times, without the number?'

'Yeah. Or a feeling for how many adult members it took to sing the song. They had places where only the males were singing; places where only the females sang. And places where they both sang.

'If one person died, they added one of the young ones—one of the more grown-up young ones, so that they always had the same amount. If two people died and there was only one young one, the young one had to sing twice. They used a system to find places without tools. Some of them can still do it. That's why they would survive if you took every tool off them.'

Nerida took a sip of her water. Aedgar resumed.

'In this era, speaking of the ones that think they're more intelligent and use all these energy-consuming tools: if the tools fail or if you take the tools off them, they will die pretty quickly. They're lost.'

He stopped talking and began using Mari's hands on her shoulder and the base of her neck. Nerida knew she had pain there.

She had pain all over the body, some days.

She heard a whooshing. *Perhaps a storm is blowing in.*

After a few minutes, she said, 'It seemed that you were coordinating your movement of energy with the sound of the wind.'

Aedgar said, 'It's breathing of this body—it's an effort. Doing different things at once, being in a body, takes more effort. It's not the wind. It's the breath.'

'Your effort is greatly appreciated.'

'I know. I'll always try. Might take a few attempts.

'I don't do miracles so well.

'In Bristol, I was able to do things in one session, but then people would be afraid of you. Some would try to punish. So it can be a secret business.'

'Tell me more.'

'Say I could have done things in a single session. I preferred to do it in two or three sessions, so it wasn't considered "a miracle". Otherwise, some people would say you have done "devil's work".

'Not the one you treated.

'But the ones that thought that this person deserved to suffer—they would call it so.

'There were women who did this kind of work too.

'They were just killed, considered witches.

'So you had to find a way to limit success, even if one treatment could've fixed it. It was necessary to hold yourself back.

'If it was considered to be god's work you were doing then you were doomed, too, because then the church "took care of you". One would want to avoid that.

'It was an era when one was forced to manage success to survive.

'Actually, this is also what modern doctors do. They make people come back over and over again; except they don't do it to hide success. They try to keep the money coming.'

Nerida felt guilty. She hated that caring for the sick was how she made her living. But she had studied acupuncture, and then medicine, to be able to be paid to care for others. She was one of the few doctors who'd say that, 'I trained as a doctor because I needed a decent income.'

She needed to support Sam, her children's father, after he was injured and unable to work, as well as being breadwinner for the children and others in the family.

When she began to read scientific books and set out on her journey to get into medicine, she was discouraged by a careers counsellor and other people meant to support her.

They'd say, 'Why not be a nurse? Or a social worker? A health worker? Do you know how tough the study of medicine can be?'

'They all work as hard as doctors, with great responsibility, less pay and less power. I'll study longer. I can be a doctor,' she said.

Now, she admitted to Aedgar, 'It's a problem with making healing a business. I try to avoid it.'

'There's nothing wrong with making a business. If the things you do tend to be successful, there's nothing wrong. Those people won't need to come back to see you, and others will come.

'Your less successful colleagues make the same people come back over and over again to rescue the doctor's personal economy.'

He took a deep breath. 'S getting too hot for this body. I might leave for now.'

'Thanks for coming and for the good work you do.'

'Until another time, then.'

TWENTY-TWO

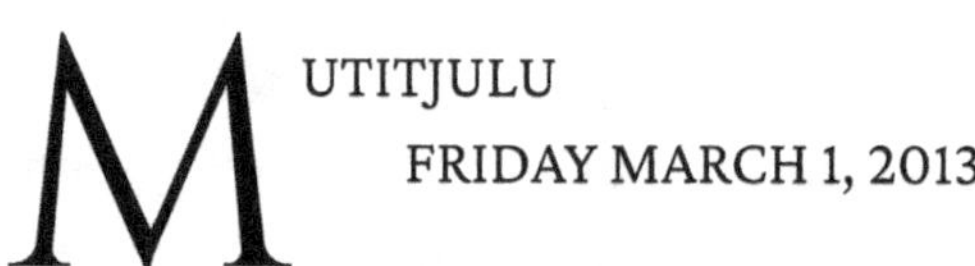

M UTITJULU
FRIDAY MARCH 1, 2013

AT NIGHT, the women heard the rain and the cooler winds that came with it, pounding and knocking the metal roof. They woke to the sound and smell of the waterfalls, pouring silver down the dark red Rock after its waterholes had filled.

Birds and kids splashed in puddles, feeling so good to be cold and wet.

The change in weather helped Mari and Nerida.

When Mari had a camera or a brush in her hand, she was well. But almost any other time she was irritable.

Nerida got on her nerves in the house. All day Mari longed for her company. And then when she was home, they snapped at each other.

She started with the bad news of the day—the world was full of violence and destruction. And went on with the problems of the house that couldn't be fixed. Or that were Nerida's fault.

'You're always so negative about everything. I can't do anything right,' Nerida complained.

'It's true, you don't,' Mari said loudly.

She seemed to say everything loudly. There was so much energy and tension built up her. She wouldn't let Nerida massage her, it only hurt. They hadn't had sex in six weeks.

Nerida was too tired to offer, anyway.

Nerida was slovenly in the house. She washed up in the dark, if she did it at all. Mari often had to wash things again because there was grease on the plates, or she didn't clean out the groove at the top of her best coffee cup, that Mari had bought her.

Nerida hardly understood the concept of having a favourite cup. She thought it was childish to care so much about nice things. All the pretty things she'd ever had were evanescent—they were second hand or cheap in the first place. She saw no point in being attached to them.

Mari understood that some things were better made than others. They had more value in them and were worth maintaining.

She had the wood panelling in her car restored when she bought it and took care to keep the dust off it, wiping it down after every ride.

When the car had a terrible smell, persisting for weeks, she disassembled the doors and took the back seats out to find the mouse that had died in there.

Nerida felt ashamed of her lack of skills in daily living. Her insecurity made her react angrily when Mari tried to show her how to do things. It took Mari years to persuade her not to throw everything into the wash together and toss in any soap, even dishwashing detergent, or shampoo, to wash her clothes.

'Didn't you notice that all your clothes were, like, shades of grey before I came?' Mari asked.

It was true. She had noticed all her bra straps were grey and didn't know what she should do about it.

•   •   •

MARI'S CHANNELLING compelled her to step away from all that busyness. When she sat down to channel, she became still.

That's probably good for her.

Nerida watched Mari's breathing slow.

And now it's like she's having yoga done to her.

As she began the channelling session, Nerida saw Mari's eyelids flutter for a few moments.

Her mouth opened and closed a little, flexing, as if to unstick her jaw. Nerida suddenly smelled sweet, blossoming flowers in the room.

The eyelids fluttered again. Then a purposeful effort to lift the lids got them up a small way, as if they weighed a tonne.

The eyes opened a tiny slit, as if the light was extremely bright.

Abruptly, the eyelids opened, showing Mari's eyeballs rolled up, as if she were unconscious.

Which I guess she is, sort of. Still, Mari sat up calmly.

It looks a bit scary, Nerida thought as the action was repeated. *But it is amazing to watch someone learning to drive the eyes, if you could say that.*

'Fascinating,' Nerida murmured.

There was a slight nod. They persisted with the effort to open the eyes. Then there was a stop, a rest, taking a breath, starting again.

The eyebrows moved a little. There was a visible push to get the eyelids up. But the eyeballs were still rolled up underneath.

The eyes scanned down briefly.

They had a rest. Then opened and closed the mouth. Tried again.

The eyes remained rolled up, but now pointed towards Mari's upper left.

Again, they rested a few seconds. It was like seeing someone learning to operate an extraordinarily sophisticated puppet.

Nerida recovered from the strangeness and used her hands the way Monica had taught her to help, coaxing the energy to roll

Mari's eyes down. A crescent moon of dark brown iris appeared.

The being lifted the eyebrows, turned and tilted the head as if trying to get a clearer signal.

About twenty minutes after Mari had gone into trance, the conversation started.

'Hello.' Someone threw a voice to connect.

'Hello. Who has been here?' Nerida asked.

'Friend. Needed some support.'

'Yes, she did.'

'We can give support.'

'Thank you. This is Aedgar now?'

'This is me.'

'I thought so.'

'What have you been up to lately?'

Nerida smiled. 'Lately—enjoying the rain very much.'

'There's more to come.'

'How wonderful.'

'Soon.'

Noise of people speaking loudly on the porch of the house intruded.

'We've got plenty of knowledge to share.'

The noise increased—joyous people shouting in a local language. Laughing.

'Are you having a party?' he asked.

'I may have to ask those people to move on if they keep getting louder.' She waited a minute or two. 'They're going.'

'They enjoy themselves,' Aedgar said.

'They do.' She went to the window to peep out.

'They are very excited,' he said.

'They are. I don't mind if they're excited somewhere else.' Dogs barked just outside the door.

'The dogs are excited, too,' Aedgar noted.

'The cool weather makes everybody happy.'

Aedgar nodded slightly. 'S been a big change. There will be more change. More rain. 'S gonna create lakes. It's gonna be more than usual. The effects of it will last longer.'

'Good.' A lovely quiet descended and wrapped them.

Aedgar said, 'Seems like the party's over now.'

The peace was deepened by a bird chirping.

'Change at this other place is continuing. Less trouble on the horizon than here.'

Nerida realised he was talking about Christmas Island. 'Should we make plans to go there, then?'

'Not now.

'Be prepared for some interesting times. Your friend is coming soon. I can still see trouble on the horizon. You shouldn't be worried. It won't take too long.

'Here, on some level, people just come and go. Someone just came, but this person will just go again.

'Place doesn't need the expectations of that person. And this place doesn't need persons of that kind. Wrong skills.

'Won't work.

'Not very clever. But clever enough to find out that the skills don't work. Used to being in crowded places, will go back to crowded places.'

'Good. If he doesn't cause damage to me and my friends, that's okay.' She knew he spoke of their new manager from Adelaide. She hadn't talked to Mari about him. Everyone knew he wouldn't last long. He spent most of his time in his donga watching cricket.

'He'll try. He'll realise quickly it won't work, though.'

Nerida said, 'There's a place southwest of here that they want to mine.' She meant Lake Amadeus, the Territory's biggest lake.

The lake, part of a complex named *Pantu* in Pitjatjantjara, was 180 kilometres long and ten wide. This sacred, magnificent place was north of Uluru, not southwest. Her sense of direction was hopeless.

'Can't sense any water—' he said. Looking from behind closed eyes, he sensed the expanse in spite of Nerida's misdirection.

'No, it's full of salt. It only fills occasionally. It's very, very big.'

'Might be the place where the lake's gonna be created by that rain. More than usual. Parts of it will last a long time.'

Nerida breathed deeply.

'There will be some changes to the area,' the seer said. 'There will be more water to this area than usual. They might have to reconsider some of the tracks.'

'Perhaps it will delay the mining. Fracking was proposed,' she said.

'The mining for the blueish material is still going to happen. Some things are laid out that way. It has to happen, for learning experience, to change things in the long term. It has to change a way of thinking.'

'I believe that's to the southwest?'

'Told you so,' he said.

'Yes, you did. A day's travel to the southwest.'

'Approximately. Or half day. The difference in time depends on the mode of transportation.

'There is no settlement there at the moment. It's still difficult to get there. It's not that far. It's the terrain that extends the travel time to get to that place.'

'Mari and I saw a black and white striped plane, like a big insect.' *It has a pole out of its nose, like a mozzie's proboscis.*

They saw it flying around above and then parked at the airport. 'It was around for a long time. People say it looks underground to see minerals.'

'It was part of the problem we are discussing,' Aedgar said. 'That substance has been detected. They still have no idea what it is. They're trying to get it out, to discover what it is. It's the wrong approach.

'This stuff changes through contact with air. They'll think it's good and interesting, for a while.

'It's dangerous.

'Too much greed around ... It will be too late for many of them once they figure out it's dangerous. There will be no cure.

'It's the ones that are responsible who are going to meet the biggest disaster.

'It will get on to the right people—who are actually the wrong people.

'They get kind of a—some people might call it something else—we here would call it a **lesson**.

'It will help them to make different decisions, once they come back. They won't be able to make any more decisions in this lifetime, though.'

'Are they going to build a road into this place, then, to get in there?'

'They will. Some of the people know about it.

'They say, from their history, there's a bad ghost living down there, a spirit. That's why there is no settlement in this area. They know.

'They don't even think about the possibility that someone might attempt to take it out. It wouldn't ever be their approach. They would just leave it alone.'

Voices in the distance reminded Nerida that people were celebrating Friday night outside.

Aedgar's voice was dark. 'There will be this kind of disaster ... So, the greedy bunch of people will have this learning experience for another lifetime. Observers might learn for their current lifetime that it would best to leave it alone.'

So, he's reinforcing the message he gave me earlier, just in case I didn't get it.

Further details about the bluish mineral were fascinating but daunting. Nerida was not particularly opposed to mining before she knew Aedgar. She found his vehemence off- putting. *He's always talking about greed like a preacher.*

Even though she felt that his condemnation of greed as a motivation was appropriate, Nerida was chary about moralism. She'd been in retreat from making judgements about people for a decade or two, as people sometimes do, looking for an easier life, when they age. *Or mature.*

What if this is total fantasy? There goes my reputation. What if it's true? Thereby hangs a lot of responsibility!

How to share it? How soon do I need to get it out so that people are warned of it? If the accident foretold happens before the conversation is published, a learning opportunity is lost. But how does a medical doctor publish such material without losing credibility as a scientist?

The seriousness of the information and the duty that came with it challenged and frightened her.

She thought of herself and a job offer. 'There's a place on the west coast of this island called Port Hedland. There's been big storms there. It's where the iron ore—'

'There will be more storms. It's caused by the imbalance. It's still not over.

'Due to the rotation of this planet and the shifting of the angle of it during the seasons, there's always been this kind of movement of the air appearing there. That would move the water, too. It was a natural thing.

'It's not natural anymore, because through the imbalance, it's getting more intense, stronger.'

'I have people asking me to work there, but we don't want to go because of the mining and the imbalance.'

'It's got a disturbed energy about it.' He spoke as if he could see it. 'It's not a good idea to become part of the disturbed energy. You might be able to start a different way of thinking there, educating. It's too early.'

'Perhaps we all can visit there later.'

'Maybe at some point. There will be more opportunities for—as I'd like to call it— sudden learning experiences.

'It's probably not the safest place to go.

'They urgently need these learning experiences, because they are well on their way to putting more disturbances up there in the area—extensions of their greed. Some areas are still intact, on an energetic level, so they might be able to fight it off. It won't happen tomorrow.

'They need to take some of these "sudden learning experiences" into consideration, so to say. It will support the good people that decided to fight it already.

'They're still not entirely sure, some of the important people. They're having an inner dispute between their love for protection and their own greed.'

'What kind of protection? Protection from what?' She supposed he meant the Traditional Owners as the 'important people.'

'They love to protect their environment,' he said, 'but they have this inner war with their personal greed. Their love and protection of the environment is much older. It will gain strength again.

'The greed was a new thing. They saw it happening everywhere. They wanted to be part of it.

'Quite a few things are going to change.

'Coming events will support the people of higher intelligence, because the ones on top (that are of lower intelligence) won't be able to explain what happened. The people will want to know what happened and why. It will give more power to the people who know about it. And sweep the other ones out of business.'

'Good. That's a pleasing prospect.'

'Indeed. There is important work to do.'

The roar of a car accelerating outside filled the room.

Aedgar sighed deeply. 'I think that was an expression of a silly mode of transportation.'

'You're right. And a silly person using it.'

'Dangerous combination,' he said. 'Someone should lock both parts of it up: the mode of transportation, as well as the person using it. 'S gonna cause heartbreak.'

The spirit did not speak for five minutes. Nerida listened to the car, still not far away and turning in circles to make dust and gravel fly.

'Thank you for the beautiful work you've done bringing the cooler air and the water—'

'There will be more.'

'It refreshes all the living things,' she said. Again, he did not speak for a longer time.

Then said, 'We're trying to concentrate, to find someone who's going to stop the crazy person from causing major heartache.'

She felt the seriousness of it, stayed quiet.

He sighed. 'Seems like something needs to happen.

'So it will be—'

A siren blared in the distance. Nerida thought it might have been on the road around the base of the Rock. There were not so many vehicles with a siren around Muti. She hoped it was not their ambulance.

He sighed again, twice. 'We got some work to do ... We'll talk to you another time.'

'Thank you. I always enjoy your company.' She was curious about what he was doing.

'Pleasure to talk to you. Thank you for being here. We are grateful for this opportunity.'

Mari returned, put the crystals on the table. Nerida greeted her as she stretched with a groan.

'Mmm. Times at the beginning I thought it wouldn't work,' Mari said. 'I felt like one of these steel balls that the dolls have was rolling around in my head.'

'Sounds uncomfortable.'

Mari laughed. 'It felt like it was bigger than those ones. I had this pain in my ear. It's gone now. And then I had it in this other ear.' She arose with exertion, adjusting her leg.

'And how's your body feel now?'

Mari ignored the question, as she often did.

She pulled vinegar out of the cupboard, laid out bowls and a pan. 'I'm going to eat. How about you?'

'Yes, please. I'd like two eggs.

'There's been somebody driving dangerously out there and Aedgar went off to try stop someone "causing heartbreak". It's something they do, apparently.'

'Oh.'

Mari swirled simmering water with a wooden spoon to poach the eggs. The room filled with the smell of coffee and toast.

Nerida pretended to read. Aedgar had alluded to upcoming complications at work. That made her apprehensive.

The workplace often felt unsafe, because of management, mostly. Her patients and Nerida created a private world of healing, even in such a harsh environment.

Penetrated by red dust, the clinic was never really properly clean.

Claire had said. 'It's not about essential oils and little fountains, our clinic. People come here when they're really suffering and we do harsh things to them. Look at how the kids scream when we give them their immunisations.' She was right.

Nerida kept giving her patients hugs sometimes, nevertheless.

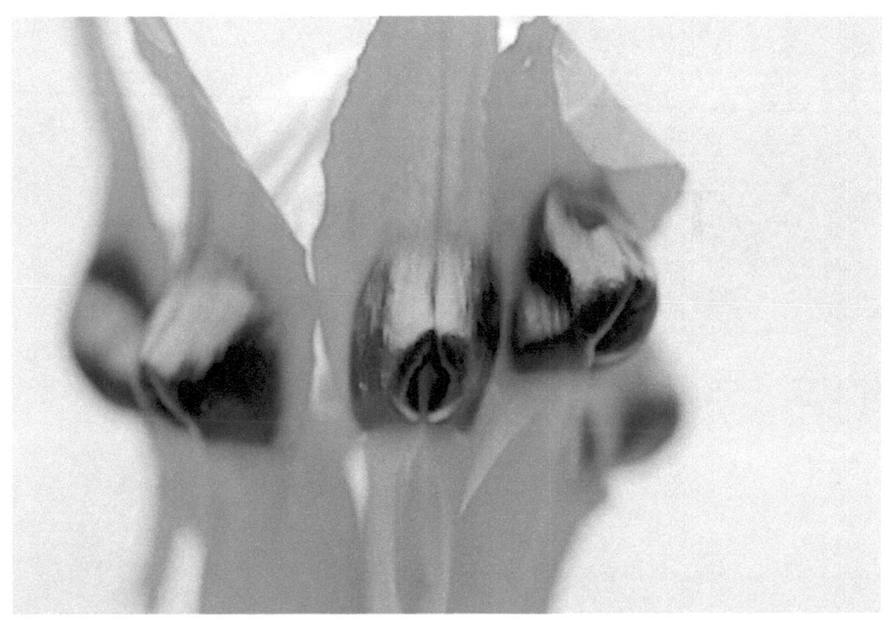

CHAPTER

TWENTY-THREE

M UTITJULU CLINIC
THURSDAY MARCH 7, 2013.

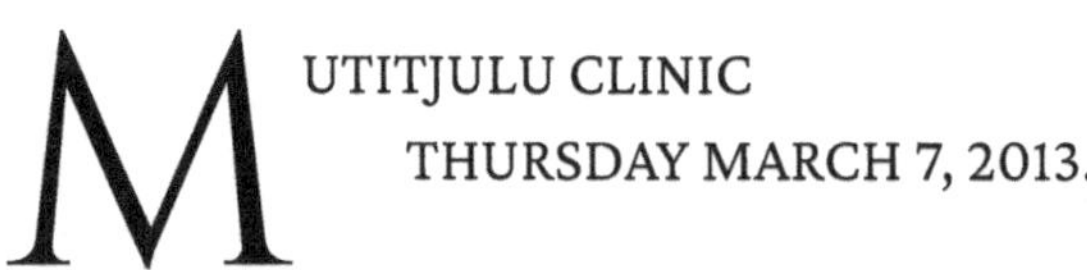

NERIDA WAS ABOUT to go to lunch when a woman walked into her room, stooped, limping and wincing. It took the doctor a few moments to recognise Desdemona, the feisty young woman who'd come in for her Pill.

Something terrible has happened. Nerida noticed a large, dark bruise on the left side of Desdemona's neck, extending down to her shoulder. Her face was puffy. Almost worst of all were her eyes—dull, absent and defeated.

Nerida gave her a gentle hug.

Desdemona lifted her thin cotton dress to show large yellow, purple and green bruises on her thigh and buttock. She had no under-wear on.

She took a sip of the water offered. 'I just got out today. I saw someone at the shop and gave her a note. My old friend from school.

She's brought me here.'

Her eyes started moving fast, side-to-side. 'I made him take me out to the shop to use my card for cigarettes and food.'

Nerida saw that it was painful to breathe. Speaking came hard, too. Desdesmona's lower lip and cheek were swollen. A large cut was crusted, healing.

'It was the second time he took me to the shop. The first time I was too afraid to look at anyone. I tried but I couldn't make eye contact without him seeing.'

Nerida's eyes widened.

'I've been locked up in the Gaines' house for I don't know how long. About two months, I suppose. What day is it?'

'March 7. It's a Thursday.'

'Last time I remember it was the end of January.' Desdemona began to cry. It was dry, exhausted crying. Few tears were left. It hurt her to sit, so she got up and walked carefully to the exam couch and back, still talking.

'You've been kept prisoner in the Gaines' house all this time? Fucking hell.' Nerida's eyes were wide.

She put her hands over her mouth. Gave Desdemona tissues, touched her arm gently, helplessly.

'They had me tied up. I was kept on the floor. I tried to climb out the window. He found me and hit me hard. I tried to climb out of the windows twice. They tied me down.'

Nerida noticed burns on her wrists, probably from a thin nylon rope. She began typing notes now, as much as she could, knowing her words should end up in Court.

Desdemona sobbed and caught her breath. 'There were days they didn't let me up to go to the toilet. I tried kicking the floor to make a noise but he beat me to shut me up. He kicked me with steel capped boots.

'He had a digging stick he used to hit me with—hard as steel. He hit me over the head with it. I blacked out maybe four times.'

She sat down again.

Nerida got up and stood behind her, gently touched her head. She saw handsful of hair missing. Desdemona's skull was lumpy in several places.

While she was up, she did a brief neurological exam, shining a light in each of her eyes, asking her to move her eyes.

'Do you think you have any broken bones?' she asked.

'I don't think so. The women in my family have very strong bones,' said Desdemona with a shadow of her former pride.

'There seems to be something wrong with my jaw. He knocked out four or five of my teeth. They're still there in the cracks between the floorboards in that house.'

'Desdemona, don't you think we should go to the Police?' Nerida asked. Her own jaw was clenched, as if she wanted to bite.

'I don't know yet. I would like to go to the Police. But they'll see me go.'

'Who are "they?" Are the ones who did this still around?'

'Him and his family. They're from interstate, but they're still here. I'm hoping they might leave soon.'

'Do you have a safe place to stay now?'

'Yes. My aunty will keep me safe. She has a gun.'

Desdemona was raped repeatedly during her captivity.

Nerida drew in a sharp breath when she realised that other adults had been in and around the house while the young woman was imprisoned and tortured.

Some commented, Desdemona explained. A woman washed her with a bucket and rags after she'd been lying in her own faeces and urine for days. The woman told the rapist the stench would attract attention. Then she was gone and he tied her up again.

The nightmare started when she was out on a Saturday night, drinking with friends. She had accepted a ride with her captor.

Desdemona described how she had eventually persuaded him to take her to the shop with him to be able to use her card, when he was out of cash. How frantically she'd tried to let people know her situation without letting her captor know.

The note she'd passed to her former school friend that day was the third she'd written. Other people at the shop had ignored her notes. She'd left one, screwed up, on the counter for the cashier, who perhaps didn't read it. A second was slipped into a woman's shopping bag.

Nerida documented as much as she could and called the hospital in town for advice about forensic care.

'I know it's hard, but we need you not to wash. The doc in town is specially trained for sexual violence. She'll want to take swabs to get his DNA. Will you go to town for that?'

Desdemona agreed.

Nerida went to talk quietly to Claire. Together they checked some of their strongest pain relief tablets out of the safe in the pharmacy.

Nerida explained to the shaken young woman how to take them, warning her about constipation and the risk of dependency. How to manage the withdrawal when she didn't need so many in a few days. Nerida wrote it all down in big, clear handwriting and put the note with the medicines in a paper bag, which conferred privacy in Community. She put a detailed letter in the bag, too, for the doctor in Alice.

'I'll arrange transport for you to town and let them know when you're arriving. You shouldn't have to wait in the waiting room.'

'My auntie Thea will take me. She's got a car.'

In a small town of less than two hundred people. Nobody knew she was there. Nerida wondered if she'd heard the thumping of the desperate captive at night. *Maybe I heard it and thought it was someone hitting the fence at Peter's place, provoking the dogs?* She swallowed; her mouth was dry.

'Can you help me check that I'm not pregnant now, though? Please?' Desdemona's voice shook. 'They wouldn't let me take my Pill.'

TWENTY-FOUR

Mutitjulu
SATURDAY MARCH 9, 2013

MARI AND NERIDA were exhausted and sad. Mari woke up grieving. Nerida didn't know what for. If she asked, Mari expressed herself in angry, bitter words.

Mari was furious every day. Nerida could see there was plenty to be enraged by.

She was worn down by being the doctor's wife. In the preceding two years, they'd witnessed some of the trauma Anangu experienced: attempted and completed youth suicides, fatal car accidents. Survivors with serious, multiple injuries. Addictions. A couple of women beaten by their husbands who almost lost their lives—Mari took one of them to Alice with facial fractures. Pregnancies lost. Unwanted pregnancy and childbirth endured.

After reconstructive surgery, the woman with the facial fractures took her husband back. Mari struggled to understand it.

'She said she'd never forgive him. She said she'd be mad to go back with that prick. He kicked her on the ground, with steel-capped boots!'

'I see this everywhere I work,' Nerida tried to explain. One of her patients had been burned to death by her husband when she worked in the Illawarra, in New South Wales. This violence was not unique to Mutitjulu, or to Indigenous people.

But sometimes systemic problems hurt people there in ways Nerida hadn't seen before.

RETURNING TO WORK IN FEBRUARY, Becca found that an agency nurse had removed all the recalls for long-acting contraceptives from the clinic record keeping system. Informing women that they were due for their contraceptive device or needle was not something done in the city, apparently. The nurse had never worked in Indigenous Health or at any remote community before.

In her defense (on the phone with Becca) she said she'd been directed by management to help make the clinic more efficient. Nerida had not seen Becca angry before.

'She said, "Those people should manage their own calendar. They have too much done for them." She has no respect for what we do, how the clinic responds to the Community's needs. It was all "these people" and "they" this, and "them, them, them." She had no idea how racist she sounded.'

Becca pushed her hand through her short, thick hair. Her brown eyes flashed. 'She said it was patronising to say women in the bush can't keep track of their own health care.'

'She's blustering to cover her insecurity. I'm glad you fought with her,' Nerida said. 'Management told her that because they didn't want to have to employ three nurses, even though the clinic is funded for them.

'They'd call it "managing community expectations". We'd call it running the clinic into the ground, so people expect nothing and get less. She's a fool.'

'A fool and a tool,' said Becca. It was as close as she got to swearing.

The agency nurse's ignorant and misguided effort to please management meant that Nerida saw two women with unwanted pregnancies because their contraception had expired and they were unaware. One was five months pregnant when she came to the clinic.

Alongside her Aboriginal ancestry, Nerida was descended from the Irish. That wasn't unusual in New South Wales, where the Kooris and the Irish convicts had a common enemy in the English red coats. From all sides of the family she saw how unwanted children sometimes grew up unwanted. *To be a child your mother has no time or energy for can mean growing up unloved.*

That month was full of drama. Their male nurse and Nerida were attacked by a brain-damaged patient at the local airport. He woke up from his sedation abruptly.

He threw rocks at them, smashed the ambulance window when Nerida was inside, and, finding a lighter that should have been taken out of his pocket, tried to set the medical evacuation aircraft on fire. When he came running at her, rock in hand, as she sat in the ambulance, Nerida made herself small and begged for mercy in Pitjantjatjara. Confused, he ran away.

The same week they dealt with several suicide attempts. And another young man hanged himself. The team tried to care for his devastated family.

The Sorry Camp was to be at a different community, which was a relief to the clinic staff. But the pressure on community people was relentless.

Nerida felt and thought her way through. She talked to Thea and Angus. The youth who died was not mentally ill in the Western way. Seeing the desperate young people through that lens, with plans for giving them tablets, was not enough.

At the clinic, Nerida tried to stay honest about their limitations as unsupported outsiders in a community that was frequently under siege (from within or without). Claire helped.

Meanwhile, management in Alice Springs called to give Nerida good news about a new clinic manager. Five years after the Community Business Manager 's office was burnt down they had finally recruited someone who might stay for the clinic. Aedgar was right about the previous fly-by-night. He lasted less than three weeks.

Now a man with no experience in health, who presented nicely, was appointed to the role. She should be pleased because he was Aboriginal, Nerida was told. As she was. *Things could get easier now. Maybe they we won't have to work so hard.*

Eric was conventionally handsome, with his flash smile and new clothes. He wore a thick, gold chain and jewelled rings.

Nerida, who loved coloured stones, wore only her wedding ring or occasionally beads the local women made when she was in Community. She found Eric provocative, flaunting his wealth.

She was trying to change her attitude to wealth, though. *Fortunatus says that you can't get rich by sneering at rich people. Maybe Eric's a good example.* She tried to be welcoming, despite her gut feeling. He made her stomach churn.

Mari hated Eric, sight unseen. She refused to host him for coffee. If Nerida mentioned his name, Mari was enraged.

'Just hearing about him makes made me feel as if every cell in my body is on a warpath. I can't explain it.

'I don't care if everyone else says he's charming. That will only last for the first week—or less. You'll see.'

'You're being irrational. He's not that bad.' Nerida disapproved. *Mari is being blindly judgemental.*

It took less than a fortnight for Becca, Claire and Nerida to realise that Mari's instincts were right.

Eric's expensive cologne at the morning meeting—he did smell nice as he enforced an 8am start—was a cover for the alcoholic binges he had at Yulara most nights.

Jasmine, whose daughter worked there, told them he was an argumentative drunk who made trouble at the bar. Vilifying Angus was one of his favourite themes. Eric often stayed at Yulara in a hotel because he had trouble walking to his car.

An alcoholic, even if he had been functioning, was a poor choice for a remote Aboriginal community under prohibition.

But Eric wasn't even functional. He came to the morning meeting, read fiats from emails sent from Alice, pretended to listen with utter incomprehension as the staff discussed patient transport arrangements, clinical procedures, medication stocks. Then disappeared home to sleep off his hangover.

One afternoon, Claire talked to Nerida about the hours they'd spent with a vasculopath with acute coronary syndrome the day before. None of them had a chance of getting a line into that poor person's arm. Nerida put an interosseous needle in his shin bone for fluids and medication. She used a local anaesthetic but it still hurt and wasn't a definitive solution. The Flying Doctor came at 3am and placed an arterial line in the man's neck to be evacuated to hospital. Claire stayed with him, got home at dawn.

'Do you think you might do training to be able to put an art line in?' Claire was at the end of her swing. Exhaustion lined her face.

'I don't think so.' Nerida squeezed a stress ball. 'Management won't let me go to a Pitjantjatjara language course in Adelaide. Or even train to be certified to put contraceptive implants in.

'I've applied. I'm never granted the time off.

'It'd take weeks under supervision to learn to place an arterial line. "It costs us money when you go away," they say.'

They put in a request to Eric for the clinic to buy an ultrasound machine for easier IV access, especially for children. Pressed for a response, he eventually emailed that the clinic did not 'have the resources for tertiary care needs.'

'Where did he get that line?' Claire said as she prepared to leave, the creases deepened between her brows. 'He doesn't use words of more than two syllables.'

Mari and Nerida had shadows under their eyes. But the support Mari gave Nerida meant she continued as the backbone of the clinic. Aedgar and Monica were compelling, and

Nerida was maturing with their insight. But she felt defensive about the source of her strength. Having Eric in the clinic made everyone feel insecure.

Other doctors have spiritual beliefs. As long as mine don't interfere with the medical care of my patients, they're nobody's business. So why do I feel like there's a target painted on my back?

EVEN WHEN SHE CHANNELLED, Mari's fatigue was evident. She committed to channel despite the episodic, extraordinary rage surging through her, which she blamed on Eric.

She closed her eyes, planted her feet. Turned her palms gently up on her thighs. Wriggled to adjust her balance. She always channelled with her artificial leg on to help Aedgar balance. 'I'd hate to fall over while I'm channelling,' she said.

Mari stopped, frowned, awoke. It was six minutes or so before she settled and Aedgar spoke. Words came slow and quiet.

'Hello.'

'Hello. Thank you for coming.'

Aedgar spoke weakly. 'It's been a while.'

'It has.'

He worked with a very dry throat and had difficulty forming words. 'I've been very busy lately.'

'Tell me more.'

'There's a shift of energy happening soon to this planet.'

'You've been preparing?'

'Yeah, some sort of preparation happened. You'll be safe here.' He was quiet for a minute or so.

Nerida asked, 'Is it that the planet is trying to readjust her balance, her axis?'

Aedgar replied, 'It's been trying for a long time.

'It started quite a while ago.

'But, yeah, some bigger kind of adjustments. Happening soon.

'You will be safe.

'Most of the people you have—hmm—energetic attachments to, like feelings, will be safe too—most of them.'

'A few will be going then?' *People we love will die?*

'It's not sure. Most of them, the closest ones are safe.'

'Is this island affected?'

'It will have some effects here, but it will happen all over the place … It will all be better—after that.'

'Should we expect more meteors?' Mari photographed meteor showers recently. *Is one going to hit us?*

'There're always some around. There won't be a major impact.

'But there will be slight changes to the whole planet, having bigger effects in some areas and smaller effects in others.

'It's like, you know an animal bothered by parasites might try to shake them off, or to wash them off, rinse itself—'

'Perhaps it's like a body that needs to get sick to get stronger,' she suggested.

'Kind of. It's less internal, it's more external.'

His energy was lower than usual. He usually filled the space. He felt further away to Nerida today, distracted.

'So you will be safe from these sorts of things,' he said. 'But there is some—hmm— bad energy at your place.'

'Hmm. Mari felt an extreme anger when she was trying to go out to let you come in today. She was hoping—'

'It's always difficult if you've got this sensitivity to energy waves.'

'Is it that somebody nearby is enraged or somebody's mad with us?'

'Several are quite angry. Doesn't have anything to do with you.

'There was kind of a collision of energies last night.'

'Here in the community? There was a fight?'

'Close by ... One person is trying to have everything happen in a different way. Person tried to hold back a little, previously. Is trying now to push their agenda through. Won't last.

'Changes will happen everywhere.

'It's hard to differentiate at the moment, because it's coming from more than one direction.

'The person who wants to have things in their own and special way is opposed by a person with the same mindset.

'Male, I think. Two male energies.'

There was a long pause as he investigated it. 'One person is angry, very angry. Feeling used, pushed into something.'

'Can you tell me more about who it is?'

'Someone who's not supposed to be here,' he said finally. 'Person will go soon.'

That should be Eric, surely. 'Good.'

'Has no attachment to the place at all. Getting in trouble with that person who's very attached to the place. Conflict of interests. Power struggle.'

That person very attached to the place. I'll bet that's Bull. Fed up with Eric talking shit about Angus.

'Try to stay out of it,' he concluded. 'Okay.'

Aedgar sighed. 'Friend is coming soon. That's gonna ease the tension. Both of you stay out of it. It must be solved by someone else.'

'Good.'

'What have you been doing lately?'

'I've been going to work.'

'Hmm. Doesn't sound happy,' he commented.

'I had an unhappy experience. One of my clients was kept prisoner and treated with cruelty. She was locked in a house. None of us here knew that she was there, being tortured. It made me very sad.'

'Some people knew,' he said with intensity. 'Some people knew it all the time.'

'That makes me even sadder.'

'They thought the person had to be taught a lesson … The people who have been involved shouldn't be at this place. It's the wrong energy for them.'

Aedgar seemed to be looking into the situation. He sighed again.

Nerida continued, 'The cruelty with which she was treated makes it hard for me to talk to people about it. I feel disappointed that such torture was tolerated by some people here.'

Aedgar summarised. 'I'd say there are two to four persons who knew, all the time. They thought there was a valuable lesson to be taught.'

'One's a man I used to have respect for,' she realised. 'I don't love him now.' Somehow, she knew it was Old Jack with the stylish belt buckles. He wasn't the perpetrator, but he allowed it.

'He thought he was doing the right thing,' Aedgar said.

'The incident had jealous thoughts attached to it from the people who knew. Not all of them are male. Older people.'

She saw their faces like photographs in her mind. *Felicity was one. So much for her tenderness with the babies when she was young on the Ernabella Mission.*

'There will be harsh punishment and they won't understand it. They've got no insight into their wrongdoing.

'Physical punishment will happen if some others find out that these people knew. Again, for you, stay out of it.'

'Okay. I do.' She sighed, in turn. 'Thank you for helping me understand a little more.'

'There is a lesson to be taught, but not the way they thought.

'There are lessons for both sides.'

What the lessons could be was opaque to her.

The ceiling made cracking noises as metal expanded. It was unusually hot outside.

'You are going to experience some (you would call it) wild weather —starting soon. It's always difficult to define "soon", but it's coming —not today, probably not tomorrow either.'

'We're planning to go to the east coast to Sydney, to listen to your colleague, Fortunatus. We'll fly at the end of the week.'

Aedgar looked. 'Not sure at the moment—could be interesting. The weather might get in the way. But it's a bit difficult from me to say with this time issue.'

'We'll see. It will unfold as it's meant to, as Monica says.'

'Yes.'

'MARI'S BEEN SO UNHAPPY, especially in the mornings.'

'I can sense that,' he said. 'It's about change. It's still about letting go of other deeply rooted career wishes. It's still a big issue—won't be talked about. But it's a very big issue, the realisation that it won't happen—accepting a new path.

'I think it still has to be done, another time.'

'Being a doctor?' *Such a gruelling course. One doctor in the family is surely enough.*

'So to say.'

'It makes her sad that she doesn't think she can do it in this lifetime now?' Nerida felt guilty for discouraging Marie from studying.

'It's hard to accept. She came back for it.'

'Oh.'

'There is some other issue.

'Person—quite a distance, I think. Male, might be an older person but not "old" in the sense of wise. Hmm. Same roots. Deet—'

'Detlev. Detlev is her youngest brother. She's worried about him. He's getting sick.'

He's a wreck. He's physically older than Mari.

'It should be taken more seriously. There is a chance to overcome it, but it should be taken more seriously.

'Some medication should be changed—quick. He's taking too much. There is an interference.'

'Between the medications?'

'It's not the body itself. It's the way the body's affected by the medications—wrong interactions. Should be changed.'

'Okay, we'll tell him.'

'Something has to be replaced … Can't figure out which one—using strange formulas.

'All these formulas are not good in general.'

'I can find out.'

Aedgar said in a flat voice, 'Very dry here.'

'It is.'

'There will be quite a bit of water soon.'

'Good,' she whispered. After a beat she said, 'We've been loving the stars.' The clear, dark nights made them euphoric.

'They are very enjoyable. Very educational, too.'

'If only we were smart enough to learn from them.'

'Never too late.

'You can see plenty of stars from this part of the planet. Much more enjoyable than in the northern part.

'But people there still enjoyed star gazing.' It felt like a mellow memory.

'The earth is beautiful everywhere,' she said.

'In different ways.'

'Yes. Mari doesn't like the snow and ice in the northern winter.'

'It's good to experience it for a limited time. Can be a good experience.'

'I lived for a year in that climate, with an icy winter. Made me wonder how humans came to live in such a harsh place.'

'They had no choice.'

'I guess.' She imagined battles, famine.

'But still, there is a choice to leave it now. Unfortunately, it's greed that keeps them there. They are too attached to things that are not important. That's why they stay there.

'Only greed can make people stay in inconvenient places.'

We are living in an inconvenient place. Am I only here for the money? 'Is that why Mari and I are here in the desert?'

Aedgar sighed. 'It's a minor aspect of it.

'It is about greed, but also learning opportunities, facing confrontation and mastering it.

'It is an interesting place. But there are places where you could live a happier life.'

That's kinda obvious. Still needed to be said. I feel privileged to be allowed and needed here. Not sure how we'll ever live somewhere more ordinary, but comfortable, after this.

Better think about it. Maybe I'm greedy for heroics. Or status. And in my self-centredness, I've denied my wife her career.

'Do you have any advice for Mari, Aedgar, to help her feel happier? I guess it's nothing we can hurry.'

'There's not much to do about it. It's about change, focussing on different things, letting go of other things, even if it's not the obvious things. Still there, has been there her whole life, so far.'

'The desire to be a doctor, you mean?'

'Yes. It's nothing anyone should interfere with.

'It must be dealt with to be able to completely focus on other things.

'But you can't deal with it. It's not your change. It's not your issue.

'The other thing is, it's hard to handle all the energies around if you have the sensitivity to get all these vibrations of other energies. It will become easier to handle it.

'But there is a **tremendous** amount of sensitivity to these things.

'It is something one must get used to.

'Need to get used to it, to be able to keep a distance.

'At the moment it's all coming at her at once, from all directions.

And it's all these, hmm, strong energies fighting each other. Of course, there will be less, at some point. And this huge sensitivity is not so much of an issue, if the energies around her calm down a bit. It will happen.

'Will take a while, so to say, nothing that happens overnight. It's a very complex thing.'

'Can she use crystals to help protect her or help reduce her sensitivity? Would music help? Or nice perfumes? Going other places?'

'I think some crystals would intensify it.'

'Right. Perhaps the quartz at the top of her bed should be put away somewhere for a while?'

'You need something for protection,' he countered.

'Moving away to other areas close by, at least for a certain amount of time during a day, could help—to have a break.'

Nerida felt a shade of guilt. *I might be neglecting her a bit. I did not take Mari's desire to study medicine seriously enough.* 'Thank you for the black and white birds—the willy wagtails,' she said, clutching at a happier feeling.

'When we don't talk it's nice to be reminded of you.'

'I'm never very far.'

'So we'll look forward to the wild weather. And I'll tell Mari about Detlev. We'll look at his medications.

'And I'll encourage her to take some breaks away from here and take her out more often myself, with more understanding that she needs it.'

'That could be a bit of trouble.

'She doesn't know she needs it. And she thinks she doesn't need it at all.'

Nerida laughed. 'Yes. She can be quite resistant to looking after herself.'

'Resistance is nothing wrong. I've chosen well.'

She laughed again. 'So have I.'

'Make sure your doors are locked at night,' he said.

'Was there somebody trying to get in last night? Mari woke, thinking somebody was knocking at the door.'

'It could have been energy trying to get help. It might have been this strong feeling of energy, without it being physically there. But someone tried to get advice from you.'

'Should I have been more available? Have I done something wrong?'

A light shone on her insecurity about people's needs in the Community. She was never enough. She feared Aedgar would judge her harshly.

'There's nothing wrong about it,' he said.

She said, 'I think perhaps it's part of that other one learning that this is not the place for him to stay.' *It's that Eric who's been fighting with Bull and Angus*, she realised.

'He knew it from the first day. The difficult thing is, he is taught a lesson but he thinks that he has to teach a lesson to someone else.'

'Is that the source of the conflict?'

'Probably, part of it. It's part of it.'

'I'm happy to stay out of it. I don't want him to teach me any lessons.'

'He can't. There is nothing that he could teach that would be useful for you or that you would need.'

That's a great relief. She could be more confident in dealings with Eric. She thanked Aedgar.

'Your friend was supposed to stay out of it, too. Will still be able to teach him some valuable things.'

'Yes, as is her way.'

'It's on a higher level.'

'It's not about, like, teaching kids in school.'

'I feel protective towards her. I hope she doesn't get hurt by the experience.' She was thinking of Claire, returning to Muti soon.

'She won't. She'll grow. Very strong individual. She won't see it as a threat.'

'Good. I'd like to see her grow stronger and expand her energy.'

'She's done a bit of that, lately. She found some guidance to her pathway. She will know better what is important and what's not.'

'Last time you left me, you were trying to sort out a dangerous driver to try to stop him killing somebody.'

'Yes.'

'How did you go?'

'Successful.'

'What did you do?'

'Changed the energy.' He made it sound like a dance move.

'Of the person driving dangerously?'

'Yes.'

Nerida was awestruck.

'A few energies had to be changed. Telling some people, making them *feel* like there are other things to do, right now. Which stops one from using that means of transportation in the wrong way. And changing someone else's urge to go outside, so these energies don't collide.'

'Uhuh. You saved a child's life.'

'He just had to continue his playing for a bit longer. And the other one had to go a different way, talk to a girl.'

'I find that very moving.' She had tears in her eyes.

'This is how it works.

'Lessons to learn shouldn't always be harsh.

'Even though a harsh lesson can speed up the learning process, if the experience is *too* harsh it can stop the learning completely.

'If an event would stop a learning process completely, it's not supposed to happen.'

'Thank you for sharing your wisdom, Aedgar.'

'You're welcome. I might leave for now.'

'I look forward to talking to you again soon.'

'My pleasure as well. Talk to you another time.'

There was a pause. Mari returned with a deep inhale, stretching.
'Hello Mar.'

'Hi.'

'Are you hungry?'

'Yeah.'

'I'm really hungry. Do you know who came?'

'I thought it was Aedgar.'

'It was, again.'

'Hmm?

'What is it?'

Nerida gazed at Mari, delighted.

'I love seeing you every time you come back.'

Mari sighed and yawned. Stretched again with a satisfied sound.
'You have a chance to miss me, huh?

'I'm thirsty, too. Can you make me a juice, please?'

Nerida got up and pulled the bottle from the fridge, keen for a
simple way to care for her wife.

CHAPTER

TWENTY-FIVE

M UTITJULU
TUESDAY MARCH 12, 2013

CLAIRE ARRIVED BACK at the clinic for her six-week swing in the afternoon. She'd barely had a break, just a long weekend. Eric was incapable of organising a humane roster.

But she hit the ground running, as always, updating orders for meds and supplies, making a list of people needing follow-up of their diabetes treatments, based on recent blood results.

Refreshed from her short visit home in Sydney, she said, 'Happy to be on call tonight. Everyone here looks tired. I'm thinking how good my life is.' She smiled, showing beautiful teeth.

'This morning I got the ferry across Sydney Harbour, past the Opera House. And this afternoon I get to drive around Uluru. Say hello to Kata Tjuta in the distance. And be here for the sunset.'

'Thanks for coming back, sista. It's a hard time for Community. And Eric is still a pain in the arse,' Nerida said.

At home, hours later, it was totally dark when Nerida's phone rang. She felt tight in her chest. *Is it Claire calling for help?*

But it was something different. The elderly lady she'd persuaded to go to Alice Springs for eye surgery next week was coming back early, without having had the surgery. It was her driver, an energetic white woman people called Peewee.

Peewee was calling because they'd hit a cow about an hour's drive down the highway. Nerida was anxious and exasperated. They were not supposed to be driving at night. Everybody in the Territory knew that. *That old lady must have pushed Peewee to take the risk. She can be very persuasive.*

Peewee assured her that neither of them was hurt. The car was damaged, but drivable.

The cow had a broken leg and Peewee had stopped to tell the owners so that they could go and pick it up. The old lady was good-humouredly scolding her for not hitting a kangaroo instead.

'That cow was too big for us two women to put on the top of the car and bring home for meat,' Peewee said, quoting the Elder with a chuckle.

They'd left Alice because the place they were staying was not going to be suitable for the old lady to be able to get to the hospital for her surgery. There was no one there to tell her when breakfast was on, or when she should go to the hospital. Half-blind and frail, she would have been better off in the Aboriginal hostel than the De-Luxe Hotel.

Peewee had another job to go to and couldn't stay with her. So they headed home.

We'll arrange her surgery in six months. She's been to the podiatrist, who's helped save her foot by debriding that deep burn we've been treating every day for a month. I guess that's what the old lady really wanted. The trip was worthwhile, even if the Eye Charity, who paid for it, would be disappointed.

There wasn't anything Nerida had to do now except wait for

Peewee to call when they arrived safely back in Muti. Around 10.30, she did so. *All is well.*

Later that night, Mari set up her camera in the back yard, its neck craned on the tripod to see over the fence. If she pointed it to the south, the stars turned in circles when the individual frames were run together in a time-lapse.

The previous night she took ninety photographs, which came to about 3 seconds when she ran them like a movie. The camera's eye saw thousands of stars. It caught shooting stars, too.

Mari was excited about the new moon's velvet black sky. She also got animated about solar eclipses (there was one coming the next morning) and meteor showers (one was predicted at the end of the week). Nerida liked it that she took these things seriously.

Mari planned to take about 400 photos of the stars that night. She was up in the small, dark hours, satisfied to see the colours and movement of stars that she'd caught.

During the day she stayed up, processing the photos on her computer during breaks from her other work. She was tired again when she channelled that night.

It was fifteen minutes or so before Aedgar seemed ready to speak. 'Thank you for coming,' Nerida said.

'Was a bit difficult.'

She could see that. 'What's going on?'

'This body is still too sensitive,' he said.

'Yes, it's causing suffering.' Mari had complained about her neck at lunchtime. Her stump was reddened, the skin dry.

'The whole body doesn't seem to be very comfortable,' he continued.

'That's right.'

'There are some issues.' He seemed to survey further. 'Too exhausted.'

Nerida was too tired herself to listen properly. 'Exhausting?'

'Too exhausted. Needs more rest, focussing on the important things. Too much distraction going on—distraction with this place and its problems.'

'I can stop talking to her about the problems in the clinic. That would help I guess.'

'Well, she should just realise that these problems are not her problems. It's not easy, of course, because of the circumstances you live in.

'It will get better, but it will take quite a while.'

'You know she stayed up all night with the stars?'

'A good way to spend the night. Can be exhausting. It's a good thing to do if you can sleep all day.'

'Yes. But she won't take the opportunity to sleep during the day because she doesn't wanna miss out on anything.'

'There are quite a few things to do in her day. And taken together with all these distractions—it's hard to find the real path.

'At the moment it just seems at times like there is a maze of pathways.

'She needs to learn how to listen better, to find guidance through that maze.

'But it is not easy. It's very complicated. It's not so easy to make a decision about what's right or what's wrong to do, because everything is attached to something else.

'Very difficult circumstances,' he concluded.

'So, did your friend come?'

Nerida nodded.

'She did. Things are better. I'm much happier with Claire around.'

'You will have another person come, that you know. Some others will leave, though.

'Too many wrong decisions in this place.'

'Yes.' *Please God let Eric leave.*

The living room blind was up. Clouds were streaks of orange on the western horizon. Aedgar said, 'The change to the planet is starting soon.'

'I'm happy for that,' she said. Everyday they heard more about the dangers to the earth—profound irreversible changes.

'These damaging things have been around for a long time. People continue to damage it.

'But other people are more aware of it.

'And the number of humans who are aware of these things is growing.

'It's still all about greed. It's one of the worst things around. Most of this damage is done to satisfy greed.'

'Yes. Yesterday Mari and I were learning about the network of clean water under the ground in Mexico (between the Americas). The swamps have been blocked up by big buildings, built for greed. And it's hard for the water to be clean now. There's a danger of water being poisoned all the way through—in the caves and the rivers underground. I thought about what you say.

'And this is how it goes. Every day there's an illustration before our eyes.'

'Sadly so. People will hear more and more about it. The masses need to be educated,' he said. 'The ones with the lowest intelligence have the biggest greed. Unfortunately, they're in positions where they put pressure on other people.

'They must be eliminated—taken out of power.

'Plenty of them have to go back to **very basic work**.

'It's an educational journey for them. And yet, they still need to discover, once they come back, that they spoiled it for themselves.

'If they only would understand.

'Most of them, if you told them this now, would think you're insane. Some of them might slow down a little bit and think about things.'

. . .

Nerida appreciated his insight. She was increasingly conflicted between her work as a doctor, her self-image as a scientifically minded person and her participation in the channelling. She noticed her troubled eyes in the mirror.

The conflict was there at clinic when she spoke to a client using her intuition. It felt good but she still doubted herself. She practised listening to her instincts in small ways.

In that flow, one morning, she asked a mum about parts of the kangaroo that would help address her child's iron deficiency and encouraged her to feed the child those parts when the family went hunting on the weekend.

Conflict came that afternoon when the remote manager in town sent a former nurse, Lorena, to audit the clinic. Nerida and the team greeted her warmly, but Lorena was cold. Her brief was to enforce KPIs. Nerida had to look them up to see that meant Key Performance Indicators.

Lorena had a narrow face and a pinched nose. She wore thick-framed, colourful glasses that were supposed to make her look interesting but only made her face look smaller. She read from a list, holding people back from their work after the next morning meeting.

They were not keeping up with some of the diabetes checks. They were not recording Pap tests in the right box on the computer (even though they were doing them). They had only reported sixty percent of clients' smoking status.

'Well, the other forty percent are probably children. Did you check that?' Nerida asked her.

'Two-thirds of the Community comes to the clinic and half of them have diabetes,' Claire told Lorena. 'We have one regular nurse, who does on call 24/7. Today, that's me. One doctor. No functioning manager. You're here to get blood out of a stone, are you?' She looked sideways at the interloper, with half-closed lids. She was leaning against a cabinet, elbows resting in a tired, open posture, her chin slightly lifted in challenge. Lorena couldn't look at her.

Nerida explained, 'We stabilise a person for emergency evacuation to Alice at least once a week. Sometimes three or four times a week. We have young ones who self harm, threaten suicide. We endure youth carrying out suicide. We look after people with brain damage induced by petrol sniffing. And their carers, who sometimes collapse. Victims of assault. Broken-hearted people.

'We do this acute care in the context of looking after people so that their chronic conditions don't deteriorate. Claire and Bec are good at it. We've got the highest rate of completed health checks and plans and the best rate of child immunisations of any Aboriginal Medical Service in the Territory. We made $300,000 in government funding for this clinic last year, but we don't have a reliable ECG machine or a proper pharmacy. Where'd the money go? How about funding another nurse? Or another doctor?'

Eric was in the corner, supporting himself against a desk. *He looks like he might vomit*, Nerida thought. *He must have heard what Claire said about a useless manager.*

Gathering his car keys, Eric left the room.

'I guess he needs a drink,' Claire said to Nerida under her breath as she left. 'I've got sick people waiting for me,' she said to Lorena.

Lorena referred to a sheaf of papers and said, 'I have list of KPIs that I mean to use to give structure, using protocols and guidelines, to your work. Given that the folder of protocols and guidelines date from before the Intervention, you will have to update them.'

Nerida laughed and said, 'I'll do that. In my free time.'

Lorena had a fetish about children's iron. Like many Indigenous children, Anangu babies were strongly bonded to their mothers with long breastfeeding, sometimes after their mother's iron stores were depleted. Lorena wanted the babies and children to be injected with iron. 'Because you can never rely on them to come back.'

'If you treat people respectfully and kindly, they do come back,' Nerida said. 'Injections are painful. They can cause allergic reactions and scars. There are other ways.'

She looked at the recall list. 'We're talking about three children, right? Give me a chance to talk to the parents and Terri at childcare. If their iron levels aren't up in two months, we can talk about an injection.' She thought of the mum she'd seen going hunting with the family.

'You can't trust them on anything,' Lorena persisted.

Later, Claire heard Lorena complain to a patient. 'That doctor is dangerous. She'd neglecting the children. She might need to be reported to the Medical Board.'

'Who was she talking to?'

'Thea,' Claire scoffed. 'Wrong person to choose. Thea looked down her nose at her and left. She only came to get her meds.'

They did some research. Claire found out from colleagues at another community that Lorena was a failed nurse. Unable to work in a rural clinic, she'd also been moved sideways from clinical work in town. Her knowledge was inadequate. And she treated Aboriginal people, like Nerida, as idiots.

'Aboriginal people get very weary of the undermining of their self-built organisations ... There's a constant stream of righteous, ignorant busybodies who come to make us conform to whatever formula they misuse from their management course,' Nerida said to Claire. 'If they've ever studied management. Most of the ones we get here have no training at all.'

'White people are like Toyotas,' said Claire, quoting a famous essay about the way outsiders came and went from remote Aboriginal communities.

'A Toyota's more reliable and gets better mileage. It doesn't think it's superior to you,' Nerida said wearily.

Nerida reflected on how she found Aedgar's use of the word 'intelligence' awkward. She thought about the concept. *Lorena is probably a good example of the kind of person he's talking about. She has power over us. And, infuriatingly, can disrupt our care. She's done nothing to earn or deserve that power. And she wastes my energy.*

TWENTY-SIX

MUTITJULU
WEDNESDAY MARCH 13, 2013

'When you say 'low intelligence' I have the feeling you are talking about people who are poor in spirit,' Nerida said to Aedgar. 'Not the conventional way of talking about intelligence—being able to read and write or doing arithmetic. Or do you mean understanding other peoples' feelings?'

'There are different forms of intelligence,' Aedgar recognised. 'There are some people on the highest levels who don't have **any** of the required intelligence. They think they know some things, but they don't.

'Because this kind of intelligence is missing, it's hard for them to get insight into what they're doing. I mean intelligence about human interactions: among each other and with the planet.'

Does he mean compassion? More than that. 'That's the only intelligence worth having, in your estimation?'

Aedgar nodded. 'Indeed. Some other skills can be brought to good use: trying to find out how things work or how they could be improved.

'But these people at the highest levels won't have the ability to learn. When the most important part of intelligence is completely missing, other parts they may have are useless.'

'Is it a matter of their evolution? Are they young souls, who haven't had enough experience?'

'It's more like—people would call it (it's not, but we're trying to explain it)—it's like genetics. Some people have it, some don't. It's just missing.' He used Mari's hands as he spoke, looking for the right word or concept.

'Mmm. So they may have lived many lifetimes, but they're just not able to mature—?'

'They failed over and over again. Something is missing in their essence. There is a lack of that kind of intelligence that can't be substituted for. It's like part of evolution gone wrong.

'These ones are going to eliminate themselves because they keep making the wrong choice, over and over again.'

Nerida cocked her head. 'Let me see if I understand. When they were cast from All That Is, they still had the potential of all of us. But they've chosen to go the wrong way, repeatedly, and that has deformed them, somehow?'

'It's an evolutionary problem. The nearest idea I could use to explain it is genetics. It doesn't have anything to do with education or other things, because they are not able to learn even the basics of that special kind of intelligence.'

'They don't learn kindness, compassion? They don't learn about love?'

'No, it's all about greed.

He paused for a beat. 'Not all of them in those positions are that way.

'Some other souls, seeking a learning experience, feel attracted to them. Those ones still have the ability to learn, to avoid the same mistakes next time around.'

Nerida, ever hopeful, pondered. 'Mhmm. And perhaps they may ameliorate or lessen the impact of the damage done by some of their greedy colleagues at times, if they have insight.'

'They have insight. It depends on their level of ability to learn, how long it takes them to figure it out.'

'So you say that these people in power, of low intelligence, who need to be removed from power, are kind of an evolutionary dead end?' Nerida found the concept astonishing.

'Yes.'

'And is this a set of physical traits that's passed from parent to child or is it something in the soul that incarnates over and over that isn't working properly? Or both?'

'It's both.'

'But they will incarnate again? Because there's nothing but evolution and learning for spirit?' *Isn't that how it works?*

'Yes, they will.'

'So even for them there's no death?'

'At some point they kind of run out of energy.'

'Uhuh?' *This is weird.*

'So there is some kind of end to it.'

Perhaps he sensed that the idea was too much for Nerida to handle, because this time Aedgar changed the subject, tangentially.

'There are some people in power who got attracted by these beings. And once they figure it out, it's very hard for them to handle—the whole experience.

'For example, there are people who go into politics. When they leave politics, they do something completely different—like something where they try to protect the environment— because they still have the insight to see what's right and wrong.

'They leave their political positions because they are kind of shocked by the cruelty and lack of knowledge of these people they felt attracted to.

'Those people have chosen this experience to learn what's the wrong and what's the right way to choose. And many of them go into areas where they, later, try to protect the environment, the planet, try to make it a better place.'

Nerida thought of bourgeois retirees, who in old age began doing things contrary to their decades of work. A former prime minister who did nothing (that she could see) to break down racist barriers during his political career, who became a campaigner to push for an end to apartheid in South Africa. She had thought him a hypocrite, too little too late. But she did judge people harshly when she was younger.

Returning to his first point, Aedgar said, 'The ones who haven't learned will go on, continuing to chase satisfaction of their greed.'

There was a lull. Nerida heard Selkie's kids kicking, running and leaping, marking their ball on the road outside.

She said, 'Some of the world religions try to teach opposition to greed. We've had teachers like Jesus, the Buddha, Mohammed who have tried to teach against greed.'

'Yes, they did,' he agreed. 'They were just caring for humankind and the planet. It's not right to call it a religion.'

'It's not right to make it into a religion, the teachings of these people?' She was irritated by being taught new concepts and was not as open-minded as she would like to be. And the previous point about politicos who become environmentalists hit too close to home.

'People must begin to understand that learning, evolving, growing is not a voluntary decision, like choosing a religion. It's something they *have* to learn, protecting the environment and the planet to make it last.'

'So, you see choosing to live in a religion as a way of avoiding dealing with what's happening to the planet?'

'People form these groups to have their own way of living, trying to live in their own world, which doesn't work out in the end because they are still on the same planet.'

Selkie called the children inside for dinner. Nerida got up to switch on a light, suddenly aware of the darkness in the house.

'There's a very broad spectrum of people who consider themselves religious. Some of them use their religiosity to do good work—feeding people, caring for people,' she argued. 'Others use their religiosity to do the opposite: to have power over people and oppress them.'

'Well, that's why the term 'religion' is not a good one,' he replied. 'It's about forming groups.

'Some of them are the good-hearted ones.

'But others form groups to reach their goal which is, once again, greed. They form groups to satisfy their greed, for the paper with the numbers on it. And for power.

'The ones that form groups to do good have less greed. 'All of these call themselves religious. That can't be.

'In some areas, if you call it a religion, you get away with a lot of things. If you have a group of the bad ones, they normally are very close with the bad ones in politics. They support each other in their way of being bad, so to say.'

'They reinforce each other's power?'

'Yes. If you have these political people who work very closely with religion, that's gonna be the group that calls itself religious and is actually bad. They try to benefit from each other—and not in a good way.'

Nerida had seen this. 'They do. They spread ideas that make people feel unhappy and isolated. People give up their power to them.' She'd sat in church as a youth, looking around, trying to figure out what people believed. She'd felt shamed and isolated by preachers, herself. When she was an activist, she engaged in conflict with religious zealots once or twice. Once, when she demonstrated for abortion rights in front of Parliament House in Sydney, antiabortionists made a circle around her and 'prayed,' ranting aggressively and shouting at her.

Her boyfriend, later the children's father, Sam, broke up the incipient exorcism, leading her away. He was a gentle, mostly passive man. She appreciated the action.

Aedgar was talking. 'Well, they have ideas. And these ideas support the ones in politics. And the ones in politics say, "These people have got the right ideas," if it's beneficial to them.

'You saw that vividly in your last lifetime on Earth.'

'Indeed, I did.'

'Henry VIII was a good example of somebody doing this.'

'Yeah, you just form another group, to get a benefit out of it.'

'Take all the property, kill the ones that don't agree, give riches to the ones who do agree,' she summarised.

'Yes,' Aedgar said. 'He's an example of one of those the planet didn't need.'

'You've said before that one of the people who was attracted to those of low intelligence (and had the idea that he could do good things) is the current president of the United States of America.'

'He's struggling. He's struggling because all these horrible things are going to reveal themselves to him. He can hardly stand it.

'He is kind of discovering new aspects of that every day.'

'Hmm. The machines that go to far-away places to kill people when nobody's there to kill them—they are his political responsibility.'

'Well, this machinery was there before. But now he's on top of it. And the one on top of it is supposed to be responsible. It's like in your job. If people make mistakes you are responsible.'

'That's right.'

'He's not a good candidate for being sacrificed. But he got this job to be sacrificed, for taking up responsibilities.

'People working with him thought, "He's the one we need the least. It's his responsibility now. If our bad ideas don't work out, he's the one that has to go."

'And because this person knows how to think, it's very hard for him to see all these things reveal themselves every day. He doesn't trust the people he works with anymore.'

'So "Court" hasn't changed so much, in so many centuries.'

'Not at all. It's still the same kind of people who are attracted to it —some of them to learn.

'And it's always the ones who lack this certain kind of intelligence who find an easy way into that system. That's how it works.'

'The current 'court' in this island, where I live, has very little genuine intelligence there.'

'There are some really bad ones there,' he said. He seemed to survey the Australian parliament.

'And then there are some people who have the same problem as the American guy. They wish they could find an easy way out of it, because they are not strong enough to handle it. They've learnt their lesson, so to say.'

'I guess it takes a lot of greed to support the damage being done to this island, that's causing an imbalance on the planet,' Nerida said.

'It happens everywhere. But you do have people here that are greedier than other ones.

Some of them are female.'

'Yes, one in particular is one of the richest women in the world.' Nerida had met people who worked for her. And hated it. She worked people for many days without a break, was haughty and arrogant in word and deed.

'Well, she hasn't done much to deserve that accumulation. She was brought up and taught by one of these individuals that's just the best example of the species with the total lack of intelligence. In the first place, she didn't have a choice. When she had a choice later, she enjoyed the bad decisions too much.

'She's satisfying her greed. She'll have to learn the hard way.'

'There's a woman working now as Prime Minister of this country. Perhaps she's not very bright.' Nerida said.

'No. That's right. She didn't have bad intentions originally, but she's forced to play the game. It's other people that make the decisions. She has to go with it.'

'She must fear losing her power, being the first woman in the role.'

'She doesn't know what else to do,' he said. 'I could see her staying there. She seems to be easy to "steer".'

'I guess these political ones will have to deal with a lot of change, chaos and difficulty in the coming period,' she said.

'The worst or toughest thing will be when it's revealed to each of them that they were the ones who made it all so difficult.'

'That's surely a between-lives kind of insight?'

Aedgar nodded in agreement. 'Then, as well. And once they are back in the next life. Once they have enough insight to understand— they will see it with their own eyes and feel it with their own body.'

'I hope the earth doesn't have to be sacrificed for their education'.

'It's suffering. That's why they have a lot of work to do. We need to try to minimise the suffering.'

'I appreciate your good work, Aedgar.'

'I am here to help.

'I think I'll go for now. This body is very exhausted.

'I'll encourage her to rest some more.'

'Please do so. Talk to you again, soon.'

Nerida got up to turn on the air-con. The sun was long gone but the torrid day hung over the country, radiating from heated earth.

Mari returned, blinking in the fluorescent light.

TWENTY-SEVEN

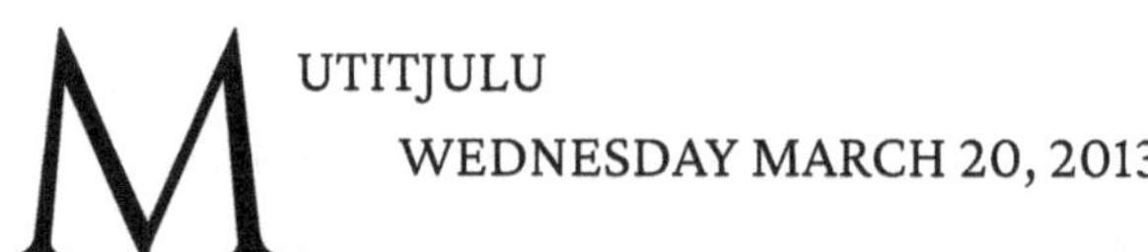

Mutitjulu
WEDNESDAY MARCH 20, 2013

Some things Aedgar says feel oppressive, Nerida mulled as she walked to the clinic. *Or is it just that he stimulates me to think? He makes me think. And I'm so fuckin' tired all the time.*

Autumn hadn't yet come. But the temperature peaked below thirty most days, which made it easier to be outside.

Peter's dogs were fewer. The local council men's had stayed up. *I'll get fitter walking, and it's not so scary, now.* She passed by bright flowers blossoming. *I wish he didn't talk about greed so much. So judgemental.*

She acted like she was humouring an old relation sometimes.

Browsing the internet the night before, she came across a book extract describing the forced expulsion of the Spanish Jewry from Andalusia in the 1490s.

Reading it, she learned more about what happened to Mari's ancestors on her Dad's side, after what Monica said. This happened: a documentary, the news or an article they saw—usually from science or history—illustrated what Aedgar or Monica had talked about.

It's called confirmation bias. Seeing what you want to see, she grouched at herself.

She felt heavier as she approached the clinic. Things piled up and seemed worse and worse with management.

The latest atrocity was a ban on non-Aboriginal people being treated at the clinic.

People like Arthur, the only person who stayed there to try to keep the houses intact, were to be denied treatment. He should go to Yulara 30 kilometres away, or Alice Springs 500 kilometres away, because they said white people cost the clinic too much. So should Selkie, totally devoted to her Anangu family, who worked untold hours at the clinic without ever being properly paid.

Clinic Manager Eric had no problem with the ban. Implementing and overseeing it was his first important job. He was focussed.

The clinic ban appalled Nerida. With a white mother and a black father, the bosses had hit her sore spot. She was irate.

Mari started pacing and talking about taking a spear to Eric if he came near their place.

Nerida understood but did not find that helpful.

She initially responded by assuming a mistake had been made, documenting the numbers to show that non-Aboriginal people did not cost the clinic anything. She was able to demonstrate that government funding meant that the clinic provided amply for everyone.

Government funding for medical care and medicines for people in remote areas was not restricted by race. It was a modest and powerful reform left over from the seventies, probably still in place because it was pleasing for primary producers and mining companies.

Claire was a wiz with finances in chronic disease management. She researched it all and brought the disparate elements of government programs together. And Nerida did as she was told. So Mutitjulu clinic made a good surplus each year Nerida worked there. The numbers were there in their record-keeping system, which was straightforward and transparent because so many remote Aboriginal community clinics did not have qualified managers.

That money should be used for a third nurse. Or a couple of part-time Aboriginal Health Workers, she wrote. She thought Eric, being an Aboriginal person, would be pleased by her advocacy for the Community.

There was no response to her letter, except for reiteration of the exclusion of longterm Mutitjulu residents from the clinic on the basis of their race. And an elaboration of it: the nurses were to grill people about their ethnicity when they came to the clinic.

Becca was very uncomfortable.

Claire, a brown-skin child of privileged public servants in recently-colonised Papua New Guinea, refused outright to participate. Her job was on the line.

Nerida reviewed the clinic's records one evening, monitoring follow up of patient recalls. She saw with a shock that Eric, with the remote assistance of the manager in Alice Springs, had read through the confidential medical files of non-Aboriginal people and others, she could see, that they considered should be excluded from care. She could even see how long he'd been in each file.

The records Eric read included that of a local (white) politician who had contracted HIV on a trip to the Philippines. Nerida diagnosed him and gave him hours of counselling and support, with a referral for medications. He came to Mutitjulu because he didn't feel sure of confidentiality elsewhere.

Eric spent twenty minutes reading his file. He must've been fascinated.

He also read the records of the Respite manager (one of the sweetest people Nerida had ever met), who'd been referred for infertility treatment after she and her husband had been trying to conceive for three years.

The Aboriginal woman—a fair-skinned Koori, like Nerida—who helped people with their Centrelink paperwork and their Basics card at the shop. Eric spent forty minutes reading about her. *Probably poured himself a drink.*

A young Asian man who worked with Arthur, who'd been treated for chlamydia.

And Mari.

Next morning at the clinic Nerida heard Jasmine shouting at Eric. She stormed out yelling, 'Fuck off!'

Eric shouted after her, 'You're sacked right now, you cunt!'

Nerida found Jasmine at the shop, buying consolatory chips. 'Do you want us all to walk out for you? We could strike.'

Jasmine explained that Eric demanded she 'Make a list of the people who are banned from the clinic "cause they're parasites." I should understand, he says. All slimy. "Being Black." Huh. As if I have anything in common with him!'

'Do you want your job back?' Nerida asked.

'Nah. I won't go there again while he's here. I can camp on Thea's verandah if I can't pay rent,' Jasmine said.

WHEN NERIDA TOLD Mari that Eric read her medical records without reason or permission, her rage escalated. Every time his name was mentioned Mari's blood pressure rose and her eyes widened. It was as if she was creating another barb on the spear, so she could tear bits of him out on it. Nerida saw it in her eyes and posture. She was shaken by the physicality of Mari's anger. But not surprised by it.

The Koori woman counsellor and support worker whose record he had also read began legal proceedings against management in Alice.

Nerida wrote letters to her union, the Ombudsman and the Anti-Discrimination Board. She woke in the small hours of the morning or didn't sleep at all. In her grey home office, she wrote furious, articulate documents.

The Rock came out of the dark as the sun rose, hard and fast.

Sighing, she went to shower before work. Her neck was sore. Her eyes and back ached.

One morning soon after Jasmine was sacked, Nerida was inspired to compose a petition against the ban, in support of everyone living or working at Mutitjulu being cared for by the clinic.

She took her text next door, where Selkie spent the morning translating it into Pitjantjatjara (on pain of secrecy).

Nerida took the petition to Respite.

From there, the uncredited, bilingual letter circulated through the Community, collecting the signatures of Elders and others who were not afraid to speak up. The signatures were sweet bush flowers.

Some were in immaculate cursive like perfectly round wattle blossoms, some signed in capitals as wild as desert roses. A few signed with an 'x,' like a scar on the Rock, with the respite manager's record of their names written neatly next to them. The completed petition, with over one hundred signatures, was sent to the Equal Opportunity Commission in Canberra.

'Black people standing up for white people. For social justice. Aww,' said Claire. She patted her heart and made a warm, sad smile when Nerida told her.

The manager of the Yulara clinic called and wrote to the Department of Health in Canberra, too. He was a dedicated man with a strong, innate sense of what was right. *Who probably has Aspergers*, Nerida thought fondly when she went to talk to him about the situation.

The modest clinic at Yulara looked after thousands of tourists a day and over twelve hundred residents. They couldn't take on the care of upset people excluded from Mutitjulu clinic on racist grounds, many of whom had complex medical histories. Muti patients were used to taking their time, after waiting, consulting with Dr Nerida and the nurses. Yulara couldn't accommodate them.

So, Nerida met excluded patients outside the clinic, near the phone at the shop or near the art centre, distributing metformin and statins. She gave Arthur his blood pressure tablets in a paper bag as if they were contraband. Their clinic was funded to provide medicines to people who lived there, regardless of their ethnicity. Nerida knew it.

Maybe it was the petition. Maybe it was Yulara clinic. Or the Koori worker's threat to sue. As it happened, Eric was away, probably grog-sick, the day the email came from Alice. The odious 'condition of care' was rescinded.

Mari baked and built a Schwarzwälder Torte (without Schnaps) and invited everyone (except Eric, of course) to celebrate.

Over cake they figured that something was rotten in the organisation. The long search for money from Alice Springs management, with the fact that they never saw any of the money earned by the clinic, played on Nerida's mind. *Almost a million dollars since I began here. Money made with, by and for Mutitjulu residents. Where did it go?*

At work, harassment from Alice Springs continued. Nerida dreaded opening her inbox. One day, there was a decree that Mari was no longer allowed to drive Nerida's work car. Or any clinic car.

The next it was 'Why does the clinic provide people with Vitamin C, paracetamol and pawpaw ointment? These consumables are too expensive for our organisation to be subsidising.'

'Because there is no pharmacy in Yulara. And people are poor. And it's our job to relieve suffering,' Nerida replied. There was no point appealing to Eric for support. He took on a dazed look and went home if she tried to talk to him.

One morning when she was alone with him, Eric told her that he'd made a discovery. The clinic was only funded for a doctor, a manager and an admin worker, thus he would have to fire the nurses, he said.

Amongst all this, it felt like Aedgar told Nerida things she didn't want to hear. She reflected on this on a drive back to the clinic. She'd made a home visit to a client with prostate cancer who lived on his land out of town. Taking him his medicine and checking up on him was a blessed change of pace.

She was queasy about Aedgar's suggestion that there was something passed on from parents in people who were unable to 'expand their energy'—wasn't there something dangerous about that idea? She feared an extreme response, the labelling and disempowerment of any humans. What would she do if Aedgar's ideas turned out to be misused? *Well, that's not gonna happen. I love him already.*

And he was somehow a friend (or even, perhaps, a creature) of the woman she loved.

Nevertheless, she got steadily more uncomfortable with some ideas he raised.

Beyond her emotional defensiveness and reactivity, she thought about Charles Darwin. Such a gentle, cautious man. And yet his theory had been taken up and thoroughly twisted by others.

What began with finches in Galapagos was misused to justify imperialist domination and racism.

At the same time, there was part of her that felt relief. *There **is** a difference between the greedy stupid ones and the rest of us.*

Here I've been thinking all along that my greed is the problem. But there's a qualitative difference between overeating and taking billions of dollars of wealth out of the earth and other peoples' skin.

Maybe her revolutionary studies were not for nothing—*the ruling class has to fall, after all.*

She was distracted from politics and philosophy by her irritating body. A literal pain in the arse. Nerida had haemorrhoids.

She had been shocked to see them in 1987, shiny pink lumps of her guts coming out of her anus, when she was pregnant with her second child.

It was one of many uncontrollable changes her body went through to bring her children into the world.

The haemorrhoids subsided as she recovered from the birth and slowly grew into her mama-shaped body.

Now, well over twenty years later, she still had a round, mother's belly. But it was soft.

Sometimes her body did crave babies. She was impressed that her eldest, daughter Ruby, managed to remain child-free into her early thirties. *I guess she learned something from our experiences.*

But now the haemorrhoids were back and worse than ever, a vivid reminder of the forceful strain of childbearing.

A few had thrombosed—formed a clot inside and turned dark as red grapes. Her bottom was so painful she cried sometimes. It hurt all day and was worse at night.

She took codeine a few nights to be able to sleep and then, of course, her shit turned to bricks and there was more crying on the toilet and lying on the bed waiting for an enema to work on a Sunday afternoon.

She needed surgery. And eventually was able to arrange it for herself.

Eric and the remote manager refused to pay sick leave, or give her any leave, because the surgery was 'elective.'

The implication was that she wasn't really sick but chose to have cuts and stitches to the blood vessels in her anus as a way of getting time off. Her union lawyer wrote the employer a letter. It took a fight, with more tedious documentation, to get paid leave.

After her surgery, Nerida returned to work promptly but still needed dressings on her bottom. She walked little and gingerly. At home, she spent her time in bed playing with her phone or lying on the couch watching telly. Mari brought cups of tea and cuddles.

IT WAS good for her spirit and her intellect, then, when Mari offered to channel.

She had a fleeting thought that perhaps Mari didn't mind, for once, having a short break from her. Mari had seen more of Nerida than either of them would have wished for during and after her surgery. Nerida felt that she was at risk of losing her mystery.

After Mari went into trance, Nerida waited more than ten minutes before Aedgar cleared the throat and greeted her, croakily.

'It's that dry place again,' he said.

'Yes. The rain hasn't come yet.'

'It will,' he said.

'It will.' *Wishing for rain is a chronic illness in the desert.*

He said, 'Some other things had to be done first.'

What does he mean by that? And what do they have to do with bringing the rain? She didn't understand how time and energy and priorities work when you're not in a physical body. Aedgar seemed god-like in his abilities but he had limits, ways of being and doing. She was curious about the nature of his existence. But didn't know how to begin to ask about the physics of it.

He asked, 'What have you done lately?

'We went on an adventure to the city.' She had almost forgotten about their exciting weekend away, since her recent difficulties.

He raised the eyebrows, 'Adventure?'

'Yes. We went to see Abbey channelling Fortunatus. It was very interesting!'

Aedgar sounded glum when he said, 'He was avoiding me.'

'I know! Nobody else avoids us, but he was avoiding us! He didn't want to talk to us.'

It was a big event. The women had front row seats on stage right. Fortunatus, being channelled by Abbey, totally refused to even look in their direction. Nerida had a question or two prepared. Her bum was not so sore then—the codeine was working—and she enjoyed being out and dressed up in Sydney.

She wanted to ask whether there was a contradiction between individuals creating abundance for themselves and the challenges of caring for the planet's environment.

And maybe Fortunatus would like to share a platform with Aedgar. But she had no chance.

The questions asked were the usual types of questions at a Fortunatus session. People asked about money, businesses, relationships. Even their cars.

Aedgar continued. 'I was tempted to use our friend as a host to ask some questions. But he was avoiding me—'

Nerida agreed. 'He didn't look our way—'

'—completely.'

'—not even once, that's right!'

'It was his day,' Aedgar said. 'It was his ideas and his thoughts. So he had the right to ignore me.'

'Yes. But it might have been so much more interesting if he hadn't.'

'It might have started a wild discussion,' said Aedgar.

'Yes!' enthused Nerida. 'It would have changed their routine completely.'

'In general, we have the same goal. But we have different approaches. He conveys his ideas in a very different way. But it is good to be able to talk to people.'

'He had a good crowd there.' There were about 1200 people at a Sydney conference centre.

Aedgar said, 'It's always a quest for education. There was a lot of energy around, mainly positive. I was surprised how positive this energy was. I guess they've all been anticipating that they get their wishes fulfilled.'

'What did you want to ask him? Did you have any questions formulated?'

Aedgar said, 'I wanted to ask him about depriving the earth, to give people different ideas. And about the goal of fulfilling one's greed and the consequences of it.'

'That would have been disruptive, Aedgar. All hell would have broken loose if you had asked that question.'

'It might have been a bit more entertaining.'

'Yes. I would have loved that.'

'Maybe another time.'

'Perhaps.'

'But you've seen it now. You don't have to do it again.'

'It seems to be,' Nerida speculated, 'as Trevor said, that it's all about manifesting things. Not much else, really.'

Aedgar explained, 'He has his own special audience. Some of them are genuinely interested in the science of channelling. Most of them are only interested in how to attract the money, the partner, business success.

'I don't think many of them were thinking about how to attract better health.'

'There were a few people there who I thought might enjoy learning from talking to you one day,' Nerida ventured.

'Why did you think that?'

'Umm, I guess their vibration was a little bit different from most. They seemed to have a little more depth. But that was just an impression.'

'Well, that's the few who are genuinely interested in the bigger picture.

'There's nothing wrong with using the idea that you will attract things with your thoughts. But, as he said, it can be overdone.'

'Yes, you heard that story of having 67 cars and 42 houses and "What do I do with it all now?" Seriously?'

'Give it to individuals in need,' Aedgar suggested. 'Mind you, you don't have to give them away for free. That would slow down the learning experience of these people who are on the receiving end.'

That was not what Nerida expected. 'I've heard it called "philanthropic karma." Karma that accumulates from, er, being too nice to people.'

She'd heard the expression and thought about the concept. She was polite to Aedgar but underneath she thought the idea was an excuse for rich people to hold onto their things. Thea had not called her Dr Tjula, the soft one, for nothing.

'You can stop people from achieving their goal or finding their path,' Aedgar said. 'Some of them will be delayed only, but for some of them it comes to a complete stop. And then they get stuck and have to do it again—'

Perhaps he sensed her resistance because he added '—which doesn't imply that you have to act in a completely opposite way.'

'There's always a place for kindness and compassion,' she said.

'Sometimes difficult to find the right way,' he said.

Nerida was incredulous. 'The right way to be kind and compassionate?'

'Without depriving them of their learning experience, yes. They need to expand their energy. If one's too kind, it will stop the expansion of their energy because that's what learning is all about.'

'You know what you're talking about here,' Nerida said. 'I have a feeling this is an area of expertise for you.'

'Well, I would say it is. One of the reasons I might not sound as cheerful as Fortunatus.'

'Yes.'

'Just another way,' he said.

'Well, for me it's a better way because your personality suits mine better,' Nerida had to admit. 'If Mari was channelling Fortunatus, I'd hardly know what to do with it.'

She envied Abbey her success. Her husband Clive was a businessman and had the skills to put her, channelling Fortunatus's teachings, in the limelight. Abbey went around the world with her rare and amazing abilities and made good money. Their body of work was well established.

Clive had died recently.

Nerida was impressed that Abbey was able to go on working without his physical presence. He had always been her facilitator. Nerida and Mari hardly understood how she could continue.

The idea of having to survive the death of their partner was the hardest thought they each had because it was inevitable for one of them. Nerida coped with it by a kind of spiritual denial, 'We never really die. We'll always be able to connect again.'

Mari was more dramatic. 'I won't live without you. How could I? Why would I want to? If you die, I'll just die too.' She said it several times over the years.

The questions asked by the audience in the Fortunatus forum were a lot less serious than the issues Mari and Nerida argued, talked and thought about.

Aedgar agreed that Nerida might not cope with Fortunatus' style. 'True. Sometimes you need to talk straight with people. You can't just package it all up, so it sounds nicer than it is.'

Nerida tried to figure it out now. 'So, manifesting things into your life by your thoughts is a true thing, but one has to be careful about, discriminating about, what one wants to attract?'

'That's why he will be able to do plenty of talks about it,' Aedgar said. 'It can be very easy once you've found out how it works—but it's not as easy as he puts it.

'Because the human mind will always have second or third thoughts that will stop that rule from working, or just give it a little detour. And then you might attract things you didn't want.'

'And that's how we learn.'

'That's how you learn. It's all about experience—'

'That's what we're here for,' she said.

Aedgar continued '—experience and how to expand energy.'

What does he keep saying that? It's starting to sound like a slogan. 'Do you know about Seth and Jane Roberts?' she asked.

'I know about Seth. I guess Jane Roberts was the host or friend ... Yes, he had another name for her—trying to remember it—' Aedgar said, 'It was an old-fashioned name.'

'A male name,' Nerida said. 'I'm going to be reading some more of Seth's work soon.'

'You've got other work to do.'

Nerida laughed at his blunt judgement. 'I need to make you a higher priority.'

'We just don't have that much time,' he said. 'We need to start to act on some things— educating people. If reading Seth might help you to realise things quicker—nothing wrong with it. But we've got important work to do.'

'Yes.'

Aedgar moved Mari's head towards her right shoulder. 'There is some strange energy about this place. It's like something is boiling underneath. It's not finished.'

'Surely, it's that Rock that we sit upon. It extends under the ground here.' Uluru was like an iceberg, with most of its mass under the ground.

Aedgar was disturbed. 'It is still too hot. The radiation is less, but it's still around.'

Nerida didn't like to hear bad things about Uluru. She remembered Blossom Wandering saying, 'It's a terrible place. Nothing lives there!'

Now, she granted, 'It's a difficult place for people to be, I think.'

'I get the feeling it's a temporary thing,' he said.

'You mean the community here is a temporary thing or the difficulty is a temporary thing?'

'People might leave at some point,' he observed. 'Some of them will definitely leave. They can't cope with the energy.'

'Some strong, very strong, people will stay. There are not many of them.

'Some children are strong too. They will be taught by the little one that's coming. Won't be that long. At least, from my understanding it won't be that long.

'But then again, what's time?'

Nerida was very much enmeshed in time. 'I need to turn off the oven because the bread is cooked. Please excuse me for a moment.'

'You're baking bread?'

'Mari's baking bread,' she called from the kitchen. 'She makes a delicious sourdough.'

'Good work.'

'Good bread, yes,' Nerida sat back down. The room was full of the warming smell.

'Once you know how to do it, it's easy. Unfortunately, most people are not interested. People could have happier lives.'

'This is an opinion that you and Mari share.'

'Yeah, combined with an ale or two, wouldn't be bad. And some meat.'

'Did you grow wheat and barley or rye for bread during your time on earth?'

'I didn't. I had sheep. Aiden grew grains. Not a lot, but enough.'

'So you had fresh grain to make bread?'

'We didn't do it. We had people who did it.

'We could have done it ourselves. It was just not the fashion for us to do so. People could have become suspicious. "They've got people who work for them. Why do they make bread themselves?" Well, I could have replied "To show them how it's done." But that wasn't my intention.'

'No. And you didn't want to insult your servants, who worked well for you.' Even now, she was checking that he wasn't mean.

'They were nice people and they were treated nicely,' he agreed. She needed to hear that.

'So, when you say that we need to begin educating soon, I guess for now I'll keep writing and we'll look for the opportunities. Keep practising, keep writing.'

'People can read it,' he said.

'You think I can begin to share some of it?'

'You should collect and write a bit more. That's why you have other things to do.

'People need to read things first. Before we can talk to them.

'Then when people have an idea what we will talk about, they can prepare—prepare questions to ask.'

Nerida was glad of this vision. 'Did you have any impression of the apparatus, the way that the Fortunatus meeting was set up?'

'Perhaps we might work with them in future.'

'We might. We might work with the host of Aiden and Monica.'

'Sounds good.'

'It would be more likely,' he said.

'She's not wanting to travel, that Dawn, and is shy.'

'But you two are happy to travel,' Aedgar said, correctly. 'You might have to start where they live, first.'

Nerida was quick to imagine them in America on tour, with Mari channelling and herself being the entrepreneur, managing their brand. She was aware of some vanity and ambition in the vision.

'Sometimes people in other countries have to understand first, before you can talk in your own country, so to say. After that, you might be able to work with these people here who were open to it.'

A prophet is not accepted in his own country. 'But the writing,' she said, 'is the first thing—these conversations and the writing.' She came back to earth.

'I would suggest so.'

'Well, I'm getting stronger, so I can work more.'

'Good. I would suggest that you exercise. It will grow your energy supply. Don't overdo it. Little walks.'

'Do you have any suggestions for Mari?'

'Once the tiredness is gone, she should start exercising, too. Not too much, just a bit. Some regular things—little walks out in the fresh air when it's not too hot. We'll try to give support.'

'As always, thank you,' she said.

'It's in our own interest, too. Give and take,' Aedgar said equably. 'I work with you. You work with me.'

'Oh, I give you something, you give me something.'

'It's more of a partnership than a "giving and expecting to receive something for it" relationship,' he corrected her.

'Okay. I was trying to translate a concept from the people who live here. They call it *Ngapartji, ngapartji*—usually translated as "I give you something, you give me something". *He's being overly literal, for a spirit.*

'It would be nice if they would do so, but they don't,' he said. 'They take from some people and never give back. People get misused.

'It's about pride. It's like, "You have to give me, but I don't have to give you..."— which is not how it was supposed to be in the first place.'

Nerida bridled. The cliché of Aboriginal entitlement was a tired one. 'But you understand that people feel the pain of having their power taken from them when they were conquered (or partially conquered)—'

'Yes.'

'—and that still makes people confused. And bitter and angry and sad.' Nerida fumed.

People have been dispossessed! We're still colonised. Why should they have to give anything back?

An Australian Government Initiative
WARNING
PRESCRIBED AREA
NO LIQUOR
It is an offence to bring, possess, consume, supply, sell or control liquor beyond this point without a liquor permit or licence.
Maximum penalty:
$1,100 - 1st offence
$2,200 - 2nd or subsequent offences
$74,800 and/or 18 months jail for supplying/intending to supply over 1,350ml quantity of pure alcohol in liquor to a third person
It is not an offence to directly transport unopened liquor through a Prescribed Area provided you can clearly demonstrate your destination is outside the Prescribed Area.
The Liquor Act (NT) as amended by the Northern Territory National Emergency Response Act 2007 (Commonwealth)
NO PORNOGRAPHY
It is an offence to bring, possess, supply, sell or transport certain pornographic material beyond this point.
Maximum penalty possession:
$5,500 for level 1 material
Includes Category 1 Restricted and Category 2 Restricted publications, X18+ films, unclassified publications that would likely be classified Category 1 Restricted or Category 2 Restricted, unclassified films that would likely be X18+ and prohibited advertisements.
$11,000 for level 2 material
Includes films, computer games or publications that are Refused Classification or are unclassified but would likely be Refused Classification.
Maximum penalty supply:
$11,000 - supply less than 5 items
$22,000 - and/or 2 years jail for 5 or more items.
Classification (Publications, Films and Computer Games) Act 1995 (Commonwealth)

TWENTY-EIGHT

M UTITJULU
SAME DAY, 2013

'It's about time to change it,' Aedgar replied mildly. 'They should listen to the idea that your thoughts will attract what you focus on. It wouldn't be a bad concept for them. It might help them to move on.

'People here wanted to go into, for them, futuristic lifestyles. But they couldn't manage so well. And now they are stuck halfway in between. Thinking about things like the Law of Attraction and having positive thoughts about things, would help them to move on, without losing their pride.

'And without losing their culture.'

Nerida was irritated by this 'stuck between two worlds' idea. It was an old-fashioned, simplistic trope. And she hated him generalising about Anangu. It was something Mari did that they fought about, generalising about people by their culture.

The best she could say was, 'I'm sure local Aboriginal people will read that eventually and think about what you say.'

'They should. It's a way back to their independence. Their brains and thoughts are different. It's as if the knowledge is hidden deep inside. If they can access it again, that understanding—that guiding your thoughts will shape your world—would work much better for them, than it will for any of the people who have been to Fortunatus' talk.

'They will have a different approach.

'Some of their minds and their thoughts are kind of diminished by abuse of alcohol and drugs. Having an ale or two is a very good thing. Having eight or ten or more is a very bad thing.'

The dogs barked outside. The waxing moon was rising.

Nerida said, 'It happened in England when the machines came and people were taken off the land and forced into the factories, that so many of them became alcoholics because they didn't know how to recover or how to live.'

She knew that the children were forced into the factories and mines—the machines only fit them. Some were required to work up to twenty hours a day. Children fell asleep and into the machines and were killed.

Gin-soaked parents stayed in overcrowded housing around open sewage pits, waking the exhausted children to send them back to work. This was the horror many Australians of British ancestry came from, but not many knew it.

Aedgar said, in his imperious manner, 'It was about having too much time.'

He annoyed her. *Where is his compassion?* 'You think? I think it was about being broken from the earth and broken from your history—'

'If you keep your culture,' he insisted, 'if you stay true to who you are, doesn't matter which part of the earth you live in.'

'But the English lost their culture, the ordinary people,' she said. 'They didn't make bread anymore. They didn't grow food anymore.

Some of them couldn't work. Only their children could work in the machines.'

'Which gave the adults too much time,' he said. 'So they spent it drinking. Then they had to have more kids, to send them to work, so they could drink more. It was a spiral into poverty, because the more children they had, the more food they needed to supply.'

Nerida understood. 'And then, they were the people who came and colonised this island—the poor, who were criminalised (and sometimes they were criminals)—they were sent to be the conquerers of the original people here.'

Aedgar paused, looking into it. 'Well, they came here in a kind of rage, already. They were trying to fight people or pass their rage onto them, to get rid of theirs. They were thinking the people here might be weaker (because they didn't have some technologies).'

The clock ticked. The refrigerator hummed. 'What a noisy place,' he said grimly. Nerida apologised. 'I hope it's not—'

'I feel sorry for you. I can go wherever I like to. You must stay here; live with that noise.'

'One day we'll have a quieter place,' she said.

'I'm looking forward to that.'

'I worry a little that noise is hard on you and the others who come,' she said.

'We're happy to talk. I think the noise is much harder on you. We can focus on the important things. It's just surprising how noisy it can be.'

'Yes,' she agreed, 'all these machines.' It had not occurred to her to feel sorry for herself. She hadn't thought much about the constant noise of machinery in her house and the effect on their health.

She was touched that he cared.

Nerida had manners. And frequently found Aedgar's company inspiring and delightful. But this conversation was riddled with conflict for her. Philanthropic karma was a sore spot. She gave so much to her patients, especially energy. Maybe he was giving her a way to consider different boundaries but that challenged her determination to practise kindness.

On *ngapartjti, ngapartji*—Aedgar made another politically incorrect but accurate assessment of some Aboriginal people who don't give back.

The idea that desert peoples' brains and thoughts were different was also grossly politically incorrect.

But then the idea that, because of this, they could manifest good things, using their thoughts, more easily and make that lore work well for them, lifted her heart. *Perhaps the ancestors used it for thousands of years. Everybody visualises success when they want to catch a fish or a kangaroo or find a crop of fruit.*

Her Aboriginal grandmother used to call people 'tinny' when they attracted good fortune, especially found money, gold or precious stones. There used to be discussion about how to become a tinny person, who would win on the horses or find a ten dollar note on the ground.

In a similar way, though, talking about the British people who became detritus of the Industrial Revolution, Nerida found herself trying to get him to understand heartbreak. It became clear that Aedgar had no time for victimhood as a way of life.

As if he sensed her upset, Aedgar said, 'Well, we're here to teach, not to make people happy. But if that happens as well, it's not that bad is it?'

She felt his lightness and laughed. 'Nothing wrong with it.'

'No.'

'It makes me happy because I can see purpose in this lifetime.' Having found her role as amanuensis for Mari's channelling, Nerida's search for her path in life—which had been a

deeper, longer-lasting ache, even worse than the yearning for Mari to come into her life—was over.

Now, she was impatient to get on with it.

'I would think you have seen purpose in this lifetime before,' he said.

She thought of being a doctor and how she battled through her training. 'I have. But this is a very interesting, an unexpected, new purpose. It expands my horizons beyond where I thought they could go.'

'Good. Means you're learning, expanding your energy.'

There he goes again with that odd, New Agey slogan. She said, 'Might be moister here next time you come.'

'The rain must come first, before that can happen. There was a little delay. We had to do some other work.'

'Are you able to tell me what it was?' She was curious about their role in the weather.

'We had to realise some things. There will some things happen that are not all pleasant. You won't notice much of it here. It's mainly going to affect the coast. But there are more things that need to realign,' he said.

'For the sake of this planet?'

'Yes.' Then he said, 'You should think about a casino.'

Nerida was skeptical. She and Mari never won anything substantial. *Well, I don't. Mari can be tinny.*

Mari had a diamond and opals that she had picked up off the ground in the Australian deserts years before Nerida knew her. She explored Australia with her parents and her previous partner in the nineties.

Mari also had a spectacular 'near win' once in Vegas. She was disqualified from winning hundreds of thousands of dollars on a technicality. The slot machine had to have a minimum amount in it for the prize to be awarded. Mari's one lucky quarter wasn't enough. The feeling of being incredibly fortunate was fleeting.

They'd talked about it.

Mari's ex was avaricious, constantly seeking money and status.

She acquired Mari as a trophy—a golden-skinned scuba diving instructor—and eventually left her for a much younger partner when Mari became disabled.

'If I'd won that money, she wouldn't have gone away until she'd spent it all,' Mari figured. 'Finding you was more important, in the big picture.'

Now Aedgar spoke to Nerida's desire to have a bucket load of money so that she could give up being a doctor and do only channelling work—her own kind of greed.

Everyone dreams of winning a big mob of cash, surely. Especially after attending a Fortunatus meeting.

'Okay,' she said. 'We went to a casino. It was fun. We began our casino education.'

'There's only a few things you need to know. It's gonna be about feelings. Feeling what to do. You can listen and feel.

'But I would still recommend going overseas.'

'Sounds good. Perhaps we could combine it with a trip to visit Aiden and his friends. They live near lots of casinos, you know.'

'So do you,' he said.

'Yes, but to go overseas is a long way from here.' She was thinking about the credit card debts. There was no end in sight to paying them off.

Aedgar said, 'Last time, you told me how pleasant it was.'

'It was! It was fun. I don't mind it.'

'Good,' he said. 'There will be more travelling involved in this work we have to do.'

'Yes ...

'Mari has said that when we're flying in that metal tube in the sky, she often feels you tapping away, wishing you could come in, have a look around.'

'I can feel things, but I can't see them. We're working on it.'

'I know. And the vision is the most spectacular aspect of it, of course. She always gets to sit near the window.'

'It's probably a good idea,' he said.

'Aaw, you would say that. It keeps her happy.'

'I guess if the weather's bad, it might not be so good to sit near the window. You might see things you don't wanna see,' he suggested.

'Yeah, that's true. If there's lightning, I sit near the window. She doesn't like lightning.'

He nodded. 'Too powerful.'

'Mmm. But she's getting better at accepting the lightning. We've had some spectacular storms here.'

Mari took photos of lightning hitting the Rock at night. Towering over the plain, it attracted lightning from all around, especially to the metal chain that had been drilled into it up 'the Climb'. Friends who worked for the Rangers or for the clinic at Yulara told harrowing tales of climbing up there during storms to rescue people who were dead, injured or just stuck on the Rock, with bolts striking the rock all around them.

One night when Mari was outside, photographing for hours with Selkie's dog, Minyma, warming her, she came running in, dragging the tripod, almost falling as she caught her balance. Minyma barked as a tremendous crash of thunder shook the house. 'The lightning! I think I might have just caught it!' she said breathlessly.

Aedgar said, 'It's about too much power that can't be controlled. If you just see it as a light show, it's not the same. If you reflect on the way it works and how much power it has, you feel differently about this "light show." That can be frightening.'

Nerida agreed. 'I guess I'm a light show sort of girl.'

'Our friend thinks too much about the possibilities—of immense powers that cannot be controlled. It can be a very distressing. If you think about these things, you can't see the beauty in it.'

'But that's changing for her.' Her photos of lightning bolts coming down to the Rock, in the storm-bruised purple sky, were inspiring, energising and unique.

'I don't think so,' Aedgar said. 'There will always be some things that don't change.'

'Well, she's taken wonderful pictures we can use to illustrate our books one day.'

'Yes, I agree.'

It was getting too hot and dry for Aedgar to talk comfortably, so they ended the conversation with salutations. Nerida got up and turned the air conditioner on with rattles and a roar.

Mari returned with a yawn. 'Hello.'

Nerida opened and poured a drink. After a sip, Mari went to the oven to take the bread out.

'Aedgar was saying—' Nerida began.

'Don't tell me. Don't tell me anything about it,' Mari said from the kitchen, holding up a red tea towel like a warning flag.

A FEW DAYS LATER, they were woken by the sound of rain. Pouring, pounding, relentless.

It was just after midnight.

Nerida went out onto the front verandah, inhaling the sweet scent of petrichor—cold rain drops on hot rocks and dust.

She stepped away from the house, in the dark, to catch more of the big, cold drops. They splashed on her face and arms, her nightdress and hair whipped by the fresh wind.

Mari strapped her leg on and got dressed. She took photos of Nerida dancing in the rain.

When they went back to bed they indulged in the cosiness of being inside, warming under their quilts, the noise of the rain a dome around them.

They woke at dawn. It was still thundering down. The road in front of the house was a rushing, rusty river.

Silver waterfalls ran like supernatural arteries over the Rock, through tunnels and caves and into holes. Clear water filled the waterholes all over and around Uluru.

The birds were almost as loud as the rain, excited.

They could hear the water on the Rock falling from the Community. After the holes were filled, some shot out in white jets from occult tunnels. Uluru was mysterious, magnificent and welcoming.

'Beautiful day!' Nerida said, bringing coffee to bed.

'I'll come and pick you up at lunchtime,' Mari said. 'We'll go out and make the most of it.'

CHAPTER
TWENTY-NINE

M UTITJULU
FRIDAY MARCH 22, 2013

CLAIRE CAME into the doctor's room to help clean up at day's end. 'Come over after work if you're not too tired.' Nerida smiled.

When evening shadows lengthened, Mari was pleased to see Claire. She brought out a fragrant, caramelised onion tart she'd made. Then prepared a salad with a homemade mayonnaise for an early dinner.

Mari was frustrated with the limitations of a photo processing program. She'd spent all week corresponding with tech support teams, researching, reading and writing on bulletin boards. She vented about it to Claire and Nerida while she sliced tomatoes and mozzarella.

'This program is total, fucking bullshit. It's driving me insane,' she said as she brought plates to the table. 'If I would cross the path of the developer of that program, he would regret it.'

'You're not joining us to eat, Mari? Are you sick?' Claire noticed.

'I'm fasting. Just today. You know, giving my guts a rest,' Mari said, patting her belly. 'I'll have some onion cake tomorrow.'

Nerida smiled softly. Mari planned to channel later in the evening.

'Did you hear that My Chemical Romance broke up today?' Claire asked, biting into the pie.

'No. Did you like them?' Mari asked.

'Sure. Fellow feeling in alienation. What's not to love? They were played a lot when I was a junior nurse in Sydney. I liked, "Vampires will never hurt you." The vampires were corporate corruption.'

'I didn't hear that. I heard that three Marines died in a murder-suicide in Texas,' Mari said. 'And 42 people were dead in a suicide bombing in a Damascus mosque yesterday.'

Mari refused to hear anything about the channelled material. But she had a strong news habit. She sometimes watched or listened to news all day.

'You're watching too much news,' Nerida said. 'One or two bulletins a day is enough.

Why d'you wanna learn all that shit off by heart? It's bad for your mental health.'

'Yeah. Why watch the news, when you can come to the clinic and be surrounded by all the drama a person never wanted?' Claire added. 'How's *your* mental health, Nerida?'

'I want to know what's going on the world,' Mari said anxiously.

Nerida got the news from Mari when she came home from work. Every day. If she'd had to work or sleep through her lunch break, Mari saved it all up.

She wanted Nerida's consciousness to extend beyond the small world of Mutitjulu.

Nerida spent her activist decades with people who lived by news bulletins. Her comrades took the news, filtered as it was through the funnel of the bourgeoisie's interests, as seriously as a doctor took calls from the nurses. Phone calls to Dr Nerida Green could be life and death. Responding to events in a way that was partisan to the working class might save humanity. So they believed.

Knowing what was going on in the world, talking, arguing and writing about what they heard, was vital to the revolutionary mission to build the party that would unite the workers, overthrow capitalism and build socialism to save the world. By 2013 it was four or five years since she'd let go of that ideology and way of life. Nerida had had enough of feeling like she was in the thick of the world's news to last her a lifetime.

It was hard for Mari, who found that Nerida couldn't talk and hardly listened when she came home from work. Despite the hugs and smiles, Nerida was emotionally and physically drained, phobic about the phone and prone to be hangry.

So they would be getting undressed or lying in bed together and she needed to tell Nerida about the fire in a refugee camp in Thailand. A white supremacist shooting people in the States. And a musician from a James Bond film who died.

'I don't care,' Nerida said. 'I can't have this in my head before I'm going to sleep.'

'When am I supposed to talk to you, then?'

For Nerida it seemed that Mari told her the 11 o'clock news whether she wanted to hear it or not. Then went to sleep, snoring softly and deeply relaxed. While Nerida, stressed beyond tiredness, blaming Mari for switching her brain on again, lay sleepless, worrying about her patients. Composing letters of complaint to management in her head.

Other thoughts kept her awake, too. She was anxious about her identity. Their financial safety. How she would ever transition from being the doctor people needed to the channel facilitator most people might think the world could do without.

After midnight she'd reflect sadly that they used to have great sex. They'd finessed and caressed their way through the years that Mari was talking in languages in her sleep, when Nerida felt that she had to check that Mari was present with her.

She was.

She never slipped away from her when they were fucking. But that sexual energy, once such a powerful force, seemed to have evaporated in the stress of their lives.

She tried to visualise something better. But the gap between their life and her dreams only made her more unhappy.

As Nerida got to know him, Aedgar began to express big ideas in strong terms–mainly negative. Lately, their sessions left Nerida wondering how she could distribute the material of this angry misanthropic being into the world.

My medical colleagues will diagnose me as deluded or delirious.

But all the New Agers working on their affirmations and positive thoughts will get irritated and dismiss us.

And who's gonna read channelled texts if not New Agers?

Major themes were unfolding, revealing themselves: Deep Time, Mining, Environmental Catastrophe, Medicine, Education, Science. Aedgar's take on them seemed almost entirely negative to Nerida.

She was aggressively trying to speak positively. To think thoughts of plenitude and zeal, to pull things out of her hurricane of riches, as Fortunatus put it.

Aedgar offered scraps of hope, she felt. But she was disgruntled.

Mari and Nerida clashed. They had always argued but now they were fighting.

Like any human, especially those exposed to repeated trauma, Mari's brain tended towards paying attention to bad news and dangerous possibilities. She warded off evil by expecting the worst and naming it in her depths, in her very mitochondria, it sometimes seemed. Trying to encourage Mari towards a 'solutions-based approach' was useless. It only incensed her.

They fought after dinner one night.

Nerida tried to talk to Mari about changing her thoughts and expressions, to better manage her anger. 'It's gotta be bad for your health,' she said. She lit a short fuse.

Mari stood up. Put her hand on her forehead.

'You have no insight into how infuriating and almost painful being here is for me.

'Sometimes I feel the vibes in the surrounding community.' She shot her arm out. Raised her voice.

'It drives me nearly mad! It's like I can feel every fight, or feel the impact of every jealousy, every nasty thought.'

Nerida felt a flash of gratitude for the insight Aedgar gave her about these feelings.

'Then you'll say it's all about lessons to be learnt. Or that having bad thoughts myself attracted all of that.

'There's a huge difference between the way my or our life is and what some interpretation of a Law of Attraction (or whatever other New Age mumbo-jumbo) says it should be. I did not ask for any of this —especially not these kinds of lessons.'

Next night, a Friday evening, Mari said she would channel. They sat in Nerida's office for a change. The office chair might be more comfortable for Mari. After only four or five minutes, Aedgar arrived.

NERIDA FELT BETTER IMMEDIATELY. 'HELLO.' She felt a twinge of guilt that she felt better with Aedgar in the room than with irascible Mari.

He came into the session as if he sensed Nerida's conflict, more charming than ever. 'Pleasure to be here. Thank you for letting me come. I am happy and grateful. Have you been making plans?'

'Perhaps. We can see some opportunities,' she said. They **did** have ideas about where they could go, what they could do.

'You're going to travel,' he affirmed. 'I can sense the desire.'

'Our friend is certainly inspired, which is always a lovely thing to see,' Nerida said.

Mari had been painting and even talking about exhibiting in the

States. She was also dreaming of a trip back to Tonga to swim with the whales.

Aedgar said, 'We wouldn't mind travelling, having little adventures. Or bigger adventures. There is certainly the desire to become rich, as well. I'm sure it will happen. You must have been inspired by Fortunatus.'

Nerida did like the idea of getting out of debt and being supported to work on her projects. She was thinking a lot lately that they should be wealthy. It was not so different to the treasure chest she used to pray for when she was a kid. 'Mari was encouraged by him and me, yes.'

Aedgar humoured her.

'Well, you definitely have good reasons to become rich—you're going to put it to good use—in our adventure in educating a lot of people ... Obviously not in what to do with 67 cars.'

'We have a broader perspective,' she said, smiling.

'You do. That's why it will happen. And you'll need to go overseas as well, working on developing some sort of program with Aiden's host.'

Nerida smiled more broadly. 'We can do good work.'

'Definitely. It will be a perfect match,' he said.

Great choice of words. Like Mari got about us when we were dating on The Velvet Lounge.

He seemed to read her vibe and said, 'I am not talking about romantic experiences.'

Nerida chuckled. 'I know.'

'There might be a minute or two, but that's certainly not what it's about,' he said.

She remembered that moment when Monica's magnificent energy focussed on Aedgar, the first time Mari channelled him.

'Do you know your Aiden?' Monica said.

What is it like to see your love of many lifetimes come in through another, to speak in human voices again after centuries? An intensely romantic moment!

Demurely, she said, 'You and Aiden are a wonderful match, skills-wise, in education.

'As Monica, she is superb at meeting people exactly where they are to raise their energy to a higher level. She's got knowledge of—'

'They—' he interrupted, correcting her.

'They've got knowledge of the time and the place they're in,' she said. 'And together with your knowledge of the needs of the planet and your commitment to healing—it's a brilliant combination.'

'There will be quite an audience interested in it,' he said.

'Yes, including me.'

'People will start to participate in spreading the education,' he foretold.

'I'm happy to see momentum building,' she enthused.

'It's all gonna happen in its perfect time,' he said gently. 'We all try to contribute our best, to make it happen in an efficient way. And easy to understand for everybody.

'Well, some people who think they are more intelligent will get very annoyed because they think they know better. But that's because they are the only ones who don't understand. They have this lack of basic knowledge.'

There it is. His articulated sense of superiority rankled her. She was afraid of being misconstrued as arrogant. *Shouldn't spiritually advanced people show humility?*

As a doctor, Nerida was blind to her own arrogance. But she periodically had experiences in the Community that helped her see her failings. With Aedgar she was painfully aware of a misplaced cockiness she used to cover her insecurity. 'So, when you refer to basic knowledge, you mean—?'

'On an emotional and energetic level.'

'Oh, okay ... There's not much remedy for that.'

'No,' he said.

Her eye fell on the modem on the shelf, where a gecko left its dirt everyday. The modem was always warm, so that gecko always had enough energy to get away from her, unlike the chilled down geckos in the rest of the house. She could never catch it.

'You should be prepared to travel more than you planned for,' Aedgar reiterated.

'Okay.'

She asked about the names of some other spirits Mari had channelled in other sessions—spirits she was just beginning to learn to converse with, if they ever came back. He responded that they could talk about them more another day.

Asking about their names, trying to get the different beings in some kind of order in her head, Aedgar replied, 'I can't tell you precisely because we are not good with names. They're not important.'

'I understand,' she said. 'I was appreciative when you told us your name with Aiden's encouragement.'

'Well, you didn't understand the first one,' he recalled.

The unreadable note Mari channelled. Something with BART and an 'R' and a 'W'. 'It was too hard for us. A good Gaelic name, I guess.'

'It is Gaelic, but an older version of Gaelic. You need the right throat and the right tongue to talk that way.'

'Aiden had no problem with it—' she said.

'Of course.'

'—and was very unimpressed that we found it too difficult.'

Aedgar said, 'He was a bit disappointed. We never get really disappointed. It was just that you asked for the name. We gave you the name. And then you didn't understand it. So, we had to use a name that was used later, different lifetime.'

'Hmm.' *So, he was Bartgrinn and then later was Aedgar. Aiden/Monica knows him by both names. Well, they would. They know each other in spirit, where it seems that all of our lives and experiences are integrated.*

Thinking of an article she'd read online that day, she asked, 'Have you heard about the discovery of an old, huge complex of ruins at the most northerly part of Britain? It's said that they've been recently uncovered.'

'It wasn't ruins when we were around,' he said, looking into it.

'I thought you might know the place. There are standing stones there—'

'A good place for education, collecting energy, collecting wisdom,' he said.

'Like a university—' Nerida speculated.

'Sort of—' he said.

'—but perhaps more interesting than contemporary universities.' She remembered that he was unenthusiastic about current education systems.

'The people in this time think it was kind of backward. Actually, it was more sophisticated than such institutions are now.

'They shouldn't be too proud of their education nowadays because what they do is not what it's about. It's very poorly taught. And it's focussing on the wrong things.'

'It's true. The teaching's all about memorisation, rather than feeling.' She knew. Twenty years, on and off, of tertiary education, struggling to reconcile her Indigenous style of learning with the limited modes of teaching she was offered.

Aedgar said, 'You need to have the emotions to be able to understand what you want to learn is about.

'Trying to squeeze things into a brain, that some people consider facts (even if these things are not the facts) doesn't add up to a good education.

'It was never meant to be that way.

'Teaching and learning. It's about energy, emotions and some kind of science—that you don't use in the way it was used in earlier days. A lot of the understanding of this science got lost.'

'You mean genuine science?' she asked.

'Yes, whatever you understand as genuine science, given how it is taught in this period. There are a lot of very important facts missing.'

Nerida found it hard not to take this personally, having been awarded an honours degree in the history and philosophy of science and technology.

She tried to keep up with him. 'My understanding is that genuine science is different to the way that science is taught at the moment. There's a big part missing at the heart of science as it's taught right now.'

Aedgar agreed. 'It's got lost on the way and some people picked up some of the facts and made up their minds how it should or could be.

'That's why many things don't work out the way they should, because your current science is based on illusions.'

'And partial truth?' She still felt defensive.

'Yes.

'If you take a little bit of knowledge from here, a little bit of knowledge from there—it's like working with herbs. You have a big pot. You use a bit from here, some herbs from there, you mix it all up and the result is something that's like poison. If you didn't intend in the first place to make poison ...

'That's how this so-called modern science—you can't say 'works' because it doesn't work. It works in some parts. But it has some *major* mistakes hidden in the formulas they use.

Nerida despaired. *How am I ever going to be publicly associated with this attitude?*

'What do you think about Einstein's work?' she asked. *Surely, he would appreciate Einstein.*

'He had some ideas,' Aedgar allowed.

Can't win a trick, can I? she thought.

'He was on a path that was close,' Aedgar upheld. 'But, when he came onto the scene, essential knowledge was already missing.

'That one was much cleverer than most. Probably because he got his knowledge from observing things and not from university education. He shows that, I've told you before, some of the best people have never been to a university.

'Well, Einstein went to universities later, to teach. But he's never been educated in a way that people think scientists should be educated.

'If you look at Da Vinci, he got his education from observing things, doing "tests", his own research. And then he put it all together. And he got some good results. But even then, some things were missing already.'

There is no perfection and he will always say so. Our intellectual gods have feet of clay.

Aedgar affirmed: 'This planet is much older than the general population thinks. There have been populations before. They were far more advanced than you are now.

'As mentioned before, it's very sad for us to watch from a distance when all this destruction happens again.

'And as before, everybody thinks, "Oh, that's the greatest thing ever. No one has ever done it before". Well, it has been done before, but nothing is left that could teach future generations about it, because it all got destroyed.'

'Monica told me one of my lifetimes I watched a massive destructive event that was caused by human stupidity.

'It was about Atlantis sinking into the ocean.' She felt quite full of herself, telling the story.

She'd asked Monica about why she, Nerida, took what she saw on the news so seriously. It was wearing her down. Why did she keep caring? Monica explained that Nerida had witnessed the consequences of human hubris before. And couldn't stand to see it happen again.

Aedgar said, 'Yeah, things got submerged. Other things exploded or imploded. It was a major disaster. People now have no idea what a big disaster it was and they're heading straight towards another one.'

Aedgar is dismissive of my self-importance because it's not a fairy tale to him. It's also not my individual lifetimes we're talking about here.

Nerida let go of her ego and felt her curiosity arise. 'Hmm.What happened to cause it?'

'The alignment of the planets got out of control. It's like a living being that had a major injury imposed on it, which was caused by the population of this planet.' He was grimly quiet.

He had learned, Nerida noted, to knit the brows. 'What was the nature of the injury?' she asked.

'The axis of the planet was turned around about 270 degrees.

'The shape of the planet was less round—it's not round but was less round than it is.

'So it started hurtling through the Universe until it slowed down again.

'It was about the balance.'

Oh my god. She was horrified. 'What did people do to cause that?'

MUTITJULU
SAME DAY, 2013

'IT WAS about deprivation of the Earth.'

Nerida interpreted. 'It was about mining, like you say it is in this period?' *You always make it an issue. Maybe I'll start to see why.*

'Mining from underground, mining on other planets, harvesting different kinds of gases—from the Universe, from other planets ...

'If you put some of them together, and you don't know enough about it, there is that big bang.

'Was big enough to turn everything around.'

Nerida's voice shook, 'Bigger than a nuclear explosion?'

'Bigger than anyone can imagine,' Aedgar said soberly.

'They had these great ideas. They thought they knew it all and everything was to be so much better after that. It didn't work out that way.

'Things got destroyed.

'You might call them—the little grids—were destroyed on molecular levels, which had a huge impact. A huge impact on the physical thing called the planet.'

Nerida tried to follow. 'Mhmm? So, the geology of the planet changed, the structure of the planet was altered—'

'Yes.'

'— on a molecular level?'

'Yes.'

'The material the planet is made of was different after that?'

'It got denser.'

'Hmm.' *That's a massive concept.*

'Yeah,' he said, 'we think some have the idea of doing something similar again, because they think, again, that they know it all.'

'You mean the ones who want to mine the moon and other planets?'

'Yes.'

'There's enough trouble here already with the ones mining this planet at such a rate,' she said.

'Definitely. People will start to say, "We can't stop the mining. It's gonna kill the economy."

'All we can suggest is, **rethink the way you live**. Otherwise, you don't have to think about anything at all anymore.'

Nerida felt like her brain was too small. *This is all very negative. Try to frame things positively.* 'Mhmm. There are individuals and small groups of people working on projects that could be part of a more rational way to live, a more sustainable way to live. These people need to be encouraged.'

'Indeed. But those people, who have more of the required intelligence, are considered freaks, little idiots, so to say, by the ones who are pushed forward by greed only (and the ones attracted to them).'

Always seeing the dark side, aren't you?

'Some of these people are quite successful,' she objected. 'I read about a project aiming to change the means of transportation in cities, so that people get around on bikes and don't need to use cars. There are bikes all over the city they can use to get around.'

'It's been around for years,' he said, almost wearily.

'Yeah.'

'Especially in some places in Europe,' he added.

Nerida persevered, and her own thoughts led her to observe human limitations, as well. 'Many years ago, in the 1920's, there was a plan to make cars from plants, and run them on plants too—sugar cane—which was much cleaner. But the people making money from the metal, rubber and petrol in the cars stopped those plans from being used.

'They bought the patents to stop the plant-based cars being produced.'

The electric tram system in Sydney, the biggest in the Southern Hemisphere, was ripped up and eliminated in the 1950s, to increase the market for private cars and tyres.

Trams were doused with sump oil and burned. In the US too, oil companies bought up tram networks and destroyed them.

Aedgar commented, 'It's always about greed. There are people who specialise in searching this planet for clever ideas, good ideas, which the greedy ones see would harm their industry. So they buy these ideas and lock them up somewhere.'

'That's right.'

'It's been done for ages. But more people are becoming aware of it now,' he recognised.

He used Mari's hands for emphasis.

'Some of the wiser ones, those who are considered freaks and little idiots by people on the "higher" levels, are attracted to those people of lesser intelligence.

'They believe those people should know, that's why they're on these higher levels, because they are supposed to know so much.

'The problem we see is that these people on the top—even the intelligent ones—didn't get there through intelligence or knowledge.

'The better of them are recruited by the ones of low intelligence, to make them do what they want.

'So, to get to the top, as it is now, you don't have to be knowledgeable and intelligent. You need to know bad people.'

Nerida thought she followed. 'Yes. And be attracted to bad people.'

'Some of them,' he granted. 'But the majority thinks they are up there because they are so clever. That's why people think those ones on the top are always right ... Or ***mainly*** right.

'Because even the last one of the majority of humans, should have realised by now that they are not always right.

'***There is an awakening happening.***

'That needs to be forced. The power needs to go there—the ***energy*** needs to go to that awakening—better to say. The word "power" is always mixed up with greed.'

This was an essential point. But Nerida felt overwhelmed, so she changed tack to something clear-cut.

'Mari and I saw a story of a woman teaching the Miqma'q language to the Miqma'q people.

'She was an inspired teacher. She had pictures of the things she wished to teach and there was a little story in each of the pictures. She didn't use written language. And she was teaching the children the language of their old people.'

This was a tender spot for Nerida, who had not yet learned her own Aboriginal language. It was bittersweet that she was learning (a few words and phrases, at least) of Pitjantjatjara, when she still didn't know her own Aboriginal language.

'Hmm. That's one of the intelligent ways to do it, where you don't have to go to a university,' Aedgar said. 'It's about clear thoughts and observation—having the right energy to do it.'

Then he returned to the spirit of his intervention. 'The education system is overrated.'

Nerida had to agree. 'People learn despite the system rather than because of it: exceptional teachers and exceptional students can do well.'

'There's not that many of them unfortunately,' he lamented.

'Yes, the health system is a bit like that too. People heal themselves despite what's done to them,' she said.

Maybe what I take for negativity is honesty, she thought.

Aedgar sighed. 'There are some things that are good about it.

'The majority isn't. Again, it's all about greed.'

Always with the greed!

Aedgar said, 'Supporting big companies by using the medication they produce makes people sicker, so they need additional and more medication.

'In many cases that's spiralling out of control because many of your colleagues don't know how these medications work, what exactly they do in the body. They just believe the advertising.

'They believe what the company tells them, because there is so much of this so-called medicine on the market available, they can't know it all.'

He was right. Many doctors were unaware of adverse effects and drug interactions. Nerida's history of drug experimentation in late adolescence made her more sensitive to chemicals. And aware of drug interactions.

She trusted her clients to honestly express their experiences because she was frank with them. Their healthcare benefitted from knowledge gained in her ostensibly misguided youth.

'And if you have a main ingredient and you exchange a minor ingredient with something else that might change the texture only, officially, or it's a cheaper additive—it will affect the main ingredient. We know they say it's not so. It's because they don't understand.'

Nerida bristled. She wanted to believe that the generic version of a drug was just as effective. Almost all her patients were on the cheapest generics.

'No one taught them how to understand it,' Aedgar said. 'So they actually believe what they say. It is sad.'

Nerida asked, 'You're saying again that there's that limitation in our chemistry?'

'Yes.'

'I studied chemistry for a while. I found it fascinating that adding one proton can change an element into the next element, with totally different properties.' She found this wonderful, this mutability of matter.

Aedgar was uninspired.

'The problem is that it changes much more. It's like all the sciences—there are things missing. They try to do their best with the knowledge that's available to them, but some of the key knowledge is missing.'

Nerida felt dumb on behalf of humanity. 'We're talking about core concepts?'

'Yes. Some of these structures they're using now were around before that massive impact.

'So these so-called elements are no longer what they think they are. There's just part of the structure left from how it was before the planet changed. They are using things that are sort of left over. These materials have some tiny things still attached to their structure from how it was before. But the scientists have no way of measuring it.'

'Are you talking about subatomic particles, like quarks?'

'Yes, you could call it something like that. That's the major problem they have.'

'Well, it's certainly one of the major problems in physics, is to try to understand what's in the heart of matter.' Nerida spoke confidently, for somebody who failed first year physics twice before she finally passed it. She tried to read Stephen Hawking's book in the 90s, too, without success. 'Quantum particles seem to follow different laws completely than what we understood to be the laws of physics.'

'Well, if you don't have the right tools to measure everything, (which they don't), you shouldn't pretend therefore that these things don't exist.

'Because they do. They might find it out one day.'

Nerida said, 'They might not have the tools to measure *you*. Doesn't mean you don't exist.'

Aedgar seemed put out. 'Well, yeah. You could put it that way.

'Somehow, we are all happy that they can't measure us. Because then they would try to manipulate us in a way that's suitable for them.'

'For profit, somehow,' she said.

'To satisfy their greed,' he said, returning to his theme.

'I'm pleased that you are immeasurable,' she said genuinely.

When Mari was channelling in her sleep, Nerida sometimes had ideas about brain scans to show what was going on when she channelled. It was a repugnant idea now. Her wife had been subject to more than enough medical experimentation and investigation in this lifetime.

'It will stay that way. We make sure it will ...

'It's like with the things for space travel, where we know there will always be that little bit missing.'

'What do you think about humans going up to the moon, as happened in my childhood?' *Wasn't that an exciting and good thing?*

'Useless.'

'Really?'

'Well, they tried to do it because it was the closest thing, so to say. There's nothing there of any use. They used it for training purposes, for things that might be used to conquer other countries, for example, and to gain some experience in what it would be like travelling to other planets, if this one might get destroyed.'

Nerida demurred. 'But the imagination of the people of the Earth was captured by seeing pictures of the planet from outside itself. Surely that was valuable?'

'It should have been a way for people to understand how beautiful this place is and that it's worthwhile to protect it,' he agreed.

'Yes. Many people had that feeling about it.'

'Did it last? Did they use it that way?'

'The ones with the power? No.'

'There you go.'

'But for the rest of us—'

'That's why we feel it was useless. It could, kind of, spur the imagination of children. That's about it.

'The valuable thing about seeing the planet from above in its whole beauty didn't work the way it should—having the wish and the desire to protect it, keep it healthy.'

Nerida wasn't giving up. 'There were some who went into space whose lives were profoundly changed. The rest of their lives they did nothing but teach about what they'd seen and the beauty of the planet.'

Aedgar replied sadly, 'They were heartbroken in the end. The ones that are alive are still heartbroken—about what they have been able to observe and what future populations won't be able to observe anymore.'

'Yes. Well, all of us with hearts here feel that, even if we're not space travellers, literally speaking. There's a constant grief and yearning for a better world.'

He ignored her poetry and was relentless, 'Yes, and they should learn and try to figure out a way to bring the rubbish back ... It's valuable, what's up there, but as long as it's up there as rubbish, it's all like parasites on the Universe.'

Nerida thought, *He's angry and bitter.*

She was reminded of an item they'd seen on the net.

'Mari and I heard about a girl who sent a kind of a little ship with a toy up through the atmosphere and down again. I think she's about ten years old. And I thought of what you said, that there are people working on bringing things back, not necessarily those who go to university, when I heard the story of that child.'

He paused to investigate it. 'It would be progress if it would be true,' he said.

'You can't tell if it's true, you can't find her? Maybe it's just a story people loved so much, they wished it would be true.'

Aedgar looked further into the energy of the event. 'Well, she tried it. She did her best. She might get better at it if she tries some more. If she would have really done that, the people at the so-called space agencies would have signed her up immediately.

' That would not have been small news to them.

'This would have been a huge story, going around the planet for weeks.'

Nerida sighed. 'Well. Perhaps people's longing for it to be true can help to create it.'

'It might, one day,' he said.

There was a lull. Nerida was uncomfortable.

She began, 'But perhaps one of the keys is people being able to listen to you, being able to read what you say and hear what you say— for them to be able to really understand the value—'

He interrupted her. 'Some people will be delighted.

'Some people won't like it at all. It will be controversial. You must be prepared for that.'

'I think you know; I've been very well prepared in my life experience for that sort of situation,' she said wildly.

Aedgar was earnest. 'There are things,' he said quietly, 'where you can have some practice. But there are things you will never be prepared for.'

'Mhmm. Well, as long as they don't burn us at the stake again. Even that's survivable I suppose, if spirit continues. We'll do our best.'

Aedgar's tone was conciliatory. 'Of course, we do. We are here to educate and to help; trying to help to sort some things out, so to say ... I think I might leave for now.'

'Thank you for coming.'

'This friend needs some more rest.' His voice was fading. She felt his energy step back.

'Yes. She'll have it. If she's willing.'

'It will always be a challenge. It's about learning how to focus. And master the technology—the kind of technology that you have there.

'It was a pleasure. Talk to you another time.'

'Until then.' Nerida got up and turned the air-conditioner on, walked around, agitated. Mari returned with a sigh. 'Hey, sweetie.'

'Hmm?'

'How are you? Sleepy?'

She looked relaxed. 'Dunno,' Mari said, in a kind of stupor.

Nerida passed her wife a drink. Mari took a draught of the black-berry cordial. 'I think Aedgar is still around,' Mari said.

'Hmm. He's never far away, he tells us.'

'Hmm?'

'Aedgar's very interesting.'

'You think?'

'Aye.'

'I don't know.'

'You didn't listen to any of it?'

Mari said, 'I know that I'm talking, but I have no idea what it's about. Like, I can hear myself talking but I don't understand it. It's like, somewhere over there.' She waved a hand to the distance.

'Somewhere far away?'

'Yeah.'

'Not concerning you?'

'No.'

'Hmm. It's a unique experience.'

'What?'

'What you do.' She touched Mari's crinkled hair. 'Are you hungry?'

'A bit.'

'Me too.'

Out in the kitchen, Nerida unwrapped cheese and ham. Grabbed a jar of pickles. A tasty sandwich would ground her. And serve as distraction from insecure and troubling thoughts.

CHAPTER

THIRTY-ONE

M UTITJULU
SATURDAY MARCH 23, 2013

It was always a grand day when she didn't have to go to work.

Nerida sat with earphones in all morning, doing nothing that made her good company.

She listened to recordings of their past conversations with Monica. Mari retreated into her painting and, after they made a deal to spend the next day out at Kata Tjuta, graciously offered a channelling session.

Aedgar came and Nerida recalled Dawn's attempts to channel him.

He said, 'I remember. Wasn't a good match. We tried to help get things going on their way ... Our friend here is a much better match. We chose well.'

'Perhaps we should use those meetings with Monica, your Aiden, to begin the book?' she suggested, sharing thoughts she hadn't talked to Mari about yet.

He agreed. 'It could make it easier for people to understand how it works. Even if most of them will never get it. It's beyond the imagination of many. They think people are sleepwalking, which is different.

'What we do is a completely different level of experience. It's a high achievement, so to say.

'It will take more time. There are still difficulties, but we are on a good path. We've done well, so far. It will get much easier. We are working on it.'

'Mari has been having a problem with the fit of her prosthetic leg and walking's been painful. Are you able to help?'

'We are supporting it on an energetic level with the energy flow, but there is a slight mechanical problem. I'm not familiar with how easy or how difficult it would be to fix that mechanical flaw. But we'll give it all our support, on the energy level.'

He took a few minutes to examine the stump of Mari's amputated leg. Nerida had a feeling of light energy in the room. *The way you feel in the company of a happy, secure child*, she thought.

He said, 'Something's not right, but it's not as bad as it seems.'

Nerida doodled a spider's web, like a star or a target, on her pad. 'Mari's using the crystals today,' she commented.

'I realise that,' he said. 'The energy's stronger. Still needs rest to get the energy levels even higher up than it is now with the crystals. We are working on it, but it needs some cooperation.

'Encourage resting. A little bit of exercise would be good, but I am aware that it may not be possible at the moment. First there should be the rest, then some things might need to be fixed, and then there should be exercise. It's still much better than it must have been in the first place.'

'It was a very hard lesson ...' *If it was a lesson at all, losing her leg.*

'She could have chosen an easier way. Would have taken longer.

'There were other possible paths to follow, to end up in the position where she is now.

'But when these opportunities came around the first time, somehow, she was not ready. Needed more learning, more compassion and other things, to understand.

'It is a good decision to become a host for us. It is not the easiest one. And it can take quite a while to get to the point to agree or commit to such a relationship. We are pleased we are here now. We are very pleased how well it works already. It will get much easier soon.

'Her whole attitude has changed. This was the part that went quicker than we thought. Given the, so to say, experience, we had in the past, about the capacity to learn enough to get to the next step.

'The capacity was always there, but there were distractions. Too many other 'opportunities'—little detours. She gained more experience through that, but it took quite a bit longer than it could have.'

Nerida asked, 'Have you been hosted by a channel before?'

'Well, with Aiden's host. We would never have chosen that host. It's not a match on the level of energy and physicality and many other things.

'We were trying to help, to bring it along nicely.

'We first thought it might not work at all, being an unsuitable match. We thought it was scary, rather than educational. So, we were very pleased that she was brave enough to still do it. It was probably not all too easy to watch and witness.'

'We tried to make it as little scaring as possible, but due to the bad match, it was a bit difficult. We don't like to use the word "difficult". It was just less easy.'

'I've been trying to learn to frame things in a positive way,' Nerida said. The channelled material she was reading implied that words had a kind of magic in them.

The couple's conflict about this philosophy reignited at lunchtime that day, when Mari threatened, 'If that's what's coming out of my mouth when I channel, I'll stop doing it. I don't agree with it.'

She was clearing the table, filling the sink.

Her voice had a cry in it. 'I think about good things all the time. I try hard.

'We never win the lottery.

'And then shit things happen, like what management has done to you.

'And all the shit things that have been happening to me all my life? Aren't you saying that's my fault? That I caused all my problems by thinking the wrong thoughts?'

She crashed pans in the sink.

Nerida tried re-framing that, 'It's more like that you have the power to have a better life by thinking of things in a positive way.'

Mari's dark eyes flashed. 'Well, fuck that. I don't like it. And if you don't want me when I don't channel anymore, then you can go away, too.'

Nerida held her from behind then, resting her cheek on the back of Mari's shoulder, her hands touching around Mari's belly. She let herself be held for a minute. Then the anger built up again. Nerida felt her wife's muscles tense.

And moved away.

Scrubbing a pot that had egg baked on it, Mari spat, 'You like Aedgar better than me. You're always so happy when you've been talking to him.'

Nerida promised herself she'd make more of an effort to show Mari her happiness, and to feel more happiness with Mari. It wasn't Mari's fault that her body hurt and made her miserable. Or that Nerida's work exhausted her.

'I'm sorry. But please don't be jealous of Aedgar. He always speaks well of you ... But you're the one I married! You're the one I spend my life with. And will stay with for the rest of my life.'

Maybe it is all too much for her. Maybe she needs a break from channelling so much to get a sense of herself back, Nerida thought.

But whenever Mari offered to channel again, Nerida felt it as a rare and precious opportunity. She would not say no. And Mari usually did feel better for a while afterwards, it seemed.

NOW AEDGAR SAID, 'It's much more educational to speak in a positive way—a better way to educate. The other way could be called a faster way. We prefer to use the better way, if possible. Sometimes the fast path has to be used. 'Specially if lessons have to be learned over and over again.'

So, painful, negative experiences are faster ways to learn? That makes sense. 'So, you are a guide...?' She'd heard of spirit guides. Maybe Aedgar was one.

'I work on many levels. Mainly, still, in a bigger scale. But you need to work on the tiny levels as well, to get success on the bigger scale. Many times, it's the tiny things that can change the bigger picture. Or the longterm success of things.'

'Can you give me an example?' she asked.

'If you try to build one of these high-rise buildings, the higher you want to go, the better the basis of it has to be.' He used Mari's hands to show the building of a tower.

'A tiny flaw in the preparation of the base can make the whole thing tumble down in the end.

'Like, they use this mix—concrete. If there's a bubble in it, it will impact the strength.

'If you put the weight of a high-rise building on it, a small bubble can cause the failure of the whole project.

'It might not happen immediately. It might take a long time to appear as a problem, but if it does, it can be devastating.

'So, it was a tiny thing someone didn't pay enough attention to. They thought it's not important in a big project. But the bigger the project, the more attention you have to pay to the tiny details. In the planning, as well as in the execution.

'If people don't make small or tiny things important enough, it can cause failure many times. You have these examples everywhere.

'You don't have to look far, so to say.'

Nerida worried about whether her attention to detail was enough for the project they were sharing.

Although she was fastidious in her work, what Mari saw at home made it hard for anyone to trust that Nerida would pay enough attention to detail. Mari was always re-washing plates or saucepans that still had grease on them, soaking Nerida's shirts and blouses to remove the stains of food she dropped absentmindedly on the front of them.

Nerida hardly ever cooked anymore because her impatience. Her refusal to wait long enough for the veggies to be cooked or for the sauce to thicken meant that her dishes were never quite right.

Aedgar looked around behind Mari's closed eyes.

'The energy of the place seems a bit better now. Like, in this moment. The change has started to come.

'There will be another change of energy, human energy. This translates to someone leaving or someone coming. Probably more than one person.'

Nerida appreciated the reassurance. The new locum nurse had not done well. It would be good when she left. And Eric was still around.

'It feels comfortable to work with our friend. We were pleased. We knew we made a good choice. But it's getting better all the time. The adjustments on our way in here will become easier, too. We are very pleased with the match.

'So's Aiden and his host and friends. Our match is as good as theirs. Better, we think. We got to this level much faster and much easier than they did.'

'Because they helped us, as well,' Nerida reminded him.

'They did. They didn't have the help that we had.

'It took them a very long time, in your understanding, to get to the level where we kind of, started out, so to say. Not that we haven't been waiting for a long time, too.

'But the progress was much easier and faster.'

'My work has been easier, thanks to you and others,' Nerida recognised. She mostly felt comfortable with patients at work nowadays, being open to her intuition. This meant that the medicines she gave were a better match. And if she was cutting, cleaning or suturing, the guiding voice in her head was clear whenever she needed help.

'You're welcome. We are here to help, to support and teach.'

'You're moving the eyes under the lids,' she noticed.

'I can feel colours, see colours. Different patterns of colours,' he said.

'You're moving towards the light of the window,' she fed back to him.

'The colours get brighter over there.' He moved Mari's head toward the window, where the afternoon light burned through the gaps in the blinds.

'They are more intense, but less bright over there.' He tilted the head towards the inside of the house and the kitchen.

'It's the yellow and orange kind of colours, as you would call it, over there. And it's the purple and blue over the other side, here.'

Nerida was pleased to see him enjoy himself. *I hope that his pleasure helps Mari feel good.* She wondered what the physiology or physics of that would be.

'Dawn's husband Trevor has a keen interest in physics,' she said.

As a younger student, she was aware of how privileged she was to have the opportunity to study. But she was disappointed with the way physics was taught. She thought it would be about Stephen Hawking and Einstein. Like, photons resonating with each other although they were separated by distance. Instead, it was nothing but mathematical formulae for boring things: a ball rolling down a plank, a rock getting faster as it fell. The teaching was stuck in the past. She eventually passed the tedious subject with a mark of fifty percent.

Aedgar was aware of Trevor's interest. 'We know,' he said. 'We have given advice before. Aiden asked for help. We gave some advice, about some molecular structures. It was a basic question. The answer to it was less basic, so it caused a bit of confusion.'

'This morning I listened to Monica talking about physics with Trevor. I swear I heard you in the recording. It was you— before we met. It was your view of the universe, it was language that you use and I recognised you in what she said,' Nerida insisted.

'We do things like this all the time,' he said placidly. 'This is how it works. If you don't have an understanding of some things, sometimes you need specialist advice. Different expertise. We don't want to give wrong answers. That would fail the purpose. Questions get asked for a reason.'

'But Monica, Aiden, held back on who you were. She didn't tell us how well she knew you. How important you are.'

'They had to. If you do something like this, it helps to discover things for yourself. It makes the relationship afterwards easier.'

'Listening to the recording reminded me about your lifetimes as a Druid. Can you tell me more about that?'

'We will get to that later.'

'Something more to discover, then,' she said.

'Every time.

'We are still adapting to each other, even if it is an almost perfect match. Once things get easier, we will be able to use the full potential of what's available.'

'Are you talking about being able to walk around, to talk to people?' *Like Fortunatus?*

She was wondering when they would be able to have shows for a living, touring in a motorhome like Abbey did.

'We will be able to have it all,' he said reassuringly.

'We are in the process of,' he waved the hands along the sides over

Mari's head '— sorting out these kind of little drawers in this brain that haven't been used before … We're trying to blend the information that's available, about the linear, how it is at the moment, to be able to apply our knowledge in a way that's easier to understand. Because it is important that it will be understood.'

'Hence the concrete and skyscrapers?' She was impressed by the modernity of that.

'Yes. We gathered some information, too, about how to use the things that are available already and how to apply it to examples, to make it easier to understand our knowledge.'

'I'm privileged to be a witness to such a process,' Nerida said sincerely.

'Not many of us are lucky enough to find such a match, and a host that agrees to do this work, so there are not many humans that can witness these kinds of things. If you see it that way, you might consider yourself privileged.'

'I do—it's rare and wondrous.'

'It doesn't happen that often, unfortunately for us. Many of us would have things to teach. But they can rarely find a match. Some find a match, but they could never get their host to commit to that kind of work.

'These humans are too scared.

'They think they are, what they call, adventurous. They are not.

'Climbing up a mountain, for example, is a physical exercise. It's not what should be called an adventure.

'Adventure is something you go on and you don't know what to expect. You're open to any kind of experience.

'And most importantly—you learn from it. And you'll be able to use what you've learned afterwards. It should expand your energy on a different level, not on a physical one.'

'Surely dealing with the limits of the body leads to expansion of consciousness.'

She had time to think about what the body could teach while the wound from her hemorrhoidectomy was healing. It was a humbling experience.

Aedgar said, 'There are examples on this planet of humans who have expanded their energy levels. They use the potential of what was available for them to learn and to expand this energy without being able to use the physical body.

'The body is a barrier if you consider it to be one. It makes it easier in this lifetime to, as they say, get around. But it's not a necessity to expand your energy and to learn and grow to the potential you're given.'

'Are you talking about someone like Stephen Hawking?'

'He's one of them. He's a good example. He's using his potential. Humankind could learn a lot from his example.

'But they prefer to use physically strong humans as role models. Which means they can climb up high, run fast or throw something a long way.

'All very useful skills to have in the old days when they went hunting. They're not so much use anymore.

'So they've chosen, as good examples to follow, many who can run or move very fast, but don't use their potential to expand energy and learn,' he said.

Nerida understood. 'The mainstream society is all about pretty, handsome, sexually attractive people who can sing loudly or pretend to be others, in order to tell stories.'

'I wouldn't say it's impossible to combine all these things,' Aedgar observed. 'But most human beings focus on one thing only, so they lack experience in other things.

'They are not interested, so they don't use their abilities to learn. They don't use the potential that was given to them in the first place. They get stuck on a single level.

'What can a human learn from someone who's considered to have the perfect physical constitution? People might be taught that if they look different they are not perfect.'

Nerida suppressed a groan of recognition.

'But those 'imperfect' ones—we don't think that is a real thing—they might be much more advanced in their knowledge and in expanding their energy, because they concentrate on more things than that one,' he went on.

'It's not all about physical appearance.

'It would be possible for those so-called 'perfect' ones to grow and learn, if they'd consider focussing on different levels, trying to expand their energy on all levels.

'But generally, they refuse to do that because they get their greed satisfied by the ones who admire them.'

Nerida thought of well-paid celebrities. *It seems an easy life to the rest of us.*

'They might even get more of that paper with the numbers on it, just for having a certain kind of physical appearance. They think on a single, simple level and get rewarded by others. It means they don't or can't expand their energy. They are stopped.

'They don't learn to broaden their experience. Why would they? They think they have it all.

'But then they feel empty. They are the ones that have the most regrets at the end of a lifetime, once they realise what they missed out on.

'Some have a 'perfect' physical experience. But then they might realise they are on a wrong path, a kind of dead-end road.

'If this is discovered suddenly, some of them decide quickly to come back and try a different path.

'You've plenty of young ones like that, (as you'd say, given the time pattern you have here). Many of them just decide to leave and come back with a different goal.'

Decisions made on a soul level. Nerida thought of Marilyn Monroe, of course. Jimmy Hendrix and Janis Joplin. Kurt Cobain, Heath Ledger. Tupak Shakur. *All the beautiful young ones.*

'They find out very abruptly,' Aedgar said, 'that they are on a wrong path. They can't expand their experience. They are not able to learn and expand their energy.

'That's what they come for. And so, they feel that they need to leave because they're on a one-way, dead-end path. They have to leave and come back.'

So, if you're so far from your purpose in life that you can't get to it, like because you won't let go of your greed, or you've got caught up in superficial things, sometimes you just die? Then get born again, be a baby and go through it all, to have a chance to learn what you came for. She did not interrupt.

Aedgar seemed to read her thoughts: 'You might find plenty of examples of human beings, sporting kind of an almost perfect physical appearance that leave quite early in that lifetime.

'Because they realise they have built their whole learning experience and ability to expand their energy on physical appearance.

'When the cells don't split up that quickly anymore, they age. And then they realise, sometimes quite early, that they're at a dead end.'

That's his first acknowledgement of ageing after all the 'time doesn't exist' talk, Nerida thought. *It's a relief to hear it.*

'You can't stop this ageing process. So if your whole learning path, is based on your youthful appearance, it has to be a failure.

'But that's the thing they learn,' he said kindly. 'They won't do it again when they come back. They've grown beyond that experience.'

Nerida said, 'I know a lovely example: Jim Morrison. There's a disabled man in Los Angeles who sings his songs, the same way he did.'

She and Mari saw him busking, singing Doors songs with remarkable talent and verve. 'You'd swear it was Jim come back. He loves the songs so much, has such a feel for them. He's homeless. I saw him happy, though. He brings joy. Could it be the same spirit?'

Aedgar did not stop to look. *Perhaps there is a need to protect that soul's privacy,* Nerida thought.

'Some choose to have a short appearance. They prove to themselves and others that it doesn't take the perfect, or almost perfect physical appearance to have success.'

A short appearance, like me? Oh, he means they're not in this world for long.

'So they grow and expand their energy by showing other people what's possible,' Aedgar said. 'They teach that it's possible to achieve a lot without that almost perfect physical appearance.

'It's an easy way for them: coming back for a relatively short time in the linear to expand their energy a lot.'

Aedgar left her soon after with his usual elegant salutations.

Drying dishes later, Nerida reflected on the heartbreak it causes when someone leaves so young.

She opened a cupboard. The thick stacked plates clattered. She sighed, recalling their clinic maintenance man and snake-catcher, Biggie's father. And that young man's lithe movements and ready smile. *How could he feel that he was at a dead end? He had competing career offers, competing families. Was he overwhelmed by his choices?*

Or was he fatally disappointed to find that his physical beauty, an appearance and charm near perfection, made learning and growing more difficult or impossible?

THIRTY-TWO

STUART HIGHWAY, SOUTH AUSTRALIA
SATURDAY MARCH 30, 2013

THEY WERE RETURNING HOME across an infinite plain of coloured pebbles in the late afternoon. On the way home from a city excursion. Suddenly Mari, driving, was waved down and pulled over.

Nerida met an agitated coach driver in the middle of the empty road, her shoulders hunched against the sudden cold. His blue jacket was rumpled, his posture defeated. He pointed down the road as he spoke. Then patted his pockets as if he needed a cigarette.

Nerida came back and called into the driver's window to Mari, 'They need a doctor. Pass me my coat, please.' The unseasonal, frigid wind slapped Nerida's face and neck as she came to the passenger side of the car. Zipping her coat, she wished she had doctor's gloves. Or anything else to protect her.

'Bad accident. It's not the coach. There's a car over in the scrub, see?' Nerida said to Mari, who turned. She pointed to a copse of roadside mulga trees about sixty metres behind them. Bright blue paint-work appeared amidst the stocky old trees.

'It's flipped on its roof,' Nerida explained. 'Two nurses were on the bus. They've been here a couple of hours already. They want me here.' She drew in her breath, bracing herself against the frame of their car. 'There's been a death.'

'Do you need me?' Mari asked. Her instinct was to go with her wife, whose grey eyes were wide with urgency.

'You've got no insurance. Stay here for now,' Nerida replied. She looked over the inside of the car. 'We've got nothing here. The nurses at home have the doctor's bag in the ambulance.' She was talking to herself, really. She reached to squeeze Mari's hand momentarily, then turned down the road. 'I'll sing out if I need you to come.'

Nerida headed towards a small group of people huddled together for shelter against the bitter wind. Her legs dragged against resistance, that was more than just the wind. She had the sick fear she always got in an emergency.

A voice in her head said, *You don't know enough.*

The wind screamed from Antarctica across the plain. She folded her arms tight across her breasts.

As Nerida approached, a person broke away and walked towards her, her brown head down. Nerida made out three others, two wrapped in blankets. *Can't see any body lying or broken on the ground. That's a relief. Not much we can do, anyway—no drugs, no equipment.* She bit her lip.

The brown-haired woman approached in slow motion, as if her legs were in the same mire Nerida felt she was in.

'Hi. You're a doctor?'

'Yes. I'm a GP. My name's Nerida Green. I'm from Mutitjulu. I deal with the occasional emergency. Is there any way I can help?'

She shook the nurse's hand—cold skin on cold.

'I'm Linda. I'm traveling with Sarah, over there. We're both RANs, remote area nurses, you know? Thanks for stopping. There's not much

... We've done everything we could.' She kept her voice low, as if the wind might carry her voice to the accident victims.

'Everything anyone could do, I think.' Her body blocked the scene behind her, even though they were still thirty metres from the others.

Nerida could saw the hatchback, jammed into the trees, its windows broken, roof flattened, columns bent. A circular hole on the passenger side spiderwebbed the windscreen.

The abrasive ground between the road and the ruined car was strewn with goods: crockery and cutlery spilled in the dirt; a plastic box disgorged lipsticks. A suit jacket flapped around the bottom of a tree. Unnumbered pieces of paper blew away across the plain. The noises of fabric, branches and paper seemed loud in Nerida's head.

'We work at remote communities up the road. We're on our way back from a break in Adelaide, catching the bus up to work for a few weeks,' Linda sniffed. Her eyes looked irritated by the wind. 'We just work a few weeks at a time,' Linda repeated uselessly.

She stopped and looked out over the plain, as if wishing she was somewhere else. She took a deep breath and, meeting Nerida's eyes, said, 'Oh, there's a baby dead.'

Nerida felt a gasp of grief escape her chest and mouth. A sick tightness crept up from her belly. 'Oh god,' she said.

'We did everything we could,' Linda repeated. 'We tried to resuscitate the baby when we arrived. You know, the parents needed it. We did that for almost an hour before we had to stop. It's so tiring.

'I mean, he was already dead.' Linda's voice choked and tears spilled. 'His father had to go looking for him in the bushes.'

She drew a deep breath. 'The coach driver has called the flying doc. There's a place they can land, just up the road. They're sending a plane.'

'Do the parents have injuries?' Nerida asked.

'A couple of lacerations. Scratches and bruises. No loss of consciousness that we know of. Sarah's washed their cuts. We had some antiseptic and saline in the bus First-Aid kit.

'They could have internal injuries of course, so they have to go to hospital…' her voice trailed off.

Nerida touched Linda's arm and they fell into a hug, then walked to the young parents, who stood with Nurse Sarah.

The mother held her child tightly to her chest, wrapped in a cosy, peach-coloured blanket. The baby's face peeped out, showing long lashes and fat cheeks in a round face.

Mum was crying so hard she could hardly talk. 'You're the doctor, yes? Please can you try? Please, look. Please help him. Can you make him better?

'Shouldn't we do more resuscitation, doctor?'

Nerida came close. She touched Mum's arm and leaned over the infant's sweet face. She was afraid to move the blanket in case he had injuries she didn't want to see. His skin was perfect. *Please don't let him be bloodied or broken.*

'There's not a mark on him,' Sarah bent towards Nerida and whispered, reading her thoughts.

The doctor touched the baby's cheek with her ungloved finger. He was colder than her hand. 'Do you have a stethoscope?' she asked Linda. She did. *One of those crappy instruments they give nurses, no better than a child's toy.*

Nerida put it in her ears and opened the blanket, which was warmed by the mother's body. She carefully placed the thin diaphragm, made of aluminium and white plastic, on the infant's chest, under his shirt and singlet. Then listened for a long minute. Heard only the rustle of her fingers gripping the instrument.

Next, she pushed the stethoscope into the folds of the baby's fat, icy neck, where his pulse would have been. Lastly, she lifted one of his eyelids gently, glimpsing the lifeless blue-grey eye.

She stroked the child's soft curls and looked up into his mother's streaming eyes. 'Such a beautiful child,' Nerida said.

'Can you resuscitate him, doctor? Please can we try?' she sobbed.

Her husband, standing close by her side, studied the doctor's face. Nerida let her sadness show.

'He's gone,' she said. She shook her head, her hand on the mother's blanketed arm. She looked across the plain, wondering whether to say what she really thought. 'This one's spirit is far, far away. We can't call him back now.'

'Really? Nothing? Really?' his mother said. Her hair, undone, whipped her face, stuck to her tears.

'Wouldn't there be any medicine when the flying doctor comes that might help him?' the father asked.

'No, nothing. He's gone from this life.

'He must have brought you so much love,' Nerida said. 'I'm sorry. He would have died instantly when he was thrown out of the car. His spirit flew away out of his body then.'

Nerida stood with the small family. They talked and cried together. She felt the father's back and neck, checking for fractures. He grimaced when she felt his ribs. *Looks like several are broken.* She listened to his chest, felt his belly, chilled and soft.

Nerida was a little surprised when Linda said, 'Do you think me and Sarah might go? Could you stay with them until the evacuation team arrives?

'We're trying to reach Kendumber before sundown. You know, it's no good driving after dark. There's other people on the bus who've been waiting a long time.'

'That'll be okay. My wife and I can stay at the next roadhouse.' Nerida could see Mari's dark head in their vehicle.

The nurses embraced their patients and walked wearily back to the bus. Linda stopped at the car to explain the situation to Mari and thank her. As the bus departed, the desert plain was suddenly bigger and emptier.

The parents tried to comfort to each other. Nerida asked again if they had pain anywhere. She palpated the mother's spine and skull, felt her ribs and pulse.

Nothing broken in her, clinically speaking.

'Can we keep him with us? When the plane comes? It's so cold. I want to keep him warm,' she asked.

An hour later, the sun was low and orange over the plain, when the Flying Doctor Service arrived in a local station owner 's vehicle, driven from the small plane they'd landed twenty kilometres up the road. There was a nurse, a pilot and a doctor, each carrying bulky equipment bags. The station worker driving them removed his battered felt hat, gave a small nod.

Nerida gave the doctor a handover of what she knew about the young family and the accident, while the new nurse went to talk to them.

'They may have swerved to miss a cow. Or maybe the driver fell asleep at the wheel and drifted onto the soft edge of the road. They say they were driving about one hundred and ten kilometres an hour,' she said.

'Lovely couple,' she continued with the wind stinging her eyes. 'He got a new job in the city. They stayed up all night, packing. They put everything they own in the back of the car. It was piled to the ceiling. They didn't have room for the baby's capsule in the back.

'They had seatbelts on, but the little one was on Dad's lap, without one, in the front. Mum was driving.'

Nerida swallowed. She looked up the road to where Mari now waited, imagining the small blue car coming down the undeviating road.

Then she twisted around to see the deep tracks in the dust where the car left the road. A mess of marks showed where it had flipped on its roof and slid, still on its roof, to the place where the shell of the vehicle stopped against the short, thick trunk of a tree.

Nerida's voice shook. 'The baby went straight through the front windscreen, probably on the impact of the car turning over. Parents self-extracted. Dad had to go searching for him in the bushes. He was already cold when Dad picked him up.

'They're both a bit shocky but holding their own. Dad's got broken ribs on the left, but he seems to have good air entry. No head injuries as far as I can tell—neurologically grossly normal. Spines and necks okay.

'Abdomens soft, not tender, except near Dad's ribs. Moving all their limbs. Strong, regular pulses.

'A few lacs the nurses washed. Plenty of bruises. She's got a big hematoma from the seat belt across her upper abdomen and chest.

'Please allow them to hold the baby until they get to the hospital.'

The retrieval doctor nodded, speaking quietly, 'That'll be alright. Poor little thing doesn't need to be strapped in anywhere anymore.

'The hospital's pretty good. They'll be able to keep him with them, even after they've arrived—probably for a day or two. Til they're ready to let him go. Well, you know, if anyone is ever ready.' The nurse buckled the young father into a neck brace, with the pilot lending a hand.

Nerida said goodbye, kissing each of the patients, including the child's smooth, cold forehead. Walking up the road, she thought of her own children, Ruby and Jim, all grown up. She felt sad and deeply grateful.

As Nerida climbed into the car, the glow of the sunset spread all along the plain, as if the horizon was the fiery end of the world. She snuggled against Mari's warm body. Mari wrapped her arm around her and drew her close. The handbrake dug into Nerida's hip.

'Not much you could do, huh?'

Nerida started to cry.

'Good that you were there for them,' Mari said and kissed her, stroking her hair and warming Nerida's face with her palm.

THIRTY-THREE

MUTITJULU
SUNDAY APRIL 7, 2013

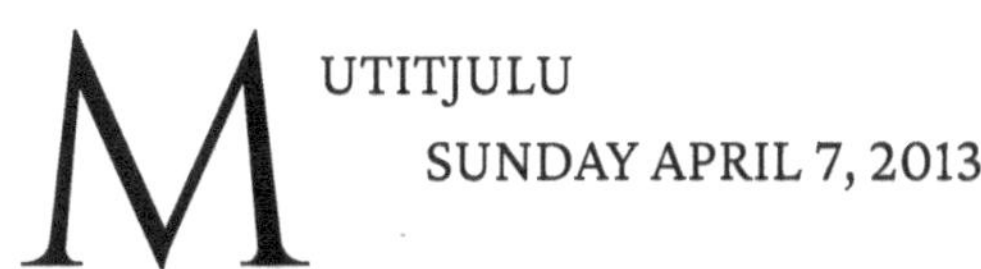

NERIDA POTTED pumpkin and cauliflower shoots she'd grown from seed in a sheltered spot at the side of the house.

It was unlikely they'd grow to be edible. Weather and water were inconsistent, especially for such big, slow-growing, vegetables.

But they'd made it so far, these tender shoots. Thickened their stems and grown proper velvety leaves. As she patted them into the potting mix she suddenly felt her heart swell for the baby who died on the road. *There is so much grief for him.*

Where there is love, there is grief. She tried to accept it.

Aedgar's talk about the souls that don't stay long had prepared her for supporting the child's parents. The knowledge he gave helped her be there completely with them in those soul-scarring moments.

She came into the house and cut herself an apple and some cheese. Mari was fasting.

Hopefully, there'll be a session this afternoon.

Only an hour or so later, Mari was in trance.

Her crystals were put emphatically on the table after three minutes or so. They clunked, in a movement unlike Aedgar 's usual delicacy.

Something's up.

Mari's movements were faster than usual, including lifting and shaking the shoulders, stretching the arms out and circling the hands to warm up the wrists.

After a serious throat clearing, five minutes in, the spirit spoke up. 'Hello then,' they said.

'Hello then,' Nerida responded. 'You're looking very fluent and comfortable in that body today!'

The spirit spoke in a different, soft and serious voice. 'I'm looking … for a spare body,' they said.

A bit shocking, to put it that way. 'Oh, really?'

'You've been reading my books,' they said, sounding pleased and proud. The room was quiet. More flexing, looking around.

'Not a bad match.' Like a patron newly arrived at a resort.

Nerida was trying to process. Aedgar didn't have any books yet, except in her dreams and aspirations. Amazed, she asked, 'Is this Seth?'

'This is Fortunatus.'

Nerida gasped. 'You're kidding!' She let out a roaring laugh. 'I'm very surprised!' It was as if Bob Dylan arrived on the doorstep.

'Do I sound like I'm kidding?'

'No. Not at all.' Still laughing, she sputtered, 'I'm honoured to see you. And surprised, as you can tell.'

Sharply, he replied, 'You'd better be.'

'Yeah. Astonished. I am.'

Fortunatus made a quick, forceful exhalation.

'How wonderful,' she said. 'And unexpected.'

Fortunatus paused a moment. Then spoke at a fast pace. 'I had this idea the other day.'

'Uhuh. Tell me about it.'

Intensely, he said, 'I could feel the energy. When this Abbey was talking at that place.

'So, I thought I might give it a try.

'Not bad.

'Bit limited in the movements.

'*I* am used to walking around.'

He tried to open Mari's eyelids, which fluttered like she was dreaming. 'I'm used to seeing, too.'

Nerida watched but the eyes didn't open.

'That's a bit of a blow, I'd say,' he said.

Nerida would not interrupt him. She was quiet, thinking *Do we even want Fortunatus to be channelled with us? What's happened to Abbey?* She said, 'Well, I'm sure it will be possible, at some stage.'

'I'm just trying to be a little bit of a spy, as you do.'

The way he spoke was almost a bit sinister. *What have we here?*

She laughed nervously.

'I'm trying to find a spare body for other possibilities. Probably.'

After a beat, he admitted, 'It is a bit discouraging, having people asking the same questions over and over again.'

This time, Nerida laughed with recognition. 'Yes.'

He said bleakly, 'I don't think they've learned anything at all.'

'Ah,' she said.

'Well, some of them do—'

'Yes.'

'But it's a minority.'

'Yes,' she said. There was another long pause. Then she spoke with admiration: 'And yet, you have a huge audience.' It was true. Fortunatus' teachings had influenced mainstream culture, especially in the US. His books and recordings sold in the millions.

And if even one in a thousand of his readers learns anything that helps them grow, his influence is huge, hard to estimate. She couldn't help thinking, too, that Abbey had a beautiful home. And would never want for material things.

'It's because of my chosen specialty,' he said with a glimmer of pride.

After a couple of beats Nerida commented, 'Your specialty was a good match for the time and place.' She recalled Aedgar saying, 'He's trying to get to the masses. Someone had to.'

'Of course,' Fortunatus agreed.

'Do you have other things you'd like to teach about?' Nerida asked.

'I've thought about other things.

'The point is, the Law of Attraction could be used in different, or better, ways.

'But I got kinda stuck. Well, not me.

'It's the people asking the same questions over and over again, who are stuck.' He sounded weary when he said that.

Nerida was familiar with Nietzsche's idea of the eternal return. Sam was studying philosophy (and experimenting with large doses of LSD) when they met.

He was inspired by Nietzsche. Following Sam's guidance, she read about the concept.

As she understood it, one should live life so well that living the same moments over and over, in every detail, would be a source of joy. The idea was appalling when she was nineteen, but she had reflected on it occasionally, over the years.

Fortunatus was not enjoying his version of the eternal return. They'd witnessed it at the show they attended in Sydney, where people asked the same narrow, materialistic questions. 'What will happen with my small business?' 'Is money coming to me in this court case?' 'When will I win the lottery?'

'They lost view,' he said, quirkily, 'on the important things in life. And on the bigger picture. They are worried about all these tiny things that don't mean anything, at all.'

'Yes.'

'I mean, I am **not** supposed to use this body,' he declared. Nerida understood that. And was intrigued.

His tone was respectful, then. 'It's a relationship. But after realising what happened to Clive, I'm not sure how long it's gonna last.'

Nerida found herself counselling him! He trusted her to listen; she was moved by that. 'With Abbey, you mean?'

'Yes. Well, she's travelling around. Keeping herself busy. And busy and busy.'

'Mhmm.' She liked the way he repeated a word to intensify the feeling. Anangu did that sometimes in several of their languages, including English. 'But she's really, really lonely, lonely, lonely.'

Nerida felt sad for Abbey. 'Yes.'

'Almost brokenhearted,' he said. She understood.

'So, she's covering up. Doing all this work,' he said. He was quiet for a minute or so, reflecting. 'I know you've got a primary source that has important things to say.'

She felt proud of Aedgar, their 'primary source'. Appreciated Fortunatus' recognition.

There is harmony in the world of Spirit. 'Yes, that's right,' she said softly.

'I was just trying to view the opportunity.

'Finding out if it's possible to change at some stage.'

'And apparently it is,' she said.

Now, he was the one who said, 'Surprising.'

'Yes. And delightful.' She was enjoying the feeling of him being there now. He had her trust.

'Yeah, I think so, too. Yeah, I could feel this energy at that place.'

Did he mean Mari or Aedgar as the energy he could feel?

He went on, 'Somehow, I felt attracted—'

Nerida butted in, 'But you ignored—'

Fortunatus said, '—but, on the other hand, I had business to attend to.'

Nerida understood. She and Mari had talked about it. 'It would have caused a ruckus,

so to speak, if you'd engaged with us that time. Might've changed a lot of things.'

'I had to negotiate with your primary source.'

Nerida was glad to understand that. 'Thank you.'

'I had to promise that I won't take over.'

And she was very relieved to hear that. 'Thank you.'

'But they'd agreed that we might share at some point in the future.'

'That's interesting,' she said. 'And exciting …

'One of the things Aedgar talked about was the power of the Law of Attraction for the people living in this area, who are Indigenous, the Original People of Australia. That they might be able to use it in a way that would help them and help the Earth.'

'Well, they would be pre-destined to use it. If they would be just a little bit more clever. They just don't get it.

'It's a worry.

'They have kind of deteriorated somewhat,' he said.

Nerida sighed. 'Yeah. There's been damage done.'

'They're doing a lot of the damage themselves, actually,' Fortunatus commented.

'Nowadays, yes.' She had to agree. She thought of the Blair sisters and their love god.

Of Jack, who couldn't give up the smokes. And a young one who cut and spoke angrily towards themselves and others.

Pitjantjatjara used the same word, *pika*, as a noun for pain and sickness, and as an adjective for rage.

Fortunatus said sadly, 'If they knew how powerful they are, they could make a big change. Your primary source was right. Of course, **we** are right.

'They would be the perfect people to use it. I'm just a bit worried they might use it for the wrong purpose.

'Some of them would like to compete. We do things to expand energy, not to compete with other "races", so to speak. Which is the part those ones don't get.

'They are trying to compete in a contest they're not made for. They have other advantages. Unfortunately, they are not using them.'

He paused, then said, 'I think your primary source should easily be able to use more of the functions of this body.

'It's quite easy to access.

'I'll leave it to your primary source to open the eyes. Can't be that difficult to work it out.

'He's very intelligent.'

She agreed.

'Very, very intelligent. Intelligent, intelligent, intelligent.'

Nerida smiled. 'We love him.'

'Ah, he's got very nice energy. Besides being so intelligent.'

'Yes!'

'In your linear life, this would be an exceedingly rare combination.'

She concurred again and asked, 'Do you know our friend Monica, also?'

'Indeed, I do. It's a great privilege to get into this plane you live on and find a body—being able to work with ... to talk. Of course, we know each other.

'We know everybody, more or less.

'But especially the ones privileged enough to find that partnership. We know each other well.

'We all have our different specialties, though.'

'I have been reading your books. It's true,' Nerida said. 'I mistook you for him because I was reading Seth's book yesterday.'

She was feeling pleased. 'But we have a whole stack of your books here at our house.' She bought a couple from the big tables of merchandise at the meeting in Sydney and had others she'd purchased, mostly impulsively, online. She dipped into them for energy and inspiration.

'That's a bit surprising, somehow,' he said.

'Because your primary energy knows about the Law of Attraction, of course. But he's interested in it in a different way—that resonates more with his partner.'

So, Mari has her own take on Law of Attraction. And Aedgar resonates with it.

'And it's not my way of thinking about it. Or, at least, it wasn't.

'Until I realised that I get asked the same questions over and over and over and over again.

'No matter where I go.'

'Hmm. When you say "his partner", you mean Mari, this friend whose body you use?'

'I suppose so, yes. We are not that familiar with names. You tend to need them.'

'We do,' she said. 'Well, I've been studying your work because it's fundamental to my understanding of what we do in the world. I must understand what Abbey does. I need to understand what you've created, with her and Clive.'

Fortunatus was proud. 'Cause we are pioneers.'

Nerida felt he had a right to be. 'You've broken new ground,' she said.

'You'll be pioneers of your time,' he said. 'Even if it kind of interlaces with our time. You're not that far apart.'

It was true. Abbey was only ten or fifteen years older than Nerida and Mari. They were contemporaries in many ways. Nerida drank up his praise.

'There is great ability,' he said of Mari. 'Hopefully for me too at some point. So, all I can do is encourage you to use it. Use it. Use it. Whenever you can.

'It's a partnership that's also a source of health, pleasure. And wealth, if you use it the right way.

'There is great potential. Big potential. Big, big, big potential. Use it.'

Nerida felt ashamed of her impatience with Aedgar's repetition (about time not existing, energy expanding, learning). *Fortunatus is not afraid of repetition.*

'Mari had planned to be a doctor,' Nerida confided. 'And she's grieving the loss of that opportunity.'

Fortunatus made a harrumph. 'It's all rubbish. If you're privileged to work in this kind of—hmm—technique, or environment—on this Earth plane, you are more than any doctor could ever be.'

Nerida smiled knowingly. 'Yes.'

'You are more than any engineer could ever be. You are more than anybody else.

'Because it's a very, very, very rare--very rare! --possibility to use this. It's an ability that's a gift. She should see it as a gift. This ability is so much ahead of everything else.'

He was quiet a moment. Then, 'Doctors,' he clucked. 'Rubbish, rubbish, rubbish.'

Chuckling along, Nerida said, 'Ah, you're funny.''

'I think I've seen and experienced enough now,' Fortunatus said abruptly. 'I can feel it's usable at some point.

'I already have had negotiations with your main source. We might share a little bit at some point in the future.

'So, I think I'll leave you. I might be back at some point. But you keep on working with your main source.'

'We do. It's an honour and pleasure to meet you,' she said. She felt a glow of love from the energy.

'I knew.' He clarified. 'I could feel you had some questions. But I couldn't interfere with anything. I had business to do.

'And I couldn't expose Abbey to a ... well, we wouldn't call it a disaster, but ... a lesser success, maybe?

'Well, that's all I have to say for now.'

'Lovely to meet you, Fortunatus. Until next time.'

'Nice to talk to you. Might take a long time to talk again.'

'Yes.' She felt his energy step back.

Quietly, he said, 'Keep on doing this work. It is important.'

There was a minute or two of silence as Mari returned. Nerida greeted her brightly. Almost in a whisper, Mari said, 'Hey. Who was that? That felt different.'

Nerida grinned. She got up to get food and drink out for Mari. 'Tell me about your experience, and I'll tell you about mine.'

She pulled out cheese, butter and mortadella. Started arranging them on a plate. Sun- dried tomatoes. Eggplant roasted yesterday.

Mari observed, 'Actually it was … less gentle. Less gentle than Aedgar or the others. Even the cat was gentler.'

Nerida nodded. She cut the camembert into wedges. 'That was an assertive energy. Confident.'

'Aaw, it felt like something very strong.'

'Yes.' Nerida opened a jar of pickles and put some in a small dish Mari had brought from Germany.

'It didn't feel like a bad one,' Mari said. 'But it was very different, somehow. I had a name in my head before it started.'

Nerida held her breath. 'Can you remember the name?'

'Fortunatus. But that can't be because they don't change who they go with.'

'No, not normally. It was Fortunatus.'

Mari groaned. 'Oh, fuck.'

Nerida bent over the kitchen bench laughing. 'Yeah, that's what I thought when I found out who it was! He arrived with great confidence and energy and said, "You've been reading my books." I thought it was Seth. I was reading *Seth Speaks* yesterday … No.

'It's Fortunatus.'

Laughing more at the look on her wife's face, she said, 'He was looking for a new body. But he had negotiated—'

'For a new body?? Does that mean—?' Mari was horrified.

'Possibly, in future, he might use you as a channel,' Nerida explained. 'You are very suitable, he says. It's easy.

'He noticed your energy at the meeting and was attracted to it.

He's had long negotiations with our "primary source." Who, he says, is "intelligent, intelligent, intelligent."

'I'll tell you more about it when while we're eating. You might want to listen to the recording, cause it's astonishing.'

Mari would not listen to the recording. When Nerida asked her about it again after dinner, she said she found the episode disturbing.

'I felt angry that he could do that to Abbey.

'I wouldn't want Aedgar to come through someone else. It could open the door to all those pretenders, wannabees who can't really channel.

'I don't want them to try to steal from what Aedgar says, or Fortunatus. Saying "Oh, Aedgar came to me this morning," on Instagram. And coming up with bullshit.

'I can't have it!'

CHAPTER

THIRTY-FOUR

M UTITJULU
SUNDAY APRIL 14, 2013

A week later, the flies surged as camels came into the district, attracted to the lush green grass springing up around Uluru.

'So, what is it with you and the fly spray?' Mari asked her wife, who was chasing flies around the living room with the yellow plastic swatter. 'It's just there by the door. I used it to kill a mosquito this morning.'

Nerida was too short to reach the upper parts of the room. She waited until the fly came into her reach. Then waved the swatter to and fro, approaching the fly.

'If you move it like this, they don't see you coming,' she said quietly, demonstrating her method with a satisfying blow. She picked up the dead fly with a tissue.

'When I was six, my grandmother sprayed the rooms. She did that at sundown every night in the summer, to kill the mosquitoes before we went to bed. She used this old-fashioned pump spray. It made thick clouds. She closed the doors to kill them, fifteen minutes before we went to bed.

'Maybe she sprayed too late that night. For some reason, I was in a little room by myself instead of being with the other kids. The room stank! I felt like I could hardly breathe. I complained to my mother more than once. She told me "Just lie down and go to sleep."

'The insecticide was so strong. I coughed. I felt like droplets had got into my throat. It was sore. I was convinced I was being poisoned. I started to cry in bed.

'One of my great-grandfathers was gassed in World War I. And took years to die. Maybe I'd heard that. Anyway, I was convinced this poison would kill me.

'I didn't want to go out because I thought they'd growl at me. But I thought if I was going to die, that was serious, and they should know. So, I dried my tears and went out to where the adults were.

'I said, "Fly spray is poison, isn't it?" It was if you got too much of it, they said. But I'd be all right and I should go back to bed.'

'Didn't someone give you a cuddle?' Mari asked.

'I was too old for cuddles by then.'

'You were six.'

'Yeah ... So, I'm lying in bed with the air poisoned around me, convinced I'll die that night. I cried a lot. I prayed to several kinds of gods I'd heard about. Reflected on what a short life it had been.'

Mari smiled fondly.

'It was my first idea that my life would end,' Nerida said. She put a leg on a chair and leaned to swat the last fly. 'Anyway, the swatter's more fun.'

As the sun got lower in the afternoon, Mari channelled Aedgar. It took ten minutes or so to hear that soft, rounded, 'Hello.'

'Hello,' she said warmly. 'Welcome back.'

'Thank you,' he said, gaining strength in the voice. 'It was difficult to get in, cause she had trouble getting out.'

'Really?'

'Yes. What have you been up to lately?'

'We've had great adventures.' She grinned. 'What's the nature of these adventures?'

'Well, one was a visit from someone we were not expecting at all. You might know about it.'

'Hmmm. It was about as tough as it gets for negotiation.'

'I'll bet.' She could hardly imagine brokering a deal with Fortunatus.

'Had to promise to make it short. And it's a one-time thing for now.'

'Good. We were a little shocked.'

'We didn't do all this preparation for someone else. But we still do support one another.

'It's a gift that's too precious to use it as a—hmm, let's say it like, "Can I ride your bike for a while?"

'That's not how it works. Nothing to be messed around with or lightly to be shared.

'We are trying to establish a serious and profound relationship, trying to extend it. We've been preparing it for a long time. So, it did take quite a bit of negotiation.

'We hope you haven't been too disturbed by that.'

'I thought it was interesting.' Nerida's eyebrows rose.

Aedgar said, 'For me it was kind of a confirmation or affirmation of these things being possible. And that there is interaction, so to say, between us.'

'Yes.' The experience gave insight into the interaction of the non-physical beings, beyond the relationship between Aedgar and Monica/Aiden. It shone a light into that mysterious world. And showed that Mari was as gifted as another famously successful channel.

'You've been busy I think, also.' Sometimes she could sense it.

'Quite a bit, all the time. There are some good things going on. Some bad things, too, as we speak.'

'You mean just locally here?'

'No.'

'In the planet?'

'We would call it a shift in nature forces. Others might call it an unpleasant event.'

She knew there was an extreme winter continuing in Europe. She'd heard talk of a link between melting of the Arctic ice and extreme weather events—storms and power outages killing people in Canada and the eastern US.

But Nerida wanted to talk about something good. Her mind needed narrower horizons. 'There's been a victory on this island. Up in the northwest,' she said. 'There was a plan to take gas out from under the sea. People have been fighting against it. Would have killed all the sea life.'

'Yes.'

'Seems to have been postponed at least.' Plans to drill for undersea gas off the coast of Broome, had been foiled by protest. It was a place of turquoise water, red rock and white sand, and handsome mixed-race people.

'It might never happen.'

That was a happy thought. 'We hope so,' she said.

'But there will be fights about it.' He perceived the seeds of coming conflicts. 'There are some others lining up already to take over, who think they have more stamina to fight against this win.

'But they are companies that have had "accidents" before, so we think all their so-called stamina won't help.

'People will find out about their past failures in and realise that they haven't learned. Or changed anything they do.'

'Mhmm. Broome's a place very dear to Mari's heart. She wondered if you might have played a role in that fight.'

'Well, you might go there sometime. It has a good energy, this place,' he said, neatly side-stepping the question. 'It would have changed dramatically.'

'Yes.' She felt that he or others like him had given support to the protesters and said, 'Thank you for helping.'

'You're welcome.'

When they were in Broome last, a friend who was a descendant of the Karajarri clan from south of Broome, showed them around an important coastal site, a tall midden, a broad hill of shells and tools tens of thousands of years old.

Their friend's uncle told stories recalling Port Hedland, down the coast. He visited there as a child. 'It was just as beautiful as Broome,' he said. 'But then when they brought the iron ore into the port in such quantities in the sixties and seventies, it killed the fish. That's what this place'll be like if they set up the gas rigs—a marine desert.'

Now, Nerida said, 'I'd almost given up. I didn't think there was any hope.' She sent fifty dollars to those fighting against the gas mining, posted links and sent messages of support.

Aedgar replied: 'If the right forces or energies join up together, it's never too late. But sometimes there is not much "time" (in your understanding) to join these good energies or forces together.

'It was close, but it works for now.'

'People up there did a good job,' she noted. It felt like she was asking for recognition for herself, too. In past battles, she'd stood on picket lines and joined blockades. Stayed up all night producing inspiring propaganda. A part of her felt like she should still be doing that.

'Indeed,' Aedgar agreed. 'But they should keep their eyes open. Victories of that size are not easy to come by.'

'And not so easy to maintain,' Nerida noted.

'That's the main problem.' He seemed to be looking into it. 'They might use a backdoor next time, the ones that are lining up already.

'It had some political taste to it. Someone wanted to present himself in a better light for upcoming events.'

'Are you talking about the boss of the company?'

'No. Some people want to have more power over the region—pretending they are well-meaning. For them this victory was not about rescuing the environment. For them it was about changing the deal for one with more profits.'

'Oh really. Okay.'

'But there are some good people around. They will keep an eye open because they must.'

'Mhm, because they care about the earth there.' Nerida's heart was always open. But the bad actions of humans skewered it. She was trying, as well, to think and speak positively, as Fortunatus said people should do.

Aedgar agreed. 'But they have an enemy within—'

'Mhmm,' Nerida winced. *In goes another skewer.*

'—trying to figure out how they work, what they think about and what the next move will be, to tackle it in a different way next time.

'But it might mobilise more people of the good energy. They made an impact— temporarily—but they made an impact. It's a good role model for others coming.'

'It's encouraging,' she said hopefully.

'Yes. So, we know about the plans, what they're trying to do. But this is a stage where our side can make a change if they don't just all go away and pack up, so to say.

'They need to be on watch,' he said.

Nerida was amazed to hear a spirit speak of 'our side'. She wondered if she should send a post or letter to the environmentalists. *Would they believe it? They should hear this warning.*

'You know sometimes people play this game where they kick the ball? And then they achieve a goal and they're all celebrating. And while some of them are still celebrating the other team puts a goal into theirs.'

He temporised. 'This is something that could happen. Of course, I tried to explain it in an easy way, no one's gonna kick a ball in real life, it's the mechanism.'

'I understand. Would you like me to directly send a message to the people fighting up there, about this?'

'Don't tell them it was me,' he said shyly.

'Really? They're not ready for that?'

'Some of them are. I am not sure if you are ready.'

'Mmm.' *I guess he can read my reservations about going public with the channelled material in my energy.*

After a beat, he said, 'So, you'll have another friend coming soon.'

'I'm very happy about that, yes. He's declared himself.' Her cousin-brother Greg, a physiotherapist (as well as a Traditional Aboriginal healer), was coming to work at Muti for a few weeks.

'Good. There will be an achievement for everyone involved in it. Means people are expanding energy and knowledge, which is always a good thing. Cause everyone's here to learn.'

Greg called her from Sydney, where he had a whirlwind romance during Mardi Gras. Now he was coming to see them, alone and licking his wounds, as usual. A beautiful man, Greg was chronically single and lonely. *He always goes for the pretty ones. He wants a handsome man as a trophy.*

'He needs some positive lessons. He's had some negative lessons. Painful ones,' she said.

'His angle of looking at things is changing slowly.'

'Yes.'

'It could be a little bit quicker,' Aedgar said drily.

Nerida laughed. 'Yes.'

'But he's a bit lethargic in changing things.'

'Yes. I noticed a change, though, when I talked to him.' Greg said on the phone that he was tired of seeking love with all the wrong people.

'It's about time. Took him quite a bit.'

'Yes. Same mistakes over and over.' She had heard all about that from Greg before.

'For some people it's the only way to learn, choosing the hard way, so to say.'

'I'm happy if he doesn't bring the hard way with him.'

'He won't.'

'That's wonderful.' She was so pleased Greg was coming. Could imagine the hug already.

Then she remembered Clair's visit the previous evening. 'Our other friend was here last night. And you declared yourself!'

'Well, I was here. It wasn't me that declared anything, but—'

Claire came over to tell them about a visit from two ngankari at the clinic that afternoon. Nerida had been working at the Respite Centre when they stopped in to the clinic for medication, on their way to Ernabella.

Nerida knew the healers. She knew Charlie very well. She even felt a frisson of jealousy that they had not sought she and Mari out.

When they been talking excitedly about ngangkari, Mari told Claire that she was a channel. It came bursting out as if she'd been pushed.

Aedgar continued, 'She has something to learn. She gained insight that she wasn't expecting.'

'Yes—seemed to be a shock.'

Claire didn't want to hear about channelling. She put her hands over her ears, closed her eyes and went 'La, la, la.' It was a joke. But it wasn't.

'I don't want to know about it. I always knew that would come back to bite me,' Claire said. But then refused to explain what she meant.

'She has a very nice energy that person,' Aedgar said. 'But she's running away from positive learning experiences. She chooses the painful and difficult way to learn, as our other friend does. She could get to a much higher level easily if she would change her attitude towards certain things.'

'For example?'

'About being worthy of being loved, loving herself. She thinks she has to do huge amounts of work—which she does. She does very good things. But this is not how to gain love.

'She has respect. She gets respect through that.

'But respect is not the same as love, universal love. She's happy enough, but quite lonely at times. There hasn't been a, so to say, significant other, around for quite a while. She needs support on an emotional level.

'She needs a partnership that gets onto an emotional level. She's searching for something that she's found a long time ago. She doesn't know that this is the part she is searching for, that's why she is running away from it.

'She will notice it at some point, but she could have done so quite a while ago.

'She'll think about things now.'

'Good. Mari was hoping she might talk to you sometime in the future.' Nerida understood Aedgar's analysis of her workaholic colleague. She wondered if he meant that Claire might be gay. Or maybe there was a companion in her past she turned away. Claire never talked about her love life.

'Might happen,' he said. 'There are lots of questions. She's been hiding a secret for a long time … She put up so much protection around herself, like a wall, that sometimes even the good things can't come through.'

THIRTY-FIVE

M UTITJULU
SAME DAY

'Another friend of yours might have started something—a different way of thinking.'

'By talking to Claire, you mean?'

'Yes. Showing her a different attitude—great teacher, experienced and wise.'

'Is she here in the community?' She had a couple of old women, Elders who loved Claire, in mind.

'He's left.'

'Oh! My dear friend, that was here on Friday?'

'Yes.'

'My so-called husband.' She laughed. Charlie was Nerida's classificatory husband in Aboriginal way. She was kind to him. But not that kind: the relationship was never sexual or romantic. And she didn't buy him a car, as he had hinted that she might.

'Husband?'

'Until Mari took me, he might have been—'

'Happens all the time,' said Aedgar, warmly.

'Yes, yes. He's a very special one.' But she never loved him the way she loved Mari.

She never loved anyone the way she loved Mari.

'He wasn't quick enough,' Aedgar commented.

'No.' *Was I supposed to be with Charlie somehow?*

'He's on a different path anyway,' Aedgar went on. 'He had other things to do. You too. It couldn't work out that way.'

Nerida smiled and agreed. 'But he is delightful.'

'He still respects you,' Aedgar said.

That's all I needed to hear. 'And I him.'

'That's how it should be.'

'Yeah. I'm happy he's stayed on this planet, even without his friend who left. Must have been very hard for him.'

Charlie's closest friend, another beloved, talented ngangkari, died suddenly just over a year before.

'He had other work to do as well. He's doing important work,' Aedgar explained about their friend who'd passed.

'He is.' They'd asked Monica about him. 'And it's true, Charlie made a big difference to Claire.' *A light came on in her that day.*

'Yes. He showed her that it's not all lost. She looks at the people here. She loves them.

'And all she can see is despair and everything is lost. He showed her that there is still hope around, there is still culture. There are still some old, wise ones supporting the younger ones.'

'Yes. And we gave her a book and he's in the book—the next day.'

The women had gifted Claire with a book about ngangkari, featuring Charlie and the the other healer who visited, as well as their friend who died. It was a big, expensive book. Nerida bought it as a gift for Claire (on an impulse, she'd thought) earlier in the week.

'Yes. What a coincidence!' Aedgar said.

'And then she found out about Mari channelling.'

'I have to say that was a bit of a nightmare, catching up with her.'

What an interesting way to put it. She wondered about the reality of his experience in that realm. *Did he try to talk to Claire, and she shut him out the way she had tried to shut out Mari? Poor Claire. Dear Aedgar!*

'Really?'

'She still has the wrong idea about that kind of work. There are plenty of people out there who pretend. She might have met one or the other being who was on the wrong path.

'It will help her understand things, knowing that people she thinks are people of dignity, knowledge and—kind of—wisdom—'

Nerida chuckled.

'—can do things like this too. You don't have to pretend you see things in crystal balls and use lots of fire and smoke. And then not be doing the real thing anyway ...'

'Mhmm. Well, I hope I have a chance to talk to her about again.'

'She may come back at some point to talk about it.'

'Okay.'

'Give her some time to reflect on things.'

'All right. Thank you for your advice.'

'It wasn't advice. It was trying to explain some things.'

'Hmm. I'm not sure I see the difference.'

'Advice means being given a clear direction on how to go on things, which we do at times, but it's rather rare. Mostly we try to give explanations, so people can find their own path. Makes them happier because they think it's their own choice and their own idea.'

'And it is, kind of,' she said.

'It kind of is, of course. It's a learning experience, all the time. Giving a clear direction, "advice"—is telling someone exactly what to do, without having their own experience in between. It deprives them of learning.'

'Well, that's bad.' She saw that. She'd thought about what he said earlier, that being too kind to people could get in the way of their learning. It helped her separate from the complicated troubles of some clients.

'We still give advice. On rare occasions.'

Nerida frowned. 'I need to restrain myself from giving advice.'

'How come?'

'Well, I'm in a job where the role is sometimes giving advice to people and little else.'

Aedgar teased it out. 'People need encouragement to go on the path of learning, so they can learn through experience. If you encourage them to do things that won't hurt them, they will do it again. And so, they learn that if they act or move or behave that way, it's less painful. That makes it a learning experience.

'If you say, "Here's the only way to do it,"—that won't work.

'Saying, "You do it exactly this way", gives them no chance to think, "Oh, I could try this," and then learn. By trying it, they discover more about it.

'But telling them, "That's how you do it and nothing else", makes people rebellious. So, they won't learn. The nature of people is having learning experiences, trying out things to find their path.'

Nerida added, 'And rebelling against those who would tell them what to do.' Nerida was thinking of the quality control nurse Lorena, who had been back in Community. She told Anangu to say "please" and "thank you," if they came into the office of the clinic.

'Yes, because it deprives them from learning.'

'Mmm. No wonder you think so little of our education system, which mainly consists of a teacher telling children what to do, all day.'

Aedgar opened the hands expansively. 'It's about helping them to find the way to do things, gaining wisdom and building on it. If you tell someone, "This is the way you do it", but this person needs to be on a different path and needs the experience, even of failure, of course —this person needs to have the opportunity to try other things.

'That one is supposed to go on a different path than the teacher is.

'As the distance between what someone else tells them to do and what they're supposed to do—the gap—gets bigger, they get lost. Because they are too far away from the path they're supposed to be on. They're continuing on someone else's path.'

'They're being misdirected?'

'Yes.

'Teaching is about giving ideas of how things work. And then the student can find out that it works in a different way for them.

'This approach would mean an expansion of global and general knowledge. Everybody could add something from their special path.

'Instead of someone giving you a path and everyone learning the same thing because that's what they are told.

'That's why humankind is stuck.

'Some people would have different knowledge that they could add to the whole experience—making the whole wealth of knowledge bigger—which means expanding.

'Expanding knowledge and expanding energy, that's all it is about.

'But there's not much expansion if everybody is learning to go on the same path, having the same view.

'There are many great (you call them that) scientists, you know, who found out about things because they followed their own path. They had a different view on things, they approached questions from a different angle.

'Education systems tend to stop that way of thinking, because it is more convenient and easier to control if everybody is following the same path.'

'Yes. Whether they want to or not.'

'Indeed. Our precious host had trouble with this.'

'She did.'

In her many years at school in Germany, Mari only ever had two teachers she liked. One of them had hurt her by not believing she wrote an essay he knew was brilliant.

The topic was the social effects of the Third Reich. She wrote it from her observations of people in her village, including her family. 'You copied all this from someone else,' he insisted angrily.

She was furious and heartbroken, But Mari's alienation started much earlier. Every springtime in school, she stared out the window in class, wishing she could be out with the butterflies.

She spent too many summers in a hospital bed, not sick, but recovering from orthopaedic surgeries, unable to go outside. Teachers called her lazy.

At age 8, Mari was smacked over the head with a book by a music teacher who didn't like her voice. The blow made her ears ring. She never sang again after that.

'Teachers acted like I was having an easy time, like a holiday, when I was away in hospital,' she told Nerida. 'Nobody ever asked about what happened to me there.

'My mother would see the teacher in town. "I don't understand why they never stop to ask about what had happened to you while you were away," Mum said. They didn't want to know. They didn't like me.'

Nerida caressed her throat and chest, reflecting.

'This whole lifetime,' Aedgar said. 'In the lifetimes before, as well. It's about being pushed into a direction. And having to struggle with the thought that you're meant to be on a different path.

'Everybody else is telling you, "No, no, you should keep on following the path you're on, that's the only right path to follow."

'There's a big internal struggle in knowing, sensing, the right path to follow, and still being treated at times as someone who doesn't know anything and must be told everything. Because they say, "Why is that one digging around on that path? That's a dead end. Everybody follows this other path!"

'This precisely expresses the wrong decision. You don't follow a path just because everybody else does. This has led to very bad experiences in the past, of course. History is full of bad examples.'

'Like, soldiers going to war,' Nerida said.

'Yeah, because one, or a handful, of persons tell them, "That's the path you must follow. That's the only right thing to do." And they don't have a choice after that. Many of them die without knowing what their real path would have been.'

Nerida tried to see a broader picture, looking back over a century of wars. 'Perhaps that's one of the things that's led to a degree of awakening. Maybe souls who lost their lives in all these terrible wars are coming back and not wanting to repeat the same mistake.'

'A few do—currently there are not enough of them. I'm not talking about more people dying, to be able to come back and choose a different path.'

'Yes, but we need more of that wisdom, that understanding,' Nerida reflected.

'Indeed. Some people are meant to be on a scientific path. Some people are meant to be on a creative path. All these different pathways that were chosen.

'Everyone must find their own path. You can't follow someone else's path. That's wrong.

'Because if you do, then you will need to find a way out of it, to re-start again.

'Which delays the gaining of wisdom and expanding the energy.

'There are easier ways to go.

'All these little humans, you know, they need guidance, they need examples, so they they can each make up their own mind about which path to follow.

'It's not about telling them, "Yes, go off and do whatever you like." They need some very basic knowledge to start building up their own.

'Then they can easily follow their path, going in the direction they are supposed to.

'Give them examples.

'Tell them, "If you go in this way, there might be results going in this and this other direction. If you do it the other way, you know, there might still be parts you don't like, but here are pathways others have taken from there."

'Show them a variety of pathways. That's the kind of knowledge they should be given in the educational system, so they can choose a way or a base they can build on.'

Nerida asked, 'Are you familiar with the "roles in essence" that Michael talked about in the books that were channelled?'

'They are there, yes.'

'Is it useful for children to know people from different "roles in essence" as a way of helping them express themselves?'

Aedgar agreed. 'It would be useful. If you think about people who educate these young humans, they tend to teach things they've learned from their own experience and their own pathway.

'Say they tried a different path when they were younger and they had a bad experience with it. They went back to the path they were supposed to be on. But they might block out that other path (with their bad experience) from other young humans, who could learn from it.

'They won't offer this possibility anymore because they think it's wrong. But just because it was wrong for them, doesn't mean it is wrong for everybody. To be driven by personal experience is natural. But now you have these little pupils or students sitting there, I don't know, twenty, thirty or forty of them—and one teacher with one pathway.

'It should be the other way around.

'Like, there are all these teachers! And every little human being goes to this one for a while, to that one for a while, there for a while—so they get to participate in a broad variety of pathways.

'Then they can figure out for themselves, "Well, this is the way I wanna go." At a later point when they've had all these ideas of different pathways, they can go back to the one they were resonating the most with.

'So it's not one teacher, forty students, it's forty teachers for one student. That's the way it should work.'

'I like that. It's great to see you speaking with the hands so well, too, I must say.'

'I can do it.'

'You're becoming fluent,' she said.

'I am holding on to these ones—' he meant the crystals Mari held in her hands to channel sometimes, a gift from Monica. 'I like the touch of them.'

'Good.'

'Anything else?' he asked. 'Besides education? I could go on about education for years.'

'Good. I expect you will. That should be part of our plan— education, science, medicine.'

'They're all important things,' he agreed. 'Different approaches on one hand, but the same approaches on the other hand. Many teachers, one student.'

'I've been trying to play a musical instrument today.'

'I don't think one day is enough,' he said.

So much for the joy of learning. 'You're right. Might have to try another day and then another day.'

'It's the continuity of things that counts if you try to play or learn an instrument. And it's the same, you must find the one that's suitable for you. Otherwise, you'll have a painful time, trying to learn and then it still won't work in the end, because it's not your pathway.'

'Well, I have sore fingertips, but I had fun. It's a little stringed instrument—'

'Having fun is a good thing. Having a painful experience with it, is not,' he said. 'I mean, I told you that painful experiences can make you learn faster. It doesn't apply to musical instruments.'

Nerida laughed.

'It was about the higher experience of learning, of having experiences in this life, not about learning tiny little things—'

'—that hurt your fingers,' she added.

'Or your lips,' he said, 'whatever you learn. Our precious host, I think, had some bad experiences with the lips.'

'Mhmm. She used to play a wind instrument called a saxophone. She doesn't do it anymore.'

'Yeah, and there was this other instrument.'

'Trumpet, I think.' Nerida smiled at the thought of spirit Aedgar popping in to see teenaged Mari wrestling her trumpet.

'If you press your lips against these metal pieces, you need a while to get used to it. That can be painful, too.

'Probably wasn't the right thing anyway. The continuity is missing. If you look at great musicians, they tend to do it their whole life.'

'And more than one lifetime, I'm sure, sometimes,' she said. Aedgar agreed.

She was thinking of child prodigies. Mari was a child prodigy. But her talent was cars. She was able to identify the make and model of a car by the sound it made before age two. In a village of car factory workers, her father won beers, betting on baby Mari's uncanny ability.

'We have other things to do,' she said.

'It was all part of her preparation, so to say.'

Nerida stirred in her seat. 'Mari was telling me today how, as a child, she stole medical journals from doctors' waiting rooms, to take home and study. And I said, "Yes, that was your medical vocabulary for the work you're doing with Aedgar."

'Was I right?'

'Well, she was supposed to do that kind of profession. That's what she came back for. She started preparing for that at a very young age. It was propelled by the bad experiences she had with some misalignments in the body, as well.

'She thought learning the language could speed up the whole learning experience, for getting into that profession and making it better.

'She would be the one with more knowledge than all the others. There was great potential, no doubt about it.

'But it won't happen. There are other things to do.'

Things more important than me playing the ukulele, Nerida thought.

'Did you hear Fortunatus' response when I asked him about Mari planning to become a doctor?'

'I have to admit, I didn't.'

'He said, "Rubbish! Rubbish, rubbish, rubbish. Doctors!" I laughed.'

Aedgar wasn't laughing. 'Trying to follow a path you're supposed to be on and trying to learn, shouldn't be called rubbish.

'Some people in this profession don't do a decent job. They have the wrong approach, the wrong attitude. But you still can't call it rubbish. Because it's not all of them.'

Nerida was gratified to hear him say that.

He went on, 'Trying to educate and entertain the masses at the same time will give you—hmm—a different way of talking about things and trying to explain things. Over the years he had to adapt to his so-called main audience, his main students.'

'Yes. He seems to have been inspired by your intelligence, though. You've changed his mind about some things,' Nerida said.

Aedgar lifted an eyebrow. 'Well, who wouldn't be?'

'Only those of low intelligence would miss it,' she laughed.

'We don't have individuals or groups of low intelligence on that level with us. They are floating around somewhere else.'

'Mmm. Many of them on this planet, unfortunately,' she said.

He whispered, 'Yes, indeed.' He turned the head towards the window.

The orange twilight shone on Mari's black curls. It was the golden hour. *Mari's favourite time.*

'Are you enjoying the light, Aedgar?'

He sighed. 'Well, I'm not able to see it, am I?'

'You can't see it at all?'

'I can kind of feel energy—being lighter or darker—like the environment. I can "see" it in a different way, the energy, when I am not in this body. But to actually see it I would need to be able to use the eyes. So, I can feel energy, but I can't see. I might at some point. I could say that would add a nice touch, but we don't need it.'

'It's not the most important thing.'

'No. It's a nice side effect that we can have at some point if we choose to have that experience in the body of the host. But the most important thing is that you want to teach and educate people.'

'I've been learning about book publishing, beginning to educate myself a little. There's a meeting of writers coming up.'

'There are people who know about these things. You don't have to know it,' he said regally.

'There's a meeting of some of these people coming up not far from here. I might go along to that.' It was a Writer's Festival in Alice.

Aedgar asked, 'What would be the goal of your learning experience out of going there?'

'Hmmm—'

'Wrong answer.'

She laughed. 'Do you want me to be more focussed?'

'A reaction like this means you're probably not sure that there would be a learning experience at all.

'Could still be entertaining, though,' he granted.

'We'll see. Mari has not expressed an opinion yet about whether we should go. So I'll ask her what she thinks. We do everything together.'

'You don't have to. It adds a nice touch to life, but you don't have to. You're together because you're on a similar path.'

'But it's not the same path?'

'Very close, so.'

'She's making plans for us to go and see the whales.'

'We try to help.

'But it's you, you make the decisions. We try to give inspiration, little possibilities of directions. But you're the ones who make the decisions. After being shown things, being told things—'

'— gathering information—' she chimed in.

'—so to say, yes.'

'Do you have advice for our friend in the care of her body at present?'

'Rest! More rest. It's always been a struggle in this lifetime. It's not a thing that will be solved easily.'

'She's come a long way, in the last five years or so,' Nerida said.

'She had to be slowed down unfortunately,' he said.

Nerida recalled the feverish beauty who came to Australia, following her heart to be with her.

Mari slept short hours then, never drank fluids other than for pleasure, and worked like a demon, with no idea of or interest in rest.

She also remembered her in a back brace with fractured vertebrae in the orange house before they came to Muti.

'Is that why she had that fall and hurt her back, because she was moving so quickly in another wrong direction?'

'It was about slowing down,' he said. 'Slowing down, trying to listen. It's a noisy, noisy world here, not only in this place. It's sometimes hard to hear that so-called inner voice.'

'A person's spirit chooses to slow the body down abruptly?'

Mari's fall was as shattering as if she'd hit a wall.

'It could happen. Sometimes it's more forceful than intended. It's hard to do the fine tuning on these things.'

People were talking and there was the twitter of birdsong outside. Dogs barked. Aedgar stretched and flexed Mari's neck and shoulders.

'Thank you for the work you do on her body. It helps.'

'Hmmm. The dogs are not happy,' he noted.

'What happened?'

'Something disturbing happened to them. There is some thing going on that they don't like.'

'Yeah, many of the dogs were killed.'

The vets visited and put neglected dogs down, after discussing which ones should go

with Community members.

About thirty of Peter's dogs were taken to Alice Springs, 'to find good new homes.'

'Hmm. That's not the reason. Something else. Can't figure it out right now.'

'Okay.'

Aedgar sighed. 'Anyway, I might leave you for now. Pleasure to talk to again. I'm always around or at least not far away.'

'Until then.'

'Talk to you another time,' he said, fading away.

Mari returned with a soft inhalation and a sigh.

'Hi sweetie.'

'Hello.' She stretched and yawned. 'It's dark. Was there a sunset happening?'

'Yeah, not a spectacular one. The orange light was pretty, though.'

Placing her crystals on the table, 'Oh,' Mari said. Her eyes glittered. 'It's a shame to miss a sunset.'

THIRTY-SIX

M UTITJULU
THURSDAY APRIL 18, 2013

NERIDA STILL SHOOK her shoes out before putting them on, but she was able to wee without lifting the seat to check for scorpions.

They were less anxious, more comfortable. They stopped worrying about the piles of paper and clutter at home. And Nerida had a new level of acceptance of the noises around—people walking by; the chaotic, noisy dogs; scratching of the birds or insects exploring the wire grids on the windows. Mari was still easily woken by voices, though, (or even footfalls in dust) outside the house at night.

The summer had been hot enough to warp the metal sills of their windows. Nerida thought about the notion that the Rock pushed every living thing away, generating its own protective radiation, as Aedgar said.

When Autumn's cool breezes came, there was profound relief. Feelings of contentment, arising as if stored in their bodies from previous winters, nourished and encouraged them to feel grounded and optimistic.

There was a setback: Council had a plan to put a streetlight in front of their house. The idea was appalling, a desecration of the deep darkness of the desert. Mari intensified her efforts to photograph the desert stars from around the house before they were rendered invisible by the invading electric light. She went outside for every sunset, calling Nerida.

The twilight colours were more intense in autumn: the pink haze in the air and orange pieces of cloud were radiant reminders of flying coloured leaves in more temperate regions down south.

At the clinic things were easier for Nerida too. They'd lived there for two years. Clients were getting to know her. Younger people, who were generally healthy and didn't go to the clinic, were becoming used to her appearance around the community. Most people had an idea of what made her mad and how she acted when she was angry, which helped them feel safe, given her position of power. She'd earned her reputation for helping people. The significant change, though, came from the management side.

Eric spent a stormy Sunday night yelling, pleading and sobbing drunkenly outside the nurses' house.

Winds blew from several directions, rattling the houses and fences. Eric shouted, raising his voice above it.

Mari said, 'Surely this is the end of that arsehole.'

He bawled, 'Sorry. Sooo-ry.' Reprimanded himself incoherently. It went on for miserable hours. Peter's dogs barked the whole time.

Barry and one of his wives came out and yelled over the fence. 'Get out of here, Eric, you're pissed. Go away. I've got a heart condition you know!'

'You're on their side, Barry! You cunt! You take their side like everyone else.' He made moaning wails of self pity.

Barry's door slammed. Eric pounded on his fence for ten minutes. Barry's dogs went wild.

'If he comes here, I'm calling the police. I don't care if they pepper spray him,' said Mari as they lay awake in bed.

'Better that than you getting to use your weapons on him, right?' Nerida laughed a little. Mari had lately been talking about carrying their axe around to defend them. 'The doors are locked, honey,' Nerida said, as Mari put on her leg to get up and check them again.

Eric went back to the nurses' little house and set up camp there, shouting, calling and sobbing on the doorstep.

At eight o'clock in the morning he was curled up there, passed out.

'You not going to work, Eric?' Nerida called as she opened the back gates. Then revved her engine to drive out.

In the clinic office, everyone pored over an email. The CEO of their parent organisation 'was dismissed amid credible claims of embezzlement and corruption. A larger picture of harassment of longterm, dedicated health workers is emerging,' the email from Head Office said.

Jasmine came in with the Alice Springs newspaper on her tablet, and they read more.

All the other doctors, three managers and several nurses in other remote clinics in Central Australia had resigned or been sacked because of the poisonous atmosphere top management had created. Some people were badly broken by it.

The CEO and her remote services manager had been on a hunt for the 'missing' money the CEO had spent and were inured to the suffering they caused in the process.

The boss squandered over two million dollars on trips she took with her friends. And had lost almost another million with an online gambling habit.

The CEO and her cronies had recruited in their own image. People like Eric, who would do anything for money.

He was gone by lunchtime that Monday.

Those who had been determined to get rid of Dr Nerida Green were departed.

A new manager arrived a fortnight later. He had his flaws but was mentally stable and honest enough in his communication. These qualities made him outstanding by comparison to those who had come before.

Something deep within Nerida relaxed and let go. She no longer worried at night. She had nurses working with her who she trusted. Claire was back and working together with Rebecca for once. And no one would sack them. On that night when Eric and the storm roared they'd sat up together eating cookies Bec had baked, doing a jigsaw, keeping each other calm.

'I always knew we could call you,' Bec said said to Nerida.

'And that Mari would come with her axe if needed,' Claire added.

Jasmine was back, reprising her role as the world's roughest and toughest medical receptionist.

In the following weeks, medical colleagues, nurses and allied health workers—the podiatrist, physio, psychologists—began visiting again. They were relieved to see Nerida well and congratulated her on their survival.

She could let go of the fight for the clinic's existence.

But then, unexpectedly, Mari walked to the clinic one afternoon. As she passed his place, Peter's dogs barked and snarled because she was injured. She limped more than usual on the dirt road.

Mari was scared, and that frightened the dogs more. Her eye was splashed with melted butter while cooking. It burnt over her pupil, clouding her vision. She came with her hand clamped over her eye, trying not to cry.

Rebecca set her up with a stream of saline to keep irrigating it. Nerida came out of her consulting room to find her wife leaning sadly over the sink. 'Is it still hurting? Keep doing that. No, don't stop.'

A visiting eye doctor happened to be in Yulara that day. He drove the thirty kilometres to come and see Mari after he finished his shift there, at Nerida's request.

Mari was impressed with his gentleness and kindness.

Finally, a positive experience for you with a doctor who's not me, Nerida thought. *What a way to grow!*

After a few more restful days, Mari unbandaged her eye and offered to channel on the following Sunday afternoon.

LETTING HERSELF FALL INTO TRANCE, she moved her hands, arms and neck in gentle stretches. Like chair yoga in a deeply relaxed state.

Except that she wasn't there.

Her hands moved around the right side of her face, neck and shoulder, coming back to work specifically around the socket and pass gently over the lid of her burned eye.

After more than ten minutes, Aedgar greeted Nerida. 'We had some repair to do. Can't fix it entirely at this stage.'

'Thank you for your efforts. She's a work in progress.'

'Scars have lessened,' he said. 'Would have been a pity to damage those eyes before we get to use them.

'We'll need some more time, maybe, maybe some help from an "outsider."'

'What have you been up to lately? You seem to be busy.'

'Mmm. It's hard for me to explain how it is happening, but I did get some of your words out to interested people.' Nerida had begun a private Facebook page and invited a few hundred people—only a few of whom she knew personally. She was not sure how to explain to Aedgar what social media was.

It was invigorating to take the first steps in posting some of the material Mari had channelled on the internet. But she was anxious. *Will anyone else understand it? Or be interested? Or even find it amidst the sea of information, propaganda and marketing lies?*

Aedgar asked, 'Are you ready for it?'

'Yes, I think so.'

'Are you sure?'

'Yes. I wouldn't have done it if I wasn't sure.'

'It might get bigger than you think,' he cautioned.

Nerida laughed nervously. 'Yes, I think so.'

He seemed to investigate her efforts. 'I think you've got connections with some of the good people. Unfortunately, there are a few others as well, but not that many. They will lose interest in a while.'

'Are you able to feel people resonate with your words?' Nerida was curious.

'I can feel some of the energy within yours. But I'm around in the Universe. It's a big place, as you would say, and I've met one or the other. Of course, not the ones in linear life but some of their—hmm—teachers, so to say—the ones that give them ideas.

'They still think they are their own ideas, quite a few of them. They're not aware of it. Which in their situations is unimportant, as long as the truth gets out there.

'We don't care about the "vehicle" that's used. Or the path it takes.

'Well, I understand that you have different methodologies and technologies (even if they're not very advanced) to get things out there.

'But you need to be ready.

'And be aware: it's getting much bigger than you think.'

'Mhmm.' She was daunted. 'Do you have any comments,' she asked, 'on the selection of materials that I've distributed so far?'

She'd selected a dozen extracts from conversations she'd transcribed, looking for pieces that served as a story within themselves. It was a challenge because she found when transcribing the recorded talks that Aedgar had a graceful way of reflecting back on an earlier point, sometimes to amplify an idea they explored. Or make a joke. *People will miss out on that until I can put these into books.*

She was fastidious. She found evocative photos she could use (legally, always crediting the photographers). She began by wanting to use Mari's work to illustrate the page. But Mari felt the loss of control of her images too keenly. Even putting the spoken knowledge out there terrified her.

She was pacing when she said, 'It's bad enough that you feel you have to put that out there with our names on it. Understand me. I like our life. I don't want some homophobic, racist trolls fucking with us. And whatever that word is for woman haters.'

'Misogynists.'

'That's right! A lot of people out there hate us, just for being who we are, you know.'

'I've been attacked that way before,' Nerida said. 'I can handle it.' She didn't tell Mari how, when she was a political activist, she had nightmares of being chased down and murdered by street gangs or fascists.

Nerida argued for using her own name. Their own names. Letting the material show who they were. Her approach to the work was that her honesty and integrity were integral to people understanding the veracity of the experience. It was a romantic view of being an artist. But it was also an aspect of her culture.

'Indigenous people are known for the whole of who they are. And respected, or not. It's not like the mainstream, where someone can be successful in business or politics and goes home and beats his wife. People know each other properly! I can't keep this secret forever. People need to know where it comes from. And that it's real!'

'And if you never work again? And if the press and the government decide to go after you?'

'We'll be all right. We're strong.' Nerida tried to talk Mari down, which fuelled the fire.

'And how do you know we'll be all right? Because some spirit tells you? When I don't even know what I'm saying? How do you know it's not me with a split personality or something?'

'I know what mental illness looks like. You're not mentally ill. You're pissed off.'

That was the background discussion in their house the weekend of Nerida's creation of the Facebook page.

Aedgar said, 'Well, I am fine with what I'm saying. The question is, are you sure you've chosen the right things?'

'I'm confident.' She nodded, realising that she was.

'Well, that's how it's supposed to be. If you feel confident, you shouldn't ask me. Trust your instincts.

'I can just give you one piece of advice: Get the teachings and the knowledge out there. Don't overdo it.'

'So give them time to respond to and digest—' she began.

'People need time to think about things, to reflect on them,' he said. 'If it's too much it gets overwhelming. People don't get the meaning of it.'

'I can slow down now. I wanted to get a body of our work out—' She posted every day, following an idea the publishers were pushing, that authors need to build a platform. It cost her time in the evenings after work and advertising money that she didn't tell Mari about.

They'd learned that authors were expected to promote and sell their books. The publishing companies might publish a book (for measly royalties) when the author had over ten thousand people who looked like they would buy it.

The non-physical being was more practical.

'Can you cope with the disappointment of some of these people? People who expect you to keep up the pace?'

It was funny, his concern for her keeping up with the masses. She'd had one or two likes. Four on her most popular post. Some people shared the work without comment, as if it was filler.

Aedgar said, 'I am in no hurry. I have plenty of material as well. I can do more. But the only question is: Are you up to it?'

Nerida paused. *Everything I've done in life has been preparing me to do this work.*

Still, Aedgar's review of her level of preparedness was making her nervous. 'Well—'

'You're not.'

She laughed. 'Of course, I am.'

'It took too long—'

'Of course, I am! I'm very happy doing this and I've had lots of preparation and training.'

'I'm pleased to hear it,' he said.

'But—the most important piece I've held back for the right time. I'm not sure. I need your advice on when the right time is to talk about the mining of the blue dangerous stuff.'

'Hmm. It's kind of—'

'I think I should wait.' *Publishing that will be riskier than posting about reincarnation and new models of education.*

Aedgar continued '—bluish, bluish-green? It's hard to describe it exactly. We use different descriptions of colours. We measure them by energy. But it translates to something that you would consider bluish.

'So, hmmm, that could range from a grey-black colour with a blue shine or tinge, all the way up a bright-blue or aqua colour. That's the energy range that would translate to 'blue'.

'So it doesn't have to be exactly blue, but it has to be that **direction of blue**, that spectrum. That's what the energy translates to.'

Nerida was impatient with him. 'Whatever colour it is, I'm holding on to that material for now, until it becomes clearly relevant.'

Aedgar suggested, 'You can put out little hints. Don't use the whole message, yet. Then people will be prepared when it happens. The good people will be prepared.

'You don't want to put out a warning to the bad ones, because that would not serve the purpose of the learning experience.

'We don't want to warn them or even, as you would say, save them, because that would deprive them of an important learning experience. But little hints here and there would be usable.

'When it happens, people will say, "I've heard about this before, there was something …" And then you can come out with that story. But don't put the whole message out now.

His voice was grim. 'Don't stop these people from having their learning experience.

'This would be the worst thing to do.'

She let go a breath she hadn't realised she was holding. 'Mmm. I have to say it's given me a lot of pleasure to go over your words. To start to connect them up with people and get them out in the world has been so enjoyable.'

'It will become more pleasing all the time. You'll be surprised.

'There will be people who are going to oppose it, but for now you don't attract them. Other people will attract them, and other people will deal with it.'

'That's kind of them,' said Nerida.

'They do it for their experience, for expanding their energy,' Aedgar explained. 'It is important for them. Some of these good people will teach you things, too. They'll learn as well. So, it's a support system to expand energy and to learn.'

'Yes ... We have people reading your words already from other countries.'

'Good.'

'The Americas especially.'

Aedgar nodded. 'That's where many of these good people live.

'Unfortunately, people in important places don't have this "technology". But they will get the vibration of it. You might go there one day.

'You'll find them. And you'll all feel like you've known each other before. Even if you never met them, even if they didn't read these messages, they get the vibration and the energy of it.

'I know that sounds very abstract to you.'

Nerida had experiences like that with the ngangkari. She realised that Aedgar was probably talking about Indigenous people, protectors of the forests, lakes, deserts and mountains. And the ocean.

Many of them, like some clients and friends at Mutitjulu, didn't have access to the internet.

• • •

NERIDA ASKED, 'Can you explain how some humans on the planet now can still understand and assimilate knowledge by vibration?'

'They haven't lost the ability in the first place because they need to rely on these skills to survive,' he replied. 'People in other places on this planet have given up on these skills because they now rely on other things that they think are easier.

'Learning can be easy. It comes naturally, normally, so people can develop and expand their energy.

'But if it's getting "blocked out" there is no learning experience.

'It *is* getting substituted by, blocked out by, this technology—which is a one-way thing.

'You lose the variety of the skills you originally had by relying on something that's appealing because it seems to be so easy and quick. It deprives people of having the whole experience. People don't realise because it, because the distractions are so handy.

'People in remote areas can pick up vibrations of energy. But many people, even here in this area, and in other places in the world, can't pick up these natural vibrations anymore.

'There is too much disturbance in between them and the source of vibrations. You have radio waves. You have magnetic waves. It's all interfering. It's all stopping people getting these energy vibrations that they're supposed to have.

'That's why some people don't respond to anything anymore. They get overwhelmed.

'Unfortunately, it even touches the people that don't use the technology at all. They just live in the area. It's a kind of pollution by technology. All this radiation is being produced.

'Those that make these things are thoughtless in putting it all out there. They have more damaging effects than anyone could imagine.'

THIRTY-SEVEN

Mutitjulu
THURSDAY APRIL 18, 2013

Nerida found this conversation difficult. She had emphatically declared herself ready and willing to be Aedgar's amanuensis.

All this talk of dangerous, invisible waves was in looney territory, though. *Am I really ready for this? How far out can this go?*

She was afraid to be associated with opponents to 5G towers, even as she suspected their concerns had a grain of truth in them. What if Aedgar ends up appealing to nobody but the anti-5G protestors? After spending so much time and effort learning to conform, Nerida was afraid of losing power and being marginalised. Again.

Aedgar said patiently, 'I am not asking anyone to go back to the times when humans lived in caves. They should just put some more thought into the kinds of energy and radiation they put out there. There is a lot of damage that will reveal itself in the long term.

'You'll have a huge rise in people with psychological problems.

Brains that do not work normally anymore but react, creating strange actions in affected people.

'It's on an emotional level. People get disturbed on emotional levels.

'You'll have this huge rise in—you could call it—brain damage. This will show in a rise in criminal acts, in violence, in all these things. Many people don't know why they are acting that way. Some of them actually don't have an idea that they are doing it. Some of their brain waves are kind of erased.

'It's as if the vibration of that brain, you know, and the vibrations of some of those manufactured waves, eliminate each other.' He moved the hands in surges: intersecting, crossing, increasing.

'People have these "waves" that create their emotional level—as they are supposed to be and where they should be. Sometimes now they don't have these kinds of brain waves in this area anymore, which makes them crippled emotionally.

'They hurt people, sometimes even kill them, without realising.

'If you talked to them afterwards, they'd say, "That's not me. I haven't done that."'

'It's a kind of psychosis—a break from reality.' She leaned forward, the curious doctor.

'Yeah, whatever you call it down here,' he said. 'But that's what happens.

'People tend to carry these devices around with them all the time. There's a big number of people doing it. And—I haven't got the words to describe it. I must think of an example.'

She was aware of sunlight on her skin, in patterns through the window blinds. 'Well,' he declared, spreading Mari's hands like the storyteller he was, 'if you have a big crowd of ants. They all go about their business, so to say, these ants. And then someone goes and puts kind of a grid of fine lines of sugar syrup there.'

He used the fingers to show the massing ants and then acted out dropping honey in lines.

'The ants all start to do something else, following the lines of sugar syrup. And they don't realise anymore what they were supposed to do.

'That's a population of ants that's doomed. Because they follow these sugar lines all the time (or while you put them there). Once the sugar's gone, the ants will be gone too, when they don't find anymore what they've become addicted to.

'They're gonna start to kill each other because they don't remember the business they were about to go on before the sugar grid came.

'Does that make any sense to you?'

Nerida assented. 'It's clear.'

'I'm just trying to find easy, understandable examples for severe problems.' He rubbed Mari's nose.

'Yes. I like it when you do that.'

'What?'

'When you find easily understandable examples for severe problems.' She felt lighter.

'I thought you meant scratching the nose of my friend.'

'I quite like it when you do that, too.' She smiled broadly.

'It was a necessity.

'So, people develop this kind of technology. They have this one-way thinking ability, they try to make sure that the tool or device or transportation or whatever-the-thing-is works.

'That's all they do.

'They never think about interference or consequences in the long term.'

Nerida saw dust motes floating and thought it remarkable that she could feel fine now, with Aedgar so dark and grumpy. *Something about the vibes in the room when he's here is sustaining. Feels like love.*

'If you, or people in such remote places, work with the vibration of the energy of the place, they can get the part of the energy that's supposed to expand their energy, that makes them grow.

'Not in a biological way—I mean, they don't get taller.'

Now he's making Dad jokes. 'Yeah.'

'But they grow. Because they can make a distinct choice.

She was listening carefully. *So, we can grow, just by being in this beautiful place, but we need to do something that matches us to the place.*

'When there is all this radiation and vibration and such around you, put out by other peoples' technology, you don't get to pick the ones that are important for your growth. You get other people's important energy waves. That were never supposed to end up with you. You might go on a wrong path.

'I shouldn't say "you might," because people do.'

Nerida wrote down what he said. *Some big concepts here.* 'Mhmm. We're talking about energy waves that are generated by the earth or from Source or other people—?'

Aedgar jumped in '—the whole Universe. That's where people originally picked up these waves or vibrations, from the Source they should learn from.

'But now, with people putting all the rubbish out in the Universe that's just left there and with all the radiation and vibration and everything that's going on here now from the so- called technology ... people don't know where to go anymore.'

So many people don't know why they're here. 'It's hard to find Source,' she said.

'And it's still, as always, fuelled by greed.

'Someone puts something out there.

'This person or group makes sure that this specific part works and they get the maximum out of it. The maximum out of it means the paper with the numbers on it—or power.

'So, that's what they do. And they don't think about what they actually put out there. And they don't think about interference with other things. And they don't think about longterm damage.

'If they were really intelligent—in the way we talk about intelli-

gence—they would consider interference and any long-term problems that might arise from that.

'It would require them—not to stop exploring and not to stop
evolving, that would be wrong—but to think about things in a
broader way. They shouldn't lose sight of the whole thing.

'People focus on one thing, one part only. On one small area.' He
made a pincer movement with Mari's fingers.

Nerida could feel his frustration, even a distant fury. It was a
bubbling force of Nature, like magma within the Earth. She never felt
afraid. Sometimes fear came afterwards when she processed the
import of what he said.

'That's how a lot of damage is done. You have the imbalance in
the earth that occurs from mining: taking things out, not putting
things back. And then, putting all these waves and radiation all
over it.

'That's not how it's supposed to be.

'That's not how it works. It takes more intelligence to work on a
different level, to evolve and expand without all that harm. There are
more intelligent ways.

'I have to think about it, further along, how to explain this.'
Perhaps he sensed he'd lost her.

'It's a challenge to find simple examples to explain the problems
with this way of "inventing" things, making them work. The problem
is that people don't understand the basics.'

How many times is he going to say this? She felt impatient but she
didn't know what for.

'As I said with the Periodic Table in chemistry, they use it, but
these things have already been changed. They don't know the origins
of it, that have been there, you would say, *ages* ago. This planet is so
much older than this population thinks.'

Nerida didn't like Aedgar referring again to all the previous civilisations that had made the same mistakes. She didn't like being
reminded that the Periodic Table was inaccurate because of cata-

clysmic man-made disasters. It was all too uncomfortably like the realm of Erich von Däniken.

She'd never read his work. She only saw the reaction against him on television. She was attracted to von Däniken's ideas, to the extent she understood them, as a child.

But she was an educated adult now. She didn't want to be associated with people who believed in Atlantis, an idealised Ancient Greek fairytale, or Lemuria, which she had never heard of before these channelled beings started talking about it. She didn't want people to know that she believed in aliens. *What if Aedgar ends up talking about nothing but aliens?*

Aedgar explained patiently, 'They think they have an idea, just as the population before that thought they knew it all. And before that. We're trying to teach that it's wrong to make the same mistakes over and over and over again.

'It is so painful to watch! It's all been done before.

'You might say, "Oh well, we just start from scratch again." That's what the last populations had to do.'

Nerida remained empathic and polite. 'Very frustrating,' she said.

'Yeah, indeed.'

Nerida changed the subject, though, because the crescendo of frustration and sadness was almost too much to bear, with her sense of individual smallness and impotence. She remembered another of Trevor's suggestions. 'How about television, Aedgar? Do you know what it is?'

'It's about bundling colours and building pictures,' he said.

Nerida liked the characterisation. 'Do you think we should keep our children away from it?'

She had no television in the house when Ruby was little. But by the time her second child, Jim, came along, she was distracted and numbed out, traumatised by her partner Sam's accident and the chronic health problems that followed. Poor little Jim was plonked down in front of the telly sometimes for longer than he should have been, especially when Ruby was at childcare and Nerida just wanted a rest.

Aedgar granted, 'There are some things they can learn from it.'

Damned by faint praise. But rather than talk about radiation, he talked about advertising.

'It generates a desire,' he said, 'to have things they see, experience things they see— that they are not supposed to have or to experience yet. It's about peer pressure as well because most people did watch it. And if some other child has something and they see it, of course they want it too.

'It's in the nature of humans. That's how they acquire knowledge.

'In earlier days it was like, "This person knows so much, has so many skills. I want to have the knowledge and skills, too." This sparked their interest in expanding their energy.

'All it sparks now is, "I want to have that new toy, because they have it. Now."

'But this thing you call television is not your worst enemy.

'Worse things are out there, much worse.

'And it's good to be able to get some information quickly if it's needed to evolve and survive.'

Nerida sensed that he was talking about the net now. Maybe phones.

'But if you get it all very quickly, you can't make a distinction anymore between what's important and what's not. And you don't have the time to reflect on the important things.

'Firstly, you don't know anymore what is important; secondly, it keeps coming. It keeps coming without stopping.'

'Yes, information overload.' She thought of arguments she and Mari had about the news.

'Yes,' Aedgar said. 'Some humans just shut up their brain, close it down, sit somewhere trying not to think about things and trying to protect themselves from this overload.

'Some people are very sensitive to it.

'You know, you have two types of people that other people on this planet tend to **lock up**, because they don't seem to function.

'You have the ones that can't seem to differentiate between the radiation and vibrations they get from energy anymore: the emotionally crippled ones.

'And then you have the very sensitive ones who just close themselves up, shut everything down around them.

'Those are the two main groups you lock up.

'The ones that shut themselves down are less dangerous because if you take them out somewhere to a quiet place, they will be able, over time, to open up again. Along with the sensitivity, they do have the emotional background, so to say.

'The others can't figure things out anymore and have eliminated some of the energy vibrations in their brain—they are on a path where they can't get it back.'

Nerida was sad. 'It's a wasted life,' she commented.

'So to say. Indeed. It's very hard for us to watch that.'

'Cities must be particularly bad for this sort of thing,' Nerida guessed. Mari loved cities, but had never lived in one.

Aedgar agreed. 'You wouldn't want to stay too long in these places.

'But it's spreading. There are some areas where you'd think you're in the middle of nowhere, but this big grid or net is spanning the globe.

'You, here in the desert, will still be influenced by it. It will be less, but the influence is still there.

'People develop these devices and they wanna make sure they work. But the devices make these vibrations and radiation. They put it out there—they think that's what it takes and that's what, you know, puts them apart from their peers. It's actually not how it works.

'They put more danger out there. And with all the rubbish and these other things they put up in the Universe, the problem is spreading.

'There are still areas where you have less of that problem. But sitting in a place you would consider the middle of nowhere on this planet, doesn't mean there is no interference at all. There is just less.

'There is a level of interference you could cope with in one or the other way. But there is no place anymore where you can get away from it, on this planet.

'They should work on this. It's a problem.'

Nerida stumbled, 'We need a technology that has less—'

'—side effects,' he said. 'It doesn't mean you have to put a shell up to your ear to talk to someone. As I said, you don't have to go back and live in caves. It means you need to identify the right source of energy for the device you're using. And not use the wrong energy for it and make it work by using more of it.

'Find the right one, use the right amount, that's the way to go. That would minimise the harm.

'And, as I also mentioned before, as long as there are still beings and humans even thinking about solutions, it's not too late. There will be a way out of it. But you must attract the right people to work on these projects and make this place better, safer to live.'

Nerida clutched at the ray of hope he offered. But all the talk about excessive and dangerous radiation coming from their devices made her irritable.

Will I end up wearing a tinfoil hat?

She said, 'Mhmm. Did you know you have a new surname?'

'What?'

'I've called you Aedgar Wisdom. I hope you can forgive me.' Facebook required a second name for the page she had set up in Aedgar's name.

Aedgar said, 'If you were a human being, it would be very hard to live up to that.'

'Hmm. Just as well you're not.'

'I do have some of it,' he reflected. 'We all have some of it. Some have a bit more and some have a bit less. Some think they have it and they don't have it at all.

'But some of us out there have quite a bit of it. You could call it a longterm acquirement—by expanding energy and continuing learning.'

Oh, he's talking about wisdom. Not being human. It's cute the way he's deciding out loud whether he's up to the name.

'Well, I don't—I kind of like it,' he said. 'Because, as you would say, I don't have to live up to it because I am not alive in your understanding of life. I am not in the linear. So, you could give me any kind of name and I would handle it.'

'Mmm,' Nerida murmured. 'And the standards for wisdom in this linear existence are fairly low.'

'Low. Quite low.'

'Not to take away from your actual wisdom, at all,' she said. 'But it's not so hard to look good—'

Aedgar warmed to the theme. It was not so much that he interrupted her, as that Nerida often jumped in while he was still thinking, or formulating—*what is it they do?*—what he was to say.

'Well, some of it was acquired down here, during linear lifetimes,' he said. 'I didn't have that many. Some of us came back a lot more than I did. I am more the earth type. And I care more about the bigger picture and about energy that can be created by bringing individuals together. As I said before, I can't say I don't care about the individual, because in the bigger picture that one might be the weakest part, so I have to take care of all of it.

'It was about the bubble in the concrete base. It's about foundations and how to build on them. This should be a way you can understand it?'

'Yes.'

'Good.'

In the lull, she asked, 'Are you an "entity," Aedgar? Is it fair to call you that?'

Aedgar sighed. 'Not exactly … An entity is a group of souls that have been reincarnating, coming back to the linear life, a lot. And it's many of them.

'Some of them had lives on this planet, some of them had lives on other planets. But they are mainly reincarnated souls from the same group, so to say.

'I've been to plenty of places. I've been part of the earth. But I didn't have that many linear lifetimes. "Entity" is a name that was given to groups by humans. We don't use these kinds of names or descriptions because they are not important.

'But in your understanding, I wouldn't consider myself an entity. On some level, yes. On other levels, no.

'For us, it depends on what kind of energy you've had expand within your soul, which kind of "places" (it's hard to translate it), which kind of place or setting you've done work …

'We went to learn, to experience, to expand. What actions did we participate in?

'That's the consciousness that is forming these groups.

'So, as I haven't been mainly reincarnating into linear lives and kind of bundling up with other souls that have done it, I wouldn't consider myself what you call an entity.'

'Perhaps you're more special.' Nerida loved to flatter him. It was usually quite sincere.

He was impervious to it, anyway.

'Different,' he said. 'You can call it different, in your kind of under-standing.'

The orange twilight had turned mauve on the clouds. It was dark outside now.

'Do you have advice for Mari in the care of her body and herself?'

'We'll try to take care of it, but it's still about resting,' he said.

'She wants to stay up to see the stars tonight. If the clouds clear.'

'Hmm. Not a bad idea at all.'

'There are only a few things that are more beautiful than watching the stars. It's part of nature. It gives you an idea of the bigger picture and they're pretty to look at.'

'And there's more to see, the more you look,' she said.

'Indeed.'

'Mari thought she saw you in the horse head nebula, the big red one.'

'Who knows?' He was mysterious.

What is he? 'You might have been passing by that day, when she took the photo?'

'We get around an awful lot, as you would say … Because for us, time is not an issue. It's about placing energy somewhere, not about travelling the way you do.'

'So you put you attention somewhere and your energy follows?' Nerida tried to figure it out.

'It's the opposite way: you put the energy there in the direction, and then the attention follows.'

'Aah, your consciousness goes where you've sent your energy?'

'Yes. Although you can't say consciousness. We are operating in a different way. We pick up energy by the vibrations of energy. And if we want to, we send some back. And sometimes it's worth paying attention to it, so to say.

'This is how we travel, for your understanding, huge distances in so-called "no time". We don't have the time that you talk about. We have a different concept of time.

'We think it's kind of funny if you talk about distances in "lightyears".

'Measuring light in years means measuring light in time, but time doesn't exist.'

He's talking in riddles now. 'And nobody actually travels that way, anyway, by lightyears?' she asked.

'We don't.'

'So, it's an artificial construct?'

'Yeah. You needed the concept of time.'

'You have to handle it. These are longterm issues. Time was created to get measurements, now you need to deal with the limitations of time.'

Nerida felt her mind bending like her back in the bridge pose. 'But the limitations only arose because of our construction of time?'

'Of the way you think about it, yes. I mean, how can you construct some thing that doesn't exist?'

'Surely people do that all the time?' she countered.

Aedgar said, 'It's the thought that's been put in there. Putting a thought in means putting energy in.

'There was a lot of thinking about time going on, so that gave it a lot of energy, which should have been spent somewhere else.

'But we have more important things to do, for now.

'We have to put balance back.'

He sighed. 'I think I might leave, for now ... Make sure you are ready for your new adventures.'

Sounds daunting. 'Thank you for your company. I enjoy it very much,' she said.

'I'll talk to you another time.

'I might do a bit more maintenance, maybe get some more help before I leave.

'Pleasure to talk to you.'

After a series of gentle stretches with deep, rhythmic breathing— almost like Tai Chi— Mari sleepily returned about ten minutes after Aedgar stopped talking.

Nerida still had reservations about what she thought was a crackpot conversation. She did not include the talk about radiation in material for the book she was planning or post an extract on the website. It would take her a long time to accept being the facilitator of material so 'unscientific'. *So much for my open-mindedness about different knowledge, perception and ways of healing,* she said to herself. But she was still scared. She'd been given a hard time for wanting to give kids oral iron supplements instead of painful injections. What would the Medical Board say if they heard about this?

Resistance notwithstanding, deep down she felt that what Aedgar said was true.

Of course, the people who designed and manufactured their devices wanted to maximise the electro-magnetic power of the satellites, the towers, the devices themselves.

She knew that many believed 'more is better' without understanding all aspects of the forces they worked with. Money was always the decisive factor.

Health and environmental dangers of each new technology were often revealed in the consistent or excessive, and consequently harmful, use of them. Sometimes the dangers were known, and profit-driven manufacture went ahead anyway. *Cutting corners in haste. That has been our pattern.*

Later, Nerida appreciated Aedgar's hints at the aetiology of the severely unbalanced youth, perpetrating massacres in their time.

She eventually posted an extract on the website, linking Aedgar Wisdom's Facebook page.

A reader took offence, though, at Aedgar (and thus Nerida's) use of the words 'emotional cripple'.

If he'd read the material, he would have seen that Aedgar's words were compassionate, especially compared to other words people would use for adolescent, psychopathic mass-murderers.

The critic concluded: 'Your page is unscientific nonsense and I hope everyone who visits it can exercise some critical thinking'.

Exactly what I might have written a while ago. The same words. Her critical thinking was one her defining characteristics, she thought. But that was not her problem.

Well may Aedgar have sighed toward the end of conversation, as she changed the topic to accommodate her psychological discomfort, picked pieces out of the body of science and history in a melange with metaphysical, personal and private concerns. Was this going to end up like Fortunatus with his small-business people? Except that Aedgar would be asked about work dynamics, health concerns and the stars?

It was not a bad thing that she returned to the stars for orientation and comfort. She was good at expressing the larger and smaller concerns of a human.

But, approaching middle age, Nerida still had to grow in her sense of worth, broaden her perspective and experience true humility.

The spirits were helping her, but she was, as they might have said, both impatient and a slow learner.

She felt irritable and stagnant. She'd forgotten what she used to know, that pain is stuck energy.

THIRTY-EIGHT

MUTITJULU

GREG ARRIVED on the morning flight from Sydney to Yulara and got a ride to Mutitjulu with an attractive baggage handler.

'Beautiful weather!' He opened his arms as he got out of the car, embracing the view of Uluru, stately and wild, orange against the hard blue sky.

Nerida laughed and hugged him tight.

He stiffened in her arms. 'Careful. Lil bit tender. Cracked a rib going over the front of my bike in Centennial Park about ten days ago.'

'Oh, no!' Mari smiled. 'Let me offer you a coffee and pain relief.'

'Maybe you can give me some acupuncture later,' he said to Nerida as they entered the house.

At an early breakfast that morning—they got up to tidy the house —Mari asked Nerida not to tell Greg about the channelling yet.

'I'm having this problem. I need to know people want to be with me for my own sake, not just for the channelling,' she told Nerida. 'I know you love me. But it's even hard for me with you because you get so high when you've been talking to the spirits.'

'Not always,' Nerida said. 'I mean, I do always love you! But, with the channelling, how did you put it? It's not all pancakes and unicorns.' She hadn't told Mari about the threat of mining the bluish material. *What's the point of telling and making her anxious?*

Mari opened a jar of blackcurrant jam and spread it on buttered sourdough. 'You know Greg. He's going to love Aedgar. I'll hardly get to be with him at all once they meet.'

Nerida made a moue. 'He'll always adore you. I don't think you need to worry about him running away with Aedgar and never letting you come back.

'But you're right. He will love your channelling once he knows. And he's supposed to work while he's here. I've got a sheaf of referrals. Probably twenty people who will get so much better when he looks after them.'

She agreed to keep their secret life private for now, even with her cousin-brother. He was, after all, a master of secrets himself.

Over coffee, Mari showed Greg the brown-skin, green-eyed baby boy doll she'd named after him.

'Oh my god, that's amazing!' Greg said, reaching out his hands. 'He's so sweet. And you've made his head heavy! Look! It just rests on your shoulder.' He patted and jiggled the doll as if it needed to be burped.

That evening, over a dinner of crispy-skinned pork and potatoes sautéed with butter and parsley, Greg asked Mari what she liked about living at Mutitjulu.

Mari looked happy. There was that smile Nerida missed.

'I think it is a lot about the people who live here. Rough, strong. Warm-hearted. Some of them with that cheeky sparkle in their eyes,' Mari said. 'And there's so much to see and learn about the area's nature. And life in the desert. It's so different from previous places I lived and worked.'

Greg nodded, helping himself to brussels sprouts and a savoury sauce.

Mari continued. 'And I've worked out the oven. Most days now my baking goes well. I rotate my bread or cakes twice, at a certain angle, to bake evenly. The house smells of sourdough bread once or twice a week.'

'She's lovely for me to come home to,' Nerida said, outlining the aqua wave tattooed on Mari's forearm with her fingertip. 'You know I never asked for a partner who cooked. It was such a great surprise that Mari's a brilliant cook.'

Having gorgeous Greg around gave Nerida a warm glow. Perhaps they needed visits from family who knew them well and loved them. She'd missed that kind of support.

THEY MADE sure Greg was gone out next evening when Mari settled in to channel. He headed out towards Kata Tjuta with the attractive baggage handler, Tony. Mari made them a picnic dinner to eat in the back of Tony's ute.

After a warm welcome, Aedgar asked: 'So what have you been doing lately?'

'I've been cleaning. Sorting papers. Organising information. Making a space to do my work better.'

'Organising space sounds good,' he said.

'Yes.'

'Cleaning sounds good. It means killing germs.'

'That's right.' She was delighted that he would engage on such a prosaic level.

'The other things didn't sound so interesting.'

'They weren't but they were necessary.'

'Papers?' he enquired.

'Mmm-hmm. Bloody papers.'

'It's sad,' he said, suddenly serious. 'They have been trees.

'You'd think that these humans, at this time, would be able to use more of their brain. They wouldn't need to sort all these papers all the time. They could just memorise it easily. And access the information whenever it's needed.'

'I guess that's a skill people had in the past,' she commented.

'Well, it was necessary. If you had information you needed to keep it,' he said.

'During your lifetimes on earth I suppose knowledge that you used to heal was not to be written down,' Nerida speculated.

He agreed. 'It was passed on by telling people how to do it. It was lifelong learning. Kept the brain active.

'There have been periods where they used stone to carve things into. It might have helped with their craftsmanship, but it wasn't very useful to help recall things. I mean, who would want to carry stone plates around?'

'I don't even want to carry papers. I'm sorry. I interrupted you.'

'Well, these stone plates weren't made to carry around anyway. It wasn't very useful.'

'Are you talking about in Britain or Sumer or Egypt or China?'

'Partly Egypt. Partly. Egypt were the late ones. There was a period long before that where this planet had a population that used these kinds of things.'

'Oh. The Lemurians?' *Monica and Aedgar talk about Lemuria. I'm still not sure if I believe in it.*

'At your time, you don't know about them. You don't realise they were existent. Because you assume a wrong so-called age of this planet.'

Nerida began to interrupt, 'Yes, you spoke—'

In less than a minute, as usual, Aedgar managed to alarm her and trigger her defences. She interrupted, like a doctor did, as if she knew all about Lemuria and didn't need to know any more. Or didn't want to hear any more.

Thinking about the conversation later, she realised that her interruptions were an unconscious way of putting her fingers in her ears and saying 'La, la, la'. *Just like Claire.*

Nerida wanted everything to be balanced and harmonious and resolved. She wanted the world to be saved but didn't want to participate in the learning process of helping it happen.

No wonder Aedgar sees me as impatient. Maybe that's a kinder way of referring to my egoistic resistance and posturing.

Aedgar said, as he had said before (when she didn't really want to know, either), 'Populations on this planet have been around much longer than people now anticipate or understand. Yes.

'If people now think they are the first ones doing things, I just have to repeat, it's all been done before. Not only once. Many times.

'It's much longer periods than would be measured in human generations.

'There have been plenty of generations before. And in every generation, everybody of them thought, "I am the first one, I've invented this".

'Which is not entirely true.

'Each so-called invention was just one of them **remembering** things.

'This is how inventions and discoveries, as you call them, are made.

'Some people have kind of an awakening of their soul or spirit and then they suddenly remember some things.

'They remember why they came back. They remember what's been done before. They don't invent it.

'The time of inventions, real inventions, ended long ago.

'That's why so many mistakes get repeated as well, when a soul comes back and remembers the **wrong** things.

'Sad to watch, somehow.

'I wouldn't want to say that I was free of these kinds of mistakes during some of my lifetimes. I mean, remembering the wrong things. It happens to everybody.

'It's just a matter of recalling, realising that your memories are the wrong ones and you have to focus on the right ones. Some people don't manage that during a lifetime. They just keep following the wrong path.'

'I think some people don't manage that in several lifetimes.' She was thinking about her mother, who never seemed to learn to listen. Later, she thought about her own difficulty with overeating. Perhaps she was hung up on feelings from lifetimes when food was in short supply.

'Indeed, there are quite a few like that.

'As I said before, some souls are very slow learners. They practise something that they would need to learn and grow from but they never get to the point where they've learned enough to grow and expand their energy. For them, that lifetime is just a practice run.'

'That's a gracious way to put it,' Nerida mused. 'It must be quite frustrating to watch sometimes.'

'Patience is an important thing,' he said, slowly. 'Sometimes—we are not impatient— but sometimes we think, "That's very slow. You'll probably have to do it again several times." But as time doesn't exist, where we are, impatience is not such a big issue.

'We just keep watching it over and over again. "Oh, he's doing that thing again, or they are doing that thing again. Oh, well, that might take a while, so we can focus on something more important, in between."

'We are on standby, so to say. If we see souls are truly having a proper learning experience and they're about to really expand their energy and grow—that's when we help.

'With the other ones we just watch, mainly.

'If it gets too bad, sometimes we have to help. But there's always the fine path, so as not to deprive them of learning experiences.

'Some of them do really bad things. That could mean they don't want to come back anymore.

'But they must. They have to learn.

'Everybody's got some properties that are worth keeping and remembering. So we help if someone is on a wrong path, having a wrong experience that would stop this soul from coming back to follow the proper path. Because it's that growth of energy that we're focusing on, that's what's needed to change things.'

'It's very interesting to me,' she said sincerely.

'It's what we would call, in our place, common sense.'

'But not at all common here and now.'

'No. Not at all.'

'How are you going with your project? Well, I know you have an infinite number of projects.' She didn't know. She was supposing. She was making conversation.

'The main project for all of us is to expand energy and support growth through learning experiences.'

'Is it fun?' She didn't think about what he said. She was humouring him, missing out on the meaning.

'It can be. Yes.'

'Good ... We had some marvellous shooting stars last night. Mari caught some of them.'

'I bet you did,' he said good-naturedly. 'Once you've started observing the stars it's hard to stop because you'll always discover things you've never imagined. It expands the horizon of the individual. If that happens, it expands the horizon of the planet as well.'

'The more you look, the more you see,' she said.

'Yes indeed. I couldn't have said it any better.'

'Mari's enjoying them very much,' she said. Mari's photos revealed blue, purple, white, red or yellow arcs across the sky, as stars and planets moved.

'I agree,' Aedgar said. 'It's a good thing to do. It teaches people that they are part of the universe. And it teaches them as well how big or how small a part of the universe they are.'

'How big or how small depending on your perspective and what you need to learn at the time, I guess.'

'Indeed ... You are in a privileged place to observe.'

'Mari hasn't recovered from the installation of the electric lights. It's causing her—'

'It's a big mistake.'

'It is.'

'A big mistake,' he repeated.

Perhaps he can feel Mari's frustration and disappointment. They wrote to Bull and the Council asking for the streetlight to be installed somewhere else. It didn't work.

Someone in town had got funding and now there were streetlights all over Community, in the name of safety. It made it hard to see the stars.

It wouldn't have helped Desdemona.

And it meant that the people who played cards stayed up all night sitting on the ground under the new lights. Gambling opportunities rose exponentially.

The worst, for Mari and Nerida, was the towering, super-bright light erected and turned on directly in front of their house, right at the spot where Mari used to sit with Selkie's dog and take photos of the Rock at night. It made them want to leave Muti.

All Nerida could say was, 'They might lose their power supply soon, somehow.'

'Yeah,' he said, almost in concert, 'It could happen any time.'

The clock ticked. Someone was revving an engine in Barry's yard, outside the kitchen window.

Not for the first time, Aedgar said, 'Noisy place.'

'Too many machines,' Nerida agreed.

'Yet they seem to be of too much importance for the humans living on this planet now.

'Some of them are useful, indeed.

'We are concerned about the energy they use. And radiation they produce.'

Nerida nodded. 'Yes. You talked once'—*when was it? Did I dream it?* —'about energy available from in the air. There were a few people working on that, but they were not taken seriously enough, you said.'

'Yes, that's true.'

'I hope they're continuing to try.'

'There will always be some of them trying. They need to be supported, to be listened to. You can use energy from the sun, from water. Air movements or wind. The heat that comes from the centre of this planet. But it needs to be used wisely.'

'How about the force of the waves in the sea?' she'd heard about that, too.

'Yeah, and then there's the combination of the water and the air movement. That's going in a good direction.

'So far, the devices that they are working on are too big. It takes some clever thinking—or remembering—to figure out that there is an easier way with smaller devices to create the same amount of energy, which is less disturbing to the environment.'

Nerida's imagination was firing. 'I have in my head an image of a net that catches energy as the water flows through.'

'You talk about a net, like for catching fish?'

'Yes.'

'Not the right way. You're thinking in the wrong direction.'

'It's just as well it's not my job to figure it out, huh?'

'Lucky, isn't it?' he said, making her laugh.

'It is kind of a grid. But it's not made of a material that you know. It's created by a part of the gases that are in the water already. It would use the magnetic field of the earth to create that grid. Then you just need to harvest the energy with a small device whenever it's created.

'There is no need to put these huge turbines or concrete blocks into the ocean. These create a problem for marine life.

'Even that other kind of a grid, that I'm talking about, should be used wisely. It should be used in the large streams that are going around this planet. (I have to figure out the names that you call them by now.) But it's these huge streams that kind of circumnavigate this planet.' He turned the hands, crossing and passing in a large, circular motion.

'Yes, currents.' There was a current coming down the east coast of Australia and one coming up the west coast. She knew that because Mari paid attention to the migrations of the humpback whales to and from Antarctica.

'They're the ones that should be used. It'd be enough to power everything necessary on the whole planet—'

'Wow.'

'—if devices were built that would use energy wisely.

'Still, people are on the wrong path.

'Some of them think about it. But as with many things, they don't think about an easier solution, which would always be the best solution. The less material, the less energy you need to put into these things to produce them, the better. If you need a lot of energy to power the technology you have, then it's the wrong technology. They're still searching in the wrong directions.

'Some of them have the idea that big, impressive machines are needed to convince other people on this planet that this is the right way to do it.

'If someone remembers how to create that grid inside the ocean with everything that's already there in the ocean, needing only a small device to harvest it, people will think, "That's too easy. My child could have done that. So it's not worth anything."

'That's the attitude that has to change.

'They shouldn't look too far away. The solutions are quite close. And they are quite easy to put up, once one of them remembers.

'That one might be called a fool. People will be envious of someone having such an idea because of its power and simplicity. And because they didn't think of it.

'As I said, the intelligent people rarely come out of universities. It's observing nature that will give this planet the breakthrough: learning through experience and observing the things around you, not building machines that are bigger and faster.'

'Beautifully said.'

'And in my opinion or, so to say, in our opinion, it might well be a child that remembers it.

'Of course, the knowledge will be stolen by a big company immediately—but it's very likely that this idea comes from a child. Maybe twelve, thirteen years old.'

He paused a moment. The bush mechanic outside hit something repeatedly, metal on metal. 'That was an age when, back in one of my lifetimes, children became kings,' Aedgar said. 'They got married. They would have been kind of grown-ups during some timespans, so to say, because the life expectancy wasn't high. They had to learn quickly, through even, (probably) worse experiences than people have here now, speaking of bad experiences to learn quickly.

'So this attitude has changed. We, or you, would consider the person inventing, or better to say, **remembering** that way of generating energy now, as a child. Who would have been seen as a grown up, previously.

'There have been other times, though (to speak in your words), when the life expectancy was much higher on this planet.'

Nerida was irritated by the way he had trouble saying "time". Being enmeshed in it herself and enjoying life now that she was growing up (decades beyond but somehow behind, she felt, the kings and queens of yore), she wanted to live a long time. 'How long should a human body last if it's well cared for?' she asked.

'You know there have been populations on this planet before. When they destroyed their population, it had an impact on, what you call, the genetic material. That's why life expectancy got shorter. Significantly shorter.

'Now, it's getting longer. It probably won't reach the life expectancy it was previously. The population needs to learn much more to get back to that point.

'Life expectancy's grown a little bit because the hygiene and things like that are better now.

'You have people in some areas that grow to a very old age.'

'We do.' Nerida knew.

'And surprisingly, it's the ones that use less technology. I mean, surprising to you, not to us. They use less of what you think is the peak of technology.

'Some of them are hard-working. Most of them work closely with Nature. That's how they get to what you would call an old age.

'It's like less is more of everything.

'We have some trouble with giving you exact figures because time is a strange concept to us.'

'I understand,' she said. Being understanding was part of her job, after all.

Aedgar went on, 'I've had lifetimes before so I can say, from that experience, that the numbers are not that important either.

'But, since you ask, it is easy to achieve a three-digit number, with the given material you have.

'The more you *force* into a life: speaking about technology, use of energy that you're not supposed to use and the *avoidance* of learning through experience, from nature or life— living on fake experiences— the shorter that lifetime gets.'

Nerida enjoyed television and movies as much as anyone in full-time work. It was disturbing to think that the hours she sat watching television might shorten her life. Mari made her go out to see Nature, though, once or thrice a week.

Once she was out, it was satisfying to see how the desert oaks were maturing or how the late afternoon light shimmered on the puddles after rain. *More satisfying,* she thought, *than to be entertained by what Aedgar called "fake experiences".*

'Perhaps because it's not achieving what a lifetime is supposed to achieve, the spirit is not growing,' she said, feeling her way towards understanding.

'We will say it this way: we must cut it short because there is no progress. People would need a fresh start.

'And maybe before they come back, they need to have a chance to remember and rethink what they are about to do in the next life, what they've done in the previous life, and what they should achieve, talking about expanding energy and growing.'

'Mmm, making some plans, making some agreements,' she put in, as if she knew what he was talking about.

'It's about finding your right path. We don't talk "agreements."' He was gruff.

'Oh. Michael talked about agreements.' The phraseology was from *Messages from Michael,* the book of channelled material she'd talked about with Dawn back in Burbank.

'What you understand as under an agreement, is that someone gives you an idea which is entirely this person's idea, and not your idea at all, and then you must go conform with that idea. That's agreeing. That's not how it's supposed to be.'

'Okay.'

'It's not like, "I have an idea and that's what you're going to do." Because that's what people mean now when they say, "I agree". Some people are forced into that kind of "agreement."'

'Which doesn't help their growth?'

'When both sides put the same amount of life experience and thought and energy into something, that creates kind of a path, that's shared.'

Mari and I do that.

Aedgar continued, 'Telling someone what to do is not entirely right because everybody has a different path that's the path for them.

'You can't choose the path of someone else or for someone else.

'You might support the other person to grow their energy, but it's going to deprive yours.'

She was following him with care, thinking about her relationships, and the last point hit hard. The concept that a person would be off their path if they devoted themselves to someone else, giving them all, was new to Nerida. *I never wanted to be Mother Theresa. But I imbibed enough Christian ideology (or is it just human decency?) to think that sacrifice and devotion to others was a good thing.*

A knock on the door interrupted them. *That never happens*, Nerida thought. Greg expected to spend the night with his friend.

She excused herself to Aedgar and opened the door.

Behind the screen door was the former CEO of Alice Springs management.

THIRTY-NINE

M UTITJULU
MONDAY MAY 6, 2013

'We're on an overseas phone call,' she told the woman dismissively. But curiosity got the better of her. 'What are you doing here, anyway?' *You should be in jail.*

The embezzler, a short, stout Aboriginal woman in a colourful dress, said, 'I got a job as financial officer at Respite Services. People always said you were nice, so ...'

Nerida had only met the former CEO once or twice. She hadn't been interested in getting to know Nerida, for reasons that had become obvious.

'I can't talk to you now.'

'Make an appointment if you want to see me at the clinic. I'm very busy there. Plenty of sick people,' Nerida said. *Unbelievable! How did she get a job as a finance officer?*

She closed the door and came back to the table. Mari was still in trance and Aedgar waited patiently to pick up where he left off.

Focus now. She looked at her notes. 'Stop being too giving! It doesn't help,' she'd written.

Aedgar said, 'This won't get you anywhere. If you made that person's energy grow but you deprived yourself, then in the end there is no growth of energy.

'It will just be the same total of the energy.

'All the energy that's created adds up in the end, to make a positive impact. But this doesn't help that.'

Nerida tried to process this. Earlier, he'd mentioned in passing that the time spent in a lifetime was not so important. Now, he said that giving your energy away—in devotion to caring for others, say, without exchanging and thus creating energy—could not achieve a lifetime's goals or purpose.

And Aedgar had said—she glanced at her note where she had marked it with an asterisk—that all of them, she and Mari, him and other spirits, existed to 'to expand energy and support growth through learning experiences.' *He means that directly, sort of literally. Can you call it 'literally' when energy is growing in the non-physical realm?*

We are all growing energy in the Universe when we learn. And that is our purpose. But giving energy so someone else can grow, without growing your own, is useless.

From a universal point of view.

The thoughts came and went in her mercurial mind.

She grasped for something to say. 'I see,' she said. 'But the physicists say—and I know what you think about physics I think—'

'There are some good ideas in it. It's just not correct the way they use it,' he said.

Nerida persevered, 'They say that energy cannot be created or destroyed in the universe.' It was the second law of thermodynamics, she recalled from those repeated physics tutorials, years ago.

'They say energy can only change from one form to another. That the total amount of energy in the Universe doesn't change.'

Aedgar spoke with a mild tone that belied the intensity of his message. 'That's not entirely true. That's why we're here. We're here to help.'

'Yeah. So it's not true at all,' she said.

'No.'

'There's a possibility to expand the energy in the Universe?'

'There is the possibility to expand it,' he confirmed.

'At the moment, there is, unfortunately, a negative expansion of the energy from this planet, which must be turned around into growing energy again ... We are here to teach and to help.'

He spoke with gravity appropriate to the importance of what he said. She struggled to cope with the enormity of it. *So we're the needy ones. We're not just taking from the earth. We're taking energy out of the Universe.*

She stumbled, 'So this little planet, this earth—'

'It's one of many,' he had to say.

'—has an effect, though.'

She felt protective and resistant on behalf of the whole planet. *Planet Earth is deemed altogether too insignificant by this conscious being of the multiverse.*

Thinking on it later, she imagined Aiden in the background, saying, 'She's a bit shocked. Let's get Nerida back to basics.'

'This planet does have an effect,' he said. 'It's part of a whole thing. And as I told you before, if you don't take care of the small things, the big things might not work out in the end. Because there are tiny bits missing in the basis, or the fundamental plan, so to say.'

She moved her chair, straightened her spine.

'We will call it foundation,' he said. 'It's like with the concrete in a high-rise building. If one small part is missing or damaged, the whole thing is in jeopardy.'

'Yeah. There was a building collapse in India last week. It was very sad.' She wanted to bring him back to a human scale again.

'It happens. Wrong planning, wrong materials. Wrong use of materials as well. Failure in checking the foundations. It almost always ends in a kind of disaster. Or a quick learning experience, which is a nicer way to put it.'

Nerida raised something now that had been worrying her from her reading. 'Seth and Fortunatus both say that the souls involved in such a catastrophe generally have a vibrational match to the coming disaster somehow.'

'They do. They agreed on that, as you said.'

Did I say that? Oh, he means about the 'agreement'.'

'They agreed to take part in someone else's path, to go along this path together. It ends up with some energy (the one they offered to teach) being expanded and the other energy being deprived; so there is no net gain of energy.

'It is a learning experience for some. A quick learning experience. But those that are tagging along, not on their path, are deprived of their energy. They will need to come back to expand their energy level again. So there is a delay, sometimes quite a significant delay, in the overall expansion of energy.'

Nerida tried to follow. 'Because of these sorts of disasters?'

'Because of these, what you call, agreements,' he said.

'So, people giving up power to somebody else—?'

Aedgar inclined the head gently. 'To help them grow. They do help others to grow but they deprive themselves in these particular circumstances.

'It doesn't mean that a teacher, teaching children, is depriving his or her own energy. They're teaching them and still gaining energy. While giving the children a chance to expand their energy as well.

'We're talking about the things that we call "quick learning experiences."

'Like these people shooting everybody in America?' Nerida suggested.

'They are slow learners. They have the wrong ideas,' he said. 'They follow things that they think are emotions. But the impulses are created by the technology they use, so there is no—how should I put it? —no real emotion involved.'

'It's all an artificial sort of creation. Their brains are injured, a side-effect of misused technology,' she said.

'Yes.' Aedgar explained, 'In this case, some so-called victims are quick learners.

'They try to support them (the shooters), giving them a quick learning experience.

'Because the ones who became criminals were too slow, totally on the wrong path. They need a chance to start over. The experience can make them fast learners or, we could say, fast expanders of energy. In exchange, the others need to have a chance to come back as well.'

Nerida listened carefully. 'Is that why somebody well loved, say a great teacher that everybody treasures, might die in that kind of situation?'

'Yes.'

'That's very generous of them.'

'It is. If people used energy and technology wisely, those others wouldn't have to be so generous.'

'Yes. They wouldn't create this terrible emotional, or pseudo-emotional, storm—'

'No it wouldn't.'

'—that creates criminality.'

'No.'

Wow. That's a radical spiritual perspective. Nerida sighed. 'It's an interesting mess we've got ourselves into, isn't it?'

'There will be a way out of it. But it will take time, indeed ... It's strange how often I have to use the term "time".'

'You find it jarring,' she offered.

'Because it's something that doesn't exist,' he said, as if it was obvious.

'Yes. I appreciate your effort to communicate with us, living that way. Is it irritating to you?'

'It's not irritating. We're here to teach and to help and we're not impatient. We just sit,

or hover, and watch, observe.'

'Looking for opportunities to expand your own energy?'

'Kind of. It doesn't matter that much for us anymore. There is not so much need for us to do so.'

Nerida laughed. 'You're as big as you need to get, huh?'

'Kind of ... Well observed.'

Nerida swiped a tiny fly away. 'Sometimes living in this environment I'm forced to consider insects. Mosquitoes, flies, fleas, bugs of all kinds.

'There's an Aboriginal man I heard about whose totem animal is the fly. And I thought, "What can you learn from flies? What could they tell me?" They tell us about imbalance, I guess.'

Aedgar said, 'They teach you to take more care of the beloved animal. Because otherwise you and the animal will get punished.

'And you have an imbalance on this planet of these of insects and bugs.'

'The "beloved animal" as opposed to the "despised animals" like insects and bugs?' She was puzzled.

'They have a reason to be around,' he said. 'They give humans and animals quick learning experiences.'

She chuckled. 'They do. Irresistible learning experiences.'

'Yes.'

'Like disease does, I guess.' She saw patients learning from their illnesses every day. *Surely the haemorrhoids I had removed were a message from my body that my situation was a bleeding, out-of-control pain in the arse. Probably about my conflict with management.*

'Yes. These things show you that you're on a wrong path, living the wrong way.

'It's very generous of that beloved animal to take part in that learning experience. They try to teach the humans. It's like this thing you call an "agreement."'

'Mmm. They give their energy?'

'So to say.'

'Because sometimes they fly right in front of you and let you splat them and then they're gone?'

'Yes.'

'Yes. I understand now.' *Which is not say I like it. The idea of having to consider the consciousness of bugs is a bit much, really.* Nerida wanted to enjoy her human privilege, sometimes, at least.

'Some nights, when we're out watching the stars, I think, if I get my vibration right, these mosquitoes won't harm me.'

Working on the idea that she could make herself immune to mosquito bites by changing her thoughts (and subsequently her vibration) was an example of the kind of experiment Nerida did with the idea that her thoughts created her reality. *If we create our own reality, why not live in a dimension without flies, mosquitoes, cockroaches and scorpions?*

She'd managed to avoid 'fast learning experiences' with scorpions, but they and other beloved animals were beyond her control. If the citronella oil or DEET didn't work, she had a house with glassed windows and sealing doors. She could go inside. She was more fortunate in that respect than many of her clients at the clinic. Historically, broken windows and doors took Arthur months or years to repair.

Aedgar differed. 'It's not about your vibration. It's about the vibration of the place you're in. There is an imbalance in this place. There is too much of one thing and not enough of another thing. So you suffer.

'Insects are there to help plants grow. And feed the birds. You have animals that kill these birds.'

Feral cats. She understood.

'And then, you have animals that, how should I put it? They're fertilising the earth around you—more than is needed.'

'Yeah.'

'I didn't want to get that graphic about it,' he said primly.

'Thank you. You're talking about the camels.' There were a million feral camels in Central Australia.

'And other animals.'

'Yeah, the cows.'

She loved to eat the cows. Northern Territory steak was flavoursome and healthy.

She understood why people worshipped aurochs for a thousand years before their descendants, the cows, kept close to the temple for adoration, became domesticated.

Cattle were so bad for the arid places, though. They drove Aboriginal people off their Country, fouling the waterholes and breaking up the delicate soil. *Such an endearing, placid animal to use as an instrument of dispossession.*

Nerida understood why many Anangu had contradictory relationships with the cattle. She loved their meat and cheese. Their leather. There was a generation of Anangu who lived and worked on the cattle stations. They built the cattle industry and were justly proud of it.

She thought of Jack, the former stockman. And couldn't shake the conviction that it was him that Aedgar said was involved in the 'punishment' of Desdemona.

Aedgar was still seeing the cow manure from far, far away. 'So that's attracting these insects.

'And it creates more of them. They are not there to help the plants grow. They annoy humans and animals.

'Then there are other animals, not supposed to be there, who kill the birds that should eat the insects, and keep them at bay, so to say.

'It's an imbalance. The imbalance creates them.

'Before that you had one or two fleas helping together as the beloved animal to teach the human. Now you have a hundred fleas. And because it's too much, the person is not able to learn from it.'

'We have to address this,' Nerida concluded.

'Yes. You need to have the balance back.'

'Some animals here are wrong for this environment,' she said.

'They shouldn't be here at all,' he said. 'Same for quite a lot of the humans.'

'You have a point. It's easier to control the animals.'

'The animals are brought by humans who are not supposed to be here either. They're supporting each other on the wrong path; growing the imbalance.'

Nerida looked for the ray of hope. 'Some of us are taking small steps.'

'Yes.'

'Re-using things.'

'Yes.'

'Trying to conserve the water.' She worked on changing her tooth-brushing habit—not running the tap while she was brushing. It was surprisingly challenging.

'Yes,' he chimed in.

Nerida felt impotent. 'It feels like I can't have any effect on my own.'

'Everybody thinks that way. That's the problem,' Aedgar responded. 'Every raindrop would have the idea that it can't cause a flood.

'Of course, they don't have ideas, in the way humans have. But even if every raindrop thinks it can't cause a flood, together they will.'

'Mmm. I like that metaphor. You're poetic. I enjoy that.'

'I wouldn't call it poetic,' he said, tersely.

Nerida smiled. 'Because you're a scientifically minded being. That's your bent.'

'I used to be interested in arts as well. But the arts are distracting.'

'You think?'

'Using their creativity to create nice things, makes pleasant feelings for people. It helps to stop and take a breath. And then they can start again.

'Having these good feelings by being creative expands the energy. So once they are able to take a breath, so to say, while expanding the energy, they can do so much more afterwards.

'Those who would consider themselves as scientists, or scientific working people, (which I don't think they really are at this time), should use creativity as well. It would expand their way of thinking and grow their energy. And it might put them on the right path.

'If people are too much into one thing, they can't see what's on the right or on the left of them.

'They only see what they focus on. They go past the solution that was so close, by looking for it further away, where it is unlikely to be found.

'Well, that's something I can say because I know. They don't remember.'

Nerida ventured: 'Sometimes art can be an opportunity for remembering. Aboriginal paintings Mari and I have in our house represent the vibration of landscapes, to help people feel the land.'

Aedgar considered it. And differed. 'It's sad because it represents the landscape as it was before.

'If they drew or painted these landscape maps, not out of their memory or as they've been told, if they looked at it now to paint, you wouldn't recognise it. It would look different.

'There are small areas where it would still look the same,' he saw. 'But in the main areas it won't ... it would be very different.

'The feelings they'd get from their places now would make less colourful paintings. The colours and so-called energy of the place have changed as well as the shape.'

'Oh. You're talking about places which have been occupied and used?'

'Or deprived of their energy,' he added.

'Mined, you mean?'

'Yes. Looking at mines, in some places it's obvious that it has changed. But other places where it's not so apparent are changed, too.

'When energy is taken because the earth has been deprived at other places, the energy of this place is altered as well, this other place which is so special to them.'

Nerida said, 'Oh, so even though that sacred site was not directly mined, because the earth was deprived of energy nearby, it's affected it, changed its energy and vibration?'

Aedgar extrapolated. 'If you remove all the forest in big areas, you deprive this other area.' He used the hands.

'It creates less humidity in other places (for example). So you change the energy of these other places as well.'

'Mmm, and if you change the climate in a region, you change what can live there,' she reflected.

'Yes.'

'Yeah, that's common sense. I get that.'

'Is it?'

'It is.'

'We don't feel like people understand that's how it is ... If it would be common sense, they wouldn't destroy the forest as they do.'

'A lot of the places that are still being painted, in the artworks, are remote places somewhat removed from—' again, she sought reassurance that things weren't so bad.

'They are painted out of the memory of the artist,' Aedgar said.

'Oh yes. And from stories told,' she agreed.

'Yes. Which can help that place because it expands the artist's energy. The artist feels better so it expands, somehow, the energy of this place a little bit.'

'Mmm. Because the artist feels connected with that Country and its stories?'

'Yes. And the artist feels it from the original. It's coming out of the memory. Sometimes the memory of those that went before and passed it on.'

'Perhaps that visualisation of the place as it used to be can help to recreate it, that place?'

'Yes.' But then he corrected her. 'It's about maintaining. Recreating would take more energy.'

'That's an important distinction,' she noted.

'Unfortunately, it is. So, in some cases, it could be a very bad idea if people living here go out to places they paint or draw, because then they would get different feelings about it.'

Nerida understood. In the city she could see or feel where creeks used to run or where houses had been built on ceremonial grounds or filled wetlands. 'Grief.'

'Yes. And then grief would go into their artwork, it would change the energy, and they can't expand their energy. They can't make the energy grow. That deprives that place even more.'

'Does sadness stop energy from expanding?' Nerida asked.

'It's kind of a stagnation. A blockage,' he said.

'That's interesting. I always felt I grew from sadness and grief. In my youth I felt grieving for what happened to me or others helped me learn.'

Aedgar nodded. 'You had quick learning experiences from bad things. Grief was part of it, and sadness. You grew from a learning experience, not from the sadness or the grief.'

'Oh, I see.'

'This is what you would call in your profession a side-effect.'

'Uh-huh.'

'It makes you realise that something has happened, something has changed. It's a sign to stop, take a breath, try to get back on the path you're supposed to be on, to be able to expand your energy again.'

'But it's hard to let go of the sadness of a situation where, if I understand you, people can't visit their country because it will hurt their country to physically visit it.'

'If they visit their country, and they see, "We have to maintain it, we have to care for this place," then it's not overtaken by grief. Sometimes, going there makes people realise that something needs to be done. But it must come from themselves. A decision they make because it's their path.

'If someone else comes from a different place, saying, "I have a great idea, we'll go and visit your country," that means they agree to an idea on a path that's not theirs.

'There are well-meaning people out there doing damage with their actions. They should stick with their path at their place.

'Am I a bit too harsh?'

AM I one of the well-meaning people doing damage with my actions? This is not my place. My Ancestors' Country is by rivers, and among mountains in the South East.

She said, 'Um, maybe it has to do with soul age. There are exceptional individuals from other places who can come and help because they listen and respond.'

I'm an Old Soul. I'm wise enough to do no harm.

Aedgar gave her no false assurance. 'Few. Very few,' he said. 'Some want to put themselves into a different life, so to say.

'They chose a wrong path previously. They're still on it. And they are trying to, you can't say "cover it up"—but it is something like it. They want to be seen in a different light.'

'They want to be seen to be doing good,' Nerida offered, leaving her ego behind.

'Yes.'

'They're missionaries, you could say.' Other people, whitefellas, called people coming to the Outback "missionaries, mercenaries or misfits." She and Mari took their place with the latter.

'But, they don't do good,' Aedgar said. 'They follow a wrong idea. Don't talk about missionaries!

'Some of them were quite good, *some* of them, because they had a good energy. What you would call a "good heart."

'Many others just followed rules. That meant they didn't have a good energy. You could translate it to *not* having a "good heart".

'Humans working together need to follow their energy, not rules given to them by anyone, especially not the Church.

'The Church is a very disturbed institution trying to control rather than help. In trying to control, they give out a little bit of what's commonly seen as help. But it's like, "I give you this if you behave the way I want you to."

He went on. 'Many people see only what they give out and think, "They are very charitable. They are lovely people." They don't see what they demand. Some ask a lot of the people. They expect those they help to give back to them, to grow their energy.'

'Again, they're depriving the people of energy—' Nerida was catching on.

'Yes.'

'In forcing an agreement.'

'Yes,' he said. 'Even before that, though, they give people the wrong idea.

'It's not only churches. Other facilities do that too.

'They give people a wrong idea of what they need in the first place. Then the people think, "Oh, I can't live without that," even if they did so, for ages before. These institutions demand "support" from people, who keep giving in order get the things that they now *think* they need.

'It's give and take in a dead end, a one-way dead end.

'There's always more coming from one direction than from the other. One side only gives to cover up. To get the things they need to grow their energy out of the other side. It's a bit like with the insects: balance is disturbed.'

'Yes. I always thought of flies as like fundamentalist Christians,' Nerida recalled impudently. She wrote a kind of operetta with a chorus of flies singing satirical songs when she was twenty, travelling in India.

'They wouldn't like that.'

Nerida laughed. 'The flies or the fundamentalist Christians?'

'I guess both.'

'Yes, that idea's from when I was much younger. Many of those ideas have since been superseded. But there's some kind of metaphor to be made about imbalance.'

'Yes.'

'The give and take, with more take.'

'Yes.'

'And no expansion of energy as a result,' she concluded.

'Yes. Unfortunately, people think they are doing good because they only see the surface.

'Really good-hearted, good-energy people join them, only to be deprived of their energy too. That's why I said that about the missionaries. Not all of them are bad, only the ones that play by the rules made by someone else.'

Nerida concurred. 'They hurt the good-hearted people. Including people they say they're there to help.'

Mari was hurt by simplistic, brutal religious people. In kindergarten, a nun hit her with a metal dustpan and then locked her in a cupboard as punishment for playing with the boys' toys. She was forgotten in there until her mother came looking for her after school.

In high school, when she was thirteen, a clergyman slapped Mari's face for asking where Adam and Eve's descendants came from—given that they only had sons. His handprint marked her for hours.

When Nerida was an acupuncturist (before she was a doctor), she had a client, a dry- humoured, gentle lesbian, who had an abortion when it was still illegal in New Zealand.

Pilloried by the media, she was jailed by the state at age 19. A religious, misogynistic frenzy scarred the woman for life.

She suicided in midlife, hounded by severe depression. The trauma of that experience was a major trigger of her lifelong struggle for mental health.

Nerida said to Aedgar, 'If what you say about following rules is correct, then perhaps the structure of law in this society is something we should change.'

'There is a wrong understanding of that,' he answered. 'Societies, as you call them, need some rules—but it shouldn't be overdone. Too many rules to follow, making people adhere to that rule-constructed, certain path, will stop them from growing and participating as they should.

'A few holes need to be put in the earth to secure a building. But it shouldn't be too much. Having four poles and one in the centre might make a good foundation.' He illustrated the layout of a square, or diamond, with another pole as central support, with the hands.

'Too many poles in the earth could make an unstable foundation, as vulnerable as putting a building right onto the earth without any base at all. You might just push it and it falls over.

'A few things anchored in the earth in the right places makes the building secure and lasting.

'You need space for different thoughts and different pathways, which is not given at the current time.

'Excessive rules are made and enforced by scared people. They want to collect energy and be supported to grow their own energy by depriving everybody else.'

'Is that what fear does?' Nerida asked. 'Does fear set up a dynamic of deprivation of other people's energy?'

'Yes. "I want it. I need to protect myself. I need to make myself stronger than you." Some people are still willing to give that energy to them for a learning experience. But they deprive themselves, which causes imbalance.'

'Good to stay away from the fearful ones?'

'Yes.'

'Hard to avoid in my profession.'

He lifted a brow. 'You can make them even more fearful. And they won't come back so often ... So you don't have to deal with them so many times when they try to deprive you of your energy.'

Nerida was amused. 'Uh-huh.'

Aedgar sensed her concern that his proposal was rough. 'It's a matter of keeping balance. It's not about hurting people or doing bad. It's about keeping balance.'

'How is this body?' Nerida enquired for Mari. Her wife had stopped telling her when she was in pain to avoid distressing Nerida. Mari just got angry instead. Nerida tried not to take it personally but wasn't there yet. They were so close, so entwined, that Nerida had difficulty keeping her own independent feelings. She practiced.

For example, Mari was from a family of vivid swearers. It was cultural. The Swabians were earthy, colourful people. Her Gypsy family were horse traders, entertainers and negotiators.

Nerida's family were influenced by the mission her father grew up on and the Cold War atmosphere both parents were raised in. They never swore.

Nerida enjoyed cussing as a grown up. But Mari used two or three gruesome expletives where Nerida might have used one. It was noticeable when Mari was in pain. Or watching the news. Sometimes Nerida flinched, when Mari intended only free expression and release.

'Mmm. Still needs rest,' Aedgar said. 'There are still paths in the body needing special attention. We've seen it worse before, like years ago. It's still better than it was back then. But it's not the way it's supposed to be. It takes quite a bit of care.'

'She's doing well with your help. I can see you expanding her energy day by day.' Nerida saw Mari responding to ideas that she channelled without having to consciously hear them.

The night before, for example, they watched a documentary by a journalist who was interested in the idea that there'd been technologically advanced civilisations before the present one, and was uncovering the evidence.

'Good. For us it's a give and take on equal levels. That's what we call a relationship.'

'Mmm. I'm learning today.'

'It's about time,' he said.

Nerida laughed.

'You shouldn't take that too seriously,' he said warmly.

'I won't. I'm learning every day.'

She heard birds chirping happily outside and the wind soughing through the oaks and mulgas. Finally, she asked, 'I wondered whether you and your friends have something to do with those showers of meteors, whether you use them to try to restore balance. I know you're not gods, but you do move energy around in the universe.'

'We do,' he confirmed. 'It is a regular maintenance thing. Sometimes some of those flying rocks get out of control too, because of the imbalance. We work on balancing the energy, so that it doesn't happen that often.'

'We see them here almost every night.'

'It's a good place. Because it's dark and it needs to be dark.'

The ding of a kitchen timer went off.

'I might go for now,' Aedgar said.

'I've enjoyed your company very much as always,' she said sincerely.

'I enjoy it too. Thank you for the opportunity. We'll be back soon. Even if I'm never that far away.'

'Thank you.'

'You're welcome.'

Nerida hopped up to turn the oven off. Mari had a chicken

roasting with potatoes, carrots and onions. Moist heat flooded the small kitchen when she opened the oven door.

Mari returned slowly, looking relaxed. 'Hi,' she said with a sigh.

'Great session,' said Nerida, beaming.

After dinner, Nerida put on a jacket and jeans. Joining Mari in the yard under the starlit sky, she thought about what Aedgar said. *He explained that giving your energy away to someone else expands their energy at the expense of yours. Well, I do that all the time in the clinic. And with my family. Better stop doing that.* The Universe does not gain; the purpose of living is not fulfilled.

She looked up at the Milky Way, spilling over Mutitjulu, over Uluru, over these two women living their modest, (if well fed), remote lives. She saw the Seven Sisters as a brilliant, bluish-white blur amongst the uncountable stars.

'Wow, did you see that?' Mari pointed where a shooting star blazed its path.

'I did. That was a great one.'

He also mentioned, almost in passing, that the energy of this planet is contracting, we are not generating energy, we're losing energy. The work she and Mari did with Aedgar, then, was about turning that around.

If people understood the concept of growing from learning experiences, consciousness can increase energy on the planet.

Hence his refrain, 'Gain knowledge to grow energy.' And that's why we need to learn from our experiences. It's not just about us. Life became profoundly more meaningful as Nerida strove to understand what Aedgar said, the fundamental concepts he tried to convey.

She smiled at the stars.

He has the knowledge and power to blow my tiny mind.

FORTY

M UTITJULU
MONDAY MAY 13, 2013

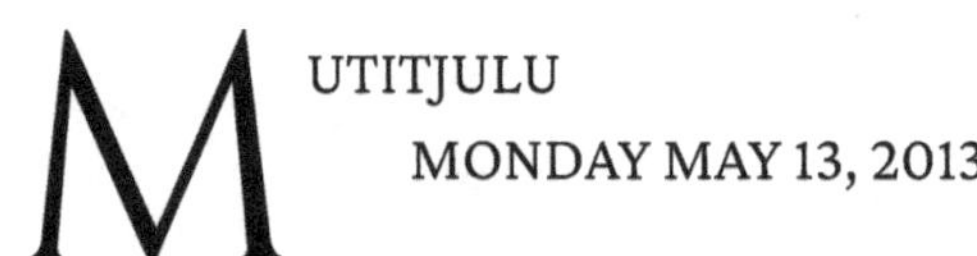

NERIDA WOKE in the early light and saw her wife's face relaxed. As she watched through hooded eyes, Mari turned away from her.

Nerida moved closer and put her arm around her, holding her through the quilt, so Mari stayed warm. The morning air was fresh on their faces.

She moved subtly towards Nerida's touch, unconsciously gravitating to her, then relaxed back into deeper sleep.

They stayed snuggled that way until the minute before the alarm went off. Nerida got up, shut it off before it started and dressed for work.

Winter was coming. The searing heat was past. People slept better. Flowers and new leaves sprouted.

The women saw more reptiles as lizards and snakes got sleepier and slowly made their way to their hollows for hibernation. Some birds made nests.

The desert had two spring-like seasons, this one and the one preceding *Mai Wiya*—that hottest time. She was still learning the name for the cooler time around April and May.

There was a lovely upwelling of energy in the earth and in the people. She felt it when she saw purple flowers on the way to work.

She walked by Peter's place, unafraid of his dogs. She'd visited him a few times at home now.

'Did you know that the Queen had more than 30 dogs?' Peter said enthusiastically when she was there last. Many of his dogs had short legs, showing their royal, corgi ancestry.

It was a beautiful place to be any time other than that period of extreme heat. That hot time caused strokes and heart attacks.

This Autumn, Nerida pottered in their yard before and after work, nurturing determined sprouts in the sandy red soil. Still tired, she worked to restore her energy. The garden helped.

And even if Nerida felt better in her warm house, the cold time was worse for many of the mob's health. A lot of people slept rough.

If there was a Sorry Camp in winter, Bull and the Council gave people big, fluffy acrylic blankets. They got a lot of wear, those blankets.

Everyone lived in jackets and beanies. People built fires. But many still shivered at night.

The suicides she'd seen were in winter. Claire had asked then, 'Why's it always so cold when this shit happens?'

But now that young woman who'd threatened suicide with an electrical cord in summer, Maleah, came to see Nerida. She needed a reference for a scholarship to a Perth boarding school.

'Is it a good school? You won't be lonely?' Nerida asked. 'Boarding school can be an adventure. But only if you want to go.'

Maleah's broad grin reached her eyes. 'Nah. I'll like it. One of my cousins is there. They've got a pool and tennis. They have dances with the boys.'

'Must be good things are happening for you. I'm glad you've decided to stay in this life now.'

The young woman nodded earnestly. 'I'm not thinking about those things anymore.'

Something's brought her back to be in this world. I hope she'll keep attracting good things, Nerida thought in the early evening, clearing away the remains of summer's zucchini, tomato and bean plants.

A buzz of voices and activity suddenly surged on the other side of the fence. Barry had one of his tour groups camping there.

An old man in poor health, he was a willing magnet for people looking for spiritual answers. Tourist groups came to learn, sometimes literally, at his feet.

Guests camped on the stony ground of his untidy yard, with a hired portable lavatory at the end of it.

They paid a lot of money to come to the camp (the prices were on the net). Mari and Nerida were sceptical about the value.

Greg thought it was hilarious to tease the women with fanciful stories, flirting with them over the fence. Nerida heard him talking about a horny echidna 'with pricks all over him,' who was never satisfied. At the end of the story, the echidna was hit by a car.

'You shouldn't make shit up like that,' Nerida scolded him. 'They get enough gammon-Aboriginal bullshit and pseudo-spiritual seduction from Barry.'

'Well and he gets paid for it,' Greg giggled. 'One of the women said, "Can you have cars in dreamtime stories, then?" I told her she should ask Barry about it.'

Mutitjulu was a private place. Only the art centre was open to the public. Even to go there you had to make an appointment. Uninvited people weren't allowed. Greg was in Muti with a permit to work as a physio for a three-week block.

He stayed at Mari and Nerida's place sometimes, or just came home to shower. It took pressure off his blossoming romance with the Yulara airport baggage handler. But they were spending most nights together. Tony was a gentle Anangu man. His house was crowded. Most nights, they camped in the sand hills in private places Tony knew. 'It's properly romantic,' Greg said.

Tony was only a year or so younger than Greg, which was a kind of breakthrough, Nerida and Mari thought. He usually went for guys ten years or so younger than him, in their twenties. Nerida knew he had felt safe with the emotional distance of being the more knowledgeable, experienced partner. Of course, they all grew out of the infatuation and rejected him. That was the pattern he'd been stuck in.

'Don't you break Tony's heart. He's a good man,' Nerida said. 'And I'll bet he knows a lot more than you about lots of things. Good for you, finally being with someone you'll learn from, my brother.'

Ten or twenty years ago, when she was starving for spiritual knowledge and almost desperate to know her purpose, Nerida would have considered paying thousands of dollars to sleep in Barry's barren yard, looking for connection with Central desert cultures. It was possible to catch glimpses of the Rock if you went to the corner of Barry's yard, climbed on the fence, and craned your head. She was grateful she hadn't needed to go there. It was hard to imagine how it would have messed with her head to experience Mutitjulu that way.

Many of Nerida's patients were controversial figures. The town was full of contradictions and strong personalities. Bull was one. The rangers hated him for shooting pigeons. Barry was another.

He moved onto the piece of land he claimed and constructed his house without paying rent or discussing his decision with anyone in the Community. Barry called himself a Traditional Owner when he wasn't one. People wanted to throw him out. Or worse. But when it came to taking definitive action, Anangu felt sorry for him.

He was removed from his family as a child, poor thing. Everybody knew that screwed a person up. So, he was tolerated.

Nevertheless, running his Aboriginal spiritual enlightenment business without consultation or permission was provocative. He annoyed people. Talked a lot about respect but didn't practice it.

Nerida guessed that Barry didn't ask for permits to bring his customers into Community because he might not have been granted them. So, the tourists paid Barry money and just showed up.

There were fights in the Council meetings about it. Bull opposed Barry having a tourism business in Mutitjulu. Barry was a chicken, Nerida reckoned, all bluff and bluster. A cock, maybe.

Mari and Nerida observed, but stayed out of local politics, grateful be allowed to live there at all. Local people mostly treated them with distance, respect, or both.

At Sunday afternoon coffee, Claire asked Mari how she was feeling about life at Mutitjulu.

Mari responded warmly. 'I like Anangu. There are some very clever people here. A few are becoming friends. I'm happy to hang around at the Art Centre sometimes when the other artists are painting, to help out and enjoy their company.'

Nerida smiled, relishing the warm apple and cinnamon cake.

Mari said, 'I'm not sure they think much of my painting. And they think photography is nothing but point and click. But I like it. I've lived and worked in beautiful places. This is one of them.

'And the house is all right.'

Claire smiled her dazzling smile. 'I'm forgiven for persuading Nerida to move here, then? I feel forgiven with the delicious baked goods you feed me. And I love being next door.'

Mari made a grunt, a concession. '*Maski.*' She'd learned the PNG expression for 'It doesn't matter,' which made Claire's smile even wider. She nodded her head encouragingly.

'The baking goes well,' Mari nodded back. 'It's taken a while to get to know the oven. And to get my sourdough culture working reliably. I like it when the house smells of coffee. Or cake.

'I've never been a housewife and don't plan to ever become one. But I like making a welcoming home for my hard-working Nerida. I greet her with a hug and fresh-cooked food. And most days she even has a smile. I can see she's satisfied with her work.' Mari walked to Nerida's side, put her arm around her shoulders and kissed her lightly on the top of her head.

After the day's work on Monday, Mari wanted to go out to photograph stars. When evening came, though, the sky was still cloudy. And Mari offered to channel.

WITHIN FIVE MINUTES, Aedgar greeted Nerida. 'Again,' he said, 'in that noisy place. Mmm.'

'Yes,' Nerida said, 'dependent as we are—'

'We are surrounded by—' he began.

'Inadequate technology,' she said.

'Indeed. Noisy, dry place.'

'Yes.'

'Lots of energy around,' he continued. 'Not all positive. Energy's getting drained from the place.'

'By the visitors, you mean?'

'By other energies,' he said. Cryptically.

'Tell me more.'

Aedgar said, 'The place is getting drained of energy by individuals trying to make their own energy grow, to gain energy from this place.

'It's a ***draining modern exchange.***'

He emphasised the last three words, as if this characterisation was a useful invention. 'It's close,' he said.

Nerida ducked her head as if a *mamu*, a pathogen in spirit form, was flying around.

'I think we might have to put a bit of protection in place,' Aedgar said.

'One individual is not, he's not so bad—he is well-meaning—but he doesn't know what he's doing. He's just trying to expand his energy.

'But it's draining the place. He's trying to gain energy from the other individuals, but they are stronger.

'Oh? And they drain him?' Nerida was trying to figure out what he meant.

'The earth and him.

'It's the problem with going to a place with an energy that doesn't match. They are trying to increase their own energy by draining the place. It is not a match on an energetic level.'

He took time to look around: eyes still closed, lifting Mari's head almost as one would move a phone, looking for reception.

'This place is not a good match for most of the individuals here. There is a lack of energy exchange,' he concluded, repeating his point.

Perhaps he sensed that Nerida was mystified.

He reminded her, 'You asked me about Stonehenge a long time ago.

'Well, it was man-made. It doesn't work anymore because energy needs to move to stay alive, so to say.

'This place is not man-made, but even here the energy must *move*. 'It's not exactly in this place, the good energy.

'The good energy moves with the rotation of the planet as well as the movement of the whole universe. So, there is constant shifting. And the radiation in the earth also creates interference with that energy.'

He paused. And she imagined the moving planet with its good, strong energy coming in waves into, through or beside Uluru.

'These individuals who came here to find something special won't find anything.'

As he spoke, she realised that he was talking about the people in Barry's yard. *And it's Barry, the one who doesn't know what he's doing.*

'Not only because they are not a match. It's just that it's not here right now.

'People need a rest.

'The earth needs a rest.

'The radiation levels are coming down and they will even come down further. This will allow the movement of the energy to change direction.

'The good energy will come back.

'Until it moves away again, when the radiation in the earth cycles back. The radiation is created by the heat.'

Nerida, still chronically tired, understood what he meant when he said that the Earth needs a rest, too. Even here at Uluru, so delicate and immense.

But she found it difficult to hear complex truths about Uluru. She still tended to idealise it. Hearing that the good energy was **gone** from the place confronted and frightened her. But the Rock did look and feel different some days. It was sometimes silky, sometimes suede.

Sometimes vibrantly compelling. Other times it felt hostile.

Those were the days she thought about the baby killed by the dingo there—with her mother crucified by the Australian State in the aftermath.

And the murder in the cave. A white colonial mercenary killed an Anangu man there in the 1930s. They saw the cave from their house.

She thought of her friends and clients who worked as park rangers.

One told her about a stormy night he had to climb up the metal chain to retrieve the body of a tourist, as lightning bolts hit the stone under his feet and thunder deafened him.

Another friend told her that she helped pick up the body parts of a climber who fell. He overreached for the toppling lid of his water bottle. His carcass (his 'shell' Aedgar or Monica might call it) was torn apart on the way down.

Sometimes that powerful place was sinister.

She went to work with her head down and her face turned away from the Rock then, finding scant pleasure in the soft red sand under her feet, the dried flowers by the path. There was still that magnificent cerulean sky. And the people she worked with and served.

'It's a cycle, then?' she asked.

'Indeed. These visiting people don't know about it. Not to say they don't know anything at all. It's not on their level of expertise, so to say.

'They pretend, all of them, that they have reached a vortex or, as some of them would put it, they have reached Nirvana. They just say it because of their peers. No one wants to admit that they can't feel the exchange of energy—which they can't, because it is not happening. Wrong time, wrong place.

'It would never work for them.

'But even for people like you, it doesn't work right now. Wrong time, wrong place.

'If you have a kind of matching energy, you can feel it's not here. You might express it like, "This mountain looks strange at the moment, it looks rougher, or darker, or less vibrant."

'It will come back soon. But it's not here right now.'

He was quiet for a moment, then spoke brightly, 'You talked to my friend.'

'Yes, we did.' The women had a session with Monica on the weekend.

'I've heard.'

Nerida laughed warmly. 'We love talking about you.'

'Why wouldn't you?'

'Yes.'

'You have a friend in common, so to say.'

'We do.'

'Though not on all levels,' he said, enigmatically.

'No ... but she introduced us.'

'To some extent,' he agreed.

'And we're very grateful for our introduction and because she knows you, we enjoy talking about you.'

'Yes.'

'She tells us funny stories.'

'Well. There are sometimes different views on things.'

'You didn't tell me.' She was laughing.

'I won't say wrong views on things. Different,' he said, with an air of propriety.

'You didn't tell me that your wife chased you with an axe once. Your sweet, innocent wife!'

'Well, she had a wrong idea about something,' he said, still maintaining his dignity.

'Mmm, she thought you were with another woman, instead of with another man,' Nerida said.

'Probably.'

'Jealousy can be a terrible thing.' She knew. She'd seen the burnt shells of the Blair sisters' cars.

Aedgar said, 'She was very sweet. Innocent.

'She just had issues at times. I wasn't sure what it was all about.

'She might have got annoyed at another point because nothing strange happened that day, except that she came out with the axe ... It was quite unexpected.'

'Oh dear.'

'But nothing happened,' he said with an almost perceptible shrug.

'Because Aiden talked to her?'

'He always did. She thought he was her best and probably only ally, against me.

'I wonder what she would have thought if she'd known. While she was always talking to the one that she thought was her ally, he was her worst enemy, so to say.

'He was very diplomatic. Sweet as honey.'

'And charming, yes?' Nerida grinned.

'Of course. So, she would have never thought about something like it.

'Jealousy can be simply terrible. I mean, she was very well cared for.

'She was even loved. Just in a different way.'

Nerida objected. 'But you had something with someone else that she could never have with you.'

'Indeed.'

'Part of her must have sensed that,' she said. 'There was always something missing for her.'

'I wouldn't put it that way. She was always safe, attended to, and nourished. She had a very comfortable life. She had wonderful, inspirational conversations.'

'With Aiden?'

'And with me, of course.'

'Good.'

'I don't know what could be considered wrong in this relationship. We even had children. And we all loved the children. Even Aiden loved the children.'

'Of course, he did,' said Nerida, from her own perspective on blended families. Mari loved Ruby, and even if Nerida's son was hard to get on with, she remained kind to him for Nerida's sake.

'Do you think it was some old issue from long ago that triggered the axe incident?'

'I don't know what she had on her mind that day because especially on that day, nothing had happened at all. We were just coming back from the city. Doing business—'

'You and Aiden?'

'—with wool. And we had been to the pub, as you would say. It was quite enjoyable. Most of the men did that when they celebrated successful business.

'We even got some wonderful silk. And then all we got was the axe. 'Didn't seem to be very grateful at that time.

'There was a moment when I thought I could have bought the scratchy cotton.'

'Oh, the scratchy cotton instead of the silk?'

He was a little desultory at the memory of it. 'It would have been a good match for that day.'

Nerida allowed, 'Well, women have hormones sometimes, chemicals in our blood that make our moods a bit overwhelming.'

Aedgar was dismissive. 'That's an excuse that's over-rated. Has been and will always be.'

'Okay,' she said slowly. 'You never felt that when you were a woman?'

'I knew about medicines—' he said.

'Oh, to moderate the effect?' She knew a bit about herbs.

'—and how things work. And how I could make things work better. These things were

quite effective. There was no excuse for hormones having taken over.'

Nerida said, 'Okay.' But was about to launch an argument. 'Sounds like—'

'Maybe it's poorly treated.' He interrupted. 'In your times.'

'Yes. I believe so.'

'So many things are going the wrong way. We must work on that.' He moved the head towards the west. 'You might get rain soon.'

He knows how to make me happy. 'Yes. I hope so.'

'Quite a bit of it. Quite soon doesn't mean tomorrow. But soon. It's building up nicely.'

She agreed. 'The clouds are beautiful.'

'What have you been doing lately? Besides talking to my friend.'

'Today I've been at my workplace; had an enjoyable day. I had a great conversation with a man who's a circus performer. He's teaching some of the boys acrobatics: juggling and jumping and flipping.'

'It's a good thing to do. The beings and humans around here, the young ones, seem to have a lot of energy.'

'Yes, they do.'

'How should I put it? It's good to use excessive physical energy to create exercise for more oxygen to the brain. Encouraging them to do this, helps them to expand other energy, as well.

'That is the purpose in this life: Growing wisdom and expanding energy. Learning the full experience. That includes learning about abilities of the physical body as well.'

Nerida did not process the first two sentences, only responded to the third. 'Their exercise delights people. They fly. They make long jumps, including over each other, climbing on each other. You know the sort of thing.'

'Sounds delightful.'

'It is. They get to travel and perform in front of very large audiences, so it's an exciting thing for these boys; for any boys, it would be.'

'Well, efforts like that, to grow energy and expand knowledge or wisdom through gaining experience in this lifetime, should be rewarded. Being rewarded means they can feel that they have done something right which makes them want more.'

'They're going to a giant football game,' Nerida enthused. 'They love football around here. And the boys are going to travel to the city with a stadium of 100,000 people to watch them do some of their tricks.'

'It's going to expand their horizon, so to say. And encourage them to do more.

'There might be one or two who'll think, "That's all too much." They'll get overwhelmed and decide to take a different path.

'It doesn't mean they have failed. They just gained some insight into different ways to discover, other ways to expand energy.'

'I wanted to ask you if that little girl, the one the others are waiting for, if she's been born yet,' she asked, changing topic to keep things concrete.

'Not yet but soon ... Your time, probably by the end of this year.'

'Close to the end of this year?

'It's hard for us to ... to add that up because time doesn't exist. And humans always try to measure time. And they always used different systems.

'You're having a very strange system right now, while pretending to be so advanced in technology. The system you're using is one of the most basic measurements possible. It allows no flexibility.

'Because the whole universe is alive, so to say, and is in constant movement, you need to be more flexible with the measurements you use.'

He sensed Nerida zoning out (and she did—he was talking about time again), so he gave a specific example. 'People say, "This summer is really cold, not like the last summers we had," or "Years ago, the summers were much nicer." Or "The winters are not the same anymore."

'Because the seasons can't happen in the same time frame as they used to.

'The planet is moving and adjusting all the time to the Universe, not to your time frame.'

Nerida was unable to comprehend that. Instead, she was still nattering to herself. *Why do they go on and on about time?* Then she thought, *Maybe that's a reflexive resistance that I should release. Because I know what he means about the arbitrary marking of a season on the calendar.*

She said, 'The old people here used to measure the seasons according to the arrival of certain plants or animals, or clouds or winds. And that's how they knew that time had passed into the next season.'

'Better still would be observing the stars,' he responded. 'It's the living Universe that's in constant movement, so for you, right now, that means watching the stars. Observing them is as close as you can get to the Universe.

'But instead, people look at a piece of paper with numbers on it, and there we go again—paper with numbers on it. It's useless. I don't know why your population favours the paper with the numbers on it so much.'

'I think you had a theory.'

'I do. It's an excuse, like with the hormones.

'It's an excuse to stay on the same track without adapting to things, without expanding energy, gaining wisdom and knowledge.

'They try to stick to the same path that someone created at a time when it might have been close to what was going on, but it doesn't work anymore, as with so many things.

'The Universe, everything, has **evolved**, moved on!

'And everyone on this planet is stuck to the same patterns.

'Patterns of measurement, putting things in so-called time frames. They don't exist, the way you do this.

'It's an illusion!'

CHAPTER

FORTY-ONE

M UTITJULU
THE SAME MONDAY

AND THEN, when he started again on the flawed fundamentals of the sciences again, she could hardly stand it. She still took it personally. Mustering grace, she changed the subject, 'You seem to be moving very fluidly tonight, Aedgar.'

He was.

'Trying to adjust some things,' he explained. 'There are areas that need it: the upper part of the spine, the neck—there's still kind of restricted blood flow on one side which isn't good for the skin, it's not good for the muscles, and most of all not good for the brain. It can lead to problems with the eyes too.

'As I'm trying to do these adjustments in some little areas, the blood flow might increase, which leads to itchy patches of skin in the face. You might have realised that.'

'I didn't realise that that was the cause. Mari will be interested to hear. She's been a little bit mystified.'

'Mystified? About what?'

'About itchy patches on her face. Among other things,' she said.

'I don't think our friend, who has agreed to lend the whole body to a being like me and some other friends, can be mystified by itchy parts on the face.' He sounded put out.

'Oh. You'd be surprised.' She laughed. Mari could obsess about little things that Nerida (and most of her community clients) would dismiss.

Aedgar was concerned. 'Could this be an issue?'

'No.'

The room was quiet. Aedgar moved strands of Mari's hair behind her ears, in a three-dimensional act of coordination Nerida hadn't seen before.

'Would you like some help?' she offered.

'No. I am used to long hair.'

'I guess you had some curls.'

'One of the few things in this body that I'm used to … We might have a friend coming in soon. Trying to adjust other parts. But it's like with the rain. It's going to happen soon. It doesn't mean tomorrow.'

Nerida sighed. 'This magnificent woman had so much suffering in life. She was born with a problem with her legs and had to endure surgeries that no one would do anymore. The surgeries caused more problems and months and months, over years, in a hospital bed.

'She was only one year old when they encased her in plaster, including her feet, up to her armpits, with just an opening for her nappy. It was supposed to be treatment for her hips.

'She contracted chicken pox in the children's ward, and they sent her home, screaming with the itch. Papa made her a stick with a soft end to scratch under the plaster.

'One time, when she was a little older, she offered her best toy—

and she loves her toys, they're alive to her—to a nurse, pleading with her not to perform a painful procedure.

'She learned to laugh as hard as she could instead of crying, so that the hands of the physicians wouldn't shake. "They thought I was mad. Dad was proud of me," she says.'

Feelings she couldn't name swirled in Nerida's belly and chest and pricked her eyes. 'Then, when she grew up, there was a stupid accident, with an injury that would have been straightforward to repair surgically.

'But the surgeon was a drunk and a drug addict. He operated on the wrong bones. Then stigmatised her. Denied the reality of her pain and disability while she tried to walk on the untreated fracture.

'After the amputation she had a problem with her neck because of the long difficult time of trying to walk when nobody could have. The surgeon left a rag in her neck, that came slowly out of the wound ... that needed another surgery.

'Just a few years ago, with me, Mari slipped and fell and broke her back. People who saw her laughed. I took her to hospital. She waited hours, standing up. Barely able to breath with pain. The doctor was one of my students. But he had to be pushed to even take an x-ray. Didn't read it. Then discharged her home with no diagnosis or treatment. "Pick up some Panadol from a service station on the way home," he said, after midnight.

'This has all gone on much too long.' Nerida was crying. 'This list of suffering and trauma. Humiliation. Is there any point in it all?'

'Yes,' he said soberly. 'Such a strong experience in every aspect means that she gains a lot of wisdom and knowledge. In the end this translates to expanding energy through all the things that are related to the experience.

'Volunteering in something like this means the whole plan of a lifetime will change. It's quite a steep learning curve. Means a vast expansion of energy. So, our friend has done well accepting it.'

Nerida sniffed. Got up for a tissue.

'Not many would or could do it,' he said. 'It takes a special energy in the first place to go for it.'

'An adventurous one,' she suggested.

'Indeed, I agree. But our friend has always been like that. There were a lot of experiences. Plenty. Giving others the opportunity to learn.

'Sometimes, it's true, our friend has taken on a little bit too much.'

Nerida accepted that readily. 'She wanted to teach the healers, or the ones who said that they were healers, doctors and nurses.'

Aedgar responded, 'Which is a very difficult thing to do in the time that you live in. Because they use very harsh methods.

'Which doesn't mean that we didn't use harsh things now and then. But it was a rare occasion.

'And the person either had a life that continued or at least a quick death.

'Not prolonged suffering in between,' she said.

'No. But now, they think they know it all.

'Every generation thinks they know it all.

'They know nothing. They miss out on the **basic knowledge**.

'They totally ignore energy, the flow of energy.

'In some parts of the planet, some populations have an idea about energy for healing.

'They try to focus on and use it. But having an idea doesn't mean it turns out as an ideal way of healing. It is a better one. It's not perfect.

'Because even they miss some important things.

He seemed to look into it, consulting some mysterious source of information. 'The way they group the energies is a bit wrong,' he said. 'The way they put together the groups doesn't balance it. I'm talking about sticking needles in energy channels.'

'As I do.'

'It's a much better way but it's not perfect. Even with this method that's quite a bit older than these so-called new technologies, they have already things missing.'

She had to bend her mind around the way he talked. *Traditional Chinese Medicine is a thousand years or more old, but Aedgar has the mindset that it will be more likely to be complete than recent, 'new' medicine, say, since the Industrial Revolution. Okay.*

'They have to group the energy levels in different ways than they do,' he asserted.

Nerida felt, when she studied TCM, that healing and learning by observation was being forced to fit into idealised philosophical or religious frameworks, like Confucianism or Taoism.

She thought of an example, 'You mean the depth of the layers of energy, internal to external?' She'd never been able to relate to what she was taught about the depth of an illness in the body.

'That's one of the issues. The other one is the groups of energy. The fire and water and—how should I say?'

'Wood and air and earth?' She liked the cycles of elements projected onto the function of organs in the body, foods, colours, the seasons and places. Concordances, they called it in English. It helped her understand Traditional Aboriginal Healing, which was also about the connections of the body with its environments.

Nerida decided not to study Aboriginal healing when she was younger. She was strongly attracted to it. But wasn't ready to make the sacrifices the training entailed.

She wasn't ready then, either, to devote herself to the care of others. Already a mother of two, she resented the feeling that she'd been born into the caring role.

'Every first daughter of an alcoholic dad feels that way,' she'd said to Mari. 'I wish I'd been tall enough to be a bus driver or a dogman.' A dogman was the on-the-ground role that needed to be completed to begin to become a crane operator. But she was too short to reach the pedals in a bus or a crane.

She consciously studied TCM when she was young enough to accept the poetry of it.

Even at twenty-two, she had an instinct that she may have had a future in hard science, although she didn't consider medicine a possibility for her own career then. That was the realm of the wealthy.

Aedgar said, 'No, not the elements. It's about—'

'Oh, the yin and the yang?' A picture popped into her mind's eye.

He agreed. 'They use the wrong counterparts.'

'Okay. So, things don't quite balance,' she said.

'Yes. Some things still work. But if they'd group the energy in the proper way, it would work a treat, as you might say.'

'Well, they tell us that it takes ten years after you've finished your acupuncture studies to begin to be good at it. Perhaps that's because you need to listen to the energy and not only use the framework that you're taught.'

'Indeed. Trust in what you feel. Don't trust the books. Some of the writers copied things from other people. They have themselves never been able to feel the energy.

'That's how things got mixed up.

'If you copy it once or twice it's still close to the original. Close. But if you translate things or rewrite it, or add ideas, once you've done it ten times then you have a completely different system. And there was that one person in between, or two out of the ten, that couldn't feel the energy, didn't trust the feeling.

'Because he couldn't trust anything, he or she couldn't feel, it means that eight people after that who **could feel** parts of it energetically, were put on a slightly wrong path from the beginning.

'They thought what was written must be true because these older generations knew these things better.

'It's like the foundation of the house. One weak part, and the whole chain of writers can change the whole thing for the worse. That's what happened.

'Chemistry's like that. Things are not the same anymore as they were when they were written down. And that was because of a change in the structure of things.

'But it's all—you use physics, you have no idea. You use chemistry, you have no idea. And you try to practice medicine and you have no idea at all because important basic knowledge is missing.

'It has been missing for a very long time.

'So everything that builds on this can't be right. Basic important information was missing in the first place.

'We have to work on that at some stage.'

'Yes.'

Nerida felt agitated as Aedgar went on, again, about how imperfect modern systems of knowledge were, how far from the truth humans were.

She changed the subject to talk enthusiastically about a conference she'd found where Mari might be able to channel for spiritually minded scientists. 'I came across some groups in my reading, who have meetings every year, scientists meeting together with—'

'What groups? What readings? You went to a fortune teller?'

'No.'

'So, what kind of reading is it?'

On the internet, she thought, probably loudly. Nerida did not feel she had control of her thoughts. If Aedgar could read her mind, he must have found her rough.

'What pleased me,' she said, 'was to find that there are meetings between scientists and those who are interested in older knowledge, one might say, intuitive or perhaps even channelled knowledge. There are regular meetings happening—'

He delved into it, vibrationally. 'It's not a bad start.'

'I thought that eventually this might be the sort of venue for our work.' She was pleased with herself.

Aedgar took a minute to consider. 'Too small,' he said. 'Could be a start. But you need to address the right people. Some of these people are very good. Others hide in these groups, who don't, so to say, fit in to any other group.'

Always so critical! She remained polite. 'Ah, so they're tolerated even though no one understands what they're saying?'

'You would say, "This person is a lunatic." In this group they think too, that "This person is such a lunatic, but maybe there is something to it." These people are more open- minded.'

'Mmm. They're generous,' she commented.

'Generous, yes. And they are trying to find the truth. So, they even try to deal with people who just go there to hide. They're the ones that don't fit in anywhere.'

'Mmm. They don't make any sense?'

'Their knowledge is not good enough. They don't make, that's right, any sense in any group. They end up there because these people tend to be more open-minded and more, as you put it, generous.

'But not all of them are like that. You might find one or the other that can help.'

Nerida accepted his grudging observation. 'That's what I thought, yeah.'

Responding to her subtext, he said, 'You just shouldn't feel overenthusiastic. It will be a small number that's suitable. Some people have their own ideas. They form their own groups so they can live their own ideas. It doesn't matter if their ideas are wrong or right because they don't accept other ideas. This happens a lot too. So, you need to be inquisitive.'

'Yes. And perhaps sceptical.' She unfolded her arms.

'Yes. You need to find out who you are dealing with. And if the people know what they pretend to.

'Some people say they know about channelling, or even that they *do* channelling, when all they've ever done was read books or listen to other channels.

'There are quite a few like that around.

'There are good people around, and you will find them. Even if they are not easy to find. The very intelligent, very good ones don't tend to form groups. Because they know what they know, so to say.

'Aiden probably told you that you need to be careful because, as you would say, it is in fashion right now, talking to us. Many try.

'Only a few can do it.'

Nerida sighed. 'We'll take our time.'

'Yes. I think I might leave for now.'

'Thank you for your company.'

'You're welcome. We always enjoy yours. So, I'll talk to you another time. Won't be long.'

'Good. Talk to you soon.' Then, 'Hey, sleepy. Hello.'

'Hey.' Mari blinked, as if waking.

'Well done,' Nerida said.

Later, folding the clean washing, still warm and smelling of sun, she thought about how Aedgar damped down her verve for the mystical scientists' meeting she'd discovered, portraying with honesty the tendency of rigid-thinking, personality-disordered or frankly insane people to be tolerated in the forgiving realm of New Age gatherings.

His independent opinions helped her keep her own.

The Buddhist ideal of trying to live without judgement did not work for Nerida. The young activist had chosen where she stood. The mature doctor made judgements and decisions about intimate aspects of peoples' lives all day.

Reflecting as she folded their socks and underwear into little piles and rolled up Mari's t-shirts, she was grateful for his free expression. There would be no books and nothing to say to the world if all the conversations were about whether they should paint the kitchen.

Nevertheless, she was frustrated by her own lack of understanding. And despite Aedgar's assurances, thinking about a book, she wondered if their conversations would ever have an audience. Also whether, if they kept doing this work (and told people about it), Mari and she would end up with any sane, reliable friends.

They went out under the stars again that later that night, driving out on Kata Tjuta Road. The meteor shower was coming to an end. Mari still caught a few on camera, coloured cuts of light in the star-saturated black sky.

Nerida was at the end of a long day. She got tired standing and being cold. Taking shelter in the car, she found a blanket, wound the seat back and looked up at the night sky. Comforted, she closed her eyes to rest.

On waking, she felt herself to be among the stars. Mari was still nearby.

The camera clicked and whirred as she made tiny adjustments to it on the tripod, took more photos and squinted into the viewfinder to change settings. She was in her zone. She could stay there all night, engaged with stars and stardust, dreaming of paintings and nebulae.

Nerida put the window down, pondering what Aedgar said about energy and knowledge. The night air was crisp on her cheek. She pulled her beanie down over her ears.

'I'll just take a few more,' Mari called.

Another forty minutes then. Nerida smiled to herself. She felt better after her snooze. 'It's very late, you know.'

Coulda bin worse. She could have attracted a woman who bred show rabbits. Or liked her algebra and calculus hard.

Or, goddess forbid, had to go skiing every year.

She could have ended up with a shopping addict, like some of the women in her family.

I got a woman who loves the stars, and the rocks. And sunsets and thorny devils. She's my perfect match.

Energy is the question of our times, she thought.

All kinds of energy, from the filthy fossil fuels we're still using to get around, to the buzz my clients and I generate at the clinic together, all the way to the energy of a person who's left their body behind. Life after death.

And Aedgar has this idea that the Universe grows with energy we create, that our spirits generate energy when we learn.

That's a brilliant concept.

Nerida looked up at the stars. The night breeze from the south pushed under her long hair. She pulled the blue silk scarf Mari had made her out of her pocket and wrapped it around her neck.

Could there be a connection between the energy we need to run our cars, light our houses, what makes Mari's camera work, and the energy we create from our learning, from our experiences?

Is there be a continuum of energy between people and things? Of course there is.

It's not a vague New Age axiom. He means it literally: Gain knowledge to grow energy. Okay. Here's me growing energy.

Nerida sighed. Happiness welled up inside her.

The curves of Mari's hips, breasts and shoulders, her bent elbows, were lit by starlight.

Nerida glimpsed her face in the light of the camera's digital screen and saw her quick movements with a small torch.

How long was I asleep? Nerida touched the car's screen to check the time.

Mari had been standing by and walking around that camera, talking to the stars as they came out and travelled across the sky, for over three hours, with no sign of flagging.

Her energy is stupendous. She must be cold.

Nerida reached into the back of the car for a heavier jacket. Mari allowed herself to be interrupted to put her arms in. 'Thanks, sweetie,' she said, zipping up.

Love is about the miraculous, multidimensional cataclysmic coming together, Nerida knew. Love is about practice, learning, growing in ourselves. *Putting on a jacket.*

Being alive involved developing skills, like Mari had to, becoming a channel. Like Nerida would have to, being a facilitator for her. And eventually becoming an author and publisher. In her own perfect time.

She climbed up the car's roo-bar and sat on the hood, gently, so as not to dent it. The car body still held warmth from the day's sun. The desert sky was so dark she saw the coloured clouds of gas around the stars. Mari's photos and paintings would show them more clearly than her eyes could see. And give people the feeling.

Nerida talked to Mari, soul to soul, in her head.

Let's continue to be so different to each other.

I wanted someone passionate and argumentative. I got you.

Seeing the world through your eyes makes me learn and grow. My world gets bigger by feeling the way you experience it. And pushing against you.

I need you to keep talking. Share your knowledge with me. Give me all your news, my beauty.

© Claudia Jocher 2021

ALSO BY MIKI MITAYN

in the *Aedgar Wisdom* series:

'This *Aedgar Wisdom* book pushed to the front of the publishing queue, to be contemporary with the Pandemic.'

—*Miki Mitayn.*

'Quirky...incredibly unique ...pits spirituality against science in a riveting adventure, featuring a multidimensional, extraordinary protagonist.With Mari and Nerida's utterly unusual lives, readers will find themselves drawn into mysticism and spiritual wisdom explored in relation to the afterlife...a plot that is stunningly imagined and intelligently executed.'

—Cristina Prescott *The Book Commentary*

AWARDS

The Conscious Virus was Awarded **First Prize** in the Supernatural & Paranormal Division, Chanticleer International Book Awards, 2021.

Aedgar said: 'But we're not supernatural or paranormal.'

'Yes, we are. Wouldn't we want to be?' Nerida asked, with a tilt of her head. 'Normal is overrated.'

Awards for *Heated Earth—Aedgar Moves In*

Heated Earth was awarded **Third Place in two categories:** 'Fantasy—Paranormal & Urban' and 'Literary Fiction—Sci-fi & Fantasy', in the BookFest International Awards, Spring 2023.

COMING NEXT!

The Others come and speak.

BOOK **2** OF THE ***AEDGAR WISDOM*** SERIES. WORKING TITLE: ***WISE ONES ARISE***

In the Central Australian desert, Mari Wildeberg channels spirits secretly. Her wife Dr Nerida Green is getting to know Aedgar, a gay dandy of Tudor times with a complicated relationship to the planet. Other channelled beings have been waiting their turn.

Bartgrinn, a druid healer.

And Isis, who may be related to a dirty-footed cat-like creature from another world.

She's all about the love.

M'Hoq Toq, a Native American medicine man, (it is the easiest of his names) returns to share his knowledge. He is imposing, with exquisite Indigenous sensibility.

In the linear world, Nerida still cares for her patients, pulled into their stormy lives. She butts her head against management and the government. And argues with her wife, who wants to be left out of it but keep centre stage in Nerida's life.

JOIN US

LOOK OUT FOR

WISE ONES ARISE
And all the following books in the series
JOIN THE MAILING LIST

Keep in touch: <u>Aedgar.com/contact</u> No ads, no spam, no affiliate marketing. Giveaways, insider news, special offers.